"*The Breaking Point* is compelling and strikingly honest. This story touches the heart and gives hope for struggling marriages. Karen Ball writes with clarity, depth, and power. It's a pleasure to recommend this engaging and memorable book."

RANDY ALCORN, BESTSELLING AUTHOR OF *SAFELY HOME*

"*The Breaking Point* goes beyond superb and engrossing—which it most certainly is—and enters the realm of heart-changing, life-altering fiction. Karen Ball has penned a modern classic and given us two unforgettable characters to root for. This is an author to watch!"

ROBIN LEE HATCHER, BESTSELLING AUTHOR OF
FIRSTBORN AND *PROMISED TO ME*

"With soul-searing honesty and commendable courage, Karen Ball dares to lift the veil on a Christian marriage where two hearts are struggling to become one. *The Breaking Point* is must-reading for any couple seeking God's ideal in this wonderful covenant we know as marriage."

ANGELA ELWELL HUNT, AUTHOR OF
THE SHADOW WOMEN

"This is a novel with purpose! Karen Ball honestly explores marriage in all of its complexity and sometimes hidden glory."

GARY THOMAS, AUTHOR OF *SACRED MARRIAGE*

"Gut-wrenching in its honesty and passion, *The Breaking Point* packs a powerful message of obedience and God's healing."

BRANDILYN COLLINS, BESTSELLING AUTHOR OF
COLOR THE SIDEWALK FOR ME AND *EYES OF ELISHA*

"Karen Ball's vulnerable, clear voice rings true in a story that will bring you face-to-face with the reality of a struggling marriage and the Father's insistent, inexhaustible grace. Authentic and revealing, this book is not to be missed."

DEBORAH BEDFORD, AUTHOR OF *A MORNING LIKE THIS*

"An honest, heartfelt novel about the craggy recesses of marriage— where God does some of His best work. Karen Ball's writing is emotionally gripping and full of insight."

JAMES SCOTT BELL, AUTHOR OF *A GREATER GLORY*

"In *The Breaking Point*, Karen Ball exposes the painful, honest truth of marriage: It's hard work. This story of lives out of control, love misplaced, and the wounds we often give each other in the name of righteous direction is carefully balanced with God's love, hope, and ministry of reconciliation. Although fiction, this powerful read is anything but. I highly recommend this book."

TRACIE PETERSON, BESTSELLING AUTHOR OF THE
DESERT ROSE SERIES AND *EYES OF THE HEART*

"*The Breaking Point* is not only a powerful story for everyone to read, it's a blueprint for those who want to take their marriages to a more Christlike level, for ailing and struggling marriages, and for helping couples to be prepared for the hard times."

LAURAINE SNELLING, BESTSELLING AUTHOR OF
THE HEALING QUILT AND
THE RED RIVER OF THE NORTH SERIES

"Karen Ball is one of my favorite authors. Her stories combine humor, poignancy, and a solid biblical background for page-turning novels. *The Breaking Point* merges all of Karen's strengths into a beautifully written story of love and redemption."

LORI COPELAND, AUTHOR OF
BRIDES OF THE WEST: *FAITH, JUNE, HOPE, GLORY,*
AND *RUTH*

"I finished *The Breaking Point* at 3 A.M. with tears in my eyes. What a wonderful testimony of God's power to heal even the most complicated of relationships. Karen Ball beautifully illustrates the truth that love is a decision and that a relationship with God offers hope for every broken dream. Every married couple and certainly every newlywed should read this book."

DEBORAH RANEY, AWARD-WINNING AUTHOR OF
AFTER THE RAINS AND *A SCARLET CORD*

THE
BREAKING
POINT

A NOVEL

KAREN BALL

MULTNOMAH
BOOKS

This book is a work of fiction. The characters, incidents, and dialogues are products of the author's imagination and are not to be construed as real. Any resemblance to actual events or persons, living or dead, is entirely coincidental.

THE BREAKING POINT
published by Multnomah Books

© 2003 by Karen Ball
International Standard Book Number: 978-1-59052-033-8

Cover design by Kirk DouPonce—UDG/DesignWorks
Cover image of woman by Deborah Jaffe/Getty Images
Cover image of man by Philip Porceda/Getty Images
Background cover images by Corbis and Photodisc

Unless otherwise indicated, Scripture quotations are from: *Holy Bible,* New Living Translation © 1996. Used by permission of Tyndale House Publishers, Inc. All rights reserved.

Other Scripture quotations are from:
The Living Bible (TLB) © 1971. Used by permission of Tyndale House Publishers, Inc. All rights reserved.
The Holy Bible, New American Standard Bible® (NASB) © 1960, 1977, 1995 by the Lockman Foundation. Used by permission.
The Holy Bible, New International Version (NIV) © 1973, 1984 by International Bible Society, used by permission of Zondervan Publishing House

Published in the United States by WaterBrook Multnomah, an imprint of the Crown Publishing Group, a division of Random House Inc., New York.

MULTNOMAH and its mountain colophon are registered trademarks of Random House Inc.

For information:
MULTNOMAH BOOKS
12265 Oracle Boulevard, Suite 200 • Colorado Springs, CO 80921

Library of Congress Cataloging-in-Publication Data

Ball, Karen, 1957-
  The breaking point / by Karen Ball.
    p. cm.
  ISBN 1-59052-033-5
  1. Married people—Fiction. 2. Blizzards—Fiction. 3. Oregon—Fiction. I. Title.
PS3552.A4553B35 2003
813'.54—dc21
                                            2003001410

This book is dedicated with love and gratitude to my husband, Don.

I wasted so many years wishing you were different—more this, less that. I'm sorry it took me so long to stop looking at you—or at myself—and finally look to the Master. But I'm grateful that when I did so, He opened my eyes and heart to the truth: His plans are perfect. He's made two stubborn, willful souls one in ways I never imagined.

Don, you fought the good fight, you stood firm in the face of great opposition, and by God's grace and your determination, you've become a man of honor and integrity, a man after God's own heart.

You've made me a better woman, a better Christian, and a better person You've shown me the true meaning of love. What a miracle to call you *beloved* and *friend*. Thank you for persevering.

I love you with all my heart.

ACKNOWLEDGMENTS

A WISE FRIEND AND GIFTED WRITER, ROBIN JONES GUNN, once said that when we write the books that stem from our truest passion, we find ourselves "floating on a sea of reluctant transparency." That's certainly true of this book.

This story is different from any I've written before. I put off writing it, in part because I knew I wasn't ready, but also because I was afraid. I didn't want to go through the emotions I knew were waiting for me if I gave in. But God is even more stubborn than I, and He made it abundantly clear that the time had come to testify to what He has done in my marriage. In my life.

I worried that reliving the dark times would harden my heart toward Don. But God is so faithful! The complete opposite happened. As I wrote, a sense of wonder and gratitude came over me. Wonder that Don and I share the love we do today, considering where we were not so long ago. Gratitude that God helped us endure so we could know this time, this delight, of who we've become as individuals and as a couple.

Beauty for ashes. That's what God promises us. And it's true. He's taken the ashes of my willful dreams and stubborn expectations and given me more beauty than I ever imagined.

I pray this story will help any who may be stumbling along the rocky path of marital discord. But when a story is based, even in part, on the writer's own life, she runs the risk of losing the universal message in a tangle of personal details. To avoid that, while some facets of this story stem from the events of my own life and marriage, it is a compilation of many stories, many lives, many marriages, many struggles. (For example, I've never been pregnant and Don has never had or considered an affair.)

Thank you to those of you who shared with me the cost of persevering; the battles to survive in a world that calls us to self-love rather than God's love; the struggles to resist the oh-so-appealing cry of "God can't want you to be this unhappy." I've found strength through each of you, through hearing what God has done when it seemed nothing *could* be done. Thank you for bearing witness to a Power that goes beyond our weakness and turns despair to hope, anger to joy, destruction to restoration.

Many people were there for Don and me through our journey. You all helped in ways both big and small, but some have been a constant support. God used you to keep us faithful to the vows we took nearly twenty-four years ago, and we thank you. My special gratitude to:

- My dad and mom, Fred and Paula Sapp, and my two brothers, Kevin and Kirk. What would I have done without you? When I was a kid, I thought all families were like ours. Now I realize what an amazing gift our family is. You are my most treasured friends. During those terrible, painful days, you were my anchor and my resting place. You still are. I thank God for you every day.
- My sweet sister-in-law, Lyn. Your quiet wisdom and loving heart bring Proverbs 16:24 to life. I'm so glad you're a part of our family.
- Our beloved church family at the Advent Christian Church in Medford, Oregon. You've known and encouraged me all my life and you accepted Don without reservation. Even in the hardest of times, you showed us both a pure, sincere love. You are the true picture of the body of Christ, and I love each of you more than I can say.
- Len, spiritual mentor, shepherd, soldier for the Master, heart friend. You spoke hard truths, brother, when I needed to hear them, even at the risk of our friendship. You followed the Master's call into battle because you knew what mattered most wasn't my happiness but my obedience. Thank you for letting Him use you so wisely and so well. I love you.
- Julee and Peggy, my heart sisters. How you've enriched my

life! Thank you for all the times you listened to my sorrow, accepted my anger and despair, and let God's light of truth shine clear in your counsel. I count myself among the most blessed of women because you are my friends.

- Our Illinois Bible study group. You saw us at our worst and still accepted and loved us. We became our best in great part because of the way you stood beside us and held us accountable.

- Don's family. You've been there for each other, supported and loved each other, no matter what. Mom, you raised some wonderful kids, and I'm especially grateful for the hand you had in making Don the kind of man who wouldn't give up, either on himself or on me; Sheryl and Arden, you opened your home and hearts to us, and both were a blessed haven. Thank you, dear sister and brother; Doug, you have such a special place in our hearts. You understood us as few have and you helped us stand; and Guy, you gave guidance and support without reserve.

  Thank you for taking me into your family, for taking us into your hearts, for giving us a safe place to fall apart, and for helping us rebuild.

- Francine and Rick Rivers. You told us, over and over, that God is sufficient, no matter what. In the darkest of times you called us to stay the course and promised it was worth it. You were right on all counts.

- Ken Petersen. You upheld us both, never taking sides. That was a precious gift.

- Our River Glen church family. God used a moment of brokenness to draw us back into Christian fellowship (thank you, David, for your honesty!), and we found such delight among you. Thank you for being transparent and for being true to His call.

- Our counselor, Steve Hoffmann. What an amazing, godly man you are. I doubt we would have survived as individuals, let alone as a couple, without you. You saw through the masks and barriers into our very hearts. And you drew us from desperation and anger into a relationship that overflows with God's promise and delight. I didn't think it was possible; you never believed it wasn't. Thank you, Steve. We owe you. Big-time.

To each of you, words can never express the depth of my gratitude for what you did, what you said, and for being there when we needed you. May God bless you richly.

Finally, a special word of thanks to the woman who, in so many ways, made me who I am: my mom, Paula Sapp. I miss you. So much. I wish you were here to read this, because you're as much a part of the story as anyone. You were the most amazing gift, the most wonderful mother. I've never known a woman who could love like you did. You were there any time I needed you. All those times my world turned upside down, your voice on the phone set things right again. You listened without judging; you loved without reservation. I still can't believe you're gone, Mom. Life isn't the same. Never will be again. So I'm looking forward more than I can say to eternity and to seeing you again. My fondest hope is that I spend these years without you making you really, really proud. I love you.

And now...we offer ourselves to the One who called us, the One who loves us so very well, the One who has restored us. And we make this our prayer:

Now to Him who is able to do exceedingly,
abundantly above all we ask or think,
according to the power that works in us,
to HIM be glory in the church by Christ Jesus
to all generations, forever and ever. Amen.

"Slowly, steadily, surely, the time approaches
when the vision will be fulfilled.
If it seems slow, wait patiently,
for it will surely take place. It will not be delayed."

HABAKKUK 2:3

The state of marriage is one that requires
more virtue and constancy than any other.
It is a perpetual exercise of mortification....
From this thyme plant, in spite of the bitter nature of its juice,
you may be able to draw and make the honey of a holy life.

FRANCES DE SALES

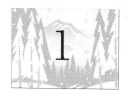

1

"Marriage...is the crucible that grinds and shapes us into the character of Jesus Christ."

GARY THOMAS

"When you put a seed into the ground, it doesn't grow...unless it dies first."

1 CORINTHIANS 15:36

DECEMBER 19, 2003
10 A.M.

WE'RE OUT OF CONTROL.

Renee Roman leaned her forehead against the cold glass of the truck window, her teeth clenched, a barrier against the tears scalding the backs of her eyes. She would not cry. She'd cried enough for a lifetime.

Two lifetimes.

She focused on the winter storm screaming just outside her window. A dense blanket of wind-whipped snow surrounded the pickup as they crept along. Visibility was nil, and gusts of wind buffeted the truck, slamming against it with seemingly determined efforts to knock them sideways.

A whiteout. How fitting. Now they could be as blind to the road as they were to each other...

Hurt tugged at her, and she pressed her lips tight against it. Blind or not, nothing was going to stop them, no sirree. Let the storm rage; their truck would still keep its steady, slow progress. Wind and snow were no match for Gabe. Nothing stopped him when he was determined—no human, no natural disaster, no act of God...

Renee's fingers curled around her seat belt. Here they were, on a treacherous road, at the mercy of the weather, and all Gabe could do was keep moving forward. No stopping to reconsider, no looking for shelter, and certainly no asking for help. Just push your way through and make everything and everyone bend to *your* will.

If she weren't so terrified, the situation would be hilarious.

A small whine drew her attention to the backseat, and she turned to place a comforting hand on Bo's furry head. Funny, Siberian huskies looked so imposing, so fierce, but under that wolflike appearance, they were serious wimps. "It's okay, boy." She uttered the soothing words, doing her best to keep her own anxiety from tainting her tone. "You're fine. We'll be home soon."

If only she believed that. A glance told Renee that Gabe was tense, too, but she knew his tight jaw had little to do with the weather. She buried her fingers in Bo's thick coat. If only she could bury her feelings as completely.

I hate him.

The words, which had nudged her heart and mind since that morning despite her stubborn refusal to grant them entrance, finally took wing.

She knew it was because of the anger. And the terror. She hated driving in the snow. Usually avoided it at all costs—which put driving in a blinding blizzard in the Oregon mountains in the "Things I Utterly Detest" category—but Gabe had been adamant. And nothing she said—no pleas to wait a day, no appeals to reason or compassion—had made a difference.

Oh, he had a list of reasons: They couldn't afford another night in the hotel; he didn't have any more vacation days and couldn't afford a day off without pay; all they had to do was leave early enough to beat the worst of the storm…

But Renee knew the real reason they were on the road in the worst storm of the year. Her husband couldn't wait to get home, to get this miserable trip over with.

To get away from her.

Tears pricked at her eyelids, and she blinked them away. He wanted to get away from her? Well, that was just fine. She was more than ready to escape his rigid, cold presence. The plummeting temperatures outside the truck cab were a virtual heat wave compared to the frigid atmosphere inside. Neither of them had spoken a word for the past half hour.

Her lips trembled. Why say anything now? They'd said enough— more than enough—that morning.

She gave Bo a final pat and turned to stare out the windshield again, then grabbed the door handle when another blast of wind rocked the cab. She started when Gabe's hand closed over hers. Swallowing a sudden jumble of emotions, she glanced at him. He kept his eyes fixed on the windshield as he spoke.

"Breathe, Renee. I need you to breathe."

She hadn't realized she'd been holding her breath. Amazing. Even in the face of a storm—both physical and emotional—Gabe was still so tuned in to her…

She forced out her pent-up air, then drew in a slow, deep breath.

Gabe squeezed her hand with gentle pressure. "We'll be okay." His gaze brushed hers, then returned to the road.

Fear, frustration, regret, sorrow…one sensation chased another, rippling through her until they were a bitter taste in her mouth.

How did we get here? How do we keep ending up in this place?

She clenched her eyes as the desperate thought scraped at

too-raw nerves. They'd been through so much…worked so hard…and she thought they were doing better. Had even dared to believe they'd make it. This whole trip to the mountains to rent a cabin was supposed to be a kind of celebration for them, a rejoicing in all they'd overcome—in all that ten years of counseling had helped them resolve.

So why had it come to this again? To this place of hurt and frustration? This place of cold distance?

Misunderstanding and miscommunication had opened the door to hurt feelings. Angry words followed, bringing resentments Renee thought were long ago resolved. Even now, thinking back on the last few days, Renee couldn't believe it took mere moments for their hard work—and her hope—to shatter. Now the tiny, jagged fragments worked their way deep into her heart, cutting, piercing, wounding her in ways she thought she'd never have to feel again.

Renee wanted to be angry. To yell and scream and throw things. But she had to acknowledge she felt only one thing: grief. Deep, wrenching grief. She stared out the window, blinking against the glaring white—and against scalding tears.

The question came again; this time she gave it voice. "How did we get here, Gabe?"

He didn't answer right away, but his jaw muscles flinched. For once, she waited. Not because she didn't have anything to say, but because she couldn't speak past the tightness in her throat.

"It's the road home."

Leave it to Gabe to give her a literal answer to a question that was anything *but* that. *Please, Gabe, please…listen with your heart instead of your logic.* "That's not what I meant—" the words came out soft and weary—"and you know it."

Exasperation escaped him in a snort. "Right. Whatever you say, Renee."

"Gabe—"

His glare cut her short. "Forget it. Whatever you meant, I

don't know the answer, okay? I never do." He turned back to stare at the road. "Not the one you want, anyway."

Bo's nose pressed against her shoulder, halting the angry words she wanted to spew. She reached back and felt his trembling, then released her irritation in a huff. Amazing how connected to them this dog was. He was so tuned in to any tension between her and Gabe. All it took was a raised voice, a hardened tone, and he was there, pacing, looking from one to the other with that wide-eyed anxiety. He'd become a kind of emotional barometer, an alarm to warn them when things were getting out of hand.

Like now.

"You're fine, Bo. Settle down."

At the harsh command, Renee felt her teeth grind and forced her jaw to relax. Did Gabe really believe using that tone would comfort the poor animal? She wanted to tell him how idiotic such a notion was, but as she opened her mouth, Bo commando-crawled between the seats until his upper body rested on the console and leaned into her.

"You'd probably better snap him into his safety harness, Renee."

As much as she didn't want to do so, Gabe was right. The harness attached to the seat belt in the backseat, and it would keep Bo from being thrown if anything should happen.

Nothing's going to happen, her mind scolded her as she unbuckled her own belt and secured Bo. If only she could believe it.

Renee turned back to her seat and refastened her belt, trying to ignore the whining now coming from the backseat. Few sounds were more pitiful than a Siberian's soulful whine, and it did what Renee's conscience couldn't: It kept her quiet.

The silence in the cab grew until Renee thought she would scream. Anything to drown out the thoughts that raged at her, shredding her already wounded heart.

He doesn't care... He can't even stand to look at you, let alone talk to you… He's so wrapped up in his anger that there's no room left for you. For anyone. It's just him and that stupid, hateful temper…

Renee closed her eyes against despair. *Father God, what do I have to do? I've made changes…Gabe's made changes…we've tried. We really have. But what good has it done? We always seem to end up in the same terrible place…* Her throat constricted. *What else can we do?*

One word whispered through her in response: *Die…*

Renee's eyes flew open at that. Die? She glanced out the window, painfully aware that was a too-real possibility right now, given the storm and the winding mountain roads they were on. One wrong turn, one jerk of the wheel at the wrong moment, and they'd be history…a pile of twisted metal at the bottom of a frozen mountain.

She shook the image away. That wasn't the answer. It couldn't be. So what—?

A sudden cry from Gabe was her only warning. That and the sickening sensation of traction suddenly lost…of wheels no longer gripping the road…of control being ripped away…

"Renee! Hold on!"

She scarcely had time to grip the door handle before they were in a spin. She'd always heard that, in moments of crisis, everything seemed to go into slow motion, but she knew now that was wrong. Things sped up. In the space of a heartbeat, their spiraling vehicle slammed into the snowdrift at the side of the road—the only barrier between them and a sheer drop-off. Ice and frozen snow shattered with a force that reverberated in Renee's very bones. She knew, with an odd sense of calm, the moment they broke through…the moment they were airborne…the moment they began to slide down the mountainside…

She didn't have time to be afraid. To think. All she could do was turn to Gabe. What she saw reflected in those blue eyes—eyes that had captivated her the first time he'd looked at her—made everything slow…stop…

Sorrow stared out at her—regret for all they'd said, all they'd never have the chance to say—and a longing so intense she thought it would break her heart.

Renee reached for him, then cried out—when a thunderous jolt slammed her back against the pickup door. For a moment, there was nothing but searing pain.

Then there was nothing.

Many of God's lessons are learned through tears.

T. L. CUYLER

"The LORD has done this."

JOB 12:9

DARK.

Cold.

Pain.

Each sensation whispered over Renee, drawing her into awareness, away from the stillness.

"No..."

Did she speak the word or just think it? Either way, it seemed to echo through her, a sound as brittle and frightened as any she'd ever known.

Her eyelids dragged open, and she blinked against the brightness, battling the fog that seemed to fill her mind as well as her vision. But what she saw didn't make any sense.

White. Everything was bathed in white. There was a suffocating blanket of it outside the truck, where snow blew and swirled.

And inside the truck…the white was there, too. On the windshield…in the air…

As Renee's dazed eyes focused, she saw why. Snow was piled on the dashboard, on her lap, and every time she exhaled, a white puff filled the air. She drew a deep breath, but as the frigid air flowed into her lungs, she was seized by a fit of coughing that racked her body.

As she struggled to breathe, she realized how cold she was. So cold she couldn't stop shivering. "G…Gabe?"

A flash of red and white came into view, and she pulled back just as Bo vaulted the seat backs and landed half in her lap, half on the floor. His frantic tongue bathed her face, and Renee grabbed at his front paws as they raked her shoulders.

"Bo, *no!* Down!"

True to his training, the husky sat with a thump on the floorboard at Renee's feet. But he leaned into her, his two-colored stare fixed on her—one blue eye, one brown—like a child seeking comfort after a nightmare. Renee dug her cold hands into his fur, scratching his neck, trying to comfort him even as she struggled to understand what had happened.

Her gaze roamed the cab of the truck…and realization seeped in. They'd gone over the edge of the road. The momentum of their spin had slammed them right through the wall of snow and ice at the road's edge. They must have gone down the mountainside…

As the reality of their situation hit her, she turned with a jerk. Sweet relief made her weak when she saw Gabe. Though he was unconscious, puffs of white hanging in the air near his mouth bore blessed testimony to the fact that he was breathing.

"Gabe?" She reached for him, then halted when pain stabbed through her, sucking the air from her lungs, making everything go faint. She drew in shallow gulps of oxygen, fighting to stay conscious.

She reached again, frustrated with her sluggish motions, as though trapped in some slow-motion segment of a movie. She crept her fingers along until they found Gabe's wrist and searched, pressed…

Yes! A pulse. When she felt it pound, strong and steady, she let herself cry.

Thank You, God…thank You…

She leaned her head back against her seat, staring up at the ceiling of the truck cab, then looked down at Bo, who watched her every move. "It's not crushed or caved in at all." She felt the ceiling. "We must not have rolled. Well, that's a blessing anyway." She shifted her gaze and grimaced. The front of the truck was another story. It looked as if it had been put in some gigantic trash compactor. Clearly it had taken the brunt of their landing.

They must have slid down the side of the mountain, taking out some of the small trees in their path. The front of the truck was accordioned back to the cab—but not into it, thank heaven, or she and Gabe might well have been crushed. Their legs surely would have been.

She glanced at Bo again and saw that his safety harness had been torn, though whether from the accident or from him chewing it through, she couldn't be sure. She nudged him off her feet and flexed her toes, feet, ankles, and then her knees. No injuries—at least not that she could feel.

Just then a gust of wind blasted the side of her face, and she shivered. Where was *that* coming from? She turned, searching…and stared. The window in the passenger door was gone; jagged remnants were all that remained. The wind and snow were taking full advantage of the opening. Hence the little drifts of snow here and there in the cab.

"No wonder I'm so cold!"

Bo cocked his head, ears pricked, as though agreeing with her wholeheartedly. She lay her hand on the dog's broad head.

"I'm glad you're okay, boy, and that you're awake—" Emotion clutched at her throat, choking her. She pressed her forehead to the top of Bo's soft head. "It helps to have someone to talk to."

Bo rewarded her whispered admission with a quick lick. She rubbed his ears, then straightened, looking at the shattered window. "I've got to cover that up, boy. Which means I need to move."

This wasn't going to feel good. She forced her aching body into action, though the response was far slower than usual. Her fingers groped for the release on the seat belt, but it eluded her. Muttering her irritation, she shifted—then gasped at the pain that jabbed through her. She grabbed at her side, groaning, pressing her hands to her ribs. They must have been bruised by the seat belt when the truck hit bottom.

At least she hoped they were only bruised.

One thing was for sure, she needed more room to maneuver. She nudged Bo with her foot. "C'mon, boy, into the backseat." He resisted for a moment, then hopped across the wide console between the seats and moved to his blanket. He circled twice, three times, and then plopped down with a long-suffering grunt.

Renee inched her hand along the seat belt and fingered the catch, trying to stir up as little pain as possible. She let out a relieved breath when she pressed the release, and the seat belt snapped free. She pushed it aside and leaned toward Gabe, grimacing at the ugly gash on the side of his forehead. Blood trickled down his pale, still face.

Jesus...Jesus...

Even as the prayer escaped her frantic heart and flew skyward, her shaking increased. Blinding panic sparked to life somewhere deep in her gut, jumping and growing like flames in a stack of tinder-dry wood. Suddenly the cab felt as if it were closing in on her, and a chilling, wailing scream was filling her mind. She sat back, pressing her spine into the seat back, forcing herself to take deep, even breaths. With each puff of white as she exhaled, she repeated one fierce word: "Calm...calm...calm..."

She wasn't sure how long it took until her pulse resumed a more or less normal beat, but when it finally happened she sighed. If only she could stop shaking. It was partly nerves, partly the aching cold that seemed imbedded in her very bones.

And shock...it could be shock...

She pushed the grim thought aside, then swiveled to kneel on the seat and reach to the floor of the backseat. Amazingly, though he never took his eyes off her, Bo stayed where he was. She grabbed the strap of the canvas duffel bag with their clothes and supplies for their winter search-and-rescue training exercises. They'd joined the organization a few years ago, and though she enjoyed all she learned, Gabe had embraced it with unbridled enthusiasm. Search and Rescue was the perfect setting for his think-through-all-the-angles mindset.

As Renee tugged the bag toward her, she remembered her reaction when Gabe insisted they always needed to keep the search-and-rescue bag with them when they traveled in the winter. She had cast her gaze to the ceiling, making no effort to hide her disdain. He was, as usual, being overly cautious, hyper-vigilant. Why on earth couldn't the man just relax and have a good time?

Now...

She glanced at her unmoving husband and her throat caught. She swallowed back the wave of panic struggling to take over. *Steady, Renee. Don't fall apart now.* She looked at Bo. "Thank heaven he ignored me and listened to his instincts, eh, boy? He sure was right about this."

Bo's steady stare never wavered.

"I know, I know; it's too bad he isn't awake to hear me say that." She turned back to the bag. "Wouldn't he just love to hear me admit I was wrong."

Heaven knew he seldom heard those words from her. In fact, Renee thought, allowing herself a small smile, hearing her admit she was wrong might even make their nosedive down a mountain worthwhile. For Gabe, anyway.

She reached out to stroke the back of her husband's hand where it lay, so very still, on the console. "I'll tell you when you're conscious, Gabe. I promise."

Returning to her task, she tugged the bag until it landed in her lap. The increasing tremor in her hands made it a challenge to jerk the zipper open, but she finally succeeded. She pulled out gloves, a scarf, a hat, snowpants, each item making her feel like a giddy child on Christmas morning.

At the bottom of the bag were a blanket, an assortment of imperishables—chocolate bars, protein bars, dried fruit, nuts, water—and a large baggie with a dozen or so pocket heat packs. She cast another look at Gabe's still form. She'd told him those packs were probably just a way for the sporting goods stores to make money on people. But he pulled one out of the package and shook it, then handed it back to her. Amazingly, the tiny envelope generated serious heat.

Gabe had been the epitome of smugness as he took the packet from her and flipped it in the air. "One of these little babies will last as long as twenty hours."

Twenty hours. God willing, they wouldn't need them for that long.

Her numb fingers fumbled with the extra clothing as she pulled the snowpants and a long-sleeved fleece top over her clothes. That done, she stuffed a few of the heat packs into her pockets, placing the rest back in the bag. As cold as it was now, when night fell it would only get colder. Better to save the heat packs until they really needed them.

Thankfully, warmth was coming back into her body. Remarkable what an extra layer of clothing could accomplish. With a fortifying breath, she reached under her seat for the small first-aid kit they stored there. Within minutes she had Gabe's wound cleaned and dressed, careful not to move his head in case there was any kind of neck injury. Relief whispered through her when she saw the bleeding on his forehead had stopped. As carefully as she could, she eased a knit cap over his thick hair.

Renee settled back in her seat, hugging herself. Now what? She glanced down at her purse and then, though she knew it was useless, reached down and pulled out her cell phone. Closing her eyes, she prayed for a miracle, then hit the power button. But when she opened her eyes what she saw on the LCD display was what she always saw on this section of road: No Service.

Teeth clenched, Renee tossed the phone back in her purse. She'd always teased Gabe that if they had trouble, it would probably happen on this stretch, where not even the booster antenna brought in a signal for their phones. "Just wait and see," she'd told him. "We'll be stuck in the middle of nowhere and have to hoof it for help."

For once, she wasn't the least bit happy about being right.

A blast of cold air and spitting snow hit her, and she took a quick look at her window, then at Bo. "I've got to find a way to block that wind, boy."

The tip of Bo's tail wagged. Obviously he agreed. Too bad he didn't have any ideas to offer. She peered into the backseat, then grabbed a ragged towel and Gabe's ever-present roll of gray tape.

"Duct tape," she heard his long-suffering voice correct her in her mind. He hated it when she called it gray tape, though she'd explained time and again that that was what her dad called it, so it only made sense she called it that as well. After all, the stuff was gray...

A scene flashed through her mind. She and Gabe couldn't have been married more than a few weeks when she'd first called it gray tape. He looked at her, eyes wide, mouth open, as though she just spit in his mother's soup or something equally unforgivable.

"It's called *duct* tape, Renee."

She wrinkled her nose, peering at the roll of tape in her hand. "Doesn't look like a duck to me."

He stared at her, then a wry smile lifted his lips. "Duct tape, with a *t*."

"Oh, of course, that makes so much more sense."

He had laughed then, and she joined him, throwing her arms around his waist and snuggling close. He looked down at her with such tenderness and ended the debate as he always did back then—back when things were so much simpler, so much easier to understand—by enfolding her in his arms and silencing her with a kiss.

Renee bit her lip. *We used to have so much fun...*

Shaking off the melancholy creeping over her, she turned to the window and got to work. It took longer than she liked to get it covered, but the band of pain that had taken up residence around her midsection wouldn't let her work more than a few seconds at a shot. When she finally finished, a thin sheen of perspiration was on her face. She was shaking again, and the thought she'd been avoiding forced its way into her mind.

Shock...I could be going into shock...

As though sensing her anxiety, Bo moved then, stretching out on top of the console and pressing his side into her. She leaned against him, grateful for the dog's warmth, and rubbed her hands up and down her arms, fighting her emotions. *Don't cry. It just makes it harder to breathe. Besides, you can't afford to lose the moisture.*

Renee gave a small laugh. None of this was the least bit funny, but she couldn't help it. That last thought had sounded so much like Gabe, in all his oh-so-practical glory. He was rubbing off on her, and for once, that was a good thing.

Pillowing her head on Bo's back, she looked at Gabe, then

laid a hand on his shoulder, struggling to draw encouragement and strength from the steady rhythm of her husband's breathing.

And yet, as they lay there in the shrouded silence of the truck cab, she couldn't help but wonder, *Is this where it ends, Father?*

Renee pressed her burning eyes against her arm, refusing to surrender to the grief that hung at the back of her heart. Grief for all that could have been…all that should have been.

But most of all, grief for the loss of all those wonderful hopes and dreams born long ago in the purity of childish innocence. Back when she was little. When she knew, without a doubt, that life was perfect.

Because Jesus loved her.

3

Every word and deed of a parent is a
fiber woven into the character of a child.

DAVID WILKERSON

Teach your children to choose the right path,
and when they are older, they will remain upon it.

PROVERBS 22:6

SPRING 1965

"JESUS LOVES ME, THIS I KNOW…"

Renee lifted her arms high, hands clutching tightly to the wood, just as Daddy had shown her. Excitement sang through her, and it was all she could do to stand still. She hated waiting. But Daddy said it would be worth it. And Daddy never lied.

"For the Bible tells me so…" She sang the song softly under her breath and lifted her face when she felt the breeze dance across her cheeks. She giggled. It was coming!

"You ready, hon?"

Renee looked to where her father stood, as tall as God, and nodded. "Yes, Daddy!"

The grin she loved so much filled his face. "Okay—" he turned away from her—"now!"

With that, she let loose of the kite she held over her head and jumped up and down, clapping as her father ran. For a moment, Renee thought her precious kite was going to fall, and then—as though invisible fingers reached out and grabbed the bright fabric—it jerked, shivered a moment, and sailed into the sky, its colorful tail of ribbons dancing a merry jig behind it.

"You did it, Daddy! You *did* it!"

Renee raced after him, leaping into the air when she reached him. She didn't even hesitate. He'd catch her. He always did.

Sure enough, his arm enclosed her and he hugged her close. "Hey, now, small stuff, take it easy! You don't want me to drop your kite, do you?"

She looked up into his laughing eyes and sighed. Was there any place so wonderful in this world as in her daddy's arms?

"Okay, hon. You want to hold the string?"

When she nodded, he set her down and knelt to put the spool of string in her hands, folding his fingers over hers. She leaned back against him, her arm resting on his knee, her head tipped back so that it leaned against his shoulder.

"It's bee-yoo-tiful, isn't it, Daddy?"

"Yes, it is."

"And we *made* it!"

Laughter filled his voice. "That we did."

"And we made it fly." Renee puffed her chest out.

Daddy's arm came to snuggle her close. "Us and God, honey. We made the kite, but He made the wind, and that's what carries it so high and makes it dance."

"Just like He carries us and makes us dance, huh, Daddy?"

His arm tightened around her, the pressure communicating as clearly as any words how much he liked what she said. "Just like that."

The string tugged on her hand as the wind coaxed her kite higher. "Oh, Daddy, it's the best kite ever!"

"For the best kid ever." He reached out to tug on her pig-tail.

"Of course, you're only slightly prejudiced," a soft voice from behind them said.

Renee turned to see Mommy walking across the green grass of the park. She had Renee's baby brother, Robert, on her hip. Renee's older brother, Randy, walked beside their mother.

"Look, Mommy!" Renee could hardly make the words come out past her excitement. "My kite is flying. *Really* high! Just like Daddy said it would."

Her mother looked so happy as she leaned down to loop her free arm around Daddy's broad shoulders. The sight made Renee's heart smile. Mommy and Daddy were always hugging, always laughing.

"Well, of course, honey. Daddy's always right."

Renee nodded in solemn agreement, but Daddy nudged Mommy, grinning like she'd made a joke. He turned his head to plant a smacking kiss on Mommy's cheek, and Renee moved to settle against Daddy again. This was the best day ever.

"It's not flying all that high."

Renee turned to glare at her brother. "It is *so* high!" Randy might be older than she was, but he didn't know everything. No matter how much he thought he did.

His snort made her want to hit him. Right on his turned-up nose. "What do you know? You're only seven."

"Oh, like being nine makes you *so* much smarter—"

"Okay, you two—" Mommy put a hand on Randy's shoul-der—"that's enough."

Renee turned back to her kite, but not before she stuck her tongue out at her stupid brother. No sooner had she done so than she felt Daddy tap her on the top of her head, the pressure both gentle and firm.

"Renee…"

She bit her lip and looked down at the ground. "I'm sorry, Daddy."

"You need to be nice to your brother, sweetie."

Renee's lower lip popped out. "Well, what if he's not nice to me?"

Daddy's voice sounded funny when he answered, as if he was trying not to laugh. "Hon, you have to do what's right, no matter what other people do. God cares about you, about whether or not you do what He says, no matter what. Okay?"

Renee thought about this, then leaned back against Daddy. Her heavy heart let loose with a sigh that seemed to come from her toes. "I like God, but it's not always easy to do what He says, is it?"

He did laugh at that, and Renee's heart danced. She loved making Daddy laugh.

"No, Renee, it's not." He hugged her. "But it's worth it. Don't ever forget that: It's worth it."

"Okay, Daddy. I won't forget." Renee snuggled back against him and watched her kite dance in the sky. It looked almost as happy as she felt.

Someday she was going to marry a man just like Daddy. And they would have little daughters and sons and take them to fly kites, just like this.

"Jesus loves me, this I know…" She sang the song to God in her very best voice. She loved that song, because she knew it was true. After all, He'd given her the bestest Mommy and Daddy in the world.

She looked up at them. Mommy stood beside Daddy, leaning against him, her hand on his shoulder as he knelt behind Renee. She let her mind take a picture that would last forever, and when she turned back to her kite, she was so full of happy that she almost cried.

Someday someone will love me like that.

And because she knew her song about Jesus was true, she knew He'd make that happen. Because He loved her.

God made failure an instrument of victory.

UNA KROLL

And now God is building you,
as living stones, into his spiritual temple.

1 PETER 2:5

DECEMBER 19, 2003
11:30 A.M.

GABE WANTED TO OPEN HIS EYES. HE TOLD HIMSELF
so, told his eyes so, but apparently neither his self nor his eyes
were listening. His lids stayed shut, blocking out the sight he
wanted to see...needed to see.

Renee. He wanted to see her. See her face. Know she was all
right.

Gabe knew something was wrong. Knew they were in trouble
of some sort. He could sense it, felt the unease crawling across his
nerves like tiny spiders skittering across a web.

Come on; open your eyes!

No such luck. Though his will was strong, his body just
wasn't responding.

Muted sounds came to him then...Bo whimpering...and then

Renee's soothing tones. Relief so powerful it stole his breath swept him at the sound of her voice, and he focused in on it.

She was talking to Bo. Calming him. Telling him they would be all right, that someone would find them soon…

Gabe felt his brow furrow. Were they lost? He wasn't sure, but he had the feeling they were. And he had an even stronger feeling that it was his fault. All his fault. He wasn't sure what he'd done, how he'd messed up—

Then he remembered. The truck. The storm. Going over the edge.

They *were* in trouble. And it was his fault.

Frustration clawed at his throat, but a heavy cloak of weariness settled over him, keeping him trapped and motionless. With the weariness came the weight of regret. And guilt.

I blew it. Big-time.

Again. Like always.

The ache in his head increased, and he wanted to cry out. But no sound came. Just the inner litany that he'd never been able to stop.

Stupid! Stupid! What made you think you could drive home in this storm? Why didn't you listen to Renee? You should have waited. Shouldn't have pushed going home today.

Pain rained down on him, screaming across his nerves, sending flashes of color through his mind. Trembling, he finally gave himself over to the encroaching darkness, but not before one last thought assaulted his dimming mind:

I guess you were right after all, Dad.

5

God is what we really desire.

DONALD M. BAILLIE

God will redeem my life.
He will snatch me from the power of death.

PSALM 49:15

WINTER 1968

GABRIEL ROMAN LAY AS STILL AS POSSIBLE.
Don't breathe. Don't move...
His eyes were nearly closed, but he could still see it. The figure. In the doorway. Even if he hadn't been able to see the man, he'd know he was there. He could smell him. He reeked of stale cigarette smoke. And beer.
Always beer.
The pungent, sickening odor filled Gabe's room. The form was a shadow in the darkness, shifting back and forth as though listening, waiting for something, anything to propel him forward, to set him off...
Gabe's lungs burned and his eyes and nose ran, but he didn't blink, didn't sniff. He wouldn't give any sign that he was awake.
So long as his father thought he was asleep, he was safe.

Time passed in agonizing seconds until his father's shadowed bulk finally moved away, shuffling down the hallway to the next doorway. Still Gabe didn't move. His aching, bruised body cried out against the stillness, but he didn't care. Better to hurt for a moment now, until he was sure. He had moved too soon before and paid the price, knew with each crushing blow that he brought the pain on himself by being foolish. Impatient. Stupid.

Gabe clenched his teeth against the frown that threatened to stir his features. *Don't move. Don't move...*

He hated being stupid. Hated being told he was stupid. Hated having the word spit at him with as much violence as the fists that punched and punished his face, his back, his arms, his gut—

A small moan broke the silence. When Gabe realized it had escaped, stark fear ripped through him, scraping his raw nerves, jolting him to a new, terrified awareness. No...

He fixed his narrowed gaze on the doorway, waiting. But the shadow didn't come. Relief hissed through swollen lips. His father wasn't coming back. He must have gone to bed.

Finally.

Gabe sat up, grimacing. He drew in a breath, then stood, grabbing for the dresser near his bed when a blaze of white agony filled his vision. He stood for a moment, sucking in air, willing the stars out of his head. Each breath brought a new surge of pain, and he shook his head.

He knew this pain well. Bruised ribs. Maybe even cracked. Well, what did he expect? He'd taken the brunt of the assault in his midsection this time. But better that than his face. Bruised ribs hurt like crazy, but at least they'd heal. And so long as he was careful how he moved, no one would know. No one would stare.

Gabe straightened, locking his mind against the pain, and started to grab a handkerchief to wipe at his eyes and nose, then winced at the pain. He moved more slowly, picking the handkerchief up. Despite the cold of the room, sweat drenched his forehead. This time Gabe let the frown come.

Weak. That's what he was. Weak and fearful, no better than a little kid. Hadn't he heard it for as long as he could remember? "Be a man. Show no fear." Yet here he stood, sweating out his near-panic like some sniveling little baby.

He crushed the handkerchief in his hand and let it fall to the floor, then grabbed his jacket and slipped it on, ignoring the protests his body made against the actions. Moving as quickly and quietly as he could, he eased out of his room, down the hallway. At the open door to his parents' bedroom, he paused, held his breath…

Snoring. They were asleep.

He went to the stairs and made his way down. He knew every creak and groan on the stairway, every spot to avoid. He wanted to hurry, but he knew better. The pain in his midsection was duller now—a constant but tolerable reminder: *Don't be stupid. Take your time. Don't wake anyone.*

Stupid. He reached the front door, edged it open, and stepped outside. That's what he'd been, all right. Stupid. What made him think he could stop what was happening? What always happened. Especially on nights like tonight.

Christmas Eve. He hated Christmas Eve. And Christmas. And any day like them. What was the point? All that garbage about peace on earth and joy to the world.

Christmas had nothing to do with peace or joy. Not by a long shot.

Gabe clamped his sore lips against the string of oaths begging to be let loose into the frigid night air. He didn't dare give in. He was too close to the upstairs windows, and for all that his dad's booze-enhanced sleep was deep, there was always the chance he would wake. And then he'd come looking for whatever had disturbed his rest…

Heaven knew the man needed his rest. You couldn't teach everyone else in the world how *they* should act and think and live if you weren't rested. Of course, when no one wanted to listen to you, when they treated you like you were some kind of rigid jerk, that left only one place—home sweet home—to prove you were best. Strongest. Not to be ignored.

The desperate need to get away, to be as far as he could be from this house assaulted Gabe. He started down the street, his feet seeming to know where he was going before he did. But that was okay. His feet had the right idea. He knew where he wanted to be...what he wanted to see.

It would help, even if it was only for a moment.

But was it too late? He glanced at the sky to see how high the moon had risen—and only then did he realize it was snowing. Big, fluffy flakes that floated down, dancing on the wind like frozen puffs from a dandelion. Gabe tipped back his head, watching the gentle descent, and let his eyes close, just for a moment, as he felt the tiny flakes land and melt on his face.

What he wouldn't give to be one of them...to just drift out of the sky, not caring where he landed. After all, snowflakes were only around for a heartbeat. One frozen moment of existence, one easy freefall, and then it was all over. They were done. Gone. Nonexistent.

The thought made him smile, but he regretted the action almost immediately. He reached up to rub his mouth, his jaw. So he hadn't taken it all in the gut. Just most of it.

He liked the way the heavy blanket of snow on the sidewalk scrunched under his shoes. So what if the wet was seeping in through the holes and soaking his socks? The cold felt kind of good...like an ice pack. Wasn't that what you were supposed to put on bruises? Ice packs?

His lip curled. Well, then, he was doing exactly what he needed to. So what if it was from the feet up?

He looked up again. The moon hung low in the sky, casting a warm glow on the empty streets. Good. It wasn't too late.

Gabe liked being out here like this, after dark, when everyone else was hiding away in their houses. He liked being alone. He especially liked not having to watch anyone, to study every nuance of expression or movement for a warning. Like he should have been watching earlier tonight. He still couldn't believe he'd let himself get distracted. He was thirteen years old. Old enough to know better. Hadn't he told himself tonight was a night to be extra careful? He'd even gone out to shovel the driveway, just to make sure there wasn't anything left undone, anything to get Dad upset.

He had worked hard and fast, determined to finish before his father's car pulled in. He hardly dared believe it when he did so, and he stood for a moment staring at the cleared concrete. Amazing. One moment it was buried, unseen beneath the mounds of white. The next it lay there, clean, free of obstacles...exposed.

Gabe chewed his cold lip, then turned from the oddly disturbing sight of that cleared driveway and stomped his way inside. He knocked the snow from his boots as he came into the kitchen, looked up to find his mother and tell her the job was done—and stopped cold.

If the empty driveway had been unsettling, what he saw now was positively surreal. Like some crazy Christmas card or commercial come to life in the most unlikely place in the world: his home.

Mom was standing there at the kitchen table, white apron tied in place, smiling and stirring, looking for all the world like those sweet-faced moms on TV. She was making cookies.

Gabe blinked once, twice. But the image remained.

A sweet fragrance hung in the kitchen, filling the room as completely as it filled his senses. Chocolate-chip cookies. His mouth watered just thinking about them.

His sister, Susan, was helping Mom. Her main duty apparently was keeping Mikey from grabbing fingers full of the dough from the large glass bowl. Mikey was a cookie dough fiend. He'd rather eat the stuff raw than cooked, and Gabe didn't think it was because he was only eight. He figured Mike would be snitching dough when he was forty. Or eighty, for that matter.

Susan was too fast for the little guy, though. She nabbed both his hands midsnitch, and as Gabe shed his coat she dragged the kid, kicking and screaming, into the living room. Gabe closed out the sound of Mike's frustration. It wasn't hard to do. He'd learned a long time ago how to block out unpleasant sounds.

It didn't take Susan long to come back, taking up her post at the kitchen table, measuring out this ingredient or that as Mom directed. Gabe grabbed a glass from the drainer, rubbed it clean on his shirt, and filled it with water, then went to perch on a chair and watch the proceedings.

Susan was always helping in the kitchen. She might be only two years older than Gabe, but she loved to play second mom, cooking and taking care of the little ones. The kitchen was where she smiled. Where you hardly even noticed the dark circles under her eyes...or the blank, empty look that came to cloak her face more and more often lately.

With the odd sense that he'd stepped into some alternate universe, Gabe watched his sister and mother as they worked. He perched on a chair, resting his chin in his hands. He liked the way they were together, the way they seemed to communicate without even talking. He liked that they accepted his presence without seeming to take notice of it. Just one smile sent his direction and then back to the task at hand.

He lost himself in the moment, watching his mother's hands as she added ingredients, stirred the mixture with a large wooden spoon. He inched closer to the bowl, bit by bit, careful not to let them see his movements.

Mikey wasn't the only one who liked the dough.

"Forget it, Gabriel."

He looked up to meet Susan's firm stare. If it had been his

mother using his full name like that, he'd know he was in trouble. But Susan always called him *Gabriel*. Sometimes he wondered if that's how she reminded herself who he was, as though using a nickname would somehow make him someone different.

"No snitching dough, Gabriel. I wouldn't let Michael do it. I can't let you." Her one arched brow told him she wasn't kidding. Normally he would have just given in. But tonight...things were different. They were different. He was different. And he wanted to play.

And tonight, though he wasn't sure exactly why, he knew that would be okay.

He gave her his best puppy-dog face, wide eyes and all. "Aw, come on. I've been working hard."

She didn't reply. Just lifted a wooden spoon and held it in her fisted hand, just above the bowl, the message clear: *Go ahead and try...if you dare.*

Gabe didn't. Play was one thing, but he knew from experience how fast Susan could be with a wooden spoon—and how long it took for bare knuckles to stop smarting.

He'd wait for the cookies to come out of the oven.

With a sigh, Gabe slid from his chair and made his way to the living room. Bill was sprawled in one of the chairs in front of the TV. Gabe couldn't help it. He stared. What was his older brother doing here? Gabe went to take a look out the front window, then he frowned. Bill's old clunker of a car was there by the curb. So he hadn't wrecked it or anything. The question returned: Why was he home?

Since Bill got his license a year ago, he was hardly ever home. He usually disappeared with his buddies as soon as school was out. Which was exactly what he'd done the first day of Christmas vacation, and Gabe hadn't seen him since then. Until tonight.

He almost said something, almost asked Bill if all his friends were busy or gone or if he'd just felt like slumming at home, but he kept his mouth shut. He liked it that Bill was home. Whatever the reason.

Mikey was sitting on the floor next to the baby. Not that Lisa was really a baby. She was seven, but she was the youngest, and everyone called her that: *the baby*. Like she didn't have a real name or something. Which was okay. She didn't seem to mind. It was as though she knew, even at that tender age, what a blessing it was to be a nonentity.

Gabe glanced at the TV and saw they were all watching some goofy Christmas special. He moved to the couch, settled into the worn cushions, and focused on the TV screen, letting the story take hold, pull him in. Without even thinking, he eased out of reality and into the fantasy. He took his place on the screen, saying the well-timed dialogue, playing the part to perfection.

Amazing how easy it was, stepping out of himself and becoming someone else. He remembered the first time he'd done it. He'd been standing in front of his fifth-grade class for show-and-tell. He hated show-and-tell. Hated how everyone stared at him. He could see they didn't like him. Thought he was stupid. Well, that day he'd had enough.

He stood there and looked at the faces until he came to Robbie Niedermeyer, the most popular kid in class. Suddenly Gabe knew what he would do. As though it were the most natural thing in the world, he made the change—let Robbie's customary self-satisfied smirk ease over his own stiff lips, let the boy's swagger settle over his own body like the soft quilt that hid him at night...

He straightened, faced his enemies, and became Robbie Niedermeyer. He'd been funny. Teasing. Just smug enough to stir respect in the other kids, yet unpretentious enough to bring approval to the teacher's features. When he finished, turning to her with a flourish, she actually stood and came to place an approving hand on his shoulder. Her glowing words still sounded in his ears: "That was wonderful, Gabe!"

He'd thought so, too, and as he made his way back to his desk, he knew he made a discovery. Being Gabe Roman was nothing. Worse than nothing. So he wouldn't be Gabe Roman any more than he had to. Instead, he'd become whoever he wanted. And it worked. Most of the time.

Except with Susan. She could always tell when he stepped into a part. "Quit acting, Gabriel," she'd always say. "I want to know how you really feel."

He hated it when she did that, blew his cover that way. Thank goodness she only did it at home.

He shifted on the couch, no longer interested in the TV show. It was too unbelievable, even for playacting. He let his attention wander back to the kitchen. He could just see Susan and their mom—hands buried safely in large oven mitts—as they slid trays of golden-brown cookies from the oven. They were talking quietly, and Mom was laughing. The aroma of freshly baked cookies seemed to swirl in the air around them, then travel out to tickle Gabe's nose.

He closed his eyes against the confusion clawing at him. Who were these people? It was almost like they had taken his lead and were playing a part, something straight out of TV— like they were one of those make-believe families Gabe and his siblings usually laughed at. "No one is really like that," they'd say with a snort.

But here they were. *His* family. Making cookies and watching Christmas specials on TV.

It was all too much. Gabe sank to the floor, huddling next to his younger brother and sister. Maybe *this* was who they were. Maybe that other family was the illusion…just some kind of dark dream that had finally gone away.

That's what he told himself anyway as he gave in to the TV special, letting the images capture and woo him, bring a whisper of joy to his face and heart.

That's what distracted him. What kept him from realizing what was happening until it was too late. Exactly when his father came home he didn't know. But there was no doubt he was there. Because the talking and laughing in the kitchen stopped.

It was the silence that warned Gabe. It pricked at his ears until awareness jolted through him and he jerked away from the TV, surging to his feet. But not in time. Even as he moved to the kitchen the silence exploded.

Obscenities. Screaming. A hand hitting flesh; fists pounding, crushing.

Things were back to normal.

He didn't enter the kitchen. He knew better. He came to the doorway and looked in. Susan was in the corner of the room, hunkered down. That blank look was back, and the emptiness in her frozen expression made Gabe shudder. She held her arms crossed in front of her like some kind of shield as she watched their father making a point with their mother.

That's what he called it: *making a point.*

"If you'd do what I tell you," he always said, sometimes during, sometimes after, "I wouldn't have to make a point this way. You just don't listen."

And then the line he always saved for Gabe. Just for Gabe. "You're so stupid. Why are you so stupid?"

Everything inside Gabe screamed at him to step inside the kitchen, to reach out and *do* something. To try and stop his father. But it wouldn't make any difference. Nothing they did ever made a difference.

Just as suddenly as it had started, it was over. Gabe's father let go of his wife, and she sagged against the counter, hands firmly planted there. Gabe knew the effort it took her to keep standing, to keep from falling in a heap at his father's feet. But such weakness would only bring more punishment.

Gabe held his breath as his father stood there, rending the air with verbal violence so heated and vile that it was almost as much an assault as the beatings. Almost. Gabe shifted his gaze to Susan, caught her glance, urged her to keep silent. *Don't move...don't make a sound...*

The whimper that escaped her was so faint, so feeble, that Gabe let himself hope his father wouldn't hear. *Please... please, God...*

Gabe should have known better than to pray. When had that ever done any good? Especially when his father seemed to have the hearing of a jackal. The man spun, launching himself across the room to grab Susan's crossed arms and jerk her to her feet.

Don't fight...don't resist...

It was all Gabe could offer as he stood there, feeling the blows his sister took as though they landed on him instead. His hand gripped the wood of the doorway so hard that the ache traveled through his fingers, along his arms and shoulders, and pushed deep into the base of his skull.

He pushed away, walking back to the living room, sinking onto the floor. Bill watched him in silence, but Gabe saw the whiteness around his brother's jaw, knew the ache of muscle and bone from teeth clenched against the fury screaming for release.

But even Bill wouldn't be able to stop it. He'd tried. Once or twice. And things had been worse for all of them. They'd seen, over and over, that the only recourse was to stay out of the way. Be silent. Be invisible.

Be nothing.

Their father was bigger, stronger, and his rage was a living thing—a huge, ravenous monstrosity that fed on whatever scraps of fear or resistance they gave it. Fed and fed, until nothing was left.

Nothing. The only place of safety.

Gabe wasn't sure when Bill moved, but he heard his brother and father meet at the kitchen doorway. He closed his eyes as words flew...words meant to humiliate, to shatter and destroy. Words of pure, unadulterated hatred.

Then the unbelievable sound. One Gabe had never heard before, never thought to hear. Bill wasn't just trying to stop their dad—he was fighting back.

Astonishment. Dread. Confusion. Wild hope. These emotions chased countless others through Gabe's veins, sending cold and then heat surging into his face. The sounds grew as the battle escalated. Gabe couldn't believe Bill had lasted this long. Could it be…?

Was he winning?

A raw victory cry lodged in Gabe's throat as he turned to look—and saw his father snatch a beer bottle from the dining room table and slam it into the side of Bill's head.

Despair slid from Gabe on a soft moan as Bill's eyes widened, then rolled back in his head. Bill went limp and sank to the floor.

He stared at his brother's senseless form. He was so still…was he even breathing? Was he dead?

Gabe sensed his father standing beside him before he saw him. He started and, before he could stop himself, looked up. Blank terror muddled his mind when he met his father's gaze, stared into those bloodshot, burning eyes.

The man stood there, dragging air in through clenched teeth, his hot, liquor-saturated breath blowing over Gabe, turning his stomach with the stench. He tensed, readied for the onslaught, but his father's eyes flickered…and then slid past him.

Gabe's stomach lurched, then plummeted. It was as if his father didn't even see him. Couldn't care less that he was there.

He should have been glad. Knew he should be filled with joy, gratitude, relief, *something* positive…

Anything other than what slammed into him with a pain so stark and raw that it nearly doubled him over.

Rejection.

It was crazy, but there it was. And it sliced through him,

sickening him, leaving his soul shredded, hanging in tatters of sorrow and hollow rage as the bleak truth ravaged his heart: *I'm not even worth beating.*

The words echoed through him, mocking him, tearing at the core of him, tormenting him until he could bear it no longer. He pushed up from the floor, straightening his legs and spine as he stood in front of his father, forcing the man's gaze to lock with his own.

I'm here. I'm here! Don't you look through me like I'm not!

But his father barely seemed to notice. He just shoved him aside, like some kind of pest, like a gnat that didn't even deserve a thought or a glance—

"Watch out, you crazy kid!"

The angry words—and an accompanying honk of a car horn—wrenched Gabe from his thoughts, and he jumped back to the curb just in time to avoid the vehicle as it sped by. He shook his head. Leave it to him to step out in front of what was probably the only car on the road this time of night.

Stupid is as stupid does.

The familiar taunt rang in his mind, but tonight the weight of it seemed unbearable. He looked at the snow-covered ground, wishing he could just lie down...let the cold seep in and coax him into a forever sleep.

A haze of white around his head caught his attention, and he realized his breath was coming in quick gasps, each exhalation making crystalline clouds in the icy air—tiny puffs that appeared and then drifted, dissipated, disappeared. He stared at the misty evidence of his existence and started when a harsh laugh escaped him, echoing around him.

He wasn't invisible. Not really. His father just treated him that way. Always had. But tonight...tonight had been the worst ever.

Gabe glanced at the houses near him. It wasn't much farther. He'd be at his haven soon.

He started walking again, trudging, trying to focus on his

steps, on the snow, on anything but the images haunting his mind. But they would not be denied, so Gabe gave in and let them return.

Thinking back on it now, he wasn't exactly sure what had happened. The clearest image he had was of something white-hot piercing his mind, his very soul, incinerating everything within him, filling him like life-giving air pouring into lungs that had lain deflated and useless. His vision had narrowed until all he saw was his father's back as he moved toward the baby. Reached down. Grabbed her by the wrist. Jerked her to her feet, his fist raised...

Gabe had been on him then, in a blaze of blinding rage, hitting, kicking, biting, slapping—using every weapon available against the beast that inhabited his father's form.

He wished he could say he'd only done it for Lisa and Mikey. To stand between them and the monster. But concern for the others hadn't been the only thing propelling him into action. Something quite different had pushed him. Something more powerful than he'd ever imagined.

Rage. It filled him. No, that wasn't quite right. It wasn't so much that it filled him as it took him over. Possessed him. *Became* him...or he'd become it.

Yes. That was it. He'd become rage. A living, breathing rage. It had been the most terrifying—and exhilarating—sensation he'd ever known. And it had done what he'd never been able to do on his own.

It made his father see him. Really see him.

Gabe replayed the moment in his mind, reliving the spark of astonishment in his father's eyes as he spun to take Gabe's assault. His father had turned from Lisa to look at him—and for one suspended moment they'd stood there, face-to-face, gazes locked.

Gabe looked from Lisa to his father. "No."

One word. It was all Gabe said, but it resonated with this new power flowing in his veins. The word was a declaration, a pronouncement to let his father know it was over. Gabe was free.

His father hesitated, took a step back, then, as though catching himself, he sneered. "So the boy wants to be a man?"

Gabe didn't even acknowledge the slurred mockery. He simply stood there, hands fisted at his sides, as the power surged through him with such force he trembled. But not out of fear. He hadn't been afraid at all. Not even when his father lunged at him. Not even when the man's greater strength and weight overpowered him, or when the blows became so many that Gabe welcomed the darkness.

None of that mattered. Gabe had won.

It didn't even matter that his father had beaten him physically. That would never matter again. Gabe had found freedom in this new place where all that mattered was the rage within. Let his father think he'd defeated him. It only made Gabe that much stronger. That much more determined.

His father would never hurt him again. Not where it mattered most. Gabe had found an ally, something to take his heart and protect it. And one day...one day he'd be big enough and strong enough that he and his friend would win the physical battle as well.

He could hardly wait. Hardly wait for the sight of his father at his feet, crumpled and bleeding...

The ache in Gabe's hands made him aware that they were clenched into fists, and he forced his fingers open, flexing them, willing blood back into them. He turned a corner and halted.

There it was.

Excitement skittered through him as he made his way toward the simple white house before him. It was a small house compared to the others on the block, but Gabe didn't care. What mattered was what was inside.

Just like with you...just like the power...it's what's inside that makes the difference.

Warm light glowed from the curtained windows of the home, and gladness sang inside Gabe. A quick glance told him the street was deserted, and he made his way to the bushes in front of a large plateglass window. He'd discovered some time ago that the bushes were the perfect location— standing behind them he was hidden from anyone walking by, but he had a perfect view inside.

He slid into place, hugging himself to dispel the chill that was working its way along his arms and shoulders, and peered inside. They were there. The family. He didn't know their names. The children were too young to be in his class at school. But he knew them all the same. Knew well the tenderness as they looked at each other, the warmth of their smiles, the frequency of their laughter. He couldn't hear the actual words they spoke, but he didn't need to. It wasn't the words that brought him such joy.

It was the people themselves. And the love.

There was always such love.

He let his hungry gaze roam the living room. Though no one was there, he knew without a doubt what he was seeing. *This* was Christmas. A tree laden with decorations—many of which looked homemade—stood proud and tall in the corner of the room. Twinkling lights peeked out from among the branches, and Gabe was captivated. It was as if they were winking at him, welcoming him.

He leaned forward, studying the presents gathered beneath the tree. There weren't a lot of them, but each one was wrapped with colorful paper and topped with a bright bow and colorful, curled ribbons. Gabe could picture the hands that had held these packages, had wrapped them with such care, creating small bits of beauty just to make others happy, to tell them you loved them…

Christmas decorations gave the normally warm room an added glow, a feeling of celebration and fun. Stars, Santas, reindeer, snowmen—they adorned walls and tables and danced from the ceiling. Christmas stockings, brimming with promise, hung from the fireplace mantel. Just above them sat a carved nativity scene, complete with a tiny wooden stable and figurines of angels, shepherds, animals. And the baby Jesus.

The soft strains of Christmas music whispered through the glass, and Gabe drank in the sound. *"O holy night..."*

Holy night. Gabe had never understood what that meant, but he was pretty sure that was what they were having here. In this little house. A holy night.

Together.

Gabe started at the sound of voices and ducked back for a moment, then, drawing a deep breath, he inched his way forward to see what was happening. The mom and dad came into the room, laughing, their two boys trailing behind them. The kids were in their pajamas, and Gabe wiggled his cold toes at the sight of the warm, snuggly slippers on their small feet.

The parents sat on the couch as the boys danced over to the tree. Each one pulled a package from the pile, then carried it to the couch. Gabe felt an odd choking in his throat when the boys clambered with careless abandon onto the couch, nestling between their parents, their gifts clutched against their chests.

He watched as the mom and dad leaned in, stroking first one child's hair, and then the other's, as the boys tore open their gifts. But the pleasure the kids took in their new toys was nothing compared to what shone on the adults' faces when they watched their sons—and when they looked at each other.

Hands clasped on the back of the couch, the man and woman leaned over their children to exchange a kiss—then broke off with laughter when the boys jumped up and crawled into their laps, throwing their little arms around the mother and father.

Gabe leaned his head against the side of the house, swallowing hard against a lump that had suddenly lodged somewhere between his throat and his heart. An odd ache was growing within him, and he pressed his lips together, caught off guard by the sudden awareness that his cheeks were wet.

He was crying. He *never* cried.

He pushed his fists against his eyes, rubbing at the tears that showed him just how wrong he was. Drawing in a deep gulp of subzero air, he let it burn his lungs, wanting the physical pain. Welcoming it. Anything to distract him.

It didn't help. He wanted to close his eyes, to hide in darkness from this bitter, cold despair that seemed to live in the cave of his soul. He'd always known it was there, been vaguely aware of it, but it had never felt like this before. It was tearing at him, clawing its way from deep inside, making him tremble with such longing that he could only stare at the night in mute wretchedness.

Just walk away, you idiot. Go home. But he couldn't. He didn't want to leave any more than he wanted to stay and suffer this torture, this watching and wanting what he knew he never had. What he never *would* have. He gritted his teeth against a surge of anger that his one haven, this one place where he came to find some sense of good, had suddenly become yet another source of pain.

Almost against his will, Gabe's focus returned to the small family, to the room and faces that shone with a wonder he'd only dreamed of, watching, weeping, until the ache inside him exploded, surging through him, taking all his yearning and confusion and loneliness and crystallizing them into one desperate prayer.

"Please...I just want someone to love me like that."

6

DECEMBER 19, 2003
NOON

"OPEN YOUR EYES, GABE. IT'S TIME TO WAKE UP. NOW!"

Renee made the words as firm as she could, but it was hard to sound authoritative when her voice kept cracking and trembling. Bo whined as though sensing her frustration, her growing desperation, and moved to nudge Gabe with his nose.

Renee reached out to stop the dog, then let her hand fall back into her lap. She wasn't getting anywhere with Gabe. Might as well let Bo give it a shot. That cold nose of his had gotten Gabe going many a morning. Maybe it would work now.

She leaned back against the seat cushion, uncertain which was worse: worrying about Gabe, about how badly he might be injured, or having to face this situation alone.

When Bo came to lay his head alongside her arm on the console, she gave him an understanding scratch. "I know, boy. You tried."

She lay her palm on Gabe's face. His skin was growing cool to the touch. She had to keep him warm. She grabbed the duffel, pulling out the blanket and several of the heat packets. She wrapped the blanket about him as best she could, then kneaded and shook the packets until the heat began to generate. She slid them between his coat and his shirt.

She settled back in her seat, rubbing a hand over her tight neck muscles. A frown worked its way across her forehead. How long had Gabe been unconscious? For that matter, how long since they'd gone through the snow barriers, over the edge of the road? She glanced at her watch—twelve o'clock. They'd left that morning around nine, which meant they'd have hit the stretch of road that was now above them around ten.

It also meant they had roughly four or five hours before darkness set in.

Renee glared at the storm that still raged around them. The snow was so thick she couldn't even tell if the road they'd been on was in front of or behind them. She realized she was tapping her heel on the floor with rapid, nervous movements. Gabe hated it when she did that. If he'd been conscious, he would have put a hand on her knee to still the action.

She pressed her hands onto her knees in his stead, willing herself to relax. "Wait…" She spoke into the silence, wishing the sound of her voice would calm and soothe her rather than just remind her how alone she was. "The truck is big and red, someone should be able to see it from the road…"

If they're looking, which they probably aren't. And if it isn't blanketed in snow, which it probably is.

She gritted her teeth against the snide voice that shivered up her spine and ricocheted off the frayed edges of her mind.

She was not going to panic. But even as she told herself that, she realized her heel was tapping rapid-fire and her knee was bouncing like a caffeine-crazed Chihuahua.

Jesus…Lord…

She dug her fingers into her knees as she prayed, almost welcoming the pain that came on the heels of the action. At least pain meant she was still alive.

Her chilled, frightened mind couldn't come up with anything more eloquent than that. *Just help us.* But she knew it was enough, just as she knew she wasn't alone. Not really. Gabe wasn't the only one in that truck cab with her.

The truth seeped into her, bringing a warmth that traveled across her ragged nerves, soothing, calming…

Renee closed her eyes, focusing on that warmth, embracing it, letting it ease the tension from her neck and shoulders, the pain in her body.

"Okay." Her voice was steadier now. "Okay, I'll wait. It won't be long until Gabe comes to, and then we can decide together what to do."

It was a good plan. She liked it. It certainly was preferable to the plan gnawing at the back of her mind—the one that had her going out into that storm by herself to find help…the one that kept saying she'd have to follow if they were going to have any chance of survival.

Shut up, she told the voice, *just shut up.* She had the feeling it was laughing at her, but she went on anyway, forcing a certainty she only wished she felt into her thoughts. *It's not up to me, it's up to God. And He won't let us die out here. I know He won't. Someone will find us soon.*

But even as she made the assertions, the sharp prick of doubt assaulted her. She brushed the snow from the dash and peered out the windshield at the blank, white world. *Would someone find them? Did she really believe God was going to save them?*

"Of course I do." If only her whispered words rang with

far more conviction and far less apprehension. With a shuddering sigh, she closed her eyes against the tears that suddenly stung them. Then, curling into a ball on the seat, she leaned her forehead on her drawn-up knees and let her eyes drift shut.

She needed sleep. Rest. To preserve her strength and clear her mind. And, for just a little while, to escape her situation.

If only she could escape her doubts as well. But she knew she couldn't. Hadn't she been trying to do exactly that for years? And here they were again, taunting her, tormenting her.

Hopelessness hovered over her. She could feel it, like some great, dark bird of prey just waiting to descend, to dig its claws into her. Renee shuddered, moving her arms to cover her head.

Lord…please help me. I don't think I can do this alone.

When we are linked by the power of prayer,
we hold each other's hand...
while we walk along a slippery path.

GREGORY THE GREAT

"I will answer them before they even call to me."

ISAIAH 65:24

DECEMBER 19, 2003
12:15 P.M.

GRACE FRAZIER WAS IN THE KITCHEN, JUST GETTING
ready to go into the dining room and sit to eat her lunch—a nice,
steaming bowl of homemade corn chowder—when she heard it.

"Pray."

She hesitated. Pray? Well, what did that mean? A frown
pinched her brow. Had she forgotten to pray this morning?
Heaven knew she was forgetting more and more things lately...
But that didn't make sense. She'd already had her devotion and
prayer time several hours earlier.

Maybe it's God.

She gave a soft snort. It hadn't sounded like God. Come to
think of it, it sounded more like... She shook off the notion. *Don't
be silly,* she scolded herself as she walked to the dining room.

Renee is out of town. You can't be hearing her calling to you.

That settled, Grace eased into her chair, then glanced at her husband, pondering. It hadn't sounded at all like him, but who else could it have been?

Apparently aware of her pensive stare, Oren looked up from the thick piece of bread he was buttering, blond brows arched, pale blue eyes regarding her with mild curiosity. "Yes?"

She shifted in her chair. "What?"

Confusion painted both his features and his tone. "*What* what?"

Grace folded her hands in her lap. "Well, didn't you just say something?"

He cocked his head. "I don't think so." A grin twitched at his bearded features and he waggled his brows. "Why? Are the voices talking to you again?"

Grace made a face at him and pulled her napkin into her lap. "Ha, ha, ha."

Oren's work-roughened fingers closed over hers, and she looked at him, her irritation melting under the tender smile he gave her. Oh, she did love this man. Irritating quirks and all.

"Ready to pray?"

She turned her hand in his so that their fingers laced together and nodded. They bowed their heads, and Grace basked in the sweet sound of her husband's voice as he gave thanks for the meal and for the hands that prepared it.

When he was done, his fingers tightened on hers in a gentle squeeze—that was their special way of saying "I love you"—and she squeezed back, then released him and picked up her spoon. The soup had been simmering most of the morning and the tantalizing fragrance had been teasing her for hours. She could hardly wait to taste—

"*Pray!*"

Her spoon clattered to the plate. "*Or-en!*"

He jumped, and the spoonful of soup that had just about reached his mouth splattered onto his shirt. "Oh, for..." He glared first at the stain and then at her. "*What?*"

A bubble of laughter rose up inside her, but she resisted it, shaking her head. What a pair they made! "Come, now. Are you going to tell me you didn't *hear* that?"

"Hon, hear what?" The faint glimmer of concern in his eyes truly looked genuine—a fact that only served to irk her.

"That...that *voice.*" She waved her hands, looking around. If Oren hadn't spoken the word, then perhaps... Was someone hiding in the room? "It practically yelled at me this ti—" She bit off the word and fixed Oren with a mild glare. "Oren Donald Frazier, are you playing another one of your infernal tricks on me? You *know* I hate it when you take advantage of the fact that I'm just a little gullible—"

"A *little* gullible?" He hooted. "Hon, if you're a *little* gullible, then Santa is a *little* fat, Rockefeller was a *little* wealthy, Bozo the clown was..."

Her glare intensified.

"...was..."

She crossed her arms.

"Um..." He met her stare, recognized a losing battle, and let whatever he'd been about to say trail off. Clasping his hands in front of him, he cleared his throat and gave her his most wide-eyed, I'm-sorry-dear-did-I-cross-that-line-again look. She might have almost believed he was sorry, too, except for that sparkle of laughter in his eyes. And the way his lips kept twitching.

Grace arched one brow and compressed her lips into a prim line. *I am not amused,* she conveyed as clearly as she could without speaking the words.

Oren swallowed, then drummed his fingers on the table, refusing to look at her. He stared at the wall, out the window, anywhere but at her. He started to whistle, but the song fizzled on his puckered lips when Grace cleared her throat.

He looked down at his hands and sat in silence for a moment...then two...then he looked up. "I'm sorry, hon, what was the question?"

She let out a huff. "For heaven's sake, Oren! I was talking about that voice. Did you or did you not hear that voice?"

He leaned toward her, the very image of sincere concern—or he would have been if he'd been able to erase the snicker from his tone. "What's the, uh, the voice saying?"

"Ohhh, you!" She stood and went to look out the window, muttering all the way. "I *know* I heard it, but why did it sound like Renee? I know it couldn't have been her."

"Grace..."

She ignored her husband's oddly hushed comment and pulled back the curtain, peering outside. Maybe one of the neighbor children was hiding outside. "Most likely it's that imp, Jimmy Bell. He's a sweet boy, but I can't even begin to count the times I've had to shoo the little barefoot dickens off of my pansies."

"Grace..."

She hesitated. No, not Jimmy. The voice had been a woman's. Or maybe a girl's. "Well, then, it must have been little Robin Lee. You know, Oren, how such an angel-faced child could come up with so many pranks is simply beyond me." She pressed her nose against the glass, trying to see if anyone was hiding just below the window. "Now, don't get me wrong, dear, I love it that the children enjoy coming to visit, to tease and have fun, but my poor pansies—"

"*Gracie!*"

She studied her husband. What on earth was he getting so worked up about? But something about the look on his face—like a man suddenly recognizing someone he hadn't seen in a long time—made her stop and turn back to him.

"Hon," he said slowly, as though working the words past whatever was rolling around in his mind, "exactly what did the voice say?"

She clasped her hands in front of her. "Pray."

"Pray? Are you sure?" Oren wasn't laughing now. In fact, every vestige of humor was gone. Instead, his eyes were wide and rueful.

Grace frowned. "Yes, pray. That's it. Just...*pray.*"

Her husband leaned back in his chair, and Grace could *tell* he knew something. So he *had* been behind it! She planted her hands on her hips—something she usually avoided because it only reminded her how they'd spread over the past few years, but right now she didn't care about that. "Oren, what are you up to—"

"Hon, I heard it."

That stopped her cold. He'd heard the voice? She marched back to the table. "Then why did you say you didn't?"

"Because *I* heard it outside, in my shop." His gaze met hers. "Just before I came in for lunch."

Grace stared at him; then, her knees suddenly too weak to support her, she pulled out her chair and plopped down on the seat. "Outside."

He nodded, those generous lips twitching. "Before I came in."

Oh, dear. "Then that means..."

She saw in his expression that the same understanding filling her mind had come to him. "We did it again, didn't we?"

He sighed and lifted his shoulders in a hapless shrug. "I figured it was just kids playing."

"So did I."

"Well, hon—" he folded her hands in his—"at least we can rest in the fact that God is patient with us."

She looked down at their joined hands, loving the way his huge paws covered hers, the way her fingers nestled in his as though every aspect of the two of them had been made to fit together.

Even their stubborn weaknesses.

Just a few months ago they'd asked God to speak to them, to move in their minds and hearts until they came to know His still, small voice with such intimacy they wouldn't hesitate to obey. It had been a bold request, but they truly wanted it. God had brought them through so much, and they wanted to give back. To Him. To His people. What better way to do that than to pray for others?

They waited, sure a response would come. But nothing happened. Not in the way they expected, anyway.

Of course, that didn't surprise Grace. God always seemed to work with her on the offbeat—when she least expected it, in ways that were surprising, unexpected…unique.

Oren said that was because God fit the working of His will to the clay being molded, and if there was one thing Grace was, it was unique. "You're one of a kind, hon," he'd say, those blue eyes shining, "and you're all mine."

No, God's answer hadn't come quickly. But it had come. Several weeks after their fervent prayer, He had sent a call whispering first through Oren's heart and then Grace's. It was nothing elaborate. Just the name of a young man from church. And the urge to invite him over for dinner. But by then Grace and Oren weren't really thinking about their request, and so each had dismissed the prodding as their own thoughts, and each let the idea slide.

It wasn't until a few days later, after church, when they realized what had happened. The very same young man stood up during prayer request time and shared how God had saved him from making a terrible decision.

"I was so depressed." Emotion choked his voice. "I felt like nobody cared, and then Mrs. Wilson called—" he directed a shining smile at the woman seated in one of the front pews—"and said God had put my name in her heart. Can you imagine that? Put my name in her heart and asked her to invite me over for coffee."

He told how their conversation showed him God was watching over him, but Grace only listened to bits and pieces of his happy report. Something was gnawing at her, distracting her.

On the drive home, she started to say something about it to Oren, but he beat her to the punch.

"You know Danny, that young man in church today?"

Grace nodded.

"Funny thing—" Oren chewed his lip as he maneuvered a sharp curve—"I almost came home that very day and asked you to invite him over for dinner."

Grace stared at him. At her far-from-characteristic silence, Oren glanced her way. "Gracie?"

"Oren, I almost did *exactly* that same thing. *I* thought of Danny. And *I* wanted to ask him for dinner."

Her husband pondered this, then pulled to the side of the road and shut the car off. "Are you telling me we both thought about asking that same boy over for dinner?"

She nodded.

"On the same day?"

She nodded again, and they both sat back.

"Well."

Oren reached out to take her hand. "So God answered our prayer. We just didn't listen."

She bit her lip and nodded, fighting the urge to cry.

"Well…"

When Grace met Oren's gaze, he gave her hand a gentle tug. "I guess next time maybe we'd best pay attention."

They'd tried. Really they had. And Grace wondered if that was part of the problem: They were trying too hard. Like watching a kettle of water and waiting for it to boil. Blasted thing *never* boiled, no matter how hard you stared. But look away for half a blink, and there it went, spitting water everywhere.

Maybe God's gentle whispers were like that. Focus on

them, try to make yourself hear them, and the only thing ringing through your mind and heart was a blaring silence. But let yourself get distracted by life, and bingo! There it came...that soft, unassuming nudge that was so easy to ignore.

Just as they'd done today.

Grace settled back in her chair as regret played tag with frustration inside her. Oren patted her hand.

"Don't fret, dear. We're still learning."

She nodded. "If only God would be a bit more obvious."

Oren tipped his head at that. "Obvious?"

She turned to face him. "You know, more...I don't know...Godlike. I mean, He sounds so much like me..."

Oren's lips were twitching again. "Oh yes, dear, I've always thought you sounded like God."

She swatted at his arm. "You know what I mean. It's easy to dismiss those little urgings because they seem like *my* thoughts." She waved her hands. "Why, I'd *never* have dismissed the voice if it had *sounded* like God. You know, powerful. Holy."

Oren didn't answer. He was frowning, in deep concentration. "Gracie, did you say the voice you heard sounded like a woman?"

She focused on his dear face. "Yes. Actually, it...it was a particular woman's voice. It sounded like Renee."

Apparent surprise tugged at his brows. "Renee Roman?"

She nodded and then almost jumped out of her chair when he gave a whoop. "Oren, what on earth—"

"Sweetheart, the voice I heard? It was Gabriel Roman! And it said the same thing: *Pray*." Awe crept across his features. "Hon, we haven't missed it. Not at all. God is calling us to pray for the Romans."

Excitement danced through Grace, and she clasped her hands—then stopped. "Oh, no..."

Oren studied her features. "What?"

She grabbed his hands. "Oh, Oren, the Romans! They've been through so much."

Oren and Grace had met the Romans years ago when they attended a Bible study together. It hadn't taken long for the two couples to realize how much they had in common, and a strong friendship grew between them. Oren and Grace opened their hearts and home to the younger couple, grateful to be able to help someone else as they'd been helped.

"I know, hon." Oren patted her hand.

"And this was supposed to be such a special time for them. What could have gone wrong? You don't suppose they—"

Oren's fingers pressed against her lips, and she swallowed back the string of questions ready to spill forth. The patience she saw in the depths of Oren's eyes warmed her heart, casting off the chill of apprehension that had begun to cloak her.

"Gracie, I don't know what's going on. But God does. And He's asked us to pray for them, so maybe it's time we stopped jabbering and got down to doing what He says. After all, there's nothing more powerful than that, now is there?" The tenderness in his features, the touch of his fingers, enveloped her.

No, there wasn't anything more powerful than prayer. The simple fact that they were here was more than enough proof of that.

With a full heart, Grace nodded, and together they bowed their heads. As they did so, a powerful certainty grew within Grace's heart: She and Oren were doing exactly what they were supposed to do. And no matter what the Romans were facing, God was with them. Just as He'd been with Grace and Oren.

And He would be sufficient.

8

One can say, perhaps, that sorrow…
played its part in setting me free.

ANNE LINDBERGH

Moses entered into the deep darkness where God was.

EXODUS 20:21

DECEMBER 19, 2003
1:15 P.M.

RENEE OPENED HER EYES SLOWLY, BLINKING AGAINST
the brightness that surrounded her.

Pain followed on the heels of wakefulness, and she cried out
against it as a mixture of fear and anger flooded her. What was
happening? Why was everything white? And why was it so
cold—?

Reality, stark and sudden, soaked in, and she closed her eyes
on a weary sigh. She'd hoped it was a dream. Prayed it was. But
there was nothing dreamlike about the wind buffeting the truck,
rocking them from side to side.

They really had gone over the side of the road. They really
were stranded in a blizzard.

She looked into the backseat to find Bo curled into a tight
ball, his fluffy tail draped over his face, sound asleep. She watched

his chest rise and fall, rise and fall...

If only she could be so at peace.

Renee glanced at her watch. Another hour had passed. Another hour, and, from what she could see through the driver's window, the snow was still falling. She looked at her husband. Another hour, and Gabe was still unconscious.

Or was he? Maybe he was just sleeping, as she and Bo had just been doing. If his battered body was just keeping him sheltered in a deep slumber, she might be able to bring him around. "Gabe?" She held her breath, hoping...praying. "Gabe, honey, wake up."

Bo, roused by the sound of her voice, jumped up and came to her, tail wagging, a low whine coming from deep in his throat. She pushed him away. "Not now, boy. Lie down."

He did as she ordered, but his worried eyes never left her as she closed her mittened fingers on Gabe's shoulder and gave him a gentle shake. "Gabe?"

When he stirred slightly and moaned, wild hope raced through Renee's veins, sending her pulse pounding in her temples. The shake she gave him this time was anything but gentle. "Gabe, wake *up!*"

He drew a shuddering breath, and she waited for his eyes to flicker open—instead, he seemed to settle back into the oblivion Renee was slowly coming to hate.

"No..."

Her hands fisted in the blanket covering Gabe, and she caught her breath at the emotions that churned within her, surging through her like liquid fire, making her feel hot and ice cold all at once. It took all her strength to relax her fingers, to let go of the blanket and not shake Gabe until he opened his eyes. She wouldn't even have cared if he yelled at her.

Anything was better than this dense, terrifying silence. Snow had settled in a thick blanket over the windshield, which meant it probably covered a good portion of the rest of the truck as well. The result was an eerie kind of muffling, as though both light and sound were being kept at bay. Renee felt encased, trapped, entombed in a place of isolation and gloom.

So this is what it feels like to be a mummy...

She turned to face the windshield, planting her hands on the dash, feeling the cold of the plastic even through her mittens.

They were running out of time.

"Where are You?" The question came out in a hoarse whisper, breaking the suffocating silence around her. "Behold, I am with you always, remember? Even to the end of the world. Isn't that what You promised?"

Guilt assailed her at the sarcasm in her tone—after all, who was she to question God?—but it was quickly pushed aside, obliterated by the pounding of her heart, the ragged breathing that tore at her lungs, the trembling that assaulted her from the inside out...a trembling that she knew had nothing to do with the icy weather and everything to do with the emotion that seared her heart and singed the corners of her control.

She'd denounced Gabe's anger for years. How many of her weekly phone calls to her parents had disintegrated into Renee complaining about Gabe, criticizing him for not trusting God enough, for not resting in God's promises and peace?

A harsh laugh broke the stillness in the cab, and Renee was startled to realize it had come from her. Wouldn't Mom and Dad be proud of her now? Of the faith she was showing?

They would understand.

Her lip curled. Maybe they would, but she didn't. She couldn't. Because she shouldn't have to face this.

She pounded her clenched hands on the dash.

"No!"

She'd gone through so much—all the years of struggling and enduring a difficult marriage...of following God into

THE BREAKING POINT   67

darkness and pain, holding fast to His promise of hope no matter how impossible it seemed—and *this* was her reward? All her effort to do what was right rather than what was expedient, and it ended *here?*

"No!"

She stared at the snow-shrouded windshield, trying to see beyond it to the wilderness. "Where *are* You?"

At first, all that met her cry was the same muted silence. And then it came. One simple word whispering through her with the softness of a baby's breath.

Peace.

She waited, wanting—no, *needing* more.

Peace…be still.

She struggled to hold on to those words, to embrace and rest in them, but she couldn't. Didn't God know she needed more than just that? She needed help! Disappointment sliced through her, leaving her already-raw nerves in tatters. But she wasn't entirely sure who she was most disappointed in: God…or herself.

She should be able to handle this. She should be doing better. But she wasn't. She wasn't doing well at all.

"I don't have *time* to be still!" A terrible bitterness caught hold of her. "Look out there. Don't you *see?* It'll be dark in a few hours. I can't just sit here."

Wait patiently…

"Wait on what? There's no telling how cold it's going to get, and I don't know how badly Gabe is hurt. He may not be able to…to—"

She bit back the sob that cut off her words. She couldn't fall apart. Not now. She had to be strong. For Gabe. For herself.

Renee swiveled to the backseat and Bo hopped out of her way as she grabbed at the canvas bag with frantic hands. Her abrupt movement was rewarded by an intense, searing pain, and nausea rippled through her. She couldn't hold back the harsh cry.

Bo rushed to her, licking at her face, tail beating out his anxiety. Renee held him off with one hand and gripped her side with the other. She tried to say something, to reassure the dog, but it was all she could do to drag shallow breaths through gritted teeth. She just hooked her arm over his shoulders and hugged him close, panting until the queasiness passed.

Thankfully, as though sensing she couldn't bear any more, Bo settled down. He lay so that she could lean on him, his head resting on his paws, his eyes flicking from her to Gabe and back again.

Poor critter. She and Gabe were his security, the ones who took care of him and made life right. They were the center of his world, and it must seem to his doggie brain as if they were definitely *not* living up to their responsibilities.

She knew how he felt.

But she wouldn't just sit here, waiting for some kind of vague miracle to save them. She had to do something. She wasn't sure what one did for bruised ribs, but cracked or broken ribs needed extra support. And ice packs.

She allowed herself a laugh at that. She'd have no trouble finding an ice pack. She could just lie down in the snow. Of course, then she'd have to deal with hypothermia.

She grabbed the roll of gray tape from the backseat, then stripped down to her shirt. It was a struggle, but she managed to wrap the tape around her midsection as tightly as she could stand it, stopping when the pain threatened to upend her stomach. When she finished, she sat for a moment, breathing slowly to still the trembling that assaulted her bruised body, staring at the towel covering her window, watching it move in and out...in and out with the wind.

When she could move without wanting to scream, she pulled her layers of clothing back on. She was ready, but for what? What should she do?

Think, Renee, think!

She shoved herself up on her knees and peered into the backseat, not even sure what she was looking for...inspiration, if nothing else. Then she spotted the backpack she and Gabe used when they took Bo for a walk. An idea began to form, and she grabbed it, opening the flap and pulling out the long, bright yellow rope they used to let Bo run free. Or as free as one lets a male husky run outside some kind of enclosure.

Renee studied the rope. That should do the trick.

She popped the glove box open, her plan falling together as she pulled out a pad of paper and a pen. Every time she and Gabe traveled this road, she'd made a game of spotting the tiny cabins tucked in the woods at the side of the highway. They were few and far between, but they were there. And most of them had been fairly close to the Rogue River, which paralleled the highway she and Gabe had been driving before they went over the edge.

All she had to do, then, was find the river and follow it. Her odds of finding at least one of those cabins should be pretty good. In any case, they were better odds than if she just sat in the truck, twiddling her thumbs, waiting for a rescue that might never come.

Not until after the spring thaw, anyway.

Renee scribbled a quick note—*Gabe, I've gone for help*—then paused, staring at the scrawled letters. That would never do. As clearly as if he were conscious and grilling her, she could hear the rapid-fire fifth degree Gabe would launch if he found a note like the one she'd just written: Was she injured? What direction did she go when she left the truck? What time did she leave? How long would she give herself to find help before coming back to the truck? What supplies did she have with her...?

Details. If there was one thing Gabe needed, it was details. She reached into the glove box again and pulled out her compass. Thank heaven for the training they'd received in

Search and Rescue. They'd always assumed that training would help them save others.

Now it might very well save their own lives.

Renee glanced outside. If she was going to give Gabe an accurate reading, she couldn't do it in the truck. She had to go out and get her bearings. She grabbed the passenger door handle and pushed, grateful when the door opened easily. She slid outside, catching her breath against the driving cold. If anything, the storm was getting worse. Dread seeping through her, she struggled against the buffeting wind, securing one end of the rope to the door handle. She looped the rest of the rope over her shoulder, then planted her feet against the gale and took a reading on her compass.

West. She needed to head west.

She climbed back into the truck and wrote a more detailed note, because she knew one thing for certain: If Gabe came to and found her gone, he'd try to find her. So it was best for both of them to let him know as much as she could.

> Gabe, I'm not injured. I've gone for help. I'm going to try to find the river and follow that to a cabin. I tied the yellow rope to my door handle and will hold on to that as long as I can. That will let you know what direction I've gone.

She wrote down the time and the compass heading she would follow, then put the note on the console, securing it under Gabe's heavy flashlight. She started to put the pad of paper back into the glove box, then stopped and stared down at the fluorescent pink paper. Gabe had shaken his head when she bought it.

"What's wrong with plain old white paper? Or even yellow?"

She'd wrinkled her nose at him. "Bo-*ring!*"

"Yeah, well, you're not putting that thing in my truck."

Renee smiled now as she looked down at the pad. Good thing Gabe had given in. She might need to leave him a note out there. A piece of white paper stuck on a tree branch would never catch his eye, but this paper? No way he'd miss it.

She zipped the pad and the pen into a coat pocket, then tied the yellow rope to the stick shift. The outer door handles weren't the kind you could tie anything to, but this should work. And closing the rope in the door would ensure it would stay in place.

That done, she turned to stuff supplies into a fanny pack. Not too much—she didn't want to be weighed down as she walked. Just the necessities. A small bottle of water. Protein bars. Heat packs. Her leather billfold with her driver's license and emergency cash. Waterproof matches. Paper and fire starters. A small flashlight, just in case she ended up out there after dark...

She slid the fanny pack under her coat and snapped the latch, then turned to Bo. He hunkered down, clearly ready to go with her. "Down, boy." He hesitated, then lowered himself to the seat. "Good boy, Bo." Renee knew that *down* was the easy part. He'd hate this next command. "Stay."

He blinked at her, then voiced his protest in one of his low yodels. Renee stayed firm, repeating the command, her voice low to show she meant business. Bo flopped his head onto his front paws, his ears flat against his broad head. Renee shook her head at the picture of pouting obedience he made.

So that's what I look like. She leaned between the seats to slide her arms around Bo's neck and hug him. The dog's bushy tail *thwap-thwapped* against the side of the cab, and he craned his neck until he could deliver imploring licks to her cheeks. Renee chuckled and sat back, wiping at her face.

"Sorry, my boy, but you can't go with me. You have to stay here. Stay."

Renee watched the dog settle into the command, reluctant but nonetheless obedient. She loved the way God worked. Well, most of the time, anyway. But she especially loved how He worked through this animal she and Gabe had come to love so much. They'd realized long ago that Bo was often a reflection of the two of them. More often than they liked to admit, they saw their own rebellious hearts, their resistance and willfulness, their stubborn determination to do things their way in the dog's behavior and expressions. The realization had made them laugh—and it made them more patient when they worked with Bo.

As God so often had to be patient with them.

Renee gave Bo a final pat, told him once more to stay, and then slid toward the door. She reached for the handle and heard the echo of that quiet voice bidding her to wait.

She bit her lip. No, obedience didn't come easily to a strong-willed heart, whether it beat in the chest of a mischief-loving Siberian or that of a human. Renee had never taken well to obedience. Like Bo, she chafed when she felt restraint. She questioned everything, wanting to know why and how and when. She much preferred to do things her way.

Thankfully, God worked with her until she could no longer resist His call. He didn't force her; He just waited her out.

For a moment she hesitated, considering. Maybe she should just stay where she was. Then she looked back at Gabe and knew she couldn't.

She needed to try to get help. It might be the wrong thing to do—probably was, considering what her heart had been telling her—but she had to try. Besides, even if it was the wrong thing to do, God would work it out. He always had.

Of course, He doesn't keep you from facing the consequences of your wrong choices…

No, He didn't do that. But all her life she'd seen Him take her willful, stubborn mistakes and turn them around and use them to help her see Him that much more clearly. He'd always been there, taking care of her. She had to believe He wasn't going to stop now.

Even if He has to work things out in spite of you?

Renee lifted her chin. Yes, even then. Because more often than not, that was exactly what He'd done. In her childhood, in her growing up...in her marriage.

She looked back at Gabe—wrapped as he was in the cocoon she'd made for him of blankets and clothing—watched the puffs of white as he breathed, and felt her breath catch in her throat.

Would this be the last time she ever saw him?

The thought sliced through her. What she wouldn't give for those powerful arms to circle her, hold her close...to hear him tell her everything would be okay in that deep, confident voice that so often brought her a sense of reassurance, even in the worst of times.

She pressed a kiss to his cheek. "I love you." Even as the words slipped from her lips, a terrible realization hit her. When was the last time she'd told him that? When had she spoken those words out loud and really meant them? She couldn't even remember. Her heart ached as though it were ripping itself free. Shaking her head against the inner recriminations straining to flood her, she pulled away from him. "I'm so sorry, Gabe. For everything."

She slid from the vehicle, shut the door behind her, and stood for a moment, one hand on the handle, the other pressed palm down against the door. "Please...please...take care of him."

The swirling snow snatched her prayer from her and enveloped her like some kind of macabre death shroud. A shiver darted across her spine, and Renee reacted almost without thinking. She turned from the blasting wind, from the white expanse that swallowed everything around her, and hid her face against the truck. Fingers clutching, she held fast to the rope—and to the fraying edges of her control.

Step back. Just step back and start walking.

She wanted to. She knew she needed to. But her feet

seemed frozen in place, captured in a solid sheet of pure terror.

How would she survive out here? What if she dropped the rope? What if she ended up lost? It wouldn't be long before the temperature plummeted to the low twenties or even lower. Even if she didn't get lost, she could freeze to death with very little trouble.

On and on it went, a litany of doom that dropped layer after layer of anxiety over her until she grabbed at the door handle, ready to jerk it open and jump back inside. To hide there. No, it wouldn't be any warmer, but at least it was safe. Familiar. And she wouldn't be alone. Gabe was there...

Gabe.

She stopped, fingers trembling on the door handle. Gabe. He needed her to be strong. To find help. Renee let her fingers relax, let go of the handle. She had to do this. She had to.

She pushed away from the truck, failure a heavy weight within her. Why did she keep fighting the same battles over and over? She was so tired of finding herself here, torn between fear and resolve. She didn't remember inviting anxiety in, asking it to take up residence within her. And yet there it was, like a yapping little dog vexing her every step. Even when she knew that what she was doing was right, it was there. Nipping at her. Scraping her resolve raw with tiny, needle-sharp teeth.

Nothing she did helped. No amount of preparation or prayer. No number of reminders that God would be true to His promises.

She knew it was true. It just didn't seem to make a difference.

Why? Renee gritted her teeth and gripped the rope. *I just want to know why. Why am I always so afraid?*

She didn't expect an answer. Not really. Because she already knew it. Knew the crux of the problem wasn't preparation, wasn't prayer, wasn't knowing what was right or wrong. It was deeper...simpler...

And much more difficult.

Only trust allows the soul room to breathe.

WOLFHART PANNENBERG

*A doubtful mind is as unsettled as a wave
of the sea that is driven and tossed by the wind.*

JAMES 1:6

SPRING 1974

RENEE LAY IN BED, LISTENING AS HER FATHER'S LAUGHTER
drifted up to her from the living room. How she loved the sound
of his laughter! It usually made her feel safe and warm. But
tonight it just made her stomach clench.

She had come home tonight after their softball team victory
celebration—they beat the school rivals for the first time in two
years!—dragged herself in the door, and told her parents they'd
won and that she was going to bed.

"My, my, that must have been some celebration," her dad
joked from his recliner. "I can't remember the last time you went
to bed this early on a Friday night."

Renee just gave what she hoped was a convincing laugh and
headed up to her room. She'd been lying here for at least an hour
now, her stomach churning, staring at the ceiling. Finally she

flopped an arm over her eyes and surrendered to the truth that had been gnawing at her all night.

I lied to my dad.

Before she'd headed out for the game, he made one request of her. He knew it was Friday night—cruising night. And he knew her friends liked to go cruising, especially if they were jazzed from winning a game. So as he gave her a hug, he said to her, "Just do me a favor, hon. Don't go cruising. If your friends want to go, just have them drop you at home, okay?"

Dad didn't ask her things like that often. But some kids had been hurt recently when cruising had turned to racing, and he was concerned. She'd smiled at him. "Sure, Dad, no problem."

If only that had been true. No sooner had she and the gang finished pizza than they hopped in the cars and headed to join the cruisers. Renee knew she should tell them to take her home, but she hadn't wanted to spoil their fun. No one liked a wet blanket.

So she sat there, miserable, pretending she was enjoying herself. And then, when they finally dropped her off at home, she came to her room to hide.

She knew her friends would think she was nuts for letting it bother her. They talked all the time about how they put things over on their parents, how they got away with stuff. But this was different.

Renee couldn't ever remember lying to her parents before.

You didn't lie…you just didn't tell him the whole truth.

Same thing. Same stupid thing.

She pulled the covers over her head, telling herself to go to sleep. She couldn't. She flopped her pillow over her face, muttering, "Sleep, idiot!"

It didn't help.

It wasn't that she was afraid of being punished. Her parents would be fair; they always were. No, what had her stomach clenching with this terrible sick feeling was one simple truth: She'd let her father down. And what would happen if she told him about it? He'd be hurt, disappointed. What if he never trusted her again?

Your dad loves you, no matter what.

Maybe so, but why put him—and herself—through what was bound to be a painful moment when nothing had happened?

I'm so sorry, God.

The truth will set you free.

She dug her fingers into the pillow. Right now all it was doing was making her miserable.

Finally, after another half hour of tossing and turning, she threw the covers back, grabbed her bathrobe, and stomped from her room. Her brothers' rooms were dark, and she could hear their snores as she trudged downstairs.

Her mother was in the kitchen, finishing the dishes. She glanced at Renee, her expression reflecting surprise. "What's the matter, honey? Can't sleep?"

She gave a quick shrug. "I…I just need to talk with Dad. You think he's still awake?"

Mom nodded. "I think so. I see a light on back there."

She forced her feet to move, even though each seemed to weigh about a ton, and made her way back to her parents' bedroom, stopping in the doorway.

Her father glanced up from the book he was reading. "Hey, sweetie. What's up?"

Renee shrugged, then came into the room, hating the unfamiliar awkwardness that cloaked her as she stood at her father's bedside. Words poured from her heart, but they couldn't push past the constriction in her throat.

He laid his book down. "What's up, Renee?"

Her stomach twisted as she pulled up a chair and sank into it. "I need to talk with you." She couldn't look him in the eyes, so she stared at the bedspread, plucking at a stray thread, as she forced the words out. When she finished telling him what had happened, she looked at him.

"I'm sorry, Dad."

His somber expression made the ache in her heart even heavier. "I won't say I'm not disappointed, Renee, but I'm glad you told me. And I forgive you."

She lay her head on his chest, sniffling into the bedspread. When she felt his hand on her hair, the question that had been plaguing her slipped free.

"Do…do you still love me, Dad?" She knew it was foolish, knew what the answer would be even before she asked it, but she had to ask it all the same.

"Oh, honey." His hand on her hair was gentle. "Nothing you could ever do would make me stop loving you. I may be disappointed or frustrated at times, but I'll always love you."

She threw her arms around him. "I love you, Boppo."

"I love you, too, sweetheart." He patted her on the back. "Now, go get some sleep, okay?"

She nodded and jumped up, then met her mother coming into the room.

"Everything okay, dear?"

Renee threw her arms around her, dancing her around the room. "Everything's great."

Her mother laughed and gave her a hug. "Good. Now get some sleep."

Renee padded back to her room, feeling lighter than the air she breathed. It was as though, without her even realizing it, the mountains surrounding the valley where she lived had been sitting on her chest. Now that crushing weight was gone. She jumped onto her bed and grabbed her Bible, then flopped onto her stomach. The Bible opened to Psalms.

Renee's eyes moved to Psalm 32, and her breath caught in her throat. She stared at the words on the clean white page.

*Oh, what joy for those whose rebellion is forgiven, whose
sin is put out of sight!*

Renee realized her mouth was hanging open. She
clamped it shut and kept reading.

*Yes, what joy for those whose record the LORD has cleared
of sin, whose lives are lived in complete honesty! When I
refused to confess my sin, I was weak and miserable, and
I groaned all day long. Day and night your hand of disci-
pline was heavy on me. My strength evaporated like
water in the summer heat.*
　　*Finally, I confessed all my sins to you and stopped
trying to hide them. I said to myself, "I will confess my
rebellion to the LORD."*
　　And you forgave me! All my guilt is gone.

Wonder filled her.

*Therefore, let all the godly confess their rebellion to you
while there is time, that they may not drown in the floodwa-
ters of judgment. For you are my hiding place; you protect
me from trouble. You surround me with songs of victory.*
　　*The LORD says, "I will guide you along the best path-
way for your life. I will advise you and watch over you.
Do not be like a senseless horse or mule that needs a bit
and bridle to keep it under control."*
　　*Many sorrows come to the wicked, but unfailing love
surrounds those who trust the LORD. So rejoice in the
LORD and be glad, all you who obey him!*
　　Shout for joy, all you whose hearts are pure!

Renee read it again, then again. Each time, she felt the
power of God's presence, the blessing of His pleasure. It was
as though He was sitting right there on the bed beside her,
telling her she'd done well.

She had been so afraid to tell her father what she'd done. Afraid of revealing to her dad—and to God—how she'd let them down. Afraid she might have damaged their love for her. How could they love her the same when they saw her for what she was: weak, faithless, foolish?

But they had. They loved her, no matter what. First her dad, and then God, had let her know nothing she did could change their love for her.

Why was I so afraid?

She hugged the Bible, lifted a finger to wipe the wetness from her cheek, then spread her still-damp fingers across the soft leather of her Bible, anointing it with the tears He had given her. Tears of gratitude. Restoration.

Lord God, don't ever let me forget this night. Don't ever let me forget that I don't need to be afraid. I can trust You, no matter what. Please don't let me—

Suddenly she laughed. Like she could ever forget what had happened! No way! Not when God had done so much, when He'd taken her from grief to joy, from prison to free-dom...

Renee snuggled down under the covers again. She flicked off the light and the darkness closed around her like a warm, silken cocoon. She'd been changed. God had touched her, and from this moment on she would trust Him. No ques-tions. No hesitation.

She'd learned her lesson, and she was glad. She didn't ever want to go through something like that again.

10

Lord, I thank You for all the trials through which You lead me,
and by which You prepared me to behold Your Glory.

TERESA OF AVILA

For our present troubles...produce for us an
immeasurably great glory that will last forever!

2 CORINTHIANS 4:17

DECEMBER 19, 2003
2 P.M.

OPEN YOUR EYES.

Gabe's body refused to obey, just as it had been doing for...well, he didn't know how long, but it seemed like a long time. Even so, he tried again.

Open...your...eyes!

It took every ounce of willpower, but his lids finally lifted. Slowly, drawing in deep breaths to keep his stomach from recoiling, he blinked against the glare of white that greeted him.

"Oooohhh, anyone get the number of the truck that hit m—"

He froze. Truck. He was in his truck. But something wasn't right.

Suddenly it all came rushing back. The argument. The truck out of control. The slam into—and through—the snowdrift at the

81

side of the road. The last thing he'd seen was Renee's wide, terrified eyes as she reached for him…

Renee!

With a deep groan, Gabe pushed himself up and looked to where she should be sitting. His stomach dropped. She wasn't there.

His pulse pounded through his veins as he took a quick inventory of the truck cab. Relief whispered through him when he saw Bo snoozing in the backseat. His gaze traveled the rest of the cab, the backseat, the windshield, the windows. That's when he saw it—the towel taped over the window in the passenger door. From the abundance of duct tape holding the towel in place, Gabe was looking at Renee's handiwork.

She was alive.

The relief that flooded his veins then was so intense it made him light-headed. He leaned against the seat and closed his eyes, concentrating on staying conscious.

A sudden wiggling weight in his lap and a wetness on his face let him know Bo was awake—and ecstatic to find Gabe up and around. "Okay, boy…relax…" He took hold of the dog's collar and gave it a tug, grateful when he felt Bo lie down. He kept a hand on the dog's head, waiting for the dots of light dancing behind his lids to fade.

Finally he could open his eyes again. The minute he did so, Bo jumped up and gave a deep yodel of joy. Gabe restrained the dog but ruffled the top of his soft head. "Hey, boy, good to see you, too."

Renee was alive…but where was she? Just then he spotted his flashlight on the floorboard. Bo must have knocked it over. He frowned. How had he done that? Gabe kept the flashlight under his seat.

He got Bo into the backseat again, then leaned down to grab the flashlight. As he did so, he caught a flash of fluorescent pink on the floorboard as well.

Renee's crazy colored paper. He'd thought she was a goof for buying a pad of the stuff. Now it was the most beautiful color he'd ever seen.

He grabbed the note and sat back to read it. Dread lodged somewhere beneath his breastbone as he absorbed the message. He looked at the windshield, but it was covered with snow, so he couldn't see out. Even so, he could feel the wind slamming into the truck.

Renee was out in this?

The thought intensified the throbbing in his head, and he pressed a hand to his forehead. A bandage. He leaned forward to look in the rearview mirror, taking in the dressing and the dried blood on his face.

He must have taken one monster of a hit. How long was he out? He turned his wrist and squinted down at his watch. A couple of hours anyway. But from what Renee had written in the note, she hadn't been gone much more than a half hour.

Plenty of time to end up in serious trouble.

Gabe refused to let the thought distract him. He didn't have much time to get things together and get going. Not if he was going to find Renee before dark.

He gathered his supplies quickly, then did one final check, forcing himself to think around the pain that beat against the sides of his temples. He was ready to go in less than ten minutes. It helped that Renee had already pulled out his backpack and the canvas bag of supplies.

Gabe slid the pack onto his back, judging the weight. Heavy, but nothing he couldn't handle. He scanned the truck cab once more, just to be sure he wasn't forgetting anything.

He gave a quick turn of his head to look in the backseat and immediately regretted it. Sharp twinges stabbed at his temples, and flashes of red exploded in his head.

Pain mixed with frustration, then escaped Gabe in an angry roar that echoed in the stillness around him. He squeezed his eyes tight, pressing his fingers into his aching temples. After a few moments, he could open his eyes. And he found Bo sitting there, ears laid back, eyes wide and alert.

A pang of regret struck him. When would he learn to think before he reacted? How often had he had an outburst only to see that cautious, alarmed look in the dog's eyes?

About as often as he'd seen it in Renee's.

A familiar weight pressed in on him, but he ignored it. He didn't have time for guilt.

When he pulled Bo's leather leash from beneath the seat, the dog almost vaulted into Gabe's lap. He laughed. If only he and Renee could be so quick to forgive. "Sit, boy."

The dog obeyed, and Gabe clipped the leash onto his collar. He was probably going to regret taking Bo with him. Last thing he needed was to worry about the dog getting away in this storm, but Gabe didn't care. No way he was leaving the dog in the truck. What if it took too long to find Renee or some kind of help? And what if, even after they reached help, they couldn't find their way back to the truck?

No. He was not going to leave Bo here to starve to death.

"It's you and me, buddy. We're gonna go out there and find her, okay? If we're going to make it, we have to work together. Got it?"

Bo gave another yodeling *roo,* and Gabe grinned. Darned if the dog didn't seem to understand—and even agree.

He pushed the door open and they hopped out of the truck. At the freezing force of the storm Gabe's head pounded like a tom-tom on uppers. He spun back toward the truck, giving his body a chance to adjust to the cold and wind. Then, the yellow rope in one hand, Bo's leash in the other, he turned, lowered his head against the storm, and started walking.

Each step confirmed what he'd feared: It wouldn't be easy going. Not by a long shot. But he pushed on, doing his best to pace himself, to ignore the way his headache crept into his stomach, making him queasy. *Just stay focused...*

It should have helped that he knew what he needed to do, where he needed to go. But it didn't. Because he couldn't escape a nagging awareness deep at the back of his mind: Nearly every time he thought he knew what he was supposed to do, he was wrong.

And those mistakes had cost him almost everything.

To believe in God is one thing. To know God another.

STARETZ SILOUAN

They began to think up foolish ideas of what God was like.
The result was that their minds became dark and confused.
Claiming to be wise, they became utter fools instead.

ROMANS 1:21–22

SUMMER 1971

GABE HATED THIS TOWN.

He snorted. Town? Hardly. It was barely big enough to call a village. A burg. That's what he lived in. A tiny, backwoods, I-can't-wait-to-get-out-of-here burg. One where everyone knew everyone else's business—and what they didn't know, they made up.

Amazing how sure the people in this town were about what they knew. How convinced they were about who was a pillar of the community and who was a bum.

Take his father. Most everyone who knew him—or thought they did—believed he was a great guy. Salt of the earth. After all, wasn't he always there at community events, always helping out, always with a big ol' smile on his face and a good word for everyone? The kids at school told Gabe how lucky he was to have such a "great guy" as his dad.

No wonder Gabe was so good at playing a part. He'd learned from a master.

He took a draw on his cigarette and blew the smoke out with a huff, watching it drift up into the night. People in this town were such idiots.

"Hey, you gonna smoke all those yourself, or you gonna share?"

Gabe tossed the pack of cigarettes to Danny. Much to his disgust, the lanky teen grabbed at them and missed. Gabe's disgust only increased when Danny leaned over to pick them up and fell on his face.

"Man, he's pickled."

This from Ray, who could hardly stand up himself. Gabe shook his head and went to snatch up the cigarettes, giving Danny a prod with his foot. His friends were idiots. But they were all he had, so he put up with them. "Get up, jerkwad."

Danny rolled onto his back, grinning up at Gabe like a stupefied Cheshire cat. "Nope. I like it here."

Gabe had gone to Danny's house right from school, not even stopping home to tell anyone where he was going. He'd pay for that, but he didn't care. He just couldn't stand the thought of being there...

Besides, Danny had told them that afternoon that his folks were out of town. This welcome news had been followed up with even more glad tidings. "And I know where they keep the key to the liquor cabinet."

That had settled it. Gabe and Ray had hopped the bus with Danny, and they'd made a valiant stab at trying every bottle in the cabinet. It was sometime halfway through the bottle of Jack Daniels when Ray had the brilliant idea of going for a walk.

Gabe should have known better. Danny and Ray were sloppy drunks. But the idea of being outside, of walking the empty streets, was just too appealing.

He stared down at Danny's sprawling form. Next time he was leaving these clowns behind and going out alone. He pulled his foot back, about to give Danny a real kick, when light split the darkness. Headlights! He crouched, pushing at Danny. "Get down, Ray!"

He peered up the street. The car was several blocks away, but that didn't matter. Nobody was out this time of night. Nobody but the cops. Gabe groaned. Great. Just great. Just what he needed...

Danny scrambled to his knees, and the three of them huddled there, watching as the car stopped at the intersection, then headed down the street. Straight toward them.

"Oh, man..." Danny sounded like he was about to cry. "Oh, man...breaking curfew and being drunk. My old man's gonna kill me."

Gabe grabbed Danny's sleeve and gave him a shake. "Shut *up*. Your old man won't do a thing. He never does." His stomach clenched. *His* old man, on the other hand, was another story.

It was definitely a cop car, and it was definitely headed their way. It was only a matter of seconds before the lights found them. He jumped when Ray grabbed his arm. Gabe spun, fist at the ready. "Are you *nuts?*"

"Over there, man! Those bushes. We can hide behind them."

Gabe followed Ray's pointing finger, and relief surged through him at the sight of a row of dense shrubs lining the street. The perfect cover. He shoved Danny to his feet and the three of them ran. As they vaulted over the bushes Gabe barely restrained a victory whoop. The cops would never even know they were—

"Aaaaahhhhhh!"

Gabe's smugness vanished in a rush of utter terror as he realized his feet hadn't landed on the ground. They hadn't landed on anything, because there wasn't anything there. Nothing but air.

The bushes hadn't lined the street. They lined the edge of a cliff.

Beamer Park. Why hadn't he realized they were on Beamer Park Road? The road that ran above the park, which sat at the bottom of a sheer rock cliff. People were always squawking about the danger. "Some little kid is going to slip, go over the edge," they whined. The town council had finally put up the bushes as a barrier, to keep anyone from getting too close to the edge.

Gabe's dad had hooted when he heard about it. Raised his can of beer to the stupidity of the townspeople, the council. "Bushes! Oh yeah, *that'll* work." He took another swig. "Like even little kids aren't smart enough to stay away from the edge of a cliff. I mean, how stupid do they think people are?"

All this ran through Gabe's mind as he fell, slamming into the branches of the tall evergreen below him, each blow bringing a new wave of pain. *God...God! Please, if You get me through this, I'll do whatever You want. Just don't let Dad find ou—*

He hit the ground.

His world exploded into a white-hot, searing wave of agony. Gabe clutched at the last shreds of consciousness, vaguely aware he couldn't move...that every inch of his body was pain.

Am I dead? He swallowed hard at the thought, gasping for air. *No, probably not. Death wouldn't hurt this much.*

Emotions jangled through him, a tumbled mass of confusion. He wanted to laugh. Almost as much as he wanted to scream. *Too bad I'm not dead, 'cuz I will be when Dad finds out about this. He's going to kill me.*

And, unlike Danny, Gabe knew his dad really could do just that. At the thought, stark fear clawed its way through him, grappling past the pain, clutching at him, telling him to get up. He tried. He really did. But it was no use. All he could do was moan.

No, wait. That wasn't him. It was Ray. Ray was moaning.

"Man…oh, man…you broke my back…"

That was when Gabe realized the voice came from beneath him. He'd landed on Ray. It was Ray's fault he wasn't dead.

"Over here! They're over here."

"Are they alive?"

Gabe managed to turn his head toward the voice, then closed his eyes against the flashing lights. The police. An ambulance. They were all there. Then they were beside him, talking, telling him they would contact his parents, that it was going to be okay.

Idiots. Stupid, stinking idiots. How could it be okay if they told his dad?

God, please…don't let Dad find out.

He opened his mouth to tell them not to call, not to say anything to his parents, but the words were choked off when hands gripped him, lifted him. Gabe screamed as everything faded, dimmed, pushed into oblivion by a searing, ravaging flash of pain.

Everything, that is, but fear. It didn't let him enter the darkness alone. It clung to him, torturing him—a terrible companion in a terrible place.

"Gabe? Honey, wake up. Open your eyes."

The coaxing voice reached to Gabe through the nightmarish darkness, pushing back the images that had been tormenting him—images of pain…of angry, punishing fists…

He shuddered, moaning. Soft hands brushed at his forehead, his cheek, and he turned toward them, almost weeping with relief when the darkness finally gave way and he opened his eyes.

His mother was there, sitting beside him, worry a heavy weight creasing her forehead. He wanted to reassure her, tell her he was fine, but when he opened his mouth, all that came out was a croak. He cleared his throat, tried again. "I'm…okay, Mom." Oh, that was convincing. He sounded like he had a whole pond full of frogs in his throat. He forced confidence to his voice, his face. "Don't worry."

The tears trickling down her face made her smile less than convincing. He swallowed against a sudden tightness in his throat. "S…sorry…"

She shook her head. "Oh, honey, I'm just so glad you're awake. That you'll be all right. You could have been—" She halted, shook her head again, then the smile was back. "Gabe, how do you feel?"

He gave a weak, hoarse laugh. "Like I went over a cliff."

Her lips twitched and she smoothed the hair from his eyes. "Yes, well, and a fine job you did of it."

He regretted his chuckle the second it escaped him. Sharp pain stabbed through him, and he gritted his teeth against a groan. "Mom, is Danny okay? And Ray?" Shifting in the bed, Gabe started to put his hands down, to push himself into a sitting position, when he realized one arm was immobilized. He glanced at it, studying the wrapping and sling that kept it bent at the elbow, secured across the front of him.

He must be on some heavy-duty drugs not to have even noticed that!

"Danny and Ray were lucky. Very lucky." He turned back to his mother as she went on. "They both have some nasty bruises, and Ray has a broken arm—"

"That's all?" Gabe didn't even try to hold back his relief. "I thought for sure I'd busted his back when I landed on him."

His mother reached out to pat his hand. "No, dear, though God only knows how any of you escaped without something like that. You had the most serious injury, Gabe. They have you on painkillers—"

"Which explains why I can't think straight."

"—because you've got a broken collarbone."

He nodded. "Which explains the mummy tape-up job."

"But it's a miracle that that's the worst of your injuries, son." Her lips trembled and he could see how she struggled to keep a rein on her emotions. "It could have been so much worse…" The words trailed off on a soft, broken sob.

"Oh, Mom." He was such an idiot! How could he have done this? Worried her like this? Didn't she have enough to deal with? And God only knew the price she would pay for his foolishness. The price she always paid when Gabe or one of his siblings did something stupid.

He looked away, staring at the wall, and slowly grew aware that he wasn't at home. He frowned, looking around the room. A hospital. He was in a hospital. He closed his eyes. Something else for Dad to blow up about. No way they could afford a hospital stay.

"Gabe? Are you okay?"

He turned back to his mother. "How long have I been here?"

"They brought you in last night."

"Get my clothes, Mom. I'm going home."

Her hand on his arm was as firm as her tone. "No, you are not!"

Their wills collided, clashed. She understood; he could see it in her eyes. But she still shook her head. "Gabriel Vincent Roman, you are going to stay right where you are."

He leaned back against the pillows, surprised at the force in her tone. "Mom…" He hated that his voice quavered, but he couldn't help it. "We can't afford this."

She looked down for a moment, then raised her gaze to his. "We'll be fine. We have insurance. The doctor wants to keep you under supervision for a few days, and if he says you need to be here, then here you'll stay. Until he says it's safe for you to come home."

He wanted to argue with her, to insist, but he just didn't have the energy. He closed his eyes. "Don't worry, Mom. I'll tell Dad." That was the least he could do. Be the one to take the first wave of reaction. Maybe he'd run out of steam before he got to her.

"Dad's gone."

Gabe's eyes flew open and he stared at his mother. "Gone?"

She nodded. "He came home from work early today. Said his boss was sending him to some training school up near Madison. He'll be gone a month. He left just after dinner."

Gone? He was gone? Gabe's mind seized on the word, on the escape it promised, but he was afraid to trust his ears.

His mother stroked his arm. "He said he'd told me about it last week. That I should have remembered…"

At the tremor in her tone, Gabe caught her hand in his. "You know as well as I do that he probably didn't say a thing about it." The uncertainty in her eyes infuriated him. "He's the one who forgot, Mom, not you."

"Gabe…"

"No, come on. That man was boozed up every night last week." He gave a snort. "He probably had a hard enough time remembering where he lived, let alone that he was supposed to go out of town the next week."

His mother pulled her hand free. "Gabriel, I don't like it when you talk that way. He is your father, after all."

Gabe held back the hot retort that shot to his lips. It wouldn't do any good. She always ended up taking Dad's side, always made excuses. He shook his head. It didn't matter. All that mattered right now was that his dad was gone. For a month. By the time he got back, Gabe would be well on his way to being healed. He'd never have to know.

"Honey, why don't you try to get some sleep? You need to rest."

He turned to his mother, saw the familiar expression in her eyes, the plea that always came into any conflict: *I don't want to fight…*

He nodded and patted her hand. "Okay, Mom, whatever you say."

She squeezed his hand as he closed his eyes, relaxed. But before sleep took over, he had a deal to live up to. He still couldn't quite believe it. God had given him his very own miracle. *God, You made it so Dad won't find out what happened. Well, You don't have to worry. A promise is a promise. You lived up to Your part of the deal, and so will I.*

LATE AUGUST 1973

Gabe stood, hands behind his back, peeking from behind the curtain to study the sea of faces as people filled in the pews. He recognized most of the faces, just as he recognized the expression so many wore: expectation. As though they were certain Gabe had something worth hearing.

For a moment total panic threatened to overtake him, but he straightened, forcing his focus away from the fear. Good thing he had a little time before he stepped out to the pulpit. He needed it to get himself ready.

Not that he hadn't done this plenty of times before. Most of the year, in fact. Ever since Jake, his youth group leader, had first asked him to do some kind of sermon for their youth Sunday service. It was a once-a-year deal that the youth group did for the church, and Jake really wanted to make this year's service an event that the folks at First Evangelical United Brethren would never forget.

Gabe had started attending First Evangelical shortly after his free fall over the edge of the cliff. He'd been in the hospital for a few days, but as soon as he got out he made his way to the small church a few blocks from his home. He didn't know a lot about God, but a deal was a deal. God gave Gabe a flat-out miracle, so now it was his turn to ante up. He figured the place to find out about God, to find out what He expected of Gabe now, was in a church.

It hadn't been easy. His dad had let him have it when he started going to church. Told him religion was a crutch for weak minds. And every Sunday when Gabe returned home, his dad gave him a sneer and asked if he'd gotten his dose of holiness for the week.

Gabe didn't care. A deal was a deal.

Besides, the folks at the church were nice enough, and before long one of the kids Gabe's age invited him to youth group. He'd stayed in the background for the first few months, until they found out about his acting ability. Suddenly everyone wanted him in their skits. He shrugged and did as they asked, amazed at the way everyone reacted when he played a part.

"You should be a professional actor," one of the young girls told him one night after youth group. "You're so...so *real* when you act."

The irony of the remark hadn't escaped him. It was true. He was never more real than when he was pretending to be someone else.

Then, at the end of a youth group meeting a few weeks ago, Jake came up to give Gabe a playful slap on the shoulder as he told him what he wanted Gabe to do. "You're a natural, kid! You do a great job in our skits. I mean, it's like you really *become* the people you're pretending to be."

Gabe had soaked in Jake's approval, and before he could stop himself, he'd agreed to do it. Of course, Gabe didn't bother telling Jake that doing skits came naturally. Put on a fake face. Make believe you feel something other than what you really feel. Say things other than what you really want to say. He'd been doing that most of his life. But giving a sermon? That was different. And the idea had petrified him.

Even so, he couldn't bear the thought of disappointing Jake. The man had done so much for him. When Gabe first started going to youth group, he hadn't been sure Jake would like him. The guy never wore anything but jeans and tennies, not even on Sundays. Sure, he added a dress shirt and a tie, but the jeans never gave way. It hadn't taken Gabe long to learn that was just a part of Jake's laid-back approach.

He explained it one night at a youth group meeting. "I like being comfortable. In my clothes. And in my faith." He looked around the room as he spoke. "I don't mean complacent, mind you. You shouldn't ever let yourself get complacent in your walk with God. It's just that I want to wear my faith as easily as I wear my jeans. To be as at home in my faith as I am—" he hooked his thumbs through the belt loops—"in these old faithfuls."

Gabe had been intrigued by the thought, and he'd stuck around afterward, talking with Jake. For the first time in his life, Gabe clicked with someone. Not because he was playing a part, but just because they clicked. Jake seemed interested in what he had to say. More than that, he seemed impressed with Gabe's questions, with the way he thought things through.

Since that night, Gabe found himself spending more and more time with Jake. He'd stop by the church, just to say hi, and they'd end up talking for hours. Jake always managed to encourage Gabe, even told him over and over that he believed in him. Gabe still had trouble believing that. Mostly because he knew that Jake would take everything back in a New York minute if he knew what Gabe—what his family and life—was really like. So he made sure Jake didn't know. Didn't have a clue.

Because while he might not believe Jake's words, he liked hearing them.

So when Jake asked him to do him this favor, to do the sermon for the youth Sunday service, he gave in to a moment of madness and agreed. He didn't tell anyone in his family. Why give them something to make fun of? But every night for weeks, after he finished all his chores and homework, after everyone else was asleep, Gabe sat at his desk, working on what Jake called his sermon. He knew it was risky to stay up past their usual bedtime, but he was careful. He shoved clothes at the base of the door to keep any light from sneaking out and used a small flashlight rather than his lamp, squinting in the dim light as he wrote. And rewrote. When it was finally done, he practiced night after night in front of the mirror. But for all of his preparation, the quivering sensation in his gut never quite went away.

Finally the big day had come, and Gabe had walked on trembling knees up to the pulpit, gripped it with fingers that felt stiff and awkward, looked out into what seemed like a thousand pairs of eyes—all fixed on him—and froze.

It was sheer willpower that kept him from throwing up right there on Pastor Paul's pulpit. But it was blind panic that saved the day, because it catapulted him to safe ground. In one frantic, frozen moment, when Gabe's mind seized and he couldn't seem to form a coherent thought or word, he did the only thing left to him: He acted.

As though some ephemeral drama coach came to stand beside him, Gabe heard the familiar directions: *Focus. Breathe. Keep your voice steady, confident. Think about Pastor Paul—his mannerisms, his inflections, even his posture…draw on those things…make them a part of you.*

Drawing a deep breath, he opened his mouth and played the part. To the hilt.

It was easy. As natural as breathing. There, standing in front of all those people, Gabe *became* Pastor Paul. Of course, the people watching him didn't know that was what he did. They thought he was just being himself. And they ate it up. They laughed in all the right places. And when they saw Gabe's perfectly timed tears—just one or two, so as not to overdo—trickle down his face, some of the women completely broke down. Even a few of the men sniffled into handkerchiefs.

It was heaven. Or the closest thing to it Gabe had ever known.

When it was all over, Pastor Paul, who'd never seemed able to remember Gabe's name before, actually threw his arm around Gabe's shoulders. "*Well* now!" He beamed at the people in the pews. "Was that amazing, or what?"

Even as Gabe thought to himself that the man had no idea just how amazing, the congregation surged to their feet and burst into applause.

Gabe stood there, drinking in the adulation like a parched young man just come in from Death Valley. His head swam, his heart pounded, and he felt ten feet tall. As the people came in droves to shake his hand and tell him how wonderful he'd been, sudden understanding filled his mind.

This was why men became preachers. This ability to move people, to make them listen, make them laugh or cry…make them love you.

"You're a natural born preacher, son! That's what you are," one white-haired lady crooned as she patted his cheek.

Jake stood there, looking at him as though seeing him for the first time. "I'm telling you, Gabe, I've never heard such powerful speaking." He shook his head. "I knew you were good, but this was…"

"This was God, my boy!" said Pastor Paul, who looked about to burst his buttons. "I think we have a star in our midst, folks. Yes sir, this boy obviously has the call on his life. And we're gonna help him answer it!"

Gabe had no idea what the man meant, but he didn't care. They loved him; that was all that mattered. And they loved listening to him, as evidenced by the fact that they kept asking him to do things during the year: read the Scripture, give the announcements, lead prayers. Each time someone came to Gabe, Jake would watch as he agreed to take on yet another task. And he watched as Gabe performed the task to perfection. Which made Gabe happy, because he wanted Jake to be proud of him.

On certain special Sundays, Pastor Paul would even ask

Gabe to give a sermon again. Special Sundays like today, his last Sunday home. Bright and early tomorrow morning he was packing everything up and heading north to college. And nearly everyone out in those pews knew about it, because they'd had a hand in it. They'd been behind him all the way, encouraging him, donating money to help him go first to college and then to seminary.

He was going to be a preacher. Just like they all said he should.

A firm hand on his shoulder drew Gabe's attention, and he turned to face Jake. The youth leader's smile was warm, but there was an odd look in Jake's eyes. Like he had something on his mind but wasn't sure how to say it.

Gabe nodded at his friend. "Jake."

The man let go of Gabe's shoulder but held his gaze. Gabe wasn't sure what he'd expected. Happiness for him, maybe. Even a little pride in who he had become. But he didn't find anything like that in Jake's brown eyes.

Instead, what Gabe saw was an odd uncertainty. He shifted, feeling suddenly uneasy. "What is it, Jake?"

He shook his head and looked away. "Nothin', Gabe. Not really." His gaze came back to Gabe's, and after a moment he sighed. "I just…" He jammed his hands in his jeans pockets. "Is this what you want?"

Gabe drew back, frowning. "Is what what I want."

Jake nodded toward the pulpit, the congregation. "This." His tone and expression were somber. "Preaching. Going to seminary. Taking a church."

He had the feeling that Jake was really concerned. About him. That he wanted to somehow see inside Gabe's heart and mind, to read for himself what was there.

But no one was allowed to do that. Not even Jake.

Gabe let a relaxed, confident expression ease across his face and put his hand on Jake's arm. "Hey, of course it is. I mean, why would I do all this if it wasn't?"

Jake frowned this time. "That's what I keep asking myself..."

Gabe gave him a playful punch. "Come on, Jake. Loosen up. I mean, you know me—"

Jake's quick stare halted whatever Gabe had been about to say. "Do I? Do I really, Gabe? Or do I just know who you pretend to be?"

The low words sent panic racing through his veins, but the same inner guidance that had led him through his first panic-stricken sermon came to save him now. *Focus. Breathe. Keep your voice steady, reassuring.* Inhaling in the relief of the familiar, he kept his tone light and even.

"Sure you do. You've been a good friend to me." He nodded toward the pulpit. "You even got me started with all this, remember?"

Jake nodded. "I remember, and that's what's bothering me." He took a step toward Gabe and his firm hand closed on Gabe's shoulder. He made Gabe meet his gaze head-on. "Are you doing this—are you becoming a minister—because it's what God wants for you, or because it's what you want? You know, because you're good at it. Because people respond the way they do. And that makes you feel good." Jake's concern was almost palpable. "I need to know, buddy, are you sure God has called you to be a minister?"

The fear that stabbed through Gabe was swift and fierce. Jake knew him so well...too well. But he didn't let himself miss a beat. He knew how the game was played. Knew what Jake needed to hear. To see.

Knew he needed to give the performance of his life.

He straightened, not letting his gaze or the confidence in his tone waver. "Yes, Jake, I'm sure. I'm following God's call." He was careful to say it with just the right tone and inflection, to avoid sounding too glib. And he kept his expression open, sincere, warm—all the right ingredients to give Jake the assurance he was looking for, to put his fears to rest.

It seemed to work, because Jake's hand fell from Gabe's shoulder, and his eyes spoke relief. "Okay, then. I just wanted to be sure. I mean, being a minister is hard enough, buddy, without going into it for some reason other than a call straight from God."

"I hear that," Gabe said, keeping his smile relaxed and loose. "Believe me, I'm no dummy. If God hadn't called me, no way I'd be doing this." He clapped Jake on the arm. "I'm not *that* crazy."

It wasn't until his friend finally left that Gabe brought his hands out from behind his back and looked down at them. His fingers were clenched so tightly that they were white. Pain shot through them as he forced them to relax.

His jaw tensed. Good thing his act had been enough to put Jake off, to keep him from seeing just how shaken Gabe really was. Because if he'd pressed any harder, Gabe might well have let those fists do exactly what they'd been wanting to do.

Nail Jake right in the center of his self-righteous face.

He turned, flexing his hands at his sides. Who did Jake think he was to ask such things, especially at a time like this, when Gabe needed to concentrate on his message? The last thing he needed was to let the anxiety deep within him run loose…anxiety that only grew stronger when he faced the truth.

Not only did he not have real answers to Jake's questions, he wasn't even sure he understood what the questions meant. Had God called him? How in the world was Gabe supposed to know that? Everyone in the church had been saying for a year now that Gabe was a natural at speaking, that he'd be a wonderful preacher. Even Pastor Paul said so. Well, didn't God speak through His people?

"You bet He does." Gabe muttered the words into the hallway, letting the truth of them ring deep inside. He moved to stare out at the congregation again, noting the smiles and nods as they greeted each other. He heard several whispers, comments that they could hardly wait to hear what Gabe had to say. He saw the anticipation on their faces, and he nodded.

"God's people have spoken. And they've told me as clearly as God Himself that I'm supposed to be a minister." He tugged at his suit jacket. No jeans for Gabe—he learned long ago that you had to look the part if you were going to play it convincingly.

The strains of the opening hymn broke forth, and Gabe closed his eyes, listening for a moment.

Am I a soldier of the cross?

The words echoed deep within him. *You'd better believe I am. And I've got my marching orders.*

That settled, he paused, let the image of confidence and ease settle over him, then pulled the door open and went to greet Pastor Paul—and his future.

12

The pleasure that a man seeks in gratifying his own desires quickly turns to bitterness and leaves nothing behind it except regret that he has not discovered the secret of true blessedness.

ISIDORE OF SEVILLE

You want what you don't have, so you scheme...to get it. You are jealous for what others have, and you can't possess it... And yet the reason you don't have what you want is that you don't ask God for it.

JAMES 4:2

DECEMBER 19, 2003
3 P.M.

CLINK. CLINK. CLINK...

Oren tried not to flinch, but it was driving him nuts.

Clink. Clink.

He peered over the top of his book, watching as Grace sat there, staring into space, stirring her tea. Again.

Clink. Clink.

She wasn't drinking the stuff. So why on earth did she need to stir it?

Clink. Clink.

"Gracie."

Clink. Clink.

"Grace."

Clinkclinkclink—

"Gracie!"

She jumped, dropping her spoon and dumping her tea all over the table. "Oh, Oren. Look what you made me do."

Heaving a sigh, he rose and went to the kitchen for a towel. Grace was right on his heels.

"Maybe we should call the police."

He cast her a sideways look. "I don't think spilling tea is a crime, Grace."

She frowned. "No, no! Not about the tea. About the Romans."

He went back into the dining room, Grace keeping pace with him. As he wiped up the tea, she started pulling paper napkins from the dispenser in the middle of the table and wiped at the spill as well.

"Well?"

He stared at her. "Well what?"

Pull. Wipe. "The police, Oren! Should we call them?" Pull. Wipe.

"And tell them what, dear? We don't know what's happening. They're not even due back yet."

She didn't seem to hear him. Just kept pulling and wiping. "Or maybe the coast guard would be better. No, they only deal with people lost at sea." Pull. Wipe. "Who deals with people lost in the mountains? Oh, what's that group called? The people who go out and search for lost people and rescue them?"

She had a wad the size of Cleveland that she was pushing around the table now. Oren restrained a grin. "Search and Rescue?"

"Oh, I know. Search and Rescue!" She gave Oren a triumphant smile. "Let's call them."

Their hands collided for the third time, and Oren gave up his cleaning efforts. He straightened. "This table isn't big enough for the two of us, Grace."

She stared, then looked down at the soggy mass of napkins. "Oh, dear…"

Oren took her hand and led her into the living room, where they sat on the couch. He sandwiched her soft hand between his. "Dear, I know you're worried. So am I. But at this point, calling the police or Search and Rescue wouldn't help. Those folks can't do anything until we know for sure the Romans are in trouble."

"Well, I'd say getting a call from God is a pretty good sign."

"For us, yes. For the police…?"

She bit her lip. "Yes, I see your point." When she met his gaze, he saw the depth of her worry in her eyes. "But we have to do *something.*"

Oren nodded. "Tell you what. How about if we call the only One who knows what's really going on?"

Grace hesitated, then her soft, sweet smile lifted her lips. How Oren loved that smile. "Of course. Why didn't I think of that?"

His answering grin was wide. "Because God knows I need to be the smart one once in a while."

"Oh, you!" She batted at his arm, then gripped both his hands with hers. "Shall we?"

Oren nodded. "Absolutely."

Together, they bowed their heads and lifted their hearts to heaven.

13

We are the wire; God is the current.
Our only power is to let the current pass through us.

CARLO CARETTO

For the Lord does not abandon anyone forever.
Though he brings grief, he also shows compassion
according to the greatness of his unfailing love.
For he does not enjoy hurting people or causing them sorrow.

LAMENTATIONS 3:31–33

DECEMBER 19, 2003
3 P.M.

"WHOSE IDIOT IDEA *WAS* THIS?"

Renee leaned against the truck, sheltering her face against the vehicle. No sooner had she slipped from the protective shelter of the vehicle than the storm slammed into her. How was she ever going to make her way in this wind?

She pressed her face against the cold metal of the door. There had to be another way. Something else she could—

Her eyes widened. Of course! She stepped back, staring at the truck—and suddenly realized she had a Plan B.

The road. It should be behind them. It was hard to tell for certain. She didn't know if they'd spun as they fell, or if they slid when they reached bottom. With the thick storm around them, she couldn't see more than a few feet away.

Still—a tiny sliver of hope seeped in—it just might work. Keeping one hand on the vehicle, she moved toward the back bumper. True, she couldn't see above her through the driving snow, but that didn't matter. If the road was behind the truck, as she thought it was, the ground would climb.

It only took a few steps away from the truck to realize the ground did exactly that. Climbed. Which meant the road was up there!

Renee peered upward, trying to spot the top of the incline, but it was hidden from her in the storm. Even so, excitement surged through her, giving her new energy. It couldn't be that far away. Not as far as the river. If she could reach the road, she'd have a chance. Snowplows *had* to be running; she could flag one down.

They'd never see you in this storm. Probably run right over you and not even feel the bump.

She recognized the thought for what it was: the voice of fear, of despair. And she refused to listen. *I can do this.* She started forward. *Even if there aren't any plows out, I can follow the road until I find help.*

But with each step, the snow grew deeper. A thin sheet of ice topped the snowpack, but it did little to support Renee's weight. Instead, it seemed to work in league with the wind against her. It raked at her pants, and then, when Renee's foot broke through and her leg sank into the underlying snow, it scraped her icy skin raw through the fabric.

Gritting her teeth, she kept going. Each step became a monumental effort as she shifted her weight, grabbed at her pants, and tugged her leg free of its bone-chilling sheath. Then it was another step forward...and another one-legged plunge into the deep freeze.

Her breath coming in increasingly rapid gulps, her knees turning rubbery, she fought with all her energy, pulling a leg free, planting her foot, and stepping forward.

Then, without warning, both legs broke through the coating of ice. Renee cried out as she sank, the ice scoring her bruised skin. She clutched at the ground, teeth gritted, and conceded defeat.

There was no way she would make it up that incline.

Gabe had always said she was mule-headed determination personified. She should have known from the first step that going up the incline wouldn't work. But hope had driven her on.

False hope. Empty hope. But hope, nonetheless.

She'd been so close...so close to finding the help they needed. Instead...

Renee drew a breath. Instead, it was back to Plan A: head west, find the river, find a cabin.

Of course, she had to get back to the truck first.

It was a struggle, but she managed to pull her legs from their wet, heavy encasement. Once free, she made her way, slowly, painfully, back to the truck.

She paused, relief washing over her, when she felt the hard comfort of the truck under her hand. Digging into her pocket, she pulled her compass out. It was hard to get her bearings with everything looking the same, all bathed in white, but she finally pinpointed a tall tree that stood out from the others. She wrapped her scarf more securely around her face and neck, ignoring the way her fingers trembled, refusing to acknowledge the panic gnawing at her nerves.

Do what you know to do.

She grabbed the rope still dangling from the car door, tugged it to test the knot, then looped the yellow coil over one shoulder. Lowering her face against the wind, she started forward. The wind fought her every step, pelting her with whirling snow and closing around her almost as soon as she stepped away from the truck. She glanced back, and alarm twisted around her heart like a thorny vine. Though she was scarcely twenty feet away from the vehicle, she could barely make it out in the blinding sheet of white.

Go back. Go back to where it's safe and wait. Help will come...

She made herself turn away from the enticement. As good as the idea sounded, she knew she couldn't do it. She had to find help.

She kept moving, pausing only long enough to take a bearing when she couldn't tell which direction was which. Even her footprints in the snow offered little help, erased almost the moment she lifted her foot by the blowing wind and piling snow.

The further she went from the seeming safety of the truck, the louder the cries grew at the back of her mind to turn around. But she wouldn't listen. She couldn't.

She just leaned into the wind, eyes squinted as she put one foot down, and then another. Her breathing was ragged, her legs heavy and leaden—but she wasn't going to stop. Not for anyone or anything. She was stronger than this storm, and she'd prove it.

Even if it was the last thing she ever did.

Now what?

Renee stared at the yellow coil in her hand.

I've reached the end of my rope. Literally. Strangled laughter slipped out as she clutched the end of the yellow lifeline in her hand.

Okay, so she'd walked to the end of the rope and still hadn't found the river. So what? All she needed to do was keep going, keep trying.

If only she could be sure which direction led to the river.

West. Keep heading west.

Renee nodded, then went back to a tree just behind her. Her stiff fingers fought her, but she managed to tie off the rope. At least Gabe could follow it this far.

Assuming he ever wakes up.

She rubbed her arm against her aching eyes, as though to erase the disheartening thought. Gabe would wake up. She wouldn't let herself think otherwise. Knowing him, he probably had done so already and was on his way to find her even now.

She lifted her head to stare at the large, heavy flakes swirling down from the muted sky. There couldn't be more than an hour of daylight left. Maybe only a half hour. If Gabe was going to find her, he'd better do it soon, otherwise...

Renee didn't even want to think about it. She stood there, trying to decide which way to go, when an icy blast of wind snatched her breath from her lungs. Every inch of her ached, and weariness seemed to have settled into her very bones. She bent over, resting her elbows on her knees.

If only she had been able to reach the road. Hard to believe it was nearly two hours since she'd tried. It seemed she'd been outside fighting the weather for days, not hours.

Renee straightened, the muscles in her back and legs offering sharp protest as she did so. She shivered, licking at her chapped lips. *If only I could sit down. Just for a minute. Just to rest awhile.* But it would be a mistake.

If she stopped now, she might never start again.

With that less-than-cheery thought, she stuck her hand in her pocket and dug out her compass. She ignored the tremble in her hands as she took a bearing due west. She was about to start out again when she hesitated, glancing back at the rope.

Maybe she should leave a note there, let Gabe know she was going west.

You already told him that in the note you left in the truck.

She frowned. True, but it might be helpful. After all, she had been known to change her mind from time to time—

The acknowledgment was cut off by a jolt of irritation. *Either he trusts you to do what you said you would or he doesn't.*

Her lips thinned. Trust? Gabe? Not hardly. Still...why

should she have to jump through hoops—especially when they were *his* darned hoops—to give the man what he needed when she'd already done so?

Enough was enough.

She spun on her heel and started walking. She didn't have time to write another note. She had to keep going, to find help.

It was up to her.

The resentment that met this thought was so abrupt and crushing that Renee stumbled. Cynical, biting words poured into her mind, as though dredged from the very depths of her cavernous soul.

Of course *it's up to you. It always is, isn't it?*

She started to form a denial, but it wouldn't come. How could it? Saving their marriage by forgiving, accepting, moving forward—hadn't it all been up to her? Wasn't she the one who had to make sacrifices, who had to give up her dreams? Be submissive. Be obedient. She'd had to do it all. That was just the way it was. After all, if she didn't do it, who would?

Gabe's face came to her then, and Renee almost laughed out loud. Not likely... She couldn't count on him to take the stupid trash out! She'd be nuts to rely on him for things that really mattered.

But even as she dismissed him, she felt a prick at the edge of her conscience. It was the same nagging reprimand she'd been feeling now for months. Maybe even years. The one that told her she didn't know *what* Gabe would do, because she'd never really given him a chance to do much of anything.

Her teeth clenched, and a sound that was half laugh, half sob escaped her. She couldn't deal with this. Not now. Not when every inch of her screamed from the strain of fighting the wind and deep snow, when she had no idea how much farther she had to go to find help.

"Stop it!" She shrieked the words into the wind. "Stop fighting me!"

The wind only howled, mocking her with what sounded like hollow laughter, pounding at her from all sides. She bent her head and plowed forward, but the icy blasts hit her square in the face and ripped the very breath from her lungs. Gasping, every muscle, every sinew in agony, she dropped to her hands and knees. Her ragged sobs rose on the swirling wind, blending with the storm's own wail to form a cry of utter despair.

Weakness crept through her arms and legs, making the ache so pronounced she could barely stand it, coaxing her to lie down and rest on the frozen blanket beneath her. *I can't... Oh, Jesus... I can't do this.*

As though someone had leaned over to whisper in her ear, she knew His response. He'd never asked her to do it. He'd only asked her to do one thing: wait.

Her spirit was pierced with a helpless frustration. How often had she felt that same urging, that same call to wait on Him? On His timing? His provision? Too often. Each time she promised Him, and herself, that she would obey. Even purposed to do so.

Each time she failed miserably.

And now...here it was again, that same command. That one impossible word: wait.

But this time it wasn't some emotional issue than hung in the balance. It wasn't even her marriage. It was her life. And Gabe's. Frustration filled her with new energy and she pushed herself back to her feet. "And if I'd waited, what then? What would have happened to us?"

The reply came as swiftly as the heated pulse pounding through her veins: *"The Spirit gives life; the flesh counts for nothing. The words I have spoken to you are spirit and they are life."*

Renee had always wondered at Christ's early followers, always felt a mixture of envy and disdain for them. How she would have loved walking with Christ! What a wonder it must have been to hear Him teach, to sit with Him and learn the truth, the way of life. To look into those holy eyes, to have Him look at you…

And yet the very people who had been given such a gift had turned from Him and walked away. Because His teachings were hard. She'd never understood it.

Until now.

She knew the words slapping her in the face were truth. And all she wanted to do was join the rank and file that had turned and walked away.

Despair devoured her; defeat feasted on the last shreds of her strength.

Renee stumbled forward to a tall, wide tree. She leaned against it for a moment, then sank down, sitting with her back against the rough bark of the trunk. The bottom branches of the evergreen swept out, hanging over her like a sheltering canopy. She drew her knees up and sat there on the cold, hard ground, thankful her ski pants kept the chill from reaching her. At least for now.

Trembling from head to toe, she let her breath out on a shuddering sigh. Exhaustion crept up her legs, crawling along her arms until it came to rest on her chest, a leaden weight that wouldn't let her move. It worked its way into her mind as well, telling her she'd worked hard enough…coaxing her to close her eyes, to rest…sleep…just for a minute…

No!

She jolted awake, shaking her head to clear the frozen cobwebs that seemed to have settled there. She couldn't fall asleep. Not yet. She needed to get warm first. She fumbled with the zipper on a pocket, then reached in and dug for a heat pack. Her billfold tumbled out, dumping its contents on the ground, and Renee let a cry of frustration sound in the snowy stillness. Why did *everything* have to fight her?

Pressing back against the tree, she tried again and this time managed to pull one of the heat packs free. She squeezed it between her shaky, stiff hands, working the chemicals together as best she could, then slid it between her layers of clothing. The welcome warmth seeped into her chilled body.

She leaned down to retrieve her billfold and ID when something caught her eye. A photo. Of her and Gabe.

It must have been tucked inside her billfold. She picked it up, then leaned back, her head resting against the tree trunk as she studied the picture. Her younger self smiled up at her. She was standing with Gabe, and they had their arms wrapped around each other as they mugged for the camera.

"I remember that day." Renee's voice sounded strange—muted, hollow—in the snowy air. She didn't care. It made her feel better to talk out loud, as though someone there was with her, listening. "That was the day we went to that state park…" She frowned, trying to recall the name of the place, then shook her head. "I can't remember. Gabe would know which one it was. He always remembers things like that—"

Her voice caught in her throat, and she forced herself to go on, to ignore the ache inside her. "It was a great place. Lots of rocks and rugged paths to hike." She could picture the day as clearly as if it were yesterday. They'd walked and hiked, talking and laughing about everything and nothing, happy just to be together.

Life had been so simple then.

Renee looked at the photo again and a tiny smile tugged at her mouth. They looked so happy. So carefree…so in love.

Her smile melted, and she reached out a finger to touch the youthful image of her husband, tracing the outline of his face, studying the happiness that filled his features, the glow in his eyes. *Gabe… Oh, Gabe, how did we get here? What happened to the people we used to be?*

She grabbed her billfold and shoved the photo back inside. Then she snapped it shut and pushed it back into her pocket. What good was this doing? And why did she have to face these things alone? Why was she the one who had to lie here, in this place of ice and snow and bone-deep cold, fighting the gnawing terror that she would never see Gabe again, never hear his voice, feel his touch—

"Stop it!"

She pulled her knees to her chest. She wanted to jump up and run, to escape the fears, the anxiety, the terrible sense of loss that gnawed at her. But she was too weary—body, heart, and soul-weary—to do anything but sit there.

Renee bowed her head. How had her marriage—a relationship she'd always longed for, something she'd always believed would be a strong, solid haven—become a constant battleground, a place of despair and sorrow, anger and resentment?

She pressed her face into her knees as the answer presented itself. How had they gone so wrong? By taking one wrong step at a time. And if there was one thing she and Gabe knew how to do, it was take wrong steps.

Big ones.

Again and again.

Life is changing so fast I need to keep track of it, to write it all down so I don't get lost. Don't forget. I don't want to forget a minute of what's happening.

I met him. The one I've been waiting for all my life. At least, I think I have. Some days I'm so sure. Other days, I don't know what I am. Confused. Hopeful. Afraid.

That last one seems stupid. Why afraid? But I am. Afraid he's not the one. Afraid he is the one. Afraid no one will ever love me. I want to know what it is to be loved that way, that special way, by a man. Loved forever and ever.

I feel like I'm afloat. Drifting...carried by whatever current or wind happens to catch me. It's as though I'm waiting for someone to come along and anchor me down.

14

God is the God of promise.
He keeps His word, even when that seems impossible;
even when circumstances seem to point to the opposite.

COLIN URQUHART

"Since the first day you began to pray for
understanding and to humble yourself before your God,
your request has been heard in heaven."

DANIEL 10:12

SEPTEMBER, 1978

THIS COULD NOT BE HAPPENING.

Renee stared at her desk, taking in box after box of envelopes and stack upon stack of printed letters. A mailing! It had to be. But she'd just done two of them in the last month!

She turned to stare at her supervisor. "Don't tell me…"

Candy leaned against the doorjamb between the reception room, where Renee's desk sat front and center, and the hallway leading to the offices. "Yup. Another mailing. Sorry about that. I know how much you like stuffing envelopes."

"Oh yeah, almost as much as I love a good root canal."

Candy's glee only made matters worse. But then, why shouldn't the woman grin like a goon? *She* didn't have to fold and stuff a bazillion letters, sacrificing her fingers and cuticles to "Dear Old Blue," as the alumni called the college. All in the hopes of prying donations from prominent, albeit parsimonious, alumni.

Well, the sooner she got started, the sooner she'd get done. Reaching for the first stack of letters, she pulled it toward her, steeling herself for the mind-numbing tedium of folding, stuffing, and sealing. But try as she might to concentrate, her attention was lured away by a nagging, persistent sound.

Glancing up, she peered out the large picture window at the front of the office. Renee could see practically the whole campus from her desk, which was a huge help on days like today. Still…what was that noise? Was someone knocking? No, hammering. Someone was hammering. Renee frowned, scanning the quad until she discovered the source. Her roaming gaze came to a screeching halt.

Oh, my…

There, in front of the women's dorm, near the concrete benches where Renee and her friends often sat and gabbed, was one of the physical properties workers. The guys who maintained and repaired the buildings. The guys everyone blamed when things broke down and loved when things were fixed.

Renee had seen this particular man before. He was nice looking—kind of handsome, really, in a rugged sort of way. His thick blond hair was on the longish side, just brushing his shirt collar. And though Renee wasn't overly fond of beards or mustaches, his was close-trimmed and she thought it suited him, gave him a mountain man kind of appeal— Jeremiah Johnson gone suburban.

The mountain man image was supported by the fact that he was almost always alone. From what Renee had seen, most of the other physi props guys hung out together. But she seldom saw this guy with them. Mostly she saw him going from one building to another. Or, sometimes late at night, she'd glance out her dorm window to the stand of trees behind the building, and she'd see him there, sitting on a picnic table. Alone.

Always alone.

Renee had first noticed his confident stride. He walked like a man who had a purpose, yet was in no hurry to arrive. More than once he'd reminded Renee of a lion, the head of the pack, walking with easy grace, confident he could face down any intruder, defend any territory.

Not that she'd paid *that* much attention to him, of course. He was just like the other guys who walked around campus fixing things, name tags perched on the pockets of their blue shirts. Or so she told herself. It was only because she saw him so often that she noticed he didn't look that much older than some of her friends. Or that, despite his age, which couldn't have been that far from hers, she had the distinct impression he wasn't a student worker. There was something about him—something...old.

They'd never actually spoken. Usually he just gave her the same distant, courteous nod he gave most anyone he passed in the hallways or going from one end of the campus to the other.

Except...

Except for one time.

Renee still didn't know why, but once, as she had moved past him on her way to class, she looked up, intentionally making eye contact. She had an odd sense of looking for...something. Some answer to the puzzle he'd become in her mind. When their gazes locked, what she saw stopped her cold. Raw emotion, feelings more intense and profound than she'd ever known, stared out at her from those blue eyes, striking deep into her heart in a way she still didn't understand. The encounter ripped the breath from her lungs and squeezed her heart with some terrible, indefinable...sorrow. That was the only way she could describe it.

She'd felt as though her heart were breaking.

The contact lasted no longer than a heartbeat. Renee didn't think she could have borne it for any longer than that. With the deep sense that she'd seen something she shouldn't have, she turned away, pretending to call to someone across the quad. But it took a while for her burning cheeks to cool, for her pounding pulse to calm and return to a normal cadence.

She'd seen him once or twice since then, but always from a distance. And—she quirked her lips as she took in the view from the office window—she'd *never* seen him look quite like this.

He was wielding a sledgehammer, lifting it just above his head then bringing it down on the concrete with smooth, powerful efficiency. His requisite blue shirt lay draped across one of the benches, leaving his torso bare. Even from across the campus Renee could see how the muscles tightened with each lift and swing of the hammer as he worked.

Lift, swing, *wham!* Lift, swing, *wham!* The rhythm was hypnotic, and she could well imagine the concrete had no option but to dissolve beneath that onslaught.

When he paused, letting the hammer come to rest on the ground, Renee jerked her gaze away, blowing out a breath at the surge of heat that surged through her and poured into her cheeks.

"Are you okay?"

She jumped, then spun to stare at Candy. "Okay? Of course. Why wouldn't I be okay? I'm fine. Why? Don't I look fine? Well, that doesn't really matter, does it?" She clenched her teeth to halt the babble. *Smooth, Renee. Really smooth.* She cleared her throat, reaching out to arrange the papers in front of her into a nice, neat pile, then looked up at Candy.

Her supervisor's face was a study in perplexity. "I guess you look fine. A little flushed...but fine."

Oh, no! She was looking toward the window!

"You just seemed a bit, I don't know...distracted, maybe."

Renee chewed her lip furiously. *Don't see him...don't see him...*

Candy's mouth tipped. "Or *mesmerized, maybe.*" When she turned back to Renee, her eyes were dancing. "But that's silly, huh? Nothing out *there* to catch one's eye, is there?"

Before Renee could think of a suitable retort, Candy patted her shoulder and moved back to her office. "So, I guess I'll just leave you to your…um…work, shall I?"

Renee didn't even reply. She just reached out, lifted the ruler from where it rested on her desk, and gave herself two quick whacks on the top of the head. With a sigh, she dropped the ruler to the desktop and forced her attention back to the task at hand.

Fold, fold, stuff, seal. Fold, fold, stuff, seal. Two down, forty gazillion to go.

Okay, so it wasn't the most exciting work in the world. So what? Was that any reason to sit there, staring out the window at a stranger like some lovestruck goon gawking at the object of her desire?

Of course not! No matter *how* compelling that object might be.

Renee picked up a pencil and started to doodle. No. Nuh-uh. Nope. She was *not* going to look again. Besides, he was probably gone. She hadn't heard the hammering since Candy had snuck up behind her, so he must be finished. Good thing, too. Last thing she needed was that incessant pounding to break her concentration. Yup, he'd left. She was sure of it. There wasn't a sound from outside.

So if he's gone, what harm could it do to look?

Renee paused, hands poised over the pile of letters. What harm, indeed? Why not just prove to herself that temptation had flown? One quick peek to confirm he was gone, and then right back to work. Right? Right.

She allowed her attention to wander back to the picture window, across the quad, to the dorm, to the benches…

He was there. He stood, relaxed, the sledgehammer leaning against his leg, as he took long drinks from a sports bottle.

Renee sat back in her chair as he pulled a handkerchief from his pocket and swiped it across his face, stretching his neck, arching his back slightly as though to work out the kinks.

Then, with so little effort that the hammer might as well have been made of balsa, he lifted the tool and went back to work. Renee rested her elbows on the desk, cradling her chin in her hands. It would take nothing less than the building catching fire to make her turn away. Even then, she'd wait until the flames were tickling her toes.

She couldn't help it. The sheer force of the actions...of the man...captured her. Every motion conveyed controlled power, giving one sure message: Here is a man to be reckoned with.

The ringing of the phone jarred Renee, and she almost fell out of her chair. For the second time that morning, heat surged into her face. Good grief. She was pathetic! He was probably married and had twelve kids.

The morning went straight downhill from there. By lunchtime her fingers were cut and raw from the envelopes, her shoulder was in a permanent cramp from cradling the phone, which seemed to ring nonstop, and her head was making like Ricky Ricardo's bongo drums. She was ready to draw and quarter the next person who walked in the door. Teeth clenched, she stalked into the break room, jerked the small fridge open, and pulled her lunch out.

"Hey, Renee, wanna join us?"

She shook her head, then grimaced at the pain that ricocheted across her temples. She managed a smile at the petite blonde who pulled a chair out for her at the lunch table. "Thanks, Angie, but I'm going outside. And do me a favor, will you?"

Angie took a bite of her sandwich. "Sure. What?"

"If the phone rings while I'm out—" she pulled the door open—"shoot it."

Muffled laughter followed her outside, and Renee felt a responding smile trying to ease across her tight facial muscles.

Her tension releasing on a sigh, she lowered herself to the stone wall bordering the walkway to the office.

She ate her lunch, grateful for the quiet, the chance to think. About the future. About where she was going from here. If only every train of thought didn't lead to the same destination: a certain blond, broad-shouldered mountain man.

She figured later it was because she was distracted that she swallowed wrong. Whatever the reason, her bite of sandwich suddenly caught in her throat, and she found herself coughing, gasping.

"Are you okay?"

She looked up—and nearly fainted. It was him. He stood there, concerned blue eyes looking down at her. She tried to say something, but all that came out was a strangled kind of *"gaaaaa."*

A small frown creased his brow. "Are you breathing?"

Barely. She tried to say so. Another croak. More coughing. Wonderful. Marvelous. Could she possibly make a better first impression? If only the ground would open up and swallow her whole.

Now, please.

Strong fingers circled her arm and something was pressed into her hand. Renee looked down to find a large cup of water there.

"Sip it. Slowly."

She nodded, her eyes expressing heartfelt gratitude as she took a small sip, letting the cold liquid seep down her tight throat.

The look on his face was one of mingled concern and kindness. "Doing better?"

Renee managed a nod.

His smile held relief—along with another emotion Renee couldn't quite define. One that said she mattered to him.

Renee shook off the odd notion—he didn't even know her, let alone *care* about her. Still, good thing he'd happened along when he did. Just when she needed help. That was some coincidence.

No—she straightened—that was a miracle. Her very own miracle, complete with electric blue eyes. Of course, she'd never imagined a miracle would look quite that good in jeans and a blue shirt.

When a wry smile worked across his lips, Renee realized she was staring. Heat surged into her face as she forced herself to look away and took another sip of water.

Clearing her throat, she gave him a sideways glance, then tested her voice. "Thank you—" it was raspy, but it was there—"for your help."

He leaned one arm on his knee and shrugged. "Don't mention it."

"But—"

He raised a hand to nudge the cup toward her lips. "No, I mean don't talk. You need to give yourself time to recover—" his smile deepened a notch—"before you tell me how wonderful I am."

If her cheeks had been warm before, they were down-right nuclear now. Renee did as she was told, but she couldn't deny the tiny, just-this-side-of-elated thrill that skipped though her.

Because sitting there under that blue gaze, she had the oddest feeling that he was exactly that: wonderful. And more than that, she felt a certainty deep inside that she was going to get the chance to find out for herself.

And that she was going to enjoy every minute of it.

EARLY APRIL 1979

"Come on, hon, you can do it."

At Gabe's encouragement, Renee nodded, then tipped her head back and gazed into a sky so blue it almost hurt her eyes. Days like this were so rare this time of year. Especially *this* year. She'd thought last winter was brutal, but it was nothing compared to this winter. The snow had started falling in late October and hadn't stopped until just a few weeks ago.

She had known that midwestern winters were harsh—full of cold and ice and snow—but she'd had no idea that she'd be walking to classes through canyons of snow. Or that winter lasted for nearly half the year. For months now the drifts had towered over her, and the gray skies grew as oppressive as the windchill. That was something else Renee had to get used to. Growing up in the southern tip of the Pacific Northwest, she never heard of a windchill factor. In fact, she thought the weathermen were saying "wind*shield* factor." Finally curiosity got the better of her, and she asked her roomie, a native Illini, how one measured the temperature of a windshield.

She was still living that one down.

When March finally arrived, Renee had watched eagerly for the snow to start melting and the dormant, brown grass to start turning green again. It had taken several more weeks, though, for the first signs of spring. Renee had been sure they'd have snow for Easter, and they still could. The forecast was for snow to start Saturday night and continue through the week.

But today was Good Friday, and there wasn't a snowflake in sight. In fact, the sun was bright and warm, and most of the snow had at long last melted away. Renee could even see tiny buds shivering on the trees—a sure sign that spring was on its way.

Her eyes drifted shut, soaking in the warm caress of the sun on her face.

"Uh, hon? Rennie? You go to sleep on me?"

A light laugh escaped her at the teasing question, but before she could answer the world shifted beneath her, and she scrambled to find a handhold in the craggy wood of the tree she was climbing. "Hey!"

Her downward glance brought a warm grin at the rueful remorse on Gabe's face. His broad hands rubbed at his shoulders, which had been her steady perch until he shrugged her off. "Sorry, Ren, but my shoulders were about to fall off with you just standing on them like that."

"Hmpf! Are you saying I'm fat?"

The curve of his lips and the look in his blue eyes sent shivers spiraling through her. No man intending to be a minister had the right to look that deliciously wicked.

"Are you kidding? With your foot that close to my face? Of course not." He reached up to pat the back of her leg. "You're light as a feather, hon."

"Hmm." She turned back to the tree, scoping out her next move. She shifted, then stepped up onto a small branch. "And you're full of beans."

"Ah, but you like beans, don't you?"

She wrapped her hands around a large branch above her, then pulled herself up and over, until she was perched on it, hanging on and gazing down at Gabe. He stood there, peering up at her, looking every inch the conquering Viking. His thick blond hair and tall, strong build bore testimony to the Norwegian blood coursing through his veins. And that smile...oh, that smile. It did amazing things to her.

"Come on up. *If* you can."

"Ooo, a challenge." His gaze caught hers and held it. "I love a challenge."

With that he moved forward, studying the tree as though it were a foe to be brought into submission. Renee leaned one elbow on the wide branch beneath her, rested her chin in her hand, and watched as Gabe began his ascent.

She still couldn't believe he was hers. The first time she'd seen him, she had been...well, impressed. A slow grin worked its way across her face. *Come on, be honest. You thought he was a hunk.*

"Hi, beautiful. Hang out here often?"

Renee turned. Gabe had scaled the tree and was perched right behind her. She shifted into a sitting position and leaned forward until their faces were almost touching.

"Beautiful, eh?" She pressed a soft kiss to his cheek. "I like that."

"Mmm—" Gabe's hand came up to cradle her face—"me, too."

His kiss was warm and heady. She closed her eyes, letting him fill her senses as completely as he was coming to fill her world.

Renee didn't know if she moved wrong or if Gabe did, but suddenly they were slipping, and she gave a small yelp as they scrambled to regain their balance on the tree limb. They both sprawled, and when their eyes met, she burst into laughter.

Gabe's smile was rueful. "Some Romeo I am. I almost knock you out of a tree."

She giggled, and he nodded toward the grass beneath them.

"Meet you on firmer ground?"

"You got it."

Gabe reached bottom first, and she looked down at him. The wind teased his hair as he turned that warm grin up at her. Wasn't this love? The way her heart turned over every time their gazes met? When he held his hands out, she slid into his embrace, wrapping her arms around his neck. He leaned back against the tree, holding her securely, and she knew he wasn't going to let her go. Not ever.

She belonged to him.

How had this happened? How was it possible to feel so much a part of someone in such a short time? She'd never known, never even imagined, it was possible to feel this way after only a month together.

And again, on the very heels of that happy thought, came the nagging inner voice, the one that seemed to intrude on her thoughts more and more.

Feel what *way? How do you feel about him, really?*

Gabe must have felt her stiffen, because he pulled back just enough to look into her eyes. "What's wrong?"

She laid her hand on his bearded cheek. "Nothing. I just...had a chill." How she hated the uncertainty swirling inside her! It seemed to have woven itself into the very fabric of her heart, her spirit. When it had first begun, she sought solace and encouragement from her friends. Unfortunately, they were no help whatsoever. Every time Renee turned around one of them was expressing one concern after another about Gabe.

A week ago, it was Sharon, from two doors down the hall, who pulled her aside and said her brother had seen Gabe at a bar. "And he wasn't drinking soda, Renee."

She dismissed the concern. So Gabe had a beer or two from time to time. The news didn't thrill her, but it didn't exactly make him Jack the Ripper, either. The man was going to be a minister, for heaven's sake. Didn't that say more about him than the fact that he'd visited some stupid bar?

Then, just a few days ago, Ian, one of her closest friends, came knocking on her door. She could tell he was troubled— he had the heavy, plodding walk of a man carrying a thousand burdens—and her heart sank. A dull ache inside warned her this would be about Gabe.

It was.

Renee sat in her desk chair and pressed her hands into her lap. Why did everyone feel they needed to warn her? To tell her terrible things about Gabe? Did they think she was stupid? That she was so blinded by being in love that she couldn't see him as he really was?

It was all she could do not to tell Ian to take his so-called concern and stuff it.

But she didn't. He was a good friend, and she knew it hadn't been easy for him to come to her like this. So she sat there, listening as he told her he'd heard Gabe laying into a student who had trashed a room for the second or third time. "I haven't heard language like that in a long time, Renee. You know I'm no saint, but this was stuff even I wouldn't say. I thought Gabe was going to take the guy apart right there." Ian leaned back in his chair. "Are you sure Gabe is the kind of man you think he is?"

Renee wasn't sure what irritated her more: Ian's prying or the fact that his question only fed the turmoil that constantly plagued her.

She felt her cheeks warm and hated that fact. Hated that it could imply she thought Ian's concern was valid. Even if she did, she didn't want him knowing that. She lifted her chin and met his concerned gaze. "Gabe isn't perfect. He's got a problem with anger, but he knows it and is dealing with it."

Ian's brow creased at this news. "You've seen him like that?" Clearly, he didn't like the thought. His next words confirmed the fact. "Has he ever treated *you* like that? I swear, Renee, if he has…"

Her stomach clenched. Oh great. Just what she needed, Ian squaring off with Gabe. She shook her head. "No, of course not. Gabe would never hurt me."

It was the truth. Yes, Renee had seen Gabe's anger a few times, had even heard the violence that poured from him when that anger was unleashed. But he'd never directed that kind of behavior or talk at her.

That didn't lessen the force of it, though, did it?

She looked away, afraid Ian would be able to read that admission in her eyes. She reassured him, told him she and Gabe were working through the issues, praying for God's help and guidance, and that everything was fine. Under control.

Relief settled over her as she closed the door behind him. She'd nearly lost it. If he'd stayed a moment longer, she wasn't sure what she would have done. Screamed, maybe. Ranted a bit. Even struck out.

But it wasn't Ian she wanted to hit. It was herself…her

doubts and fears. She had tried to surrender them to God. She asked Him to take them away. And yet here they were, brought to burning life yet again by Ian's probing questions.

She leaned her forehead against the solid wood of the door. The first time she'd experienced the force of Gabe's anger she was stunned. More than that, she was frightened. They'd been out for a drive, and in the middle of their conversation, his expression changed. Turned hard. Fierce.

Someone was tailgating them. Gabe hated tailgaters. Before Renee knew what was happening, Gabe stomped on the brakes, and she catapulted forward. If his arm hadn't been draped across the front of her like a seat belt, she might well have gone into the windshield.

The car behind them screeched to a halt, barely avoiding a collision. And when the driver gunned the engine and passed Gabe's car, he jumped into hot pursuit.

Renee had always loved Gabe's strength, the way he made her feel protected and safe, the barely restrained power he exuded. People seemed to know this was a man you didn't cross, and she liked that.

But now the very aspects she'd always loved about him seemed...out of control. Dangerous.

I'm in love with a crazy man.

Her terror must have shown, because when Gabe finally sent a glance her way, he started, and the red in his face changed to a pasty white. He slowed the car, pulled to the side of the road, and cut the engine. In the sudden silence Renee's sobbing gasps seemed deafening. When he reached for her hand, she jerked away. The despair that painted his features at her action pierced her heart, and she put her hands over her face and wept in earnest.

This time, when his arms came around her, she didn't resist. He spoke to her in the familiar, soothing tone she loved.

"I'm sorry..." The broken words were so sincere, so sorrowful, that she could only nod as he repeated them, over and over. "Ah, Renee, I'm so sorry."

When she could finally speak, he had explained, for the first time, about his childhood. Talked about the abuse. About the hopelessness. And the anger. Shared how it had built within him, how it had become his armor against terror, against pain.

How it had kept him alive.

"It became my best friend. It even stopped my dad from beating me."

Renee frowned. "How did it do that?"

"The last time he grabbed me, I lost it." Gabe's faraway expression told her he was reliving the scene. "I had finally gotten big enough, strong enough that I just turned on him and knocked him flat. He lay there, gawking up at me, and do you know what he said?"

"What?"

"'At least I know I raised a man.'" Gabe's laugh was harsh. "Like he had the first clue what it means to be a man."

Renee had listened to his outpouring of memories, torn between horror and compassion. It sickened her that anyone could subject his own child to such mindless, senseless cruelty. It grieved her that anyone—least of all this man, whom she was growing to love—had to bear such terrible emotional scars.

And it terrified her.

She'd never dreamed Gabe had this side to him. That such anger and violence dwelled inside him. As she sat there, hearing him share his darkest memories, she started to tremble.

Please, God...how can I be with him? How can I spend my life with this kind of craziness?

The traitorous thoughts pounded at her until she feared she would cry out against them.

"Renee?"

Gabe's rasping voice tore her from her turmoil, and she turned to him, met his eyes—those blue eyes that had always moved her so...eyes now clouded with pain and fear...

She moved without thinking, as though driven by some unknown, irresistible instinct. She drew him close, cradling him against her as she soothed him, comforting him like a mother speaking peace to a child afraid of monsters in the dark.

And in so doing, she made a choice. She turned her back on fear and doubt. This was Gabe. She knew him. She loved him. And she was not going to abandon him. No matter how much her mind screamed at her to do so. That wouldn't be fair to him. It wouldn't be right.

That's when it hit her. What if God had brought them together so she could show him what love was really like? To let him know he was accepted, scars and all? She tightened her arms around him even as she wrapped her heart around this new thought.

Of course! God knew Gabe needed someone to love him, to help him get past all the pain of his terrible childhood. Who better to do that than someone whose own childhood had been filled with the very things Gabe's had lacked: joy, kindness, respect, and the freedom that came from knowing you were loved no matter what. Maybe this was even why God had blessed Renee so much, so that she could then share that blessing with the man He had chosen for her.

Do you really buy that? Do you really think God needs you and only you to restore Gabe Roman?

Renee ignored the question. She knew where the voice of doubt came from, and it wasn't from God. She lifted her chin, closing her mind to the questions that kept trying to intrude on her insight, telling herself she was more grateful than she could express that she hadn't turned away. From Gabe. Or from God.

That day had marked a turning point in their relationship. Without ever saying so, they'd made a commitment to each other. To forever. Yes, Gabe's anger had shown up a few times since, but it had never been as intense, as terrifying, as that day in the car. And he'd always apologized, always told her he hadn't meant to subject her to such a display.

Each time, she accepted his apology. After all, he was doing his best. And she couldn't deny his sincerity when he promised he would do better next time.

"Hey, are you in there?"

Gabe's laughter broke into her thoughts as his warm, strong arms tightened around her. Renee pulled her thoughts away from the past, focusing on Gabe as he nestled her close.

Things would be different when he met her mom and dad. They were going to fly out there in a few months, spend some time at her folks'. She'd told them about Gabe, how special he was, but something else must have come through in her tone as well. Because when she'd talked with her mom last time, asked if she was looking forward to meeting Gabe, her mother sounded...cautious.

Renee rested her head against Gabe's chest. That was just because Mom didn't know him, that was all. She and Dad were going to love him. She knew they were.

She squeezed her eyes shut and focused on the steady beat of Gabe's heart. If only that sure, steady sound would drown out the reproachful questions pelting her mind.

Why can't you at least be honest with him? Tell him you're confused, that things are moving too fast—

"I love you."

Renee stilled, then opened her eyes. The tenderness she saw in his expression only made her feel even more wretched. "I—you...what?"

He chuckled and reached out to brush her windblown hair from her face. "I love you."

She let the words wash over her, waiting... Shouldn't she bask in the proclamation? Shouldn't she be swimming in a giddy kind of joy? Delighted beyond words? Her boyfriend just said he loved her, for heaven's sake!

She waited...and waited...but the only thing she felt was an even deeper uncertainty.

What's wrong with me? She wanted to strike out at something. But Gabe was holding her hands in his, watching her with those warm blue eyes. Renee looked at him, studying his features. She pulled one hand free to touch his face, tracing the line of his brow, his cheek, with slow, tentative fingers.

He loved her. Gabe loved her. It didn't matter what anyone else said—not even that irritating inner voice. This was right. It had to be. She'd given so much of her heart to him...*and so much of other things, too.*

She pressed the thought away and drew a deep breath, then spoke the words she'd been waiting all her life to say to a man. The words she knew Gabe was waiting to hear. "I love you, too."

She hadn't expected him to swoon at the declaration, but neither had she expected him to start laughing. She put a theatrical hand to her chest as though mortally injured and tipped her head. "What?"

His upheld hand warded off her mock displeasure. "I'm sorry, hon. It's just...well, it just occurred to me..." He placed her palm against his chest. "Do you know what today is?"

Her lips twitched. "The first day of the rest of our lives?"

Emotion flickered in his eyes, and he lowered his head to kiss her fingers. "I hope so, but no, that's not what I mean." His grin broadened. "It's Friday. Friday...the thirteenth."

Renee's mouth fell open. He was right! "That's too perfect."

Gabe tightened his grip on her fingers, tugging her toward him. "Our lucky number." He waggled his brows. "How's *that* for amazing?"

Her friends thought it was crazy that she and Gabe considered thirteen their lucky number, but she liked it. It was unexpected, different, and a bit quirky—a perfect fit for the two of them. Besides, even her friends had to admit that number kept showing up: February 13 was the first time she and Gabe had really talked; their first date was on March 13; Renee's dorm room number was 113; Gabe's address was 713 Oleander Lane; and Gabe had accepted Christ last year on October 13. On and on it went, until she and Gabe had laughingly decided that thirteen would have to be their "lucky" number.

Which only made this new thirteenth event that much more special, and she simply would not let the vague unrest gnawing at her spoil even a second of it.

Putting on her brightest smile, she nudged Gabe. "I feel like celebrating." If the slightly rebellious tone of her words surprised him, he didn't let it show. "Last one to the car buys the pizza."

"With extra cheese and mushrooms?"

Renee thought that with his hair tousled by the wind and his eyes shining with anticipation, Gabe looked like a rugged little boy, ready for whatever came. "Absolutely."

As they ran for the car, their laughter caught and carried on the wind. Renee knew she was being silly. God had brought her and Gabe together, and they were in love. What she shared with Gabe was forever.

As for those relentless questions and concerns, well, they were just nerves, nothing more. She wouldn't give them another moment's thought.

No matter how they screamed at her.

15

It takes sorrow to expand and deepen the soul.

THE HEAVENLY LIFE

Those who plant in tears will harvest with shouts of joy.

PSALM 126:5

NOVEMBER 1979

GABE WAS LOST.

Irretrievably. Irrevocably. Eternally.

He knew it the minute he looked into those green eyes. The connection hadn't lasted long, but it hadn't needed to. The minute their eyes met as she passed by him one day, something deep in his gut—something he hadn't even known existed—clicked. And from that moment, nothing anyone said to him could change his mind.

He was going to marry Renee Williams.

Of course, he hadn't known her name then, but he knew he'd find out. All he had to do was wait, and an opportunity would come. For the first time he actually looked forward to going to work. His job at the college wasn't fancy—working with boilers, fixing things spoiled college kids trashed after a weekend binge—but it was solid, honest work and it helped pay the bills. Besides, his boss was a good guy. Tough, but fair. And willing to work around Gabe's class and study schedule.

Then he saw Renee, and suddenly his job became the most important factor in his life. Because it gave him the opportunity to see her. To meet her. And, as though God Himself set it up, it happened. He'd been in the right place at the right time. He still remembered the wide-eyed stare she directed at him that day when he helped her. He knelt there, watching her, looking into those eyes, and what he saw still made his pulse jump.

Gratitude, sure. But something more. Awareness. Attraction. It danced through her eyes, and the response that nailed him was so powerful it sucked the air from his lungs and made his knees buckle—or would have if he hadn't already been kneeling beside her.

No doubt in his mind. He and Renee were meant to be together. And from the day they'd met he'd done everything he could to ensure they fulfilled that destiny. And nothing anyone said—not his roomies at seminary: "Man, what are you *doing*? This is the fourth night this week you've seen this girl"; not his best friend, John: "G-man, now is not the time for this. This girl is just distracting you from what really matters"; not even his sister, Susan: "I know you think you love her, Gabe, but do you really know this girl well enough to commit to forever? I mean, have you prayed about this?"— made the slightest difference.

Almost without realizing what he was doing, he'd strategized and then launched what amounted to an emotional assault. He knew he'd have to start slow, to move forward with carefully measured steps. Renee was young and inexperienced where relationships were concerned. He spent time with her talking, laughing. He drew her out, listening carefully as she talked about her family, her faith, her love of nature and the night sky.

When she admitted one evening that she sometimes had trouble sleeping, he'd gone out and bought some of that glow-in-the-dark paint. By then Renee's friends had started to accept him, so it hadn't been too hard to talk one into letting him into her dorm room. He used an astronomy chart as a map to paint her favorite constellations and the Milky Way on the ceiling over her bed. When she came back from class that night, she found a note from him propped up on her pillow: "Leave the light on until you're ready for bed. Then turn it off and look up, and remember how much God loves you."

Her reaction had made his effort more than worth it. As soon as she saw him, she ran and threw her arms around him. Her face pressed into his neck, she told him how she'd slipped into bed, shut off the light, and then gasped at the sight overhead. "You gave me the stars, Gabe."

But then she'd done the same for him. She gave him the stars every time she turned that tender green gaze on him...handed him heaven each time she opened her arms to him. She was everything he'd ever wanted.

It hadn't been long until she opened up to him, and the initial attraction that sparked between them had given way to deeper things. Trust. Reliance. Belonging. Desire...

Desire.

Gabe stood, pacing the room, suddenly too restless to sit still. That had been the hardest part. Dealing with the desire. He'd never known such wanting before. Sure, he knew what was right, but when he was with Renee—when she smiled up at him, when she melted against him—the lines blurred. She was so young, so passionate, and it moved him like never before to watch her discover the wonder of love—physical as well as emotional—for the first time.

He'd known it would be up to him to keep a rein on things. He was the one who was experienced at relation-ships—he'd had more of them than he cared to admit—and he promised to keep them out of trouble. A promise he'd kept. Until recently.

Gabe leaned against the wall, staring down at the floor. "God—" the whispered prayer sounded raw and miserable even to his own ears—"I messed up. Big-time."

He hadn't meant for it to happen, but it had. He let himself get caught up in the moment, let things go further than they should have. Let her passion ignite his until there was no turning back. But he'd paid for it. The look on Renee's face after it was over, the guilt and regret, the way those green eyes had filled with tears—and shame…

He swallowed hard. Her pain had cut him more deeply than any knife could ever do. He'd held her as she wept, talked with her, prayed with her, sworn to her it would never happen again. Not until after they were married.

This time it hadn't been hard to stay true to his word. All it took was the image of her hugging herself and crying that day to cool even the strongest surge of passion.

Still…

Something had changed. He wasn't sure if it was something with her or with him, but he knew it was there. He saw it every time he looked into Renee's eyes, a kind of shadow. Every time he held her, he felt it—an invisible but impenetrable barrier between them, keeping them from the growing joy they'd known until that night.

Gabe slammed his fist into the wall, then pushed away from it. Stupid, stupid… His jaw ached, and he realized he'd been grinding his teeth. He didn't care. He deserved whatever pain he got. *How could you let that happen?*

He'd been beating himself up ever since. Which was why he'd finally called Susan. He needed to talk, and his older sister always seemed to understand him, to know what to say. And, even more important, what not to say.

At least, she usually did. But this time she listened in silence, then dropped her own little bombshell into the mix:

"Have you prayed about this?" The question, his conversation with Susan, replayed in his mind. And each time, he felt the same thing: a creeping, nagging disquiet. As much as he didn't like to admit it, Susan's question had hit home. Not because he wasn't sure of Renee, of them being together, but he had to admit things had happened fast.

Because you made them happen that way.

He turned from the thought and found himself staring at his reflection in the window. He took in the frown pinching his features, the confusion looking back at him from his eyes. One minute his life was on track, heading down a path he'd determined long ago to follow, then…

Renee.

He let the chaos in his mind out on a groan that came from the very core of his heart. Since he'd met her, nothing else mattered. Nothing but the certainty that she was the one, and he'd do whatever he needed to do to win her. He'd be whoever he needed to be, say what he needed to say…

"Have you prayed about this?"

Gabe rubbed his now aching temples as his sister's words echoed again, sending that odd, uncomfortable twinge through him. "Jesus…" He stared at the night sky. "Jesus, what do You want from me?"

But he knew the answer even before he asked. Okay, he hadn't taken time to pray about Renee, about their future together. But so what? Being together wouldn't feel so right if it wasn't from God. If He wasn't calling them to be together.

"Are you sure? Are you doing this because it's what God wants…or because it's what you think you want?"

Gabe started as Jake's pointed questions from so many years ago rose from within him like specters from some recurrent nightmare. With a muttered oath, Gabe moved to throw open the window and draw in a deep gulp of the cold, clear winter night, almost welcoming the ache the subzero air caused in his lungs. Maybe it would take his mind off the ache in his gut...the ache that wouldn't go away until Renee was his.

No, he hadn't prayed, but this was right, this was God's path for them. It had to be.

So why not take a little time to pray about it?

Gabe hesitated. He didn't want to wait any longer. He wanted to go to Renee, take her hands in his and ask her to be with him, be his...forever. Ask her to be his wife. Hear her say yes, hear her promise to love and honor him, in sickness and in health, until death came to part them.

The thought of her speaking those words did crazy things to his pulse. "I do." The words rang out with a solid certainty in the quiet of his room. He leaned out the window and shouted the words into the frigid night. "I *do!* You'd better believe it! Absolutely. Not a doubt in my mind."

That's when it hit him.

Cold. A deep, aching chill. But it had nothing to do with the wintry air outside. No, this came from inside, from some-place way down in his gut. It rose with slow purpose, crawling across his nerves, raising the hair on his arms as it slithered past. With a start, Gabe glanced over his shoulder.

No one was there, of course—his roommates were all out. But even as he let loose a breath of relief, he couldn't escape the restlessness that had settled over him, pressing down on his mind and spirit. The irritating sensation grew, like a sliver that had worked its way deep into the skin—one you knew would hurt like crazy to get out.

"Father God..." He closed his eyes on the agonized prayer. Something was very, very wrong.

He had to get out. Away. Grabbing his jacket, he headed outside, accelerating as he strode down the hallway, through the door, down the stairs—and collided with Chad Madison, one of his roommates, who was bounding up the steps.

"Yo, Roman, what's the hurry, man?" Chad peered over Gabe's shoulder. "Someone after you or something?"

Gabe managed a choked laugh and shoved his hands into

the pockets of his jacket. "After me? Who'd be after me?"

"Your conscience, maybe?"

Despite Chad's wry tone, alarm jolted through Gabe, even as his sister's voice ricocheted from one side of his mind to the other: *"Have you prayed about this?"*

"What's that supposed to mean?"

Chad pulled back, his arched brows clear evidence of just how over-the-top Gabe's tone had been. Gabe held up a hand. "I'm sorry, man. I didn't mean to snap at you."

His grin sliding back into place, Chad shrugged. "Hey, no problem. I just figured you'd be studying tonight, that's all. I mean, you're the one who told me how far behind you are in church history."

Studying…he should be studying. But not church history. Gabe shook his head as the obvious finally became clear. Chad was right. It was his conscience chasing him. And the only way he'd get rid of the sick feeling that threatened to overtake him was do exactly what he should have done from the start.

He spun on his heel. It only took a moment to return to his room and grab his Bible. He passed a confused Chad as he left again, heading outside. It didn't matter how cold it was outside. He needed someplace quiet, isolated. Someplace to read.

Someplace to figure out just exactly what he was supposed to do.

I look within and I sense choices waiting to be made.

But none are clear...

...or good...

...or even desirable.

So I turn, questioning, wondering...where has logic strayed?

And why can't I hear that still, small voice whispering the proper choice?

With stakes this high, you'd think I'd know the answer.

But I don't.

16

Every day the choice between good and
evil is presented to us in simple ways.

W. E. SANGSTER

You have tested us, O God…
like silver melted in a crucible.

PSALM 66:10

DECEMBER 12, 1979

WHAT AM I GOING TO DO?

"Miss Williams, are you still there?"

Renee stared at the receiver in her hand. She knew she should answer the woman, but no words would come out.

"Miss Williams?"

Clearly the nurse was getting testy. Renee cleared her throat and forced the words past the dryness in her mouth. "I'm…I'm here. Thank you for calling."

Though she could still hear the woman's voice through the receiver, Renee set it back in the cradle. She stared down at the phone. How could something so small have such a huge impact on her life?

But it had. It changed everything. Just by ringing.

"O God…" The whispered prayer caught in her throat, much like her breakfast had done almost every morning for the past few weeks. Fighting the nausea that had become her constant companion, she looked down at the piece of paper on her desk. She always doodled when she was nervous. This had been no exception. One word was written, over and over, across the page, in big black letters.

Pregnant.

Renee crumpled the offending piece of paper and tossed it in the trash can beside her desk. She stared at it for a moment—the paper sat there, on top of the rest of the trash. And though it was crumpled, Renee could still see the word she'd written almost without thinking as she listened to the nurse's brisk voice telling her that her life was over.

"The reason you haven't been feeling well, Miss Williams, is simple: You're pregnant."

Renee jumped up, grabbed the trash can, and headed for the garbage chute in the hallway. No sense leaving that incriminating bit of paper in the trash for one of her roommates to find.

People would know soon enough.

For now she needed time...time to think. She pulled the chute open and threw the trash down it, listening as it bounced and banged its way to the receptacle below.

The odors from the chute assaulted her, and she pulled away, covering her mouth with one hand, her stomach with the other.

Breathe...breathe...

Too late. She bolted for the bathroom, barely making it in time. Renee wept as her stomach surged, emptied. After what seemed like a lifetime, she sank to the cool tile floor. Curling into a tight ball, she hugged herself against nausea—and the terrible reality—that washed over her in waves.

When she could stand, she made her way back to her room, crawled into bed, and pulled the quilt around her like a sheltering cocoon.

Pregnant. How could she be pregnant?

"God…" She pressed her face into her pillow, doing her best to muffle the sobs. "One time! We were only together one time…and we promised never to do that again. How could You let this happen to us?"

There was no reply to her whispered plea, not from the heavens. But answers abundant sprang from Renee's heart.

Don't blame God. He's not the one who ignored what He knew was right. He didn't let this happen. You did.

She rolled onto her back, staring at the ceiling, at the stars Gabe had painted there for her.

Gabe. She closed her eyes, but that didn't stop the tears from spilling down her cheeks.

How was she going to tell her parents? Her friends?

How am I even going to tell Gabe?

God gives us the cross, and the cross gives us God.

MADAME JEANNE GUYON

And even when you do ask, you don't get [what you want]
because your whole motive is wrong—
you want only what will give you pleasure.

JAMES 4:3

DECEMBER 12, 1979

GABE HAD HIS ANSWER.

He received it one bit at a time over the past month, like pieces of some inner jigsaw puzzle juggling and falling into place. Now he saw the whole picture.

And it wasn't pretty.

The first piece came a few days after that night in his room. He'd been walking out the door after theology class one day, and his prof, Asa Jacks, stopped him and pulled him aside.

Gabe liked Asa. He was one of those quiet, gentle men whose whole demeanor spoke of wisdom and experience. He'd been especially patient with Gabe when he couldn't seem to get the stuff Asa was teaching. Gabe got frustrated with himself, with his thick head and dim understanding, but Asa never seemed bothered. He'd just offer to stick around, to talk things through.

That was what Gabe expected when Asa stopped him that day, but what he received from the older man was an invitation to his house. To dinner. Gabe gladly accepted. No way was he going to turn down a home-cooked meal!

The dinner had been excellent, made even more so by the conversation with Asa and his wife, Doris. They were the most genuine, open people Gabe had met in a long time, and he found himself relaxing in their company. When the meal was finished, Asa tapped Gabe on the shoulder, then led him to his study.

There they sat in soft leather chairs as Asa poured coffee first for his guest, then for himself. Gabe took a sip. Asa was not only a good teacher, he was a man who knew how to make a good, strong cup of coffee. He settled back in his chair, savoring the rich brew, watching his professor through the rising steam.

"Gabriel, I would like to ask you some questions, if that's all right with you."

Gabe hesitated, then nodded, hoping Asa hadn't noticed his fingers tensing on the mug in his hands. The old man's pale blue eyes fixed on him, and his thoughtful expression gave Gabe the sense that Asa could see through all his barriers...right to the heart of him.

"Why do you want to be a minister?"

Gabe set his coffee mug down with slow precision, giving himself time to think. Why was Asa asking him this? What was he supposed to say?

Gabe started to say what he thought the man wanted to hear—but nothing came out. It was as though his carefully planned words had stuck in his throat. He clamped his lips shut and stared at the man sitting in front of him.

As though Asa's question had opened a floodgate, Jake's probing questions assaulted him again, ringing through his heart and mind. *Is this what you want? Are you doing this because it's what God wants for you?*

This time he didn't dismiss the questions. Sitting there with Asa's open gaze studying him, Gabe suddenly had a crazy urge.

Tell the truth.

The thought sent a chill running through him. The truth? Oh, yeah. Gabe could just imagine how the man would react to hearing that one of his students was in seminary because he'd gone off a cliff as a kid. That he'd held to the promise because his word was his word, and nothing would change that. Not even the fact that Gabe wondered almost every day if he could pull it off...if he could keep up the charade of devoted ministerial student for one more second, let alone one more day. That most nights he read those piles of books on faith and theology and the wonders of God until his brain hurt, but it never helped.

Justification. Sanctification. Consecration. Eschatology. Hermeneutics. Ascension. Eucharist. Prevenient grace. The Trinity—all just words. Empty, meaningless, utterly *frustrating* words that had been rattling around in his head since he'd started seminary, crowding his mind with confusion. Oh, he knew the textbook definitions. But understanding what they meant, the ideas behind them, why they were important...none of it made sense. No matter how hard he tried, Gabe couldn't make it seem real.

And that was driving him crazy.

So much so that most nights he ended up pushing his books aside, grabbing his coat, and making his way to what did make sense. The nearest bar.

Just like dear ol' dad, eh?

Gabe's fists clenched. No! He was nothing like his father. Of course, he wasn't anything like Asa, either.

Disgust roiled through him as he looked away. What would Asa Jacks, respected and beloved seminary professor, say if he knew what kind of man Gabe really was? If he confessed that he was far more comfortable with a beer and a cigarette in his hand than a Bible?

"It's all right, Gabriel."

He almost jumped out of his skin. Gabe met Asa's gaze…and suddenly all he wanted to do was lower his head into his hands and weep. To jump up and run from the room, to get as far away from seminary, from Asa—from himself, his doubts and frustrations—as he possibly could.

Asa leaned forward, his hands clasped loosely in his lap, his eyes never leaving Gabe's. "Please believe that you are safe here. And you are welcome. No matter what your answer to my question may be."

Gabe tried to swallow around the softball-sized lump that had lodged itself in his throat at the sincerity in the older man's tone, his eyes.

And just like that, he started talking. Told Asa everything. About that night, when he'd vaulted over the bushes and found himself airborne. About the miracle God had given him, and the promise he made. Even about the fears, the confusion…the fact that his stool at the bar was ten times the haven his seat in chapel had ever been.

Asa didn't say a word. He just sat there, sipping his coffee, listening, nodding. There was no condemnation in his expression. No disappointment. No disgust.

Nothing but simple acceptance.

When Gabe finished, he stared at the floor. He felt as though he'd just lifted the building and carried it a mile. But for all the exhaustion, he felt good. *The truth shall set you free…*

For the first time in his life, Gabe understood what that meant.

The room fell into silence, but it wasn't uncomfortable. Gabe let his eyes drift shut, felt the tension ease from his shoulders, his stomach. Free. That's how he felt.

"Thank you, Gabriel."

His eyes opened and he angled a look at his professor. "Thank you? For what?"

A small smile played at the corners of the man's mouth. "For your honesty. I don't believe telling me all this was an easy thing for you to do."

Gabe laughed at that. "No...it wasn't easy."

"But it's good and right that you did it."

Such confidence filled Asa's eyes that Gabe found himself nodding, believing.

"Gabriel, I've known for some time that things weren't what they needed to be with you." His smile broadened when Gabe started. "You've struggled in my classes since the beginning." His wrinkled hand came out to pat Gabe's arm. "I always knew it wasn't that you lacked intelligence—you are clearly an intelligent man. So I could only assume there was some lack in your heart. Your calling."

Gabe gave a slow nod. "My calling...someone else asked me about that before I started college."

Asa leaned back in his chair. "And what did you say?"

Warmth filled Gabe's face at the memory. What a glib, stupid fool he'd been. "That I'd have to be crazy to go into the ministry without a call from God."

The smile that lit Asa's features was warm, approving. "As I said, you are clearly a man of intelligence. You're exactly right." He leaned forward again, his eyes roaming Gabe's face, as though looking for a sign that Gabe heard what he had to say next—heard and believed. "My boy, I believe that when you made your pledge to God, it was in good faith. God knows that far better than I. But you must see, Gabriel, that was not a call. Not from God. It is a young boy's plea for help. Yes, God answered it, and that is a testimony to His goodness and to the love He has for you." His intent gaze pinned Gabe's. "And it is that very love that will not allow you to hold yourself to a promise you never should have made."

Gabe rested his hands on the cushioned arms of his chair as the truth of Asa's words hit home. God hadn't called him into ministry. It was his sense of honor, of fair play, that had set his feet on this path. God had lived up to His part of the deal; how could Gabe do any less? But now...

Now he saw the truth. He didn't belong here. In seminary. In the ministry.

Exactly where he did belong, he didn't know, but that didn't matter. As Gabe met the kindness in Asa's gaze, he couldn't restrain the relief. He was free.

Gratitude more deep than he'd ever known flowed over him, and he leaned forward, held out his hand. "Thank you."

Asa's hand closed over his. "May I assume, then, that you won't be in class tomorrow morning?"

"No, sir. I won't."

Asa settled back into his chair, reaching for the coffeepot on the small table beside his chair. He poured himself a fresh cup, then held the pot out to Gabe.

He shook his head and stood, feeling more excited, more energetic than he'd felt in months. Maybe years. "I should go, sir. It's getting late."

Asa studied him for a moment, then stood as well and walked with Gabe to the door. There, he stopped Gabe with a hand on his shoulder.

"My boy, I believe you are taking a first step toward finding out what your true calling is. And I believe you have one. From God."

As though God would have anything to do with me...

The dark thought dampened some of his newfound excitement, and he glanced away. But his doubt must have showed on his face, because Asa's hand gave his shoulder a comforting squeeze.

"It is clear you have some questions, Gabriel. That you have some things to work through. Please know I am here anytime you would like to talk."

As hard as it was to take in—to believe a man like Asa Jacks would care about Gabe and his struggles—he could tell the man meant what he was saying. It was an offer Gabe didn't take lightly. He had come back often, and he and Asa had talked late into the night, discussing everything from what Gabe thought about God and faith to what he wanted to do with his life now.

Bit by bit, things fell into place. Gabe left seminary. He spoke with his boss at the college, who was happy to change his part-time position with physical properties to full-time. He moved out of the dorm and took a small apartment near the college. And though he still visited the bars on occasion, he'd found himself drawn there less and less often. Instead, he spent his time reading. Ironically, the books that drew him the most were those he'd so hated while in seminary. Books on faith and truth and God. What was even more amazing was that they began to make sense. Everything made more sense now.

Everything but his relationship with Renee.

He wasn't sure why, but he hadn't told her about leaving seminary. Hadn't told her about his conversations with Asa. Gabe and Renee were still together, but he found himself pulling back, reevaluating. And finally, he was confronted by the same questions Asa had asked him about seminary: *Is this what God wants for you? For Renee?*

Gabe ignored the questions as long as he could, but one night at Asa's it all came out. Once again Gabe found himself spilling his guts, telling the man everything—every good thing, every mistake, every concern and doubt. It no longer surprised Gabe that Asa sat in silence, listening, his compassion as clear as his wisdom.

By the time he finished, he knew Asa's silence was a gift. It had enabled him to really hear his concerns for the first time. Until now, Gabe had been pushing any doubts away. But now...now he understood.

He loved Renee. More than he'd ever loved anyone or anything. She completed him. Made him whole.

No, it wasn't whether he loved Renee that had been

troubling him all this time. It was whether he should. Whether he had the right.

That night he finally understood. The question tearing at him wasn't one of love, but of right and wrong. And the answer seemed terribly clear. Regardless of how he felt about Renee, it wasn't right to ask her to commit herself to a relationship with him. Not now. Not when he still had so much to work through, so much to resolve.

If he really loved Renee, then he had to let her go. To trust that if they really were meant to be together, God would make it happen. But not until the time was right.

And that time wasn't now. Not by a long shot.

Gabe slumped in his chair, staring at the ground.

"Gabriel? Are you all right?"

He closed his eyes, his constricted throat and thickened tongue incapable of forming any words. His stomach churned, and suddenly anger sparked to life, burned through his veins, scorched the backs of his eyes. *So this is how it feels to do the right thing, God? This emptiness? This desperate aching deep in my gut?* His jaw clenched as his teeth ground down the cry of despair that begged for release. *Well, if this is what doing right is about, you can keep it.*

A touch on his arm brought Gabe's eyes open, and he swiveled in the chair, fists clenched at his sides. Asa knelt beside him. "Gabriel, why are you angry?"

The man's quiet voice broke through Gabe's defenses, and before he could stop them hot tears bathed his face. Asa slid his arm around Gabe's shoulders, bowed his head, and began to pray. "He who dwells in the shelter of the Most High will abide in the shadow of the Almighty. I will say to the LORD, 'My refuge and my fortress, My God, in whom I trust!' For it is He who delivers you."

The low voice, the words of promise and truth, resonated with such compassion, such confidence—such *peace*—that Gabe could only bow his head as the holy entreaty enfolded him, cradled him close—and lifted him to the very throne of heaven.

"Under His wings you may seek refuge; His faithfulness is a shield... You will not be afraid of the terror by night, or of the arrow that flies by day; of the pestilence that stalks in darkness, or of the destruction that lays waste at noon. A thousand may fall at your side and ten thousand at your right hand, but it shall not approach you."

The fear that had seized Gabe's spirit dissolved, unable to stand in the face of such words. The anger that had wrapped blistering fingers about his throat and threatened to choke the life from him eased, melting away like ice on a summer day.

"For you have made the LORD, my refuge, even the Most High, your dwelling place. No evil will befall you... For He will give His angels charge concerning you, to guard you in all your ways. They will bear you up in their hands, that you do not strike your foot against a stone."

Asa's hand moved to rest on Gabe's head, and the psalm became a blessing that anointed Gabe's broken heart, filling him with a peace unlike he'd ever known before.

"Because he has loved Me, therefore I will deliver him; I will set him securely on high, because he has known My name. He will call upon Me, and I will answer him; I will be with him in trouble; I will rescue him and honor him. With a long life I will satisfy him and let him see My salvation."

Asa's voice faded into silence, and Gabe knew as surely as he'd ever known anything, that God was there, with them.

After a moment, Asa moved back to his chair. "So you believe God is asking you to end your relationship with this woman."

Gabe's throat constricted again, this time with sorrow. "Yes. For her sake."

Asa was silent a moment, then he inclined his head. "I don't know what God's truth is for you. Or for your Renee. But I caution you against acting too quickly. Take some time, my boy, to listen for God's guidance."

A flicker of hope stirred. Could he have misunderstood? "How much time?"

Asa shook his head. "Only God can answer that. But if I were you, and the matter was one of such import, I would give myself to fasting and prayer. At least for a few days."

Shame caught at Gabe. How could he admit this after what had just happened? But he wanted to be honest. "I'm not sure I know how to pray. That I know the right things to say or even the way to say them."

Asa's words reflected the peace in his features. "Dear boy, there is no right or wrong way to pray. Prayer is simplicity itself. Just do with God what you do with me. Share your heart. Talk with Him about Renee, about your relationship. Your possible future together. Just talk to Him. That's all He asks." His eyes shone with a certainty Gabe longed to feel. "He will hear. And He will answer."

Gabe went home and did as Asa suggested. For a week. But no answer had come.

Until tonight.

He'd been in his apartment, talking to God, asking Him for what felt like the thousandth time what to do, when suddenly he couldn't take it any longer. He jumped up and headed for Renee's dorm. Enough of this endless waiting. He was going to tell her everything. Just lay it all out and see what happened.

But when he reached her room, she wasn't there. Deflated, he made his way down the back steps and out the door, to the grove of trees behind the dorm, led by an almost blind instinct.

Renee loved this spot. It was like a miniature forest right in her backyard. They'd come here on their first date. To talk. To look up at the skies and seek out the constellations. Gabe walked to the table where they usually sat, the table they'd been perched on when he first reached for her hand, where he felt her hesitant response the first time he drew her close and bent his lips to hers.

He stepped on the bench, then lowered himself to the tabletop. He tipped his head back, lifting his face to the heavens, staring at the stars as they winked down at him through the treetops.

"God...please, I don't know what to do."

As sudden as his next heartbeat, God answered. The words were there, and though they weren't spoken aloud, they rang through him as clear as anything he'd ever heard.

Follow Me.

For a moment all went still. Every sound, every sight, every sensation faded and melted into that one, resounding call echoing through him.

Follow Me.

Gabe wanted to. Desperately. But how? *Think, Gabe, think...*

Follow God. Okay, so God was love. Wasn't that what Asa had been saying, over and over? Did that mean Gabe should hold to the love he felt for Renee, that he should move forward and marry her?

Certainty was swift and confirming, but before he could rejoice in it, the silent voice was there again.

Take up your cross...and follow Me.

For a moment Gabe felt something he had never felt before: pure, unadulterated joy. As though some heavenly hand had reached down and touched him, caressing his face with a tenderness that nearly broke his heart. But the feeling had barely arrived when it was shoved aside by a sudden flash of gloomy uncertainty.

Pick up your cross? What does *that* mean? What cross?

The answer crawled through him, bringing resistance shuddering on its heels: Your relationship with Renee.

Gabe frowned. That didn't make any sense. Renee was a blessing, a light in a life too full of darkness and pain.

Yet even as he made the assertion, images swarmed his mind like a cloud of gnats: the two of them caught in an argument; the pained, frightened look in her eyes when he lost himself in anger; his fist slamming into the wall after a night of senseless conflicts...

That same, dark voice slithered through his mind again: Would it be like that if you two were meant to be together?

Gabe felt as though the blood in his veins had turned to ice water. The answer was glaring at him, but he turned from it. No...please...

Could it be true? Was his relationship with Renee a cross? A burden weighing him down, coming between him and God?

He slid from the table and paced, even more restless now than he'd been that night in his room. How could it be happening? How could God ask this of him? Why bring the two of them together in the first place if He was just going to make Gabe walk away?

Are you so sure God brought you together?

That was too much. "Of course I am!" He spat the words into the stillness of the night. "As sure as I've ever been of anything in my life!"

As sure as you were that God wanted you to go into the ministry?

The barbed question stopped him cold, and he felt the blood drain from his face—and the hope drain from his heart.

His feet suddenly leaden, he made his way back to the picnic table, dropping onto the bench. With a groan, he lowered his head into his hands, rubbing his aching temples with his thumbs. This couldn't be happening...

But it was.

Well, what had he expected? He'd come here looking for answers, begging God to turn on the light of his understanding. Had he thought God would let an opportunity like that just flit on by? No way. Gabe had opened himself for the blow, and God had delivered.

All that was left to him now was to choose whether or not he'd obey.

Glancing up at the window of Renee's room, he saw a dim light shining through the curtain. Usually that sight brought him a surge of joy. Tonight all he felt was dread.

His hands trembling, he reached into his pocket and drew out a cigarette. Renee had been after him to quit, and he'd been trying. But now...

What did it matter now?

He flicked the lighter, started to touch the flame to the end of the cigarette, then stopped. With a muttered oath, he snapped the cigarette in half and stuffed the lighter back into his pocket. He'd promised Renee he'd stop. Regardless of what happened with them, a promise was a promise.

He'd just have to find his comfort somewhere else. That's what he needed right now—comfort in the midst of madness.

Because that's what God had brought him. Madness.

He tipped his head back and let a slow breath out, watching as the wisp of steam rose into the silent night, poking...pointing...accusing...

You ask too much.

Gabe didn't voice the words, but they were there nonetheless. He stared at the stars, then glanced back at the light in Renee's window. His lips pressed tight, he stood and started walking.

He went into the dorm, up the stairs, not even caring if anyone saw him coming in after visiting hours. What could they do to him that could compare to what he was about to do to himself?

His steps faltered when he reached the hallway, but he drew a deep breath and pushed himself forward. The sound of his knock echoed around him, like a death knell mocking the condemned.

The door opened, and she was there.

"Gabe!"

He hesitated. Her tone, her features...they were an odd mixture of relief and dread. But before he could question her, she reached out and pulled him into the room, closing the door and wrapping her arms around him, burying her face in his chest.

"I'm so glad you're here."

Her embrace was an exquisite agony, and he forced himself to take hold of her arms and, with gentle pressure, push her away. She looked up at him, a question in her expression, and he swallowed. Hard.

"I need to talk with you—"

They spoke the words in unison and broke off together as well. For one wonderful moment they laughed, and everything was as it should be. He loved her. Man, how he loved her...

But that didn't matter.

She linked her arm in his and ushered him to a chair, then went to sit at her desk, watching him with wide, expectant eyes.

His mouth went dry. He couldn't have uttered a single word to save his life. He looked down, shaking his head.

"Gabe? Honey? Are you okay?"

He said the first thing that came to mind. "I need a drink."

Clearly, it wasn't what she'd been expecting. He cleared his throat. "Of water. A drink of water. My throat's dry."

"Oh! Of course." She jumped up and went to pull a small pitcher of water from her mini-fridge. When she handed him a full glass, she sat back down. "You need to talk to me?"

He shook his head, pointing at the glass. "That's okay. You first."

It was a cowardly thing to do, and he knew it. He just didn't care. He sipped the water, waiting, but apparently she was having as hard a time as he was. What could she need to talk about?

His head came up with a jerk and he studied her face, acutely aware that she wouldn't look at him, was staring at the floor. Had she been that pale when he arrived? And why were her hands trembling?

Understanding came in a heated rush: She's going to break up with me. Anger pierced him, and for a moment he wanted to grab her, to shake her. Then he remembered why he was there, what he'd come to say, and a wild surge of relief washed over him. He closed his eyes.

You did this, didn't You, God? This is from You. And that can only mean one thing: It's right. Renee and I don't belong together. Though the thought still hurt, he let it come, let it fill his mind. God was making it so clear that Gabe knew he needed to pay attention, to accept it.

He had to walk away.

But it's better this way. Better to let her be the one to say it. He leaned forward in the chair, resting his elbows on his knees. "Rennie—" he let his love for her, the aching tenderness she stirred in him, show in his tone—"it's okay. Whatever you have to say, just say it."

She stood so abruptly she almost overturned her chair and began to pace, her small hands clenching and unclenching.

Gabe rose and went to her, taking her hands in his, drawing her back to sit down. Then he knelt in front of her, rubbing the backs of her hands with his thumbs. He didn't speak, didn't try to rush her. Just knelt there, letting her know he was ready.

He almost lost it, though, when tears trickled down her face. Her eyes met his, and her sorrow struck deep into his heart. *Let her just say it, God. Let her set us both free.* "Sweetheart, please…it's oka—"

"I'm pregnant."

Gabe felt the air gush from his lungs. He opened his mouth, then closed it. Stared. Blinked once…twice. All the while, her words whirled around in his brain but wouldn't take root: *I'm pregnant…I'm pregnant…*

What? He scanned her face, looking for something that made sense of what had just happened. *She couldn't have said what I thought she just said. She can't be pregnant!*

Her tears flowed in earnest now, and without really knowing what he was doing, he slid his arms around her and folded her close, offering a comfort he was far from feeling.

My God…

Pregnant. She was pregnant. He didn't need to ask if it was his child. There was no doubt in his mind that he was the first—and only—man Renee had been with.

"Gabe?"

Her timid voice caught at him, ripped at his heart. She sounded so terrified. "It's okay. We'll work this out…we'll be okay…" He murmured the words over and over, amazed his voice was so steady, so calm, when all he heard in his head was screaming.

My God…

"I'm…I'm so sorry!"

He responded without thinking, without feeling, hoping his words didn't sound as empty as he felt. "It's okay, Renee. It's not your fault. We'll deal with this together." He kissed her forehead, her eyes. Pressed a gentle kiss to her lips.

He was playing the part of a caring lover to perfection. He should be proud.

My God…

He wasn't sure how long they sat like that, holding each other. All he knew was he was relieved when she set him free.

"It's late. You should go."

He nodded and stood, still uttering the same meaningless phrases of comfort as she walked him to the door. He paused, hand on the doorknob. So close. So close to freedom… "Get some sleep, Renee. We'll talk more tomorrow." He couldn't help it—his gaze traveled to her abdomen…to her baby.

Their baby.

My baby...

Emotion choked him, and he blinked back an unfamiliar heat behind his eyes. Tears. He was about to cry? He couldn't remember the last time he'd cried. "You need your rest. For the baby."

She threw her arms around him, her hug fierce. "I love you."

"I love you, too."

He walked from the room. Down the stairs. Out into the night. When the cold air hit his face, he stopped and stared up at the stars dancing in the blackness. One thought played over and over in his mind, his heart:

My God, why have You forsaken me?

Answers rose from some deep, dark inner reservoir—a bottomless well of contempt and disdain. *Forsaken you? He's done exactly what you wanted. He's answered you. Told you what you should do. About Renee. About the future.*

He couldn't hold back a harsh laugh. That was certainly true. If he'd had any doubts about leaving the ministry program, they were truly and completely gone. Some minister he'd make! No wonder God hadn't called him to it. How stupid could Gabe be to think He would ever do so? Call *him* to be a minister?

It had been a stupid idea.

At least you're free of it now.

Gabe almost choked. Some freedom. He'd gone from one prison smack-dab into another. Free? Hardly. He was more tangled now than ever.

He pulled a cigarette from his pocket, lit it, and took a deep draw. Promises were highly overrated. He'd made one to God, hadn't he? Thought he knew what God wanted of him. Leave seminary. Let Renee go. Focus on...what? He didn't know. Hadn't had the chance to figure that out. And now...

"What now?" He blew the question out in a haze of

smoke and frustration, then dropped the cigarette to the side-walk, grinding it out with his foot. "You have all the answers, right, God? So tell me, what do I do now?"

He wasn't the least bit surprised when silence was his only answer.

It is in the storm that God equips us for service.

ANONYMOUS

Follow the example of those who are going to
inherit God's promises because of their faith and patience.

HEBREWS 6:12

DECEMBER 19, 2003
3:30 P.M.

"COME ON, ANSWER. SOMEBODY ANSWER THE PHONE."

Grace waited three rings, four, five, six...

It was no use. The Romans weren't there. With a small sigh and a shake of her head, she hit the off button and stared at the phone. Renee had told her they'd be home by noon at the latest. Oren said Grace should just be patient, just wait for them to call, but she couldn't stand it.

She'd been calling since two, but there was still no answer.

Where *were* they?

At a sound behind her, quick heat rushed to her cheeks as she plunked the phone back in its base. She put her hands behind her back as she turned, but one look at Oren's face told her he wasn't the least bit fooled.

"You called them again?"

Grace didn't bother replying. She just looked at the ground.

"Well?"

She crossed her arms and met her husband's expectant gaze. "Well what?"

"Any answer?"

"Aha!" She clapped her hands. "You wanted to know, too, didn't you?"

"Gracie…"

Her smug reply told him he didn't have to admit it, she'd seen the truth in his eyes. "No, no answer."

Oren tipped his head and held out his hand. "Then you have your answer."

She frowned at that. What was he talking about? "What answer? There wasn't any answer."

"Gracie…"

"That's what I keep telling you."

"Grace…"

"For heaven's sake, Oren, if you aren't going to listen to me I don't know what…what…"

Well, really now! How was she supposed to concentrate on what she was saying when he just stood there, holding her hand, watching her with that infuriatingly patient smile on his lips? She frowned again. What had she been saying?

"That is, I don't know…"

The gentle tug at her hand brought her to a halt, and she studied her husband's features. He still looked so expectant. What was he waiting for? Grace gnawed at her lip, staring at the phone, thinking.

She had her answer…she had her—

Oh.

"Oren?"

"Yes, dear?" His smile broadened into a grin.

Well, really! He didn't have to look so pleased with himself. But even as she thought that, she knew it wasn't himself Oren was pleased with. It was her. Because he could tell she finally understood.

She squeezed his hand. "When you said I had my answer, you weren't talking about them answering, were you?"

"No, dear."

"You were talking about God answering, weren't you?"

"Yes, dear."

With another sigh, Grace straightened. "Well, then, what are we waiting for? Let's pray. And Oren?"

His lips quirked. "Yes, dear?"

"I think we need to pray that God does something...evident. Something to let Renee and Gabriel know without a doubt that He's with them."

Oren's eyes shone. "I love you, Gracie."

She gave his hand another squeeze, and this time she was the one who grinned. "Because I'm so sweet spirited and submissive?"

He laughed, drawing her into his arms. She nestled close. They fit together so well.

"Because, my dear wife, you're so you."

She leaned back in her husband's arms and planted a kiss on his bearded cheek.

"Because you're so you." It didn't get any better than that.

God, I don't get it.

I did my part. I've followed You, read Your Book, done what I'm supposed to. I've gone to church, prayed, sought Your will.

So how come my life is so far away from what it should be?

19

Here before my eyes is my God.

ELIZABETH, PRINCESS OF HUNGARY

What wonders God has done!

NUMBERS 23:23

DECEMBER 19, 2003
3:30 P.M.

THE STORM WAS LETTING UP.

At first Gabe had thought he was talking himself into thinking that so he wouldn't give in to discouragement. Every step had been a battle against the driving wind, and the aches and pains left over from the accident just got worse as he strained to keep going. It helped to have Bo with him. The husky was clearly in his element. He bent his broad head and plowed forward, pulling Gabe along with him as he lunged through the snow.

But now as he walked, he was sure it was true. The wind wasn't as fierce; the snow wasn't as dense. He could even see as much as ten or fifteen feet ahead.

His gaze traveled along the rope in front of him, and he came to an abrupt halt. Bo strained against his leash, then halted as well, looking back at him as if to say, "What's the problem? Let's *go!*"

But Gabe couldn't go, because just ahead of them the rope seemed to disappear in the thick branches of a fir.

What on earth?

Bo came to press against his legs, with that perpetually curious expression on his fuzzy face. Gabe shook his head. "I don't know what the deal is, boy. But I'm gonna find out."

He ran his hand along the rope, following it into the tree, and a hard knot formed in his gut. The rope was tied off to the tree trunk.

He'd reached the end.

So much for following the rope to Renee. He stepped back and looked around. Now what? Which way would she have gone?

The answer was quick and sure: *West. She wrote in her note that she was going west.*

Bo strained at his leather leash, and Gabe dropped to one knee, slipping his arm around the restless dog. "Settle, boy. Give me a minute to think."

Bo's rear end dropped into the snow, and he leaned into Gabe, staring up at him as though he had all the answers.

Don't I wish... Gabe gave the dog's ears an absent scratch as he looked one direction, then another, seeking some sign, some depression in the snow, some remnant of a footprint.

There was nothing.

Except the note. She told you in her note which way she was heading.

Gabe rubbed his aching eyes, not even caring that his glove was cold and wet. True enough, but he knew his wife better than to take what she wrote at face value.

He looked at Bo. "Renee is a creature of impulse, boy. She's as likely to change her mind as she is to hold to the bearing she said." He shrugged. "What do you think?"

Bo gave him a quick lick, making Gabe chuckle through his fatigue. "That's not exactly helpful, buddy."

He stood again, and his fist closed around the rope as a prayer squeezed from his heart. *Please…I can't afford a mistake here.*

There was no sudden light to direct him, no angel with an ethereal glow suddenly standing in the driving snow and pointing one direction or another. Gabe shook his head.

Typical.

Just once…just once he wished it could be different. Just once when he prayed, he wanted to be one of those people who saw God act. How many times had he sat there, listening while others talked about the miraculous ways God answered their prayers? He usually smiled, lips tight to keep them from seeing his gritted teeth. *He'd* never seen God. Not really. The one time he thought he had, the one time he thought God had spoken to him, called him, he'd been wrong.

On the heels of his anger came a soft voice echoing in his head: *You haven't seen God? What about all that's happened with you and Renee? What about the fact that you're still together? God has been at work in your life, all through your life.*

Gabe sighed. It was true. He knew it was. But sometimes…well, he just wanted God to give him something to show He was listening when it felt like He wasn't. Was that so much to ask?

He started to stand, when Bo suddenly lunged to his feet and bolted, pulling Gabe off balance. His arms flew out in front of him and, as he landed face first in the snow, Bo's leash slid free from his wrist.

Gabe scrambled to his feet. "No! *Stay!*"

Bo didn't even break stride. With a low yodel, the dog bounded into the woods.

Gabe raced after him, but it was no use. Huskies were built to run, and Bo was husky through and through. That dog could practically fly over the ground, even covered as it was with snow.

His breath came in ragged gulps and an impotent fury

swept him. Was *this* God's way of showing He was listening? Gabe wanted to shake his fists at the heavens. *What do I do now? Tell me, God. What am I supposed to do now?*

He had to find Renee. He couldn't waste time chasing after a dog. But the thought of leaving Bo out there to freeze, to starve—Gabe couldn't. Bo might just be a dog, but he was his dog. He slept by Gabe's side of the bed, was there every day at the door when he came home from work, loved to sit next to him on the couch when he watched TV...

All true, but he's still just a dog.

Indecision caught at him, but he pushed it away. *Make it simple. If Bo has gone west, then follow him. That way you'll be going after him and Renee. If not...*

Gabe grabbed the compass hanging around his neck, his movements so forceful that he felt the lanyard bite into the back of his neck. Did God hear prayers that were forced out through gritted teeth? Gabe hoped so. A good number of his were said that way.

He took a quick reading and felt a flash of rueful gratitude. Bo was headed west. Maybe God was listening after all.

At least Bo wouldn't be hard to track. The dog had plowed a fairly deep trail in the snow when he bounded away. That was something.

Not much, mind you. But it was something.

Gabe had almost given up hope of finding Bo when he heard a sound that sent his heart racing: barking. Well, half bark, half yodel.

Bo! It had to be!

Despite the ache in his head that had now traveled into his arms and legs, Gabe broke into a run. At least the wind wasn't fighting him now. The storm had finally spent itself, and though the sky was still overcast and muted, there was no more than a gentle breeze now.

He dodged trees and limbs, drawing closer to the sound with each step. Finally he saw a flash of cinnamon amid the blanket of white—Bo's coat! But what was he doing at the base of that tree?

Gabe's heart caught in his throat when he saw what—or who—Bo was lying on. Renee! He rushed forward, falling to his knees beside her.

She didn't move.

He slipped the glove off of one hand and pressed trembling fingers to the pulse at her throat, then dropped his head. The beat was slow, but it was there.

Thank God...thank God...

Gabe threw his arms around Bo and gave him a hug. "I take back everything I just muttered at you, boy!"

Bo's bicolored eyes usually danced with mischief. Now the animal's expression seemed almost somber, as if he knew just how serious things were.

Not as serious as they could have been, though.

Gabe's mouth quirked at the thought. Renee would have been proud of his optimism. Maybe she was beginning to rub off on him.

He shrugged off his pack. "I can't believe you found her, boy. It's a miracle."

Bo's bland stare, as though Gabe had just demonstrated a keen sense of the way-too-obvious, drew him up short. He hesitated as realization stirred around inside him, making its way through his muddled emotions until it planted itself firmly in his mind.

God had answered his prayer. And the way He'd done it really *was* a miracle. Male huskies were known runners, and once free they usually didn't stop for anything or anyone. Not only had Bo stopped when he found Renee, he'd stayed with her. On top of her, keeping her warm.

If that wasn't amazing enough, Bo had yelped at just the right moment so Gabe could find them.

He shook his head and started pulling out the supplies he needed to get a fire going, sorting through his emotions as he sorted the kindling. "I'm sorry, God. I thought You weren't listening. When Bo ran off—" he snapped a piece of kindling in half—"I figured You not only weren't listening, but You didn't care. And all the while, You were taking care of everything."

Gabe rocked back on his heels, then struck a waterproof match and held the flame to the small tower of kindling and wood in front of him. The flame caught, then grew.

He turned back to Renee. She was so still. He moved to kneel beside her and tugged her mittens from her hands. Her skin was ice cold. Gabe rubbed her hands between his, willing his warmth into her body. He scanned her face, noting the slightly blue tinge to cheeks and lips that usually were rosy with life.

Please, God, please…don't let me lose her.

Dark thoughts uncoiled inside him, striking with a poisonous precision. *Now you pray and say you trust, eh? Funny how you're always too late with too little, Roman. Always apologizing. Never doing it right the first time. You're worthless. A failure as a husband. As a Christian. Why should God even listen to anything you have to say?*

Gabe dropped Renee's hand and went to toss another piece of wood onto the small fire. He stared at the flickering flames, then moved back to Renee's side. He opened his coat and wrapped it around her, tucking her in against his body, ignoring the pain gnawing its way through his throbbing head.

If only he could ignore the guilt eating at him as well.

He should have reached Renee sooner. Maybe if he'd left Bo behind or hadn't taken so much time deciding what to stuff into his pack, he could have pushed himself more. So what if his head hurt? He should have gone faster—

Stop it! He leaned his head against the hard bark of the tree behind them. *I did my best.* His throat constricted, and he swallowed hard as chills shook him, ratcheting his shoulders into knots, sending the white-hot pain singing through his head again.

I did my best...

It was the truth. But that didn't help. Not when he knew it might not be enough.

But then, it never is, is it?

Gabe turned away from the dark thought, but he couldn't dredge up any kind of denial. How could he, when he knew it was true? His best wasn't good enough.

It never had been.

It's hard to build something solid when the foundation is so shaky. We made so many mistakes, so many poor choices. What makes us think we could take that kind of beginning and make it into something good?

We're not bound by our past, are we, Father? You promise we're new creations. New. The old is passed away and we're new. I want to believe it. I have to believe it.

Because if it isn't true, then I don't know how I'm going to survive one more day together—let alone a lifetime.

20

Oh God, my God, the night has values
that the day never dreamed of.

THOMAS MERTON

The LORD will work out his plans for my life.

PSALM 138:8

LATE MARCH 1980

THE CRIB WAS A THING OF BEAUTY.

Renee could hardly believe she and Gabe had made it. She ran her hand along the smooth rails, loving the feel of it, the warmth of the wood tones.

"Pretty amazing, huh?"

"Fit for a king."

"Or a queen." Gabe folded his arms around her, and they stood there, content to be together.

One night she and Gabe had been out window-shopping, when he stopped cold. They were in front of a furniture store, and there in the display was a beautiful crib. Gabe studied it for such a long time that Renee finally tugged on his sleeve.

He looked at her—and grinned. "You up for a challenge?"

With that they launched into a project that took most of their evenings, but neither of them minded. Renee loved being together like that, working together to make something for their little one.

Besides, it was a nice break from college and classes and homework. Renee had known finishing college while pregnant wouldn't be easy, but she was determined to do it. Working on the crib helped motivate her to get through her reading or paper writing in record time.

And now, the crib was done. They'd finished it just a few days ago, and finally, tonight, they moved it into the baby's room. It was the finishing touch on a room Renee already loved.

They'd painted it a pale green. "Just in case your son is a daughter," she'd told Gabe when he asked why not blue. Characters from Winnie the Pooh beamed down at them from the walls, and Renee had painted soft puffs of clouds on the ceiling.

Gabe put the tiny mattress in the crib, then stepped aside as Renee draped the fluffy Winnie the Pooh blanket in place. They fastened the musical baby mobile Gabe's mother had given them at the head, then stepped back and surveyed their handiwork.

The room was perfect.

Renee leaned against Gabe's solid arm. They had come so far. When she'd first told him about the baby, she could tell he was stunned. She was so afraid he would walk away, that she'd never see him again. But the next morning he was there, at her door. They went for a long drive and talked. She'd been shocked when he told her he was leaving the seminary but glad he'd made that decision before he knew about the baby. At least that wasn't her fault.

Finally he pulled the car to the side of the road, turned to her and took her hands in his, and asked her to marry him.

She'd dreamed of such a moment, longed for it, imagined how he would sound, how she would react. In all those imaginings, it had never been like this—Gabe so quiet, so...resigned. She studied him, looking for the warmth, the tenderness, but it wasn't there. Nothing was. No joy, no fear, no anger.

Nothing.

That frightened her more than his rages ever had.

She called her parents that night to tell them she was getting married. She didn't tell them about the baby. She couldn't. They'd know soon enough. She forced a note of excitement into her voice as she talked with her stunned parents, then wondered that she had to do so. No, she and Gabe weren't getting married under ideal circumstances, but they were getting married. She should be happy.

Once again her mother seemed to hear what Renee wasn't saying. Last night as they'd talked, she asked Renee, "Are you sure about this, honey?"

"About getting married." *Please...don't let me start crying.* "Of course, Mom."

"We'd like to get to know him first." This from her father, who was on the extension phone.

Renee heard the slight reproach in his quiet words, and her heart fell. She wanted so badly to tell them everything, to tell them why she and Gabe had gotten engaged, why they were getting married so quickly.

But she couldn't. They would be so disappointed in her. So she'd said everything she could to calm her parents' fears—and her own.

As the days went by and they planned their wedding, Renee kept watching Gabe—and her disquiet grew. She couldn't explain it, but whenever they were together, he seldom spoke. She was always the one to initiate conversation. Mostly he sat back, listening as she talked, nodding when she made decisions, shrugging when she asked him what he thought or wanted.

"I don't know much about weddings," he said more than once, a shadow of the grin she loved so much touching his mouth. "What matters most is what you want."

She'd always teased Gabe, telling him that if he wanted to make her really happy he could just let her have her way all the time. Well, he was doing exactly that, and it was driving her crazy!

What concerned her most, though, was that they didn't pray together anymore. The few times she'd asked Gabe to pray for them, he just told her to do it.

It was as though a part of him had died or gone away. As though, despite the fact that he hadn't walked away—he was still there, planning their marriage and life together with her—some part of him had closed off to her.

And to God.

She'd prayed about it, searched Scripture for wisdom, even tried talking to Gabe about it, but he just looked at her with those empty eyes and said he didn't know what she was talking about. He was fine. He was excited about the baby. Looking forward to their life.

Renee didn't believe a word of it.

The only time Gabe seemed remotely like himself was the night he suggested to Renee that they elope. To say the idea had surprised her would be an understatement. She stared at him, stunned, but her heart melted when he came to take her hands in his.

"Hon, it's hard enough for kids today. I don't want our baby...our child—"

When he broke off, too choked up to continue, Renee reached up to frame his face with her hands. "Gabe, what is it?"

The sorrow in his steady gaze had almost broken her heart, but there had been warmth there, too, and that sent her pulse racing. This was Gabe. This was the man she knew and loved.

His hands covered hers as he went on. "I don't want our child to start his life under a stigma. His parents should be married."

Renee wasn't sure when they'd decided the baby was a

he, but that's how they'd been referring to him. "He'll still be early, Gabe. People will still talk."

He nodded. "Some will. But if we marry now, he'll only be a little early. We can say he's premature, and no one can say different. Not for sure."

Though Renee's heart had broken at the loss of yet another dream—how she'd longed for a church wedding, with all her friends and family to share in the celebration—she knew he was right. They owed it to their child to do this.

So she pushed aside her doubts and nodded, telling herself the smile on Gabe's face and the warmth in his eyes was better than any wedding. She considered calling her parents, letting them know—then discarded the notion. She couldn't give them the opportunity to talk her out of it.

A few days later they were at the courthouse, waiting in a pale green room with several other couples for their turn in front of the justice of the peace.

When the clerk called first Gabe's name and then hers, Renee stood and followed him into the aisle, up to the front of the room. She clutched at her bouquet of flowers, trying to still the tremors that seemed to have taken up residence in her hands, her knees, her stomach. But as she moved into position and looked up at the black-suited man before them, one overwhelming thought rose from Renee's heart, surging through her, mowing down with startling ease her desperate attempts to repress it.

What am I doing?

She wanted to scream at the man intoning the wedding ceremony, to tell him to stop. To wait just a minute. Give her a chance to think. She wanted to turn and race from the room.

But she didn't. She just stood there, happiness pasted onto her stiff face, nodding in all the right places, and finally reciting the vows she'd loved all her life, had waited so long to say: "I, Renee, take you, Gabe, to be my lawful wedded husband, to have and to hold from this day forward, for better or for worse, for richer or for poorer, in sickness and in health, to love and to cherish, until death parts us."

In minutes it was over. The justice beamed at her and Gabe, pronounced them "husband and wife," and told Gabe he could kiss his bride—and to please pay the clerk on his way out the door.

Renee choked on a laugh. She'd gotten married at a drive through. Okay, a walk-through. She shook her head. This wasn't how it was supposed to be.

There was no honeymoon, of course. They just went back to the apartment they'd rented earlier that week—a spacious place with an abundance of windows and deep-toned woodwork on the top floor of an older home—and fixed a meal of soup and sandwiches. That night she lay in bed next to the man who was now her husband, listening to his even breathing as he slept. Only then, in the stillness of the small room, did she let her emotions flow.

Regret, grief, self-pity, anger…they all took turns wrapping themselves around her heart and squeezing. Renee pressed her fists to her damp eyes and tried to rub away the emotions, the pain, but nothing she did helped.

You're just tired. Get some sleep. Things will be better in the morning.

In a way, she'd been right. Things did get a little better. When she called her folks, they were shocked at first, then recouped quickly.

"We love you, Renee. And if you love Gabe this much, I'm sure we'll love him, too."

Quick tears had thickened her words. "Thanks, Mom."

"Tell you what, Ren, when you guys come to visit us in a few weeks, we'll have a reception, okay? I mean, seeing as we didn't get to have the big, blowout wedding."

She focused on her dad's attempt at humor, doing her best to ignore the tinge of hurt in his voice. "Sounds good to me, Boppo." She choked back a sob. "I can't wait to come home."

Now it was her mother who choked up. "We can't wait to have you here. We love you."

It had been far easier to tell their local friends they'd gotten married; it was like a holiday had been declared. Cards and gifts started flowing in, and one friend after another demanded the right to hold a party or shower.

"You may have cheated us out of the wedding, you sneaky rats," one of their closest friends said, "but you can't cheat us out of the celebration!"

And so they went from one party to another, smiling and playing the part of happy newlyweds. But though Gabe seemed more like his old self at times, more often than not Renee found herself dealing with the same emotionless Gabe who had proposed to her. And the few, fleeting moments of warmth and tenderness between them couldn't offset day after day of emptiness.

Even their visit with Renee's parents had been only a mild relief. She'd loved being back home, loved being with them, and she could tell they did their best to make Gabe feel at home. But he'd kept his distance, speaking only when spoken to.

Renee wanted to shake him, especially when she saw the glimmers of concern in her parents' eyes as they hugged them good-bye at the airport. Renee barely spoke to Gabe on the four-hour flight home. He didn't even seem to notice.

Now, after nearly four months of living in emotional limbo, Renee was about to go out of her mind. She wanted to let all her frustration out. To ball up her fists and let Gabe have it. Sure, he'd get mad. So what? She'd welcome even his anger if it brought him back to life!

Then everything changed.

They were sitting on the couch in their tiny living room, not talking, as usual. Renee had finished a paper she was working on for Lit class and was reading a magazine; Gabe was nursing his brooding silence and a soda. Suddenly Renee felt something. It was tiny…just a flutter, like a miniature butterfly had somehow made its way into her belly.

She went still and her hand moved to her abdomen. Was that…?

The movement came again, and this time Renee let out a squeal.

Gabe jumped, then turned to look at her, his brows arched. "What's wrong?"

She stared at him, her mouth open, wanting to tell him but afraid to do so in case she was wrong. What if it was just gas?

As though to prove it was much more, another flutter came, stronger this time. Biting her lip, Renee reached out to take Gabe's hand. His eyes widened as she placed it on her belly.

"What—?"

She didn't let him finish. "Wait…"

They both sat there, frozen, and when the flutter came again Renee's eyes flew to Gabe's face. The wonder she was feeling was reflected in his widened eyes, his quick intake of breath.

"Is that…?"

Delight danced through her and escaped on a giggle. "I think so."

His fingers stretched over her belly and he inched closer, bending down to press his ear over the baby. Renee watched him and felt her heart leap. He looked like a little boy catching his first glimpse of a pile of presents at Christmastime.

She couldn't hold back the smile that lifted her spirit as well as her features. *Come on, baby…talk to your daddy…*

When the movement came again, they both jumped. Gabe whooped and gathered Renee in his arms, pressing kisses to her cheeks, her forehead.

She laughed, breathless from his onslaught, and caught

his face in her hands. Her heart beat a rapid rhythm as she stared into his eyes. "Have you come back?"

Something flickered in the depths of his gaze, and she knew he understood her whispered question. He tugged her forward until she was nestled in his embrace, cradled against him. His chin rested on top of her head, and when she felt him nod, her relief eased out in a shuddering sigh.

Her arms went around him, and he leaned down to kiss her neck. "Thank you."

His words whispered against her skin, and she wrapped her arms around him. "I didn't do anything."

He leaned back so she could see his face, and the emotion there was like a refreshing rain after a long, scorching drought. "You did everything. You didn't push. You gave me time—" he reached down to spread his hand over her belly— "you gave me a son."

That had been almost a month ago, and things had been different ever since. Wonderfully so. Gabe took on the role of expectant father with unbridled enthusiasm. They read books, visited the doctor, worked on the baby's room— always together, always with shared dreams and laughter.

Renee had gone from being trapped in a nightmare marriage to feeling as though she were living in a wonderful dream. The day they went for the sonogram, Gabe could hardly contain himself. Terror battled with excitement inside her. Terror that they might find something wrong; excitement that she was about to meet her baby for the first time.

Renee glanced at the machine and her mouth opened on a silent "Oh!" Her baby was there, on the screen. *Hello, little one...*

Renee squeezed Gabe's hand. He leaned his face close to hers, and from the dampness of his cheek she could tell he was crying, too. Renee closed her eyes, holding the moment close, treasuring it. This was the most amazing thing she'd ever known!

They'd walked from the doctor's office, picture in hand,

and Gabe shared it with everyone, from the receptionist at the doctor's office to the poor, befuddled man he cornered in the elevator—

Gabe pulled her from her thoughts when he patted her tummy, his mouth quirking in playful encouragement. "We're ready when you are, kiddo."

Renee let her contentment out in a sigh. Life was good— she placed a hand over her rounded belly—and it was only going to get better.

Happiness is so hard to hold on to. It comes and goes on a whim. When it comes, I'm at peace, content. When it goes, I feel as though my world is over.

Help me shift my focus from me to You, Lord. Help me to seek my peace, my worth, my delight in You. Teach me how to live for You. Because living for me is miserable.

21

I pray God may open your eyes and let you see what hidden treasures He
bestows on us in the trials from which the world thinks only to flee.

JOHN OF AVILA

"Should we accept only good things from the hand of God
and never anything bad?"

JOB 2:10

APRIL 9, 1980

THE PAIN THAT WOKE RENEE EARLY THAT MORNING
wasn't severe. Not at first. It was just a kind of cramping discomfort that kept coming and going.

She'd experienced similar pains a few weeks ago and had gone to see Dr. Wykes, her obstetrician, right away. When she told him there was no bleeding, he assured her it was perfectly normal. "Nothing to worry about, Mrs. Roman. Just go home and relax." He sounded so sure that Renee's fears began to fade.

She'd done just as he recommended, hardly thinking about it again.

Until now.

Another cramp seized her, and Renee sucked in a deep gulp of air. *It's nothing to worry about.* She grasped at the echo of Dr. Wykes's reassurances. *Cramping is normal with pregnancy, remember?*

It had to be true; Dr. Wykes had said so. So why, she wondered as she lay here, hands pressed to her pain-racked abdomen, was she so anxious?

Within an hour the cramps had progressed from mild to just this side of agonizing. She considered waking Gabe, but one look at his sleeping form and she knew she couldn't. Poor guy was exhausted. He needed his sleep.

As quietly as possible, she slid from beneath the heavy covers and padded to the bathroom. What she discovered there sent a chill racing down her spine.

She was bleeding. The blood was bright red and plentiful.

This isn't normal. Even as her suddenly numb mind absorbed the realization, Renee was calling out. "Gabe!" She heard the panic in her voice but couldn't do anything about it. *"Gabe!"*

In seconds he was at the bathroom door, blinking against the harsh light. "What's happening?"

Renee could hardly get the words out around the terror pressing in on her. "I'm bleeding." She wrestled with the last shreds of her control as she met his suddenly alarmed gaze and gave voice to her greatest fear. "Gabe...what if something's wrong with the baby?"

He didn't hesitate. "I'll get your coat. We're going to the hospital."

By the time they walked into the ER and sat at the admitting desk, she was close to hysterics. When the kind-faced nurse asked her name, she simply sat there, blank.

"Renee Roman." Gabe answered for her, his hand covering hers where it rested on her abdomen.

After what seemed like an eternity of answering questions, the nurse showed them to a small examining room. She helped Renee climb onto the gurney, then patted her arm when another bout of cramps hit her. "You just rest, dear. And don't worry. The doctor will be here in a jiffy."

When she left the room, Gabe moved to stand beside

Renee. His long fingers closed over hers, and she tried to draw strength from him.

Scripture she'd memorized long ago came back to her now, and she drew on their promises: *"Fear not, for I am with you… The Lord is my light and my salvation, whom shall I fear? The Lord is the strength of my life, of whom shall I be afraid?… Yea, though I walk through the valley of the shadow of death—"*

No. Renee closed her eyes. *No, please…*

The curtain closing them off from the rest of the ER parted and the nurse came back in, a folded, white blanket in her arms. She spread it over Renee, tugging it up under her chin. "It's heated, so you and that baby of yours don't get chilled."

"That baby of yours…"

Renee closed her eyes. She'd never been so frightened in her life. *Please, God, please…let my baby be all right.*

Gabe's arm slid around her shoulders, and she leaned against him, clutching at his shirtfront, pressing her face into his broad chest. He stroked the back of her head.

"It's going to be okay, Renee."

She pulled back enough to look up at his face. "You promise?"

His response was quick, confident. "It's probably nothing, hon. Didn't you say some cramping and spotting was normal?"

Spotting, yes. But this was more than that. There had been so much blood…

But she didn't say that. She just nodded, holding on to his reassurances with a desperate determination. God had brought them through so much; He wouldn't desert them now. The baby had to be all right. He had to be!

When the doctor finally arrived, he asked one question after another. Renee lay back on the gurney, struggling to speak through the spasms that continued to assault her.

"How far along did you say you are?"

She looked at the doctor. "Almost six months."

When his lips thinned, her growing terror slammed into overdrive. "Doctor...is my baby all right?"

He didn't answer. He just looked from her to Gabe. Renee wanted to beg him to tell her everything was fine, but before she could form the words the curtains parted again and a young man came in pushing an ultrasound machine.

The doctor nodded. "Good. This should tell us what we need to know."

Renee gripped Gabe's hand through the procedure. She knew she was probably hurting him as hard as she held on, but she couldn't help it.

A strange, strangled sound. Her eyes flew open and she looked up at Gabe. He looked terrible, pale, and drawn. Renee turned to the ultrasound screen, seeking the cause of Gabe's obvious distress.

That's when it hit her. The baby wasn't moving. A nameless horror took hold of her. Her mind scrambled for understanding, and vague realizations began to pelt her. The baby hadn't been very active lately. In fact, now that she thought about it, he hadn't moved at all since...since...

When *was* the last time he'd moved? She didn't know for sure, and that fact made her sick. *Stupid, stupid! How could you not realize the baby wasn't moving? What kind of mother are you?*

"Doctor?"

At Gabe's raw plea, she looked to the doctor, who stood studying the screen. He just shook his head. "Your baby is small..."

"Is that bad?"

He looked up, and there was no compassion in the man's face, no pity or empathy. He was simply matter-of-fact. "I don't know yet. But the baby is smaller than it should be."

He moved closer to the screen, and in the following silence Renee thought she would go mad. Her frantic heart cried out for mercy. *God...are You there? Please...please...*

A few moments later, the doctor straightened and turned to them. He put his hands in the pockets of his coat and shrugged. "I'm sorry, Mr. and Mrs. Roman, but it appears your baby has no blood flow."

Renee heard the words but didn't understand them. No blood flow? What did that mean?

When they just stared at him in silence, he cleared his throat. "What I mean is there's no heartbeat. Your baby is dead."

Renee heard the screaming and wanted to tell whoever was doing it to just shut up, to get out and let her think. It wasn't until Gabe gripped her by the shoulders and shook her that it dawned on her: The screams were coming from her.

She looked at Gabe and their gazes locked—and Renee knew what it was to look into the face of utter despair. She reached for him then, and they held each other, their sobs and tears mixing in that tiny, terrible room. The doctor muttered something about giving them time alone and stepped out, the ultrasound technician on his heels.

She wanted to go with them. It wasn't fair! Why did they just get to walk out of the room, to leave the grief and pain behind? The answer was as swift as it was painful: Because the pain wasn't theirs. It belonged to someone else. To her. And she would never be able to escape it.

She hugged herself, aware of Gabe holding her, speaking words of comfort between his sobs. But it was as though she were seeing him, hearing him, through some kind of gauzy veil. As though he weren't really there. Or maybe it was that *she* wasn't there. Maybe she'd gone someplace else, someplace where she was alone. Safe from reality.

But she'd never be safe again. She knew it—and hated knowing it. Hated knowing that life would never be right again. Not now. How could it be when her baby—her precious gift from God that had filled her life even more than it filled her belly—was gone. She would never hold him in her arms, never sing him lullabies, never press her face to his soft head and breathe in the fragrance of creation.

Her baby was dead.

She cried out against the truth. What had she done wrong? Why had God taken him away?

And why hadn't He taken her as well?

Gabe stood in the doorway of the baby's room, staring through the darkness with unseeing eyes.

Dead. His son was dead.

They had been right. It was a boy. The doctor had told them that—then gone on about induced labor, a D & C. None of it made any sense. Not even when they wheeled Renee away. Not even when they brought her back after the procedure, and she looked at him, her eyes as hollow and empty as her womb.

Gabe's fist slammed into the wall. *Nothing* made sense! How could a baby be there one minute, and then gone the next?

"These things sometimes happen, and we never know why," the doctor had said as though they were discussing why a tire went flat on a car or why a faucet continued to drip after it had been fixed a dozen times.

Like it was nothing.

Like the baby—his baby…his *son!*—was nothing.

"Lord Jesus, *why?*" His scream, as much protest as prayer, sliced the stillness permeating their apartment. It didn't matter Renee was out cold. The doctor had given her a sedative of some sort. As responsive as she was to medications, he could turn their apartment on end and she would sleep through it. He'd even been the one who had to call her parents, to tell them about the baby.

They wept with him, prayed with him. Told him they loved him. That phone call had been the one spot of light in a very dark day.

Gabe glanced back at their bedroom door. Renee would never even know he'd left her side, come into the baby's room.

The baby's room…

He reached for the switch and flicked on the lights. He and Renee had spent so much time here, painting, decorating, making everything just right. Perfect. For their child.

They'd talked and laughed and dreamed.

He never should have let himself trust. Never should have let his heart break free from the numbing shelter it had slid into that night Renee told him she was pregnant. But when he'd felt that movement inside her, known it was their child growing…

He could no more stop his reaction than he could stop the sun from rising. His heart burst into life with an excitement and purpose he'd never known before. He was going to be a father! And as that fact planted itself deep in his heart, he made himself and his child a promise. He would be the best father a kid ever had. The kind of father he'd always wanted. A guy like Renee's dad. And one day his child would talk about him the way Renee talked about her folks—with shining eyes that spoke of love and respect.

What a fool he'd been!

He should have known better. Shouldn't have let himself feel…trust…believe. His fisted hands ached to strike out. To crush something the way he was being crushed. His gaze scanned the room, halting when it fell on the beautiful illustrated children's Bible he and Renee had chosen together.

Gabe forced his leaden feet to move. The Bible lay open on the small table next to the rocker. Renee must have been sitting there, reading, thinking about rocking their baby.

At the thought, Gabe's knees gave way and he lowered

himself into the rocker. He reached for the Bible, cradled it in his trembling hands. *Please. Speak to me. Give me peace...*

He looked down, let his eyes roam the page.

Don't be afraid. God loves you and will take care of you. If even a tiny sparrow falls to the ground, God knows. He cares.

Emotion grappled at Gabe's throat, choking him. His fingers gripped the edges of the Bible, even as his mind and heart struggled to grip the words he read.

And He cares for you even more. He has numbered every hair on your head. He loves you more than anything.

The words pierced Gabe's heart, and he closed his eyes with a groan. He wanted to believe. To trust. He wanted to lay his head in God's lap and know He would make everything right. But that was impossible. Only one thing would make it right, and it was too late.

His baby was dead. Not even God could change that.

Gabe jumped up and flung the Bible across the room.

"Why did You do this? If You love me, if You care for me, how could You take him from me? I thought he was the reason for all of this...that he was why You brought Renee into my life, why we ended up together. But now...what's the point? What's the stinking point of any of this?"

A harsh laugh escaped him. There wasn't a point. Not to his marriage. Not to his life.

Not even to God. *If there even is a God.*

Gabe went cold. No God? Did he really believe that?

He stepped back from the thought, spinning when he bumped into something hard. The crib. Gabe lifted a hand and ran it across the smooth wood. Images flashed through his mind—pictures of him and Renee choosing the wood, planing it, finishing it...the careful way they'd followed the plans, making sure every piece fit just so...the excitement he felt as the crib took shape, transformed from a pile of wood into something beautiful. Something they'd made together.

Like their baby.

His fingers convulsed on the crib, and with a roar of agony he whirled, running to the closet in the hallway. He flung the door open and jerked out the baseball bat he'd had since he was a kid.

His determined steps echoed in the dark hallway as he moved back to the baby's room. He didn't hesitate as he walked through the doorway. He lifted the bat high and brought it down, felt the impact of wood on wood jolt through his body. Again he raised it and swung, and again, and again...

He didn't stop until the crib lay in a pile at his feet. Broken, shattered, fit only for the trash heap.

Just like his dreams.

Renee lay in bed, listening. She didn't have the energy to open her eyes. Wouldn't have done so even if she did. She liked the darkness.

She jumped when Gabe cried out, heard his anguish— and wondered at what she felt.

Nothing.

Her heart was as empty as her womb.

Then, when the sound of furious pounding—of wood splintering, giving way—filled the apartment, she turned her face to her pillow, longing for the oblivion the doctor had promised her when he handed her the bottle of pills.

"One should do," he told her.

She'd taken two. But even that wasn't enough to keep her in the darkness, not totally. Her lids squeezed tight in a vain effort to halt the scalding tears, but she felt them push free, flow down her face. She dug her fists into the covers.

Please, God, this has to be a bad dream. It can't be real.

Her groggy mind embraced that thought, clutched it close. That was it! This was all a dream. A nightmare. There was no way she could lose her baby. No way God would let that happen!

All she had to do was wake up, and everything would be fine.

And if it's not a dream?

Then she hoped she never woke up again.

22

However just your words, you spoil everything
when you speak them with anger.

ST. JOHN CHRYSOSTOM

A fool gives full vent to anger.

PROVERBS 29:11

SPRING 1985

PLEASE. RENEE...DON'T BE AWAKE.

Gabe stared at the stoplight, fingers tapping the steering wheel. He couldn't believe he'd been called out again. That made five times since he got home from work tonight. If it happened again, he was taking a cot and just staying there for the night.

Twelve-thirty in the morning and he was finally heading home. He shook his head. What a day. Work was bad enough, but if he had to see that sad, puppy-dog expression on Renee's face once more today he'd scream.

Be in bed, Renee. Asleep.

Yeah, right.

He pulled a cigarette from the pack in his pocket, then pushed in the cigarette lighter. Ten to one, she'd be sitting there when he walked in. Ready to talk. To do something. To be together.

The woman was driving him nuts.

The lighter popped out, and he grabbed it, holding it to the cigarette, taking long draws until he felt his muscles start to ease. The light turned, and he drove through the intersection.

Relax. You're just tired. It's been a long day.

Yes, he was tired. But not from work. He was tired of trying to be patient and understanding.

You knew what Renee was like when you married her. Knew how important being together was to her.

Yeah, but he hadn't realized he couldn't have even five minutes to himself without feeling guilty! And what on God's green earth made her think he wanted to do any of the things she suggested? This last one was the worst. A jigsaw puzzle? Nobody did those anymore. Where did she come up with this stuff? Okay, so her parents did puzzles together. So Renee liked doing them. Hey, to each his own. But did he have to do what she wanted just because they were married? If she wanted to go do stuff, go, have fun, great. Just don't expect him to tag along.

He was her husband, not her playmate. Or her babysitter. And if she didn't give him some space soon, he'd tell her so.

Not a good idea.

Gabe grimaced. He didn't want to hurt Renee, and he was pretty sure he would if he let his frustration get the better of him. He sighed, squeezing his fingers on the steering wheel so tight that his knuckles went white.

Let her be in bed, Lord. Let her be asleep. She needs the rest. He drew in a heavy sigh. *And I need a break.*

Renee pulled her knees to her chest and looked at the clock. Again.

Three minutes later than the last time she looked.

She sighed and uncurled from the couch, standing to

stretch. She hated nights like this, when Gabe no sooner got home than he was called out again. The money from his new job at the hospital was nice—she had no idea hospitals paid their building maintenance workers so well. But she really didn't like him being on call every third week. It wouldn't be so bad, of course, if they seldom called him. But they called *all* the time.

Tonight he'd been called back in to deal with one crisis after another. This last call came barely fifteen minutes after he got home from the last one. So off he went, leaving her alone.

Again.

As he'd pulled open the door of their apartment, ready to head down the stairs to the outside door, he turned back to her. "Don't wait up for me this time, Renee. It's late. Just get some sleep, okay?"

She nodded, but they both knew she'd wait up. She always did.

Why should that bother him? What was wrong with a wife waiting up for her husband? Sometimes Gabe acted as if he could barely stand being around her. As though everything she said and did irritated him.

Other times...

She pressed a hand to her burning eyes. She was tired. Seemed as though she never got enough sleep, but then, it was hard to do so with the nightmares. She'd lost count of the number of nights Gabe had shaken her awake because she was crying or screaming. Every time she collapsed against him, and he'd hold her. Talk to her. Sometimes he read the Bible or sang to her. Then there were the stories. She loved it when he lulled her to sleep with one of his tales of adventure, where the good guy always won and the romance was pure and uncomplicated.

Why couldn't life be more like those stories? Why couldn't the daytime Gabe be more like the man who comforted her late at night?

Renee rubbed the aching muscles in her shoulders and neck. And why was she sitting here asking herself stupid questions instead of going to bed?

Good thing they hadn't tried to have another child yet. They'd talked about it, of course, but Gabe said they needed to wait. Though five years had gone by, neither of them had recovered from losing the baby. Besides, they needed to get their feet under them financially.

"Give it a couple more years, Rennie. Then we'll be ready."

He was right. Of course he was. She could just imagine what a basket case she'd be if she had little ones right now. True, she only worked part-time, but she was exhausted all the time nonetheless. From the way her friends talked, keeping up with their kids was hard enough on a full night's sleep. With as little sleep as Renee was getting? It'd be a nightmare.

No, they were definitely better off not having children right now. If only she could stop thinking about it. Longing for it. If only her heart didn't break every time another woman she knew bounced into the room with her "glad tidings."

She'd endured it when one after another of her friends started having babies. Despite the pain of her own loss, Renee threw showers for them and went shopping with them. And she *oohed* and *ahhed* over each angelic face when the babies were pressed into her arms, feeling a surge of maternal warmth as those tiny fingers curled around hers.

Renee frowned. When had that changed? She wasn't sure. All she knew was that at some point the warmth had vanished, and she'd been startled to find far different emotions flooding her when she held yet another friend's newborn.

Longing. Sorrow. Resentment. They all crowded in, and all Renee wanted to do was give the baby back to its glowing mother and head for the hills. Which she'd done.

And she'd stayed there. Each time someone called, asking

her to come over or go do something, she made excuses. It hadn't taken long for the calls to stop entirely. About the only people she talked to regularly were her parents when she called home.

Home... Renee knew she should think of where she lived with Gabe as her home. But she didn't. Oregon was still, would always be, her home. At least there when she was sad or upset, she could head to the beach or the mountains. She could walk in the beauty of nature and find some semblance of peace, of restoration.

Illinois didn't exactly offer the same havens. The state, the city, the weather, even the people often seemed cold. Inhospitable. Renee hated living here. She would have been miserable if she'd been alone.

Thank goodness she had Gabe.

She glanced at her watch. Six minutes had passed this time.

Well, she had him part of the time. She wandered from room to room in the apartment, looking for something to do. There was plenty to keep her busy, but nothing really caught her interest. What fun was it to do things alone?

She paused by the card table where she and Gabe were putting together a puzzle. *Who's putting it together?* Okay, so she was, but she hadn't given up on catching Gabe's interest. Everyone loved puzzles! Her folks had always done them together. Gotten the whole family involved. It was fun.

Gabe, however, didn't seem all that interested. Renee shoved a puzzle piece in circles with her finger. She'd tried to find something they could enjoy together. But so far all her suggestions had been flops. Far from enjoying their "together" times, Gabe seemed more and more resistant.

"I should have gotten a puzzle of a TV screen. That would have interested him." That was all he ever wanted to do: sit in his chair and watch TV.

Renee had even tried doing that with him, but the shows

he liked to watch were either boring, like *This Old House*—
please—or irritating political debates. If she wanted to hear a
bunch of two-year-olds argue, she'd go to the playground! But
let her even suggest they tune in to something else, and she
got The Look. That tense-jawed, narrow-eyed, barely tolerant
glare that told her she was being a pest.

"I'm not a pest; I'm his wife." She directed the low mutter
to the puzzle piece. "He should want to do things with me.
That's what being married is all about. Being togeth—"

"Are you still up?"

She jumped, a small scream escaping her. Gabe stared at
her, arms a folded barrier, jaw tight.

"Don't *do* that!" She couldn't keep the irritation out of her
tone. Gabe was forever coming up behind her when she was
engrossed in something and scaring the wits out of her. "You
know you're supposed to call as you come in."

His lips thinned. "It's after midnight. I thought you'd be
in bed."

Her brows arched at his sarcasm. Fine. If he was going to
be like that... She matched him tone for tone. "Well, forgive
me for waiting up for my husband."

Gabe turned and walked into the bedroom, which only
fueled her ire.

"Don't you walk away from me!"

He spun, and they nearly collided. He held his hands out
in front of him. "Walk away where? There's no place to go,
Renee. You're everywhere I turn!"

She felt her face go hot, then cold. Her arms came up to
form a folded shield between them. "What...what's that supposed to mean?"

He shook his head. "How many times do I have to say it?
When I come home from work I want to relax. To sit in my
chair. Watch a little TV. I don't want to play tennis, or go for a
walk, or ride bikes, or read a book together, or play a board
game or cards—" his voice rose as he went down the list, and

he waved his hands at the card table—"or put some stupid puzzle together!"

She bit her lip to keep it from trembling. She hated it when he yelled. Hated it. "I just want us to spend time together—"

"We're *together* all the time! We're married, for cryin' out loud. How much more together can you get than *that?*"

Tears dribbled down her face, and she turned away. But it was too late. Gabe must have seen them.

"Fine! Okay, start crying. So I'm a total jerk because I don't want to spend every stinkin' second with my wife."

His steps were heavy as he went into the kitchen, and Renee followed him. "Gabe, I—"

Clearly he wasn't in the mood to listen. "Look. It's simple. I'm your husband, not your shadow. Just because we're married doesn't mean we have to be in each other's pockets all the time."

She followed him as he paced back into the living room, almost bumping into him when he whirled to face her.

"Just do us both a favor, will you, Renee, and get a life! Find some friends. Find someone who likes the kinds of things you do and go do them together." He yanked the door to the steps open. "And quit acting like I'm some kind of criminal just because I'm tired at the end of the day and don't feel like coming out to play."

"Where are you going?" She was amazed the words could get past the knot in her tight throat. As it was, they were barely a whisper.

"I don't know. Anyplace but here!"

He slammed the door behind him, and his footsteps pounded down the stairs to the outer door. Then that slammed as well.

Renee stood there, staring at the closed door. She couldn't think. Couldn't breathe. Couldn't move.

All she could do was feel, and that was the worst nightmare of all. She felt as though she had turned to old, brittle glass, and she was shattering. Shards of her flew in every direction, ripping her apart with a pain so intense she thought she might pass out.

But she didn't. Instead she just turned and walked to where her purse lay. She opened it, dug out her wallet, and flipped to the picture section. For a moment, she stared at the picture she carried with her wherever she went—the picture of her and Gabe a few months after they were married. Before they lost the baby.

Before they lost each other.

Her fingers were surprisingly steady as she pulled the picture from its sleeve and carried it to the kitchen. She stepped on the wastebasket lever and the lid popped up. Holding the picture in both hands, Renee ripped it once.

Get a life?

Twice.

Find some friends?

Three times.

Fine. You got it. And guess what, Gabe?

She tore the pieces over and over until they were a shredded pile of little pieces.

You won't have to be a part of it at all.

Gabe sat on the porch steps outside the apartment, his head in his hands. He was going to be sick. Right there on the lawn.

He tipped his head back, dragging in gulps of cool night air.

What was *wrong* with him? How could he treat Renee like that? Talk to her like that? What had she done that was so terrible?

Love him. Want to be with him.

Oh yeah, she should be shot.

He looked at the darkness blanketing the sky, at the tiny specks of white that sparkled down at him, and he wanted to weep. Because he kept seeing, over and over, the look in Renee's eyes when he yelled at her. Said those things…

Lord, I blew it.

He was so tired of losing control. So tired of saying things he wanted to take back the second they were out.

Why couldn't You have made her go to bed?

He was so weary, heart weary. It took so much emotional energy to deal with their differences, with all the fights and miscommunication. They never seemed to get along any-more. The worst was when she tried talking about having another baby. Even the thought of it sent a chill over Gabe.

He wasn't ready to try again. Didn't know if he ever would be. With each passing day, each emotionally charged conflict between him and Renee, he felt the resistance grow. How could they bring a child into the world, especially into *their* world? He wouldn't do it. Wouldn't subject a child to the yelling, the fighting…

But what concerned him most was the anger. In him. Sometimes it took all his strength to keep himself from vent-ing that anger physically. He would never hurt Renee. He'd cut his arm off first. But what if it got out of control?

No. He wasn't ready for kids.

How do I tell Renee that, Lord? You know what will happen. We'll just end up in another fight. I'm so tired of the fights.

He was tired of this, too. Of coming to God, begging for help, asking Him to change things. To change him. Because no matter how much he prayed, nothing seemed to change.

Jesus, why don't You do something?

But even as he threw his cries to heaven, Gabe knew it wasn't God's fault at all. It was his. It always was.

And he was more tired of that than anything.

23

Wrung from the troubled spirit, in hard hours of weakness,
Solitude, and times of pain,
Truth springs like harvest from the well-plowed field,
And our soul feels it has not wept in vain.

ANONYMOUS

"But he knows where I am going.
And when he has tested me like gold in a fire,
he will pronounce me innocent."

JOB 23:10

DECEMBER 19, 2003
5:30 P.M.

SHE WAS SO TIRED...SHE'D NEVER FELT SO TIRED BEFORE.
And yet, Renee couldn't rest. Because something wasn't right. She knew it but couldn't quite figure it out. Her mind, her body, her every sense told her something was wrong, but no matter how hard she tried, she couldn't make sense of anything.

If only I could get my eyes open...

But she couldn't. Her lids had grown too heavy to lift, as though they were frozen shut.

A dawning awareness came to her then. She was lying down, but she wasn't cold. Why wasn't she cold? She should be. She was still out in the storm, wasn't she?

"Renee? Come on, hon, open your eyes."

Gabe's voice! Her heart pounded and she struggled through

the haze. She reached for him and felt someone take her hand.

"It's okay, Rennie. I'm right here."

A broken sob slipped through her, and she clutched at his hand. It was him. He was real and solid, not some dream she'd conjured up. Now if she could just open her eyes and *see* him.

With supreme effort, her lids finally fluttered, blinked, and lifted. For a moment all she saw was darkness, and panic shot through her. She was blind!

Then reason caught up with her groggy mind. No, it was nighttime. That's why it was so dark.

"Hey, there."

The familiar, tender voice enveloped her, and she turned her head toward it. The sight that met her brought a wide smile to her parched lips.

"You're awake," she whispered.

He leaned his forehead against hers. "I'm awake."

She lifted a hand to touch the bandage she'd put on his forehead, and he caught her fingers.

"And you're awake, too. Finally. I was getting worried. You've been in and out for a couple of hours."

"I missed you." Her words were thick with unshed tears, and Gabe pressed a gentle kiss to her cheek. He shifted out of her sight, then was back, a cup in his hands.

"Water. You need to drink, hon. Can you sit up?"

She nodded and planted her hands on the ground to push herself up, then stopped when the ground crinkled. She looked down. She wasn't sitting on the snow any longer. She was on a space blanket.

"Told you we might need it someday."

She laughed, then held her hand out to Gabe. "And you were right. Now help me sit up, okay?"

He stared at her, unmoving.

"Gabe?"

"What did you say?"

At the mock astonishment in his expression, she batted a hand at him. "Ha ha."

"Say it again. Just so I can be sure I really heard it."

Tipping her head, Renee gave a sigh. Well, she had promised him she'd say so if he woke up. "Youwereright-youwererightyouwereright." She held her hand out again. "Satisfied?"

The warm curve of his mouth was all the answer she needed. He helped her sit up, then handed her the cup again. She pressed her lips to the cold metal. The water tasted wonderful. Cold and clean. She looked at Gabe. "How...how did you find me?"

"I didn't. God did." He reached out to pet Bo, who Renee realized was stretched out beside her. "And this guy."

As she sipped the water, Gabe told her everything that had happened since he woke up in the cab. When he finished, he rocked back on his heels. "Pretty amazing, huh?"

It was indeed. And humbling. God had managed to take care of everything just fine.

And all without her help.

Gabe moved to tend the fire, and Renee drank in the comfort of his nearness. She had been so afraid... Her heart had longed for him to be there, called out to him to help her, and he'd come.

Thank You...

The prayer whispered through her, magnifying the gratitude that swelled within her.

She found herself smiling at his careful placement of twigs and sticks. He worked with such precision, such forethought.

They were so different.

Surprisingly, she didn't feel the frustration that too often rode shotgun with such an observation. In fact, her smile widened. Yes, Gabe's meticulous personality too often grated on her nerves. But now...

They could have been in serious trouble if not for his proclivity for considering every angle and preparing for as many scenarios as possible. Seat-of-the-pants living was fine in a more controlled environment, but out here seat-of-the-pants would only get you in trouble.

Gabe's work on the fire brought the low flames to life. She watched the fire dance across the wood, and a thrill of gladness tripped across her heart. Thank heaven he was different from her. She might know how to play, but he knew how to make things safe. And she was starting to realize both were important.

Soon warmth radiated from the snapping fire, and Gabe came to sit next to her. He held out a protein bar to her. She took it from him, leaning her head against his arm as she chewed.

Her angry thoughts from earlier in the day, when they were on the road, came back to her, and she knew she'd been wrong. She didn't hate Gabe. She might *feel* like she did at times, but that was because no one could hurt her like he could.

And that was because no one mattered to her like he did.

Renee rubbed her cheek on Gabe's arm and shifted when he moved it to circle her shoulders. She nestled against him.

No, she didn't hate Gabe. She loved him. Her reaction when she opened her eyes and saw him proved that. And really, she'd always known that was the case. Even in the darkest of times, even in the hottest anger, she knew she loved him. And that he loved her. Loving each other had never been the problem.

No, the problem was that love simply wasn't enough.

God, why did You do it?

You must have known how different we were.
You must have known what a disaster it would be
for us to get married.

So where were You? Why didn't You stop us from
going down this path? "I will lead you in the way
you should go." That's what You promised, right?

So are You telling me THIS is the way we were
supposed to go? If so, I don't think too much of
Your plans.

24

Have contempt for contempt.

FRANCES DE SALES

"They hated knowledge and chose not to fear the LORD.
They rejected my advice and paid no attention when I corrected them.
That is why they must eat the bitter fruit of living their own way.
They must experience the full terror of the path they have chosen."

PROVERBS 1:29–31

SEPTEMBER 1990

"ENOUGH ALREADY! SERVE THE BALL, RENEE, AND LET'S get this game over with!"

Renee grinned at Tom, the captain of their volleyball team. The man was the embodiment of pent-up energy. She drew a deep breath, tossed the volleyball into the air, and gave it a quick smack with the flat of her palm. She allowed herself a small moment of satisfaction as the ball floated over the net.

She loved floater serves. They looked easy to return, but they weren't.

Taking her position on the floor, Renee crouched, ready for the return—but it never came. The ball followed an erratic path over the net, then shifted just as one of the opposing players readied to hit it. He groaned as the ball glanced off his arm and hit the ground.

They'd won!

Renee's teammates exploded into cheers and congratulations, then went to shake hands with the other team. She fell in line with her friends, flexing her shoulders and back. She was tired and sore, but it was a good feeling. She'd been sitting at the computer all day, trying to meet a deadline. As much as she loved her job as a creativity and product development consultant, the stress sometimes got to her. Her boss always said it was her own fault.

"Hey, when you're known as one of the best in the business, people expect a lot from you." He'd shrug then, an amused pride playing over his features. "Such is the price of success."

She supposed he was right in a way. She'd been with Creative Solutions, Inc., for nearly five years. She traveled all over the country, giving workshops and seminars, and had just recently been asked to develop a program to help her company train new employees. She felt fortunate that she'd done so well, that people seemed to respect her and listen to her, even about important issues. But sometimes she just wanted to chuck it all—the pressure, the expectations, the responsibility—and go sell shoes.

Volleyball was a welcome change of pace today. She had known the match would be tough, and she was glad. She needed the release.

"Way to go, Renee."

She turned to Conrad Leonard. Being on a volleyball team with some of her closest friends made playing even more fun. But having Conrad, her best friend, on the team made it a blast.

Conrad and his wife, Ami, attended the same church as Renee. And though Gabe had given up on church a few years ago, he still went with Renee to the Bible study at the Leonards's home.

"So, did Gabe come to watch you play?"

Renee snorted. "And miss his TV shows? I don't think so."

Conrad frowned, and she knew it was as much at her sarcasm as anything. "I'm surprised. Did you tell him it was the championship game?"

Renee turned from his steady contemplation. Sometimes Conrad saw way too much. Thankfully it was time to hit the locker room.

As Renee made her way to her car, she heard Conrad call her. She hesitated, her hand on the car door, then turned. He and Ami were walking toward her. Renee leaned against the car, waiting.

Ami waved at her. "Want to do a Dairy Queen run with us?"

Renee perked up at that. "Sure. Lead on."

They made their way to DQ, and when they had their ice cream, they went to perch on one of the outdoor tables next to where her car was parked.

Renee licked at her cone. She loved nights like this. Nights sitting out under the stars, talking and laughing with frien—

"So why didn't Gabe show tonight?"

She should have known Conrad wouldn't let the subject drop. Not when she'd made such an obvious dodge. She concentrated on her ice cream as she answered. "He wouldn't have enjoyed it, Con. We're just the C-league, so it's not as though the game would have been all that exciting for him."

"You didn't tell him about it."

Leave it to Conrad to cut through her rhetoric right to the heart of an issue.

She sighed. "I didn't tell him about it."

"I'm sorry to hear that."

At the gentle admonishment, Renee contemplated getting into her car and leaving. But she didn't. She respected Conrad too much to run away. He'd proven himself a solid friend and a godly counselor more times than she could count. He was a man who walked the line of truth, even when it cost him—which it did when he had to say hard things to a friend.

"Look, even if I'd told Gabe, he wouldn't have come." It was the truth. Gabe never came to watch her. Not anymore.

She'd asked Gabe to come watch. Plenty of times. He'd done so years ago. But lately...his answer was always the same: "I'm too tired."

Too tired. What a laugh. How tired could you get sitting in a recliner all night watching TV? Oh yeah. Punching those remote buttons was exhausting.

She looked away. Gabe just didn't care.

"Any idea why?"

Renee started. Conrad knew her as well as anyone, but even he couldn't read her mind, could he? "Why what?"

"Why Gabe wouldn't come."

She shrugged. "He isn't interested in volleyball, Con."

This time Ami spoke up. "But he's interested in *you*, isn't he?"

Renee stared at her ice cream, which was quickly losing its appeal. Like the conversation. She hopped off the table and tossed her melting ice cream cone into the trash. So she and Gabe weren't the perfect couple. So they hardly spent time together. So what? It wasn't as though *she* wanted it that way.

She returned to the table, plopped down on top if it, and glared at Conrad. "What do you want from me?"

She wanted to retract the question the minute it jumped out. But it was too late. Conrad took his and Ami's unfinished sundaes and dropped them in the trash can. "It's not what I want that matters, Ren."

Renee looked away, gnawing at her lip. She knew what Conrad was saying: What mattered was what *God* wanted. Trouble was, she wasn't ready to ask Him. What if He asked her to do something she couldn't do? Or worse, something she didn't want to do?

Like treat Gabe like a husband rather than the enemy.

I tried treating him like a husband, and he told me to get a life, remember? I tried loving him, and he just grew colder. More critical. So I quit trying. What else was I supposed to do?

Conrad slid his arm around his wife's shoulders, but his gaze rested on Renee. "We're here for you, Renee." His words had the sure ring of truth. "It may not feel like it sometimes, but we are."

She swallowed hard and nodded.

He came to sit beside her on the table. "I know it's tough. It doesn't make a lot of sense why a girl like you didn't end up in the perfect life, the perfect marriage."

She choked on a laugh. "A girl like me?" Maybe he didn't know her as well as she thought. "Stubborn, unforgiving, demanding...?"

He didn't smile. "Creative, intelligent, sensitive, athletic, energetic. A girl with solid parents and upbringing. Having all of that probably didn't prepare you for what you're facing now."

No, it didn't. Not one of her childhood dreams looked like this. She'd never envisioned herself married to a man who didn't even seem to like her most of the time.

Ami slid onto the bench seat of the table. "You know, Renee, most people think they need intimacy on several levels. And when we don't get it, we get angry. Resentful."

How well she knew.

"But what we really need is God."

Renee frowned. "I have God."

Conrad's nod was slow, thoughtful. "I know you long to serve Him, to follow Him, but I also know how deep your anger runs."

Anger? *She* wasn't the one who was angry all the time. Gabe was! She choked back the frustration clamoring for release.

"You chose Gabe. Right or wrong, you two are joined now."

Yes, she chose him. Exercised her free will.

She shook her head. Free will? More like foolish choices. The stupidity of youth. "We never should have gotten married." Her eyes widened. She couldn't believe she'd finally said what had been rolling around in her heart for far too long.

Conrad didn't look the least bit shocked. "Maybe, maybe not. But you did get married."

"Yeah, and a fine job we're doing of it."

"Renee—" his intent look bored into her—"no person in the world can bring the love and acceptance your heart—all of our hearts—long for."

"Then what's the point?" She let the question out on a desperate whisper, hoping...praying he had an answer.

"God is the point. We were made in His image, and our hearts seek their home. They seek the love and acceptance He has for us." Conrad leaned his elbows on his knees. "Trouble is, we expect people to give us those things instead of God."

She shook her head. "I can't do this..."

His nod surprised her, as did his reply. "No one can. Life is forcing you to the edge of your perceptions and traditions about God. If He's real, He'll rescue you. If He isn't..." He shrugged. "Well, then we'll all be in a pit together."

She closed her eyes. "So what am I supposed to do?"

Ami's response was quiet but confident. "Open yourself, Renee. To God. To love."

"You've embraced contempt. Emptiness. Resentment." Each word Conrad spoke was an arrow straight through her. An arrow of undeniable truth. She'd done exactly that. Opened her arms to those things and drawn them to her breast, letting them feed on her until the joy she'd once known had been devoured. All that was left, then, was pride. And the determination that she wouldn't be hurt anymore. Not by Gabe. Not by anyone.

"But don't you see, Renee? Those things are the enemies

of your soul." Conrad's voice was gentle, but firm. "They're destroying you. I see it in your eyes; I hear it in your words. You've got to put those things out, to embrace truth instead."

She hugged herself, the hurt so deep she struggled to breathe. "Truth? I don't even know what truth is."

At his silence, she looked up, saw the challenge in his eyes…and looked away. Okay, so she knew the truth. She just didn't like it.

The understanding in Conrad's eyes eased the ache inside her. "Ren, it's okay to question, to doubt. That's a part of being human. We don't get God. And we don't get the way He does things. But never forget you were designed to be complete in Him first. Him alone. And no one else can make that connection for you. Not Gabe, not your parents—" he held her gaze—"not me. No matter how much we love you, we can't do God's work in your life. But you've got to find yourself in God first. Then you can see others more clearly. Understand their roles in your life."

When was the last time she'd seen Gabe—or herself, for that matter—clearly? Renee wasn't sure she ever had.

Ami put a hand on her arm, and Renee felt the compassion in her touch. "I know it's hard, Renee. I'm learning these things, too. But I found that when I really gave God access to my heart, when I found my contentment in Him, I suddenly realized that we're all broken and blind, just in uniquely different ways."

Renee considered her friend. Ami's words rang true.

"You know as well as we do that true wholeness only comes through Christ." Conrad looked at Renee and smiled. "But the cool thing is when we're in Him, really in Him, then we can deal with disappointment and frustration in our human relationships. Because we understand we're all doing our best, in our own broken, blind ways."

She wanted to believe them. Wanted it more than she'd wanted anything for a long time. But she and Gabe had gone so wrong. "What if it's too late for us? What if Gabe and I can never be happy together?"

Conrad leaned forward. "Ami and I will stand with you, whatever your decision. We love you. But being happy isn't the measuring stick. Obedience is. What matters most to us isn't that you're happy, but that you can stand clean before God."

Renee swallowed. Clean before God… She lowered her head. She wasn't, and she knew it.

Conrad's voice enveloped her. "God doesn't ask the impossible of us, Ren. But He does ask us to do everything *He* enables us to do. If you can honestly say you've done that, done everything He's enabled you to do to save your marriage, then walk away knowing you're clean. But if you're just tired because your strength has run, then what you're walking away from isn't Gabe or your marriage, but obedience."

They were hard words, but Conrad didn't say them carelessly. Or easily. He cared too much about her to be careless. But he also had to speak the truth.

And that's what this was: truth.

As the silence between them grew, Renee drew in a deep breath of the evening air. She slipped from the table and faced them. What was that verse? *Better the wounds of a friend than the kisses of an enemy.*

It took a good friend to care enough to speak hard truths. And she needed to hear them. Desperately.

"You've given me a lot to think about. Pray about."

Conrad stood and leaned against the table, slipping his hands into his pockets. "Are you okay?"

Renee managed a smile. "No, but I'm better." She stepped forward and hugged Ami, then turned to Conrad. His hug was gentle and solid.

Like his counsel. And their friendship.

She felt blessed to have both.

Father, he's so lost.

Every time I look at him, listen to him, all I'm aware of is pain. His pain. My pain. The pain we've caused each other. How are we supposed to overcome this?

I'm afraid. What if we can't find each other again? What if, despite our best efforts and desires, we don't make it? I don't want to be alone. I don't want to lose what we have. I mean, it may not be perfect, but it's ours.

And here's the part that really scares me: I don't know who I am without him. He's part of me — struggles, anger, disillusionment and all. Everything I do is because I'm mad at him. Or because I'm afraid I'm losing him. Or because I'm afraid I'll never escape him.

Worst of all, I'm afraid without all of that, I'll just disappear into nothing.

Help, Lord.

25

God strengthen me to bear myself, that heaviest weight of all to bear,
inalienable weight of care... I lock the door upon myself.
And bar [all others] out; but who shall wall
self from myself, most loathed of all?

CHRISTINA ROSSETTI

O LORD, you have examined my heart and know everything about me.
Search me, O God...test me...Point out anything in me that
offends you, and lead me along the path of everlasting life.

PSALM 139:1, 23-24

OCTOBER 1990

GABE JAMMED THE BUTTONS ON THE TV REMOTE AND
grabbed another handful of popcorn. He chomped down. Hard.
Again. And again.

He had to do something to vent his frustration.

Another chomp, but this time his cheek got in the way. Gabe
yelped and jumped up; the bowl of popcorn in his lap went airborne.

As did his temper. Gabe ranted and raved all the way to the
closet. He jerked the vacuum out, plugged it in, and flipped the
switch to on.

He was glad for the vacuum's loud roar. It helped drown out
the string of angry words he threw into the empty room.

Empty except for him, of course. He was always there. Alone.
While Renee gallivanted off with her buddies. The last of the ker-
nels shot into the vacuum, and Gabe grabbed the power cord and

jerked it from the wall. He probably ruined the cord, but he didn't care.

He all but threw the machine back into the closet and slammed the door.

What was it Renee was supposed to be doing tonight? He shook his head. Who knew? She never told him where she was going anymore. Barely told him good-bye as she raced out the door. At least she'd taken time to fix some kind of dinner before she left this time. He was getting tired of canned soup and crackers.

Gabe went to the bathroom and grabbed up the bottle of hydrogen peroxide. He took a swig and swished it around in his mouth, grimacing as it stung the gash he'd made in the inside of his cheek.

Why was it everything he did ended up with someone in pain?

He leaned over the sink, spit out the foul-tasting liquid, then cupped his hand under the faucet and rinsed his mouth with water. As he twisted the faucet off, he glanced up and caught his reflection in the mirror.

He took in the tense jaw, the tightly compressed lips, the glowering eyes...and felt his heart sag.

No wonder Renee couldn't stand being around him. No wonder she spent most nights someplace else, with someone else. Conrad. Ami. Oren. Grace. Tom. A dozen others. He'd lost count of the people in Renee's life—people she seemed to like and enjoy far more than him.

He sank down to sit on the edge of the tub and leaned his elbows on his knees. "She's slipping away from me."

Slipping away, my foot. She's gone, pal. But hey, you wanted her to get her own life, didn't you?

He clenched his fingers into a fist. Why had he ever said that? He should have cut his tongue out before he let himself say those things.

But it's what you wanted.

No…yes… His fist pressed into his leg, as if the pain could bring some semblance of clarity to his mind, his heart. Yes, he wanted her to stop clinging, but he never wanted her to get a life apart from him. It was as though they weren't even married. They were more roommates than husband and wife. Distant roommates at that.

He hung his head. At least roommates talked. They didn't even do that. And he couldn't remember the last time they'd touched…

I've tried and tried, but I can't stop what's happening. If only he could take back those careless words. If only he could find a way to let her know he hadn't meant it, had only been tired and frustrated.

But he couldn't. It was too late.

Gabe rubbed his hands over his face, trying to erase the fatigue…the despair.

God, please…

God? The taunt stabbed at him. *You call on God now? Do you really expect an answer? After the garbage you just spewed in the living room? Why would a holy God waste even a second on someone as vile as you?*

Why indeed? Gabe had no answers. He just didn't know where else to turn.

Well, don't turn here, pal. God doesn't listen to jerks who turn the air blue one minute then whine to Him the next. Besides, He's never had answers for you before; why should He have them now? And even if He did, why would He give them to you? Come on. Your own father didn't give a hoot about you, so why would God?

On and on it went, the voice Gabe had heard all his life. A voice of condemnation, of contempt. A voice he'd never been able to stop, to shut off.

The one voice that he hated above all others.

His father's voice.

⟨∾⟩

The apartment was dark when Renee got home. The meeting at church had gone longer than she thought it would, and then she stood in the parking lot, talking with first one person, then another. She hadn't meant to come home so late again. She'd just lost track of time.

She would have to do better from now on.

She slipped into the bedroom as quietly as possible and reached for her nightgown.

Gabe's voice, hard and cold, jumped out of the stillness and grated across her nerves.

"Finally had to come home, huh?"

She dug her fingers into her nightgown. "I didn't *have* to come home."

His snort of laughter was ugly. "Yeah, sure. You came home because you *wanted* to. Good ol' faithful Renee, the willing martyr to the end."

"*What* is your problem, Gabe?" She wasn't sure when she'd taken to yelling at him, to venting the full measure of her scorn for him, but it seemed second nature now.

For a moment there was a silence so heavy Renee wondered if it would bury her.

Then Gabe's voice came to her in a whisper. "You, Renee. You're my problem."

The words should have infuriated her, should have sent her right over the edge. But they didn't. Because as Gabe spoke them, he was crying.

Lord…

She stood there, imprisoned in disbelief. Was this for real, or was it yet another one of his acts…a part played to perfection? She'd seen it so many times, watched him adopt whatever persona he needed to elicit just the right response.

No. The ragged sobs filling the room were no act. She would bet her life on it. She'd heard this sound—this agony, this complete and utter despair—from Gabe before. Once before.

When they lost the baby.

The sound of his weeping floated around her, piercing the barriers she had so carefully crafted around her heart. And as they crumbled beneath the weight of his sorrow, she felt her knees give.

She landed on the bed, reaching for him.

"Gabe...Gabe, it's okay."

Her hands found him, tugged at him, and he came to her, burying his face in her neck, clutching her as though she were his only shield against whatever terrors were assaulting him.

Jesus, please, give him peace...

She held him to her, felt the shivering that had taken hold of him, and laid her cheek against the top of his head. His tears made their way down her neck, a river of agony too deep for words. She whispered words of reassurance, words of comfort, praying something would reach him, soothe him.

Jesus...

Almost without thinking, she started singing. Songs from her childhood. Songs that spoke of innocence and trust and safety. One after another she sang them to him, her hand rubbing gentle circles on his back. Finally she came to the one she loved most of all.

"Jesus loves me, this I know..."

She felt the power of those simple words, prayed Gabe felt it as well. *He loves you, Gabe. He loves you...*

"Little ones to Him belong..."

Big ones too, Gabe. Especially big ones with terrified little ones deep inside them. Little ones who have been broken and beaten down until they're too afraid to come out, to lift their faces to the sun and laugh again.

"They are weak, but He is strong..."

Come out, Gabe. Please, let that little boy inside come out and see that God is here, ready to protect him...

"He doesn't."

She stared at Gabe's choked voice. "Who doesn't?" She stroked his face, and he leaned his cheek into her hand.

"God. He doesn't love me. He can't."

O Jesus. What pain he must be in to believe that. "Gabe, of course He does—"

He pulled away from her, and she could just see his face in the moonlight pouring in through the window.

"How can He? Look what I've done to you. To us." His voice caught, cracked. "How can He love me when I even hate myself?" His eyes sought hers in the darkness. "When I've made you hate me."

The hollow, aching words tore at her, and she had to swallow several times before she could answer. Fear took hold of her, squeezing so tight she could hardly breathe.

She knew her silence was hurting him, and she reached out, spreading her hands on his arms, wanting to make some kind of connection, to let him know she was trying. She wanted to respond, but she couldn't. Not yet.

He flinched, but she understood. He wasn't rejecting her touch—he was stunned by it. She hadn't touched him, hadn't let him touch her, for longer than she could remember.

Gabe went still as she let her fingers trail down his arms to his hands, as she closed her fingers over his.

And still she remained silent. How could she give him the reassurance he needed? Was she supposed to just pretend the last few years never happened, that he hadn't taken her heart, her soul, in his hands and shattered them with those terrible words that night?

Yes.

She caught her breath and looked to the ceiling. *I can't...I can't...*

And as though they had been waiting in the wings for just the right cue, Ami's and Conrad's words walked onto the stage of her mind: *"Open yourself, Renee. Open yourself to the*

*One who seeks to fill you… You've embraced the enemies of your
soul and they're destroying you….put those things out, open your
eyes and heart…embrace truth."*

Truth. What was the truth?

But even as she asked that, she knew. She knew it as
surely as she knew the man sitting in front of her was terrified, fully expecting her to speak the final words of death to
their marriage.

"Oh, Gabe…" Her throat was thick with sorrow, regret. "I
don't hate you."

Silence. Then soft, quivering amazement. "You don't?"

She squeezed his fingers, leaned forward to press her lips
to the backs of his hands. Strong hands. Hands she used to
love to watch…used to love the tender feel of.

Her tears came then, a torrent of regret, of loss that she
didn't even fully understand. "I'm so sorry, Gabe. I'm sorry I
made you think…made you feel…"

His fingers pressed into hers. "Please, what I said to you
that night…"

She shook her head, but he went on.

"Those stupid, angry things I said to you. I pushed you
away. Please…please forgive me."

She couldn't stand it any longer. Couldn't stand the distance. Couldn't stand not being with him. Really with him.
She pulled her hands free from his and shifted forward. His
arms opened to receive her, and she buried her face in his
chest. For a moment his arms stayed open, as though suspended around her, then, as if he couldn't help himself, they
closed, embraced her, cradled her.

"I've missed you." The words whispered through her hair.
"Oh, Rennie, I've missed you."

"I missed you, too." It was all she could manage around
the emotions crowding her throat. Now it was he who
stroked her hair, her back, pressed soft kisses to her temple.

And when his lips found hers, when the kiss deepened,

for the first time in a very long time, she didn't pull away. She leaned into him, surrendering, seeking, longing to find, just one more time, that place where they used to live. That place of love and laughter and sweet communion.

A place she thought she'd lost forever.

26

Our real blessings often appear to us in the shape of
pains, losses, and disappointments; but let us have
patience and we soon shall see them in their proper figures.

JOSEPH ADDISON

I will wait for the LORD to help us, though
he has turned away... My only hope is in him.

ISAIAH 8:17

AUGUST 1991

RENEE STOOD SURVEYING THE TABLE. IT WAS PERFECT.
Just one more thing to do.

She struck the match and lit the two slender tapers in the
center of the table, then went to lower the lights. There. She was
ready.

The clock on the wall chimed, and she went to check the
steaks one more time. She slid the oven rack out from beneath the
broiler and sliced one of the thick pieces of meat. Gabe was going
to love this.

Steak and potatoes—his favorite. Well, nothing was too good
for tonight.

She went back to the living room, sinking onto the couch,
leaning her head back against the soft material. Music drifted
through the room, and Renee let it dance over her.

Why can't I relax?

Because you've waited so long for this night to come.

Yes, she'd waited a long time. Years. But it had been right to wait. She and Gabe hadn't been ready to start a family, not until just recently. She was still young enough to have kids without too much risk. And things might not be perfect between her and Gabe, but what relationship was?

She could hardly believe all the years they'd endured of emotional tug-of-war. She had considered giving up, lots of times. But for all that Gabe drove her nuts, she knew she didn't want to leave him. She loved him.

Speaking of Gabe...

She glanced at the clock, willing the knotted muscles in her shoulders to relax. *He'll be here. We talked about it. He'll be here. He wouldn't forget this. He knows what it means to me.*

With a nod, Renee leaned her head back again, listening for his key in the lock—and hearing only the ticking of the clock.

She was sitting on the couch, arms around her knees, when Gabe came home. One look her way, and he knew something was wrong. She had that pinched look...as if she had a headache starting somewhere at the back of her eyes.

Great. What had he done now?

He didn't say anything. Just went to put his lunch box on the kitchen counter and shed his jacket. *One time...* The thought rattled around in his head. *One time I'd like to come home and not find some kind of problem waiting for me.*

He went back to the living room and lowered himself onto the couch beside her, but she stiffened. *Uh-oh. Bad sign.* He shifted, giving her more space. He'd learned the hard way not to crowd her when she was like this. Or to touch her. It never helped.

Funny, he'd always thought a man was supposed to comfort a woman when she was upset. Do the man thing and fold her in his arms, let her know she was sheltered, protected. Didn't Renee tell him that was one of the things she'd first loved about him? His strength?

Well, she didn't love it so much now.

"You're late."

Her hushed words set the warning bells clanging in his head. Quiet was not good. When she got quiet, she was really steamed. He didn't even try to explain, to tell her about the flat tire or the crazy traffic that had almost flattened him while he fixed the tire. She wouldn't care. There was only one thing she wanted to hear.

"I'm sorry."

She turned to him, and he saw the emotions swirling in those green eyes. He loved her eyes. Even when she was angry—as she most definitely was now—they were beautiful, bright, expressive. They made him ache deep inside.

"We were supposed to talk tonight. I fixed a nice dinner…"

He cast a glance at the dining room table, and his heart sank another notch. Great. Candles…the china… "Ah, hon, I'm sorr—"

She stood with such abrupt force that he almost fell back on the couch. He followed her as she marched into the dining room and started stacking the plates, snatching up the silverware. Her movements were abrupt, jerky, like she had to fight not to throw everything in his face.

He frowned. What was going on?

"Rennie…" He reached out to let his touch tell her how sorry he was, but the moment his fingers caressed her arm, she exploded. The plates and silverware rained down on him, and he protected his face with his arms. A slamming door told him she'd stormed into the bedroom.

"What in the…?" He gave a spoon a frustrated kick, taking some satisfaction when it nearly imbedded itself in the plaster of the wall. Muttering through clenched teeth, he stooped and cleaned up the mess. He made sure to gather the knives off the table and put them in the sink. No point leaving any weapons within easy reach.

When he opened the bedroom door a crack, he saw her on the bed, staring at the ceiling, eyes wide and bleak. She looked so…hopeless. Worry vied with anger as he came into the room and stood looking down at her.

"Renee, what's going on?"

She didn't look at him. "You were *supposed* to come home early."

Her bitter emphasis set his nerves—and his teeth—on edge.

"We were *supposed* to have a nice dinner. We were supposed to talk—" she paused, but only long enough to glare at him with burning, reproachful eyes—"about starting a family."

That hit him straight in the gut, and as he stood there silent, understanding dawned on her features, and she jerked into a sitting position. "You…you *forgot!*"

Her disbelief raked at him, scoring his conscience. The implication was clear: How could he have forgotten something so important?

Trouble was, he didn't have an answer. Not one he was ready to give her, anyway. So he said the only thing he could. "I'm sorry."

Well, what else could he say? That he'd forgotten because the last thing in the world he wanted to do was talk about this again?

She stared at him, and something in that intent look sent a momentary chill through him. But then the anger came, sweeping aside everything. Everything but resentment.

What right did she have to look at him that way? How many times did they have to talk about this? She wasn't stupid. So why was she still pushing an issue that should be settled? What would it take for her to get it?

There weren't going to be any kids. Not now. Not next year.

Not ever.

The silence between them stretched on, growing heavier with each passing moment. A steady stream of things to say floated through Renee's heart and mind—questions, condemnations, pleas. But they were all trapped inside, tangled in the emotions raging through her, emotions so desperate and intense she couldn't even sort through them.

She'd never seen that look in his eyes before. That hard-edged, uncompromising glare. But she couldn't deny what it communicated. Stark understanding settled over her, heavy, choking...

God... God...

It was all the prayer she could muster. Just His name, over and over, pleading. Almost against her will, the words she couldn't let herself believe slipped from her suddenly numb lips. "You don't want children."

Gabe's only reaction was a flicker of impatience, as though she were a child uttering some obvious fact. Her fingers clenched against the urge to slap him. How *dare* he look at her like that? How dare he shred her heart, destroy her hopes, then look at her as though she didn't even have the right to question him?

Their gazes sparred, parried, and finally he gave a shrug. "No."

One word. That was all he could give her? One lousy word? No explanation. No apology. No acknowledgment that he should have told her this little tidbit of news long ago— like before they got married.

I didn't know. Sweet Jesus, I didn't know.

And then, snapping at the heels of her heart cry, came an appalling realization: *But You did.*

She closed her eyes against the sight of Gabe's rigid stance, his tight jaw, those hard eyes so full of disdain. She let her lids form a wall between them, blocking him out. If only she could as easily escape the thoughts striking at her like angry bees roused from their hive. Cold thoughts. Thoughts that grabbed her and shook her.

God knew the desires of your heart. He created you, didn't He? Gave you the family and childhood that you so love? He knew how much you wanted a family, how you've always wanted children to raise as your parents raised you.

As though to make her loss complete, the hopes and dreams she'd treasured as a child danced once across the screen of her mind, each scene dumping the stinging salt of reality on her raw, wounded soul.

She saw herself cuddling a tiny baby, singing the songs she'd so loved to hear as a toddler, retelling the stories of love and faith her parents had told her…

God knew…

She saw her child's glowing eyes, heard the lilting laughter as the toddler ran to her—just as she used to do with her dad—and jumped into her arms, sliding chubby arms around her neck and hugging her as Renee caught her.

God knew…

Everything within her fought against that terrible truth. God had let this happen. He'd let her fall in love with a man…marry him…struggle and fight to stay married…and all the while He'd known full well that in doing so, she was killing her fondest dream as completely as if she'd laid it on an altar, raised the ceremonial knife, and plunged it deep.

God…O God…how could You let this happen?

The acrid taste of betrayal burned in her throat, her mouth, and she swallowed hard.

"Renee…"

At the broken whisper she stared at her husband. Her husband. The one who was supposed to cherish her…to love and honor her…to place her above all others…

The one who had taken her dream from her.

Sudden clarity swept her. God didn't kill her dream. Nor did she. Gabe did. It was his fault.

And she'd given him the power to do it. She chose him. She married him. She had been fool enough to trust him.

Renee turned away from him. "Go away."

"What?"

She didn't look at him. Couldn't bear doing so. It wasn't that she hated him. She almost wished she did. That would have been better than the numbing emptiness that seemed to be invading every cell. "Go away, Gabe. Just…go away."

Gabe stared hard at his wife. He had never heard that tone from her before. That flat, empty monotone. As though no matter what he said or did, it wouldn't be enough.

Could never be enough.

I've lost her.

He pushed the thought away almost as soon as it formed. *Don't be stupid! Renee is your wife. She loves you.* He refused to acknowledge the desperation in the inner reassurances. *She just needs time.*

As though of its own volition, his hand reached out toward her, to touch her silken hair, to make some kind of connection between them, but he caught himself…and his outstretched fingers curled, clenching into fists. The last thing she would want right now was his touch.

Without another word, he turned and walked away from her, through the apartment, and out the door. But as he descended the stairs to the outside door and stepped into the cool evening air, he couldn't escape the picture in his mind— the image of Renee's face when she finally understood what he'd been trying for so long to tell her.

His gut constricted. He'd known the emotions that filled his wife's eyes and shadowed her features. He'd seen them often enough in the face looking back at him from the mirror.

Despair. Desperation. A gnawing, endless sorrow that threatened to consume everything...

Oh, yes. He knew them. Far too well. Had known them all his life. And he hated them. Prayed to escape them.

A harsh, humorless laugh slipped out. He could no more escape them than he could the anger. And every time that anger surged, every time it filled and overflowed him, he knew his worst fears had come true.

He was just like his father.

Gabe had never said so, never spoken the words, but he shouldn't have to. Renee had seen...he'd watched her back away, her face paling. She should understand. Should know they couldn't subject a child to that.

Too bad he didn't smoke any longer. Times like this he missed the calming effects smoking always seemed to have. But he knew those effects were temporary. And he needed something real to help with this.

He shook his head as he slid into the car, steeling himself against the sickening sensation that was squeezing his gut into knots. The sensation that he was an utter, complete failure. As a man. As a husband.

"She'd be better off without me."

But even as he spit the words into the darkness, he knew it didn't matter. He wouldn't leave. Not ever. Because the love they shared, as flawed and painful as it was at times, was better than the nothing he knew he'd have—and be—without her.

You know, I try so hard not to upset or hurt or anger him, but he ends up that way all the same. I try to listen, to understand when he's frustrated and fed up, to calm and reassure him...then I end up feeling drained and tired of hearing complaint after complaint. Maybe I'm trying too hard. I don't want him to stop sharing, but there's got to be a happy medium somewhere.

I thought things were going to be better, but they aren't. I thought we were on the road to healing, and maybe we are, but if so, then why do we keep tripping over each other? One step forward, three steps back. I'm so tired of those steps back.

I have so much to learn, and I need him to help me survive the learning. Whether he believes it or not, I love him.

My spirit has become dry because it forgets to feed on You.

JOHN OF THE CROSS

*Though the Lord gave you adversity for food and
affliction for drink, he will still be with you to teach you.*

ISAIAH 30:20

FEBRUARY 1992

"I JUST DON'T KNOW WHAT TO DO ANYMORE."

Grace watched Renee over the rim of her teacup. Fatigue had
come to settle in dark circles under her eyes; her face was pale
and pinched. How she'd changed since the first time Grace had
seen her, nearly ten years ago at a women's retreat. Then Renee's
cheeks had glowed with color and she had smiled so easily. She'd
been like a child in her ability to enjoy life.

Renee took another sip of her coffee, cupping the mug in her
hands as though trying to draw warmth and strength from it.
"Sometimes I feel like Gabe and I have come so far, like we're
doing so well. It took us a long time to get past Gabe's refusal to
have children, but we did it. Now we talk and even laugh sometimes. But it never lasts."

The pain in Renee's voice struck Grace's heart. Their friendship had blossomed—at first, anyway—because they both loved

to laugh and make others laugh. Which they used to do, often. But a few years after they met, Grace had seen a change come over Renee. It was as though she carried some deep wound inside her, something that wouldn't heal, that festered and spread until it stole the sparkle from her eyes, the smile from her face.

Grace had been worried about her—and Gabe, for that matter—for a long time. Then came that terrible day when Grace had answered her doorbell and found Renee—or a shadow of Renee—standing on her doorstep. Grace had ushered her inside, and her young friend's grief had come pouring out. Gabe telling her to get a life. That they'd never have children. Grace had listened, found herself growing angry.

Thank heaven God stopped her before she got too far down that road.

That kind of anger stems from fear, child, and from pain. Don't judge what you don't know.

Grace listened to Renee, talked with her, prayed with her. She kept on doing so over the years, watching as Renee found her footing in a career, found good friends with whom she could share common interests. On the surface, she seemed to have it all now.

But one look into those shadowed eyes put the lie to that notion.

Father God, she's so worn down. It's so sad to see her like this.

Renee set her coffee mug down with careful precision on the coaster, then turned her green eyes to Grace. "You always seem happy. You and Oren, you laugh so much, tease so much. No one could ever doubt you love each other."

Renee's sigh seemed to bear the weight of a multitude of sorrows. "Why can't Gabe and I be like that? Why can't we get past the garbage, the anger and frustrations, the little things that drive us both crazy, and just hold on to the good things?"

Grace saw the longing in Renee's face, heard it in her voice. "Because there are good things, Grace. In Gabe. In us. There's so much that's good…or that could be, if we'd just let it."

Grace set her cup down and considered her friend. "May I ask you a question?"

She nodded. "Of course. You know I'm an open book to you."

Grace knew Renee believed that, but she also knew it wasn't true. Not entirely. *Give me wisdom, Lord.* "What do you want from Gabe?"

The younger woman stared down at her hands. "I want what any woman wants from her husband: respect. A man who will stand in the gap for me, who treats me like I matter."

She gripped her hands together. Now that the words had started, they came in a heated rush, tumbling over each other as they poured from her heart. "I want him to cherish me. I want to know I can depend on him and trust him. I want him to be my friend as well as my husband."

Grace caught the hardening in Renee's tone but held her silence. Renee's hands moved to grip the arms of her chair, and Grace watched the knuckles turn white.

"I want him to talk to me like I've got a brain in my head, not treat me like some kind of idiot. I want him to be real, to be who he really is, instead of always playing a part, maintaining an image. I want him to talk to me, not yell at me. I want him to treat me with kindness, not like I'm a waste of his time and energy. And I want to know I'm more important to him than his stupid anger is."

Resentment, anger, hurt, disappointment—Grace saw them all burning in Renee's eyes.

"I want him to be the spiritual head of our home, like he's *supposed* to be. I want him…I want…" She paused, as though catching her breath, then fell silent. She stared at the floor for a moment, then shook her head. "I don't want much, do I?"

Grace chuckled. "No more than the rest of us. We may

not admit it, but we'd like our husbands to be a blend of Solomon, John Wayne, and Cary Grant."

Renee's lips twitched. "I'll take him."

"You've already got him." At her blank stare, Grace leaned forward. "Don't you see? Most of us already are married to the very men we long for, but we don't see it. We focus on what he isn't rather than what God is making him, and we ignore the fact that not one of us can be all that the other person wants us to be. Even Oren—" Grace couldn't help smiling at this—"as wonderful as he is, isn't as wonderful as I'd like him to be."

"But you guys are so great together."

"We are now." Grace folded her hands. "You know what I want to know?" She went on before Renee could respond. "I want to know what idiot came up with the idea that our main goal in life is happiness."

A small smile quirked at the edge of Renee's mouth.

"And I want to know what genius decided the best source of happiness is another human."

Renee's laughter broke forth, and Grace joined her. "Talk about the impossible dream! Expecting another person to be able to make you happy—"

"Meet your needs—" Renee supplied.

"Fulfill your dreams—"

"*And* look good doing it!"

"Has to be the biggest leap of faith anyone has ever taken." Their laughter was a welcome relief, and Grace let them enjoy it together before going on. "Renee, you know as well as I do, no one can make you happy. Happiness—true, lasting happiness—isn't found in another person." Grace knew the agreement she saw in Renee's eyes was probably about to fade. "Any more than it can be found in marriage."

Renee stiffened at that, but Grace knew she couldn't stop now. "It's a mistake to think marriage is about happiness." Renee leaned forward, and Grace held up a hand to stall the protest quivering on the younger woman's lips. "Just a minute, let me finish."

With obvious reluctance, Renee settled back in her chair.

Guide my words, Father. "I'm not saying we won't find some happiness in marriage, not at all. It's definitely a by-product of a marriage grounded in God. But the goal of marriage, that has a lot more to do with obedience than happiness."

"Obedience?" Renee's tone was as pinched as her features. "How so?"

"The Bible makes it clear that a couple's relationship in marriage is meant to be a reflection of God's relationship to His bride, the church. All our instructions as husbands and wives are compared to Christ's relationship with the church. The Bible even goes so far as to say that if a husband doesn't treat his wife as he should—as Christ treated the church, being willing to give His life for her—then that husband's prayers won't be answered."

Renee lifted a brow at that, and Grace let herself smile. "I thought you'd like that part. But there are just as many warnings to wives as to husbands. More, in fact. Warnings that we are to submit to our husbands as we do to the Lord. Because he is God's representative in our households."

Apparently that was too much. Renee came out of her chair, and Grace leaned back, watching her friend pace, knowing the struggle that fueled her furious steps about the room.

"That's ridiculous, Grace. You're telling me I'm supposed to treat Gabe like...like I would treat *Christ?*"

"No, I'm not saying that at all."

Renee fixed her with a glare. "Then what...?"

"The Bible says it." Grace lay her hands along the arms of her chair. "I know it's not easy to take—"

"Now there's an understatement."

Grace ignored the muttered comment. "And I'm not even

saying Gabe deserves to be treated that way."

That stopped Renee's pacing. She leveled a look at Grace. "That's good, because he's *nothing* like Christ."

"No, but then neither are you." Grace knew she was going out on a limb with her quiet response, but she also knew if she was really going to love Renee, to be a true friend, she had to speak the truth to her.

Renee's face flushed, and Grace wondered if she would walk out. But after a moment, the tightness around Renee's mouth eased, and she came to slump on the couch.

Grace let the silence continue, wanting to give Renee the time she needed to work through the emotions churning inside her. Finally Renee turned to her. "No—" she chewed the side of her mouth as she spoke—"no, I'm not."

Grace leaned forward to lay a hand on her friend's arm. "And neither am I. None of us is. Don't you see? None of us deserves to be treated the way we want to be treated. We're all broken and struggling and muddling through. That's why we need to focus on the only One who truly deserves our kindness, our service, our love."

Renee stared at her hands. "Christ."

"Christ," Grace echoed. "Don't you see? When we marry, it's foolish to think our spouse is going to meet our needs. That's God's job, and His alone. What God calls us to in marriage is to serve our spouse."

Grace's heart sank when Renee shook her head.

"It's not that hard, Renee. All we need to do is let Christ live in us, in our thoughts and actions. It's the old 'What would Jesus do?' way of looking at things. We let *Him* love our spouse through us."

"I've tried that!" Renee took hold of her coffee mug and lifted it to her lips, her actions abrupt, jerky. "I've tried to 'die to self—'" she emphasized each word, her sarcasm painfully evident—"over and over. For all the good it's done me." She took a sip of the coffee, though Grace knew it had to be cold.

Cold like her heart, Lord. She felt the sinking ache of despair. *I'm not getting through.*

"Take a different tack, Gracie."

Oren told her that often. How well he knew her tendency to keep hitting at something over and over, regardless of the effect. She nodded. *Thank you, dear.*

She took hold of her teacup, lifted it to her lips, and took a sip of the now-tepid liquid. She cradled the delicate china in her hands. So beautifully formed, so fragile.

Like our spirits if we don't keep them grounded in truth.

Of course. To communicate truth, go to the source.

"Renee, remember in Bible study when we talked about Israel wanting a king to follow rather than God?"

Renee pulled back, and Grace could almost see how her friend's mind scrambled to follow the shift in conversation.

"I...think so."

"Israel wanted to be like the other nations; God wanted them to trust only in Him. But He let them have what they thought they wanted. They looked to man—first a king, then to other countries, Egypt and Assyria—to uphold them. To be their allies."

Renee nodded. "Right. And all they got was disappointment and pain. Because no one could give them what they were looking for but God."

"So who are your allies?"

A frown brought the younger woman's brows together. "My allies?"

"Whom do you trust? What tells you how things should be?"

"Well...God, of course."

Grace didn't take her gaze from Renee's. "I know you mean that. I've seen how you long to follow Him and do what's right. But Renee, is God really the One you turn to when you're angry? Or do you turn to your dreams? Your expectations?"

Renee shifted. "Doesn't everyone? Don't we all come into relationships with those things?"

"Of course we do. That's normal, because we're human." *Let her hear me, Lord…let her understand.* "But we're not called to stay with what's normal, Renee. We're called to godly living, and that's about as not-normal as it gets."

Renee's misery was evident in the droop of her mouth. "I don't understand…"

For a moment frustration filled Grace, not with Renee, but with herself, with her inability to say what was on her heart in a way her friend could understand.

Give me the words, Lord…

"You've told me about your childhood, how wonderful it was, how amazing your parents are."

A smile eased the tension in Renee's features. "They're the best."

"You've told me many times you consider them a gift."

"Yes."

"What if your childhood was God's way of preparing you for your marriage? What if He gave it to you not just for you, but for Gabe as well?"

Renee stilled. "You mean…"

"What if those precious years growing up weren't about then, or even about you finding that kind of life when you were an adult? What if they were about now? About grounding you? Getting your roots down deep in the soil of what's true because God knew you'd have to stand in the face of the world's lies."

Renee pushed at her coffee mug with a finger. "They're not just in the world, Grace. I've had Christians tell me they can't believe God wants me to be this unhappy."

"And?"

"What they were saying never rang true. Not in the face of the cross, or the call to follow Him. And the Bible is pretty clear. Following Christ means joining the fellowship of suffering, not the happy hour."

Her quiet words lifted Grace's heart. There was so much wisdom in Renee, if she could only see it. Hold on to it. "Why haven't you left Gabe?"

"Because God hasn't released me from my commitment."

"So you're hanging in there, suffering for the cause?" Grace had figured her words would irritate Renee, and the flash in her friend's eyes told her she was right.

"Now you sound like Gabe, telling me I'm getting my jollies out of being some kind of martyr. But that's not true."

Grace studied Renee for a moment, taking in the stiff set of her shoulders, the glower hardening her features. "I think it's time for you to give up."

If she'd wanted to stun her young friend, she'd succeeded.

"You what?"

"There's something keeping you from finding that joy you talked about. Something that's holding you down, burying you under sorrow and pain, resentment and anger. You talk about Gabe's anger all the time, but I wonder if you see your own. You need to do so…and to give it up."

Renee blinked at her. "Easier said than done, Grace."

"I know. But dear one, don't you see?" She leaned forward. "You've spent all this time waiting for Gabe to change, and he hasn't. Maybe it's time to stop focusing on him and look to yourself instead. That doesn't mean Gabe isn't wrong; it just means he isn't yours to change."

Tears trailed down Renee's face now, and Grace wanted to go to her, to take her in her arms and comfort her as she would a child. But she couldn't. Not yet.

She held her hands in front of her and curled her fingers into a fist. "You've got a death grip on how you think things should be between you. You've held on to your hopes and dreams until they've become a club to Gabe and a prison to you. If you'll only stop clutching them—" her fingers relaxed, unfolded—"you can receive the real wonders God has for you. The joy He seeks to bring both you and Gabe."

Renee stared at Grace's open hands. "Unless a seed falls into the ground and dies…"

The whispered words resonated with an understanding borne of pain, and Grace lowered her hands to lay them on Renee's clasped fingers. "Yes. Stop looking to others to fill our needs and seek instead to serve them. And do you know what? When we do that, Christ gives us so much more than we ever imagined."

"But what if nothing changes?" Renee's ragged whisper was heavy, tortured. "What if Gabe is still Gabe, and I'm still miserable?"

Grace wished she had an answer, but she didn't. Renee wasn't the only one in the marriage; Gabe could always refuse God's call and stay closed to Him, to Renee. She sighed.

"Gabe is in God's hands, Renee."

When her friend started to protest, Grace held up her hand, giving her a soft smile to let her know she wasn't being flip or unkind. "There's only one person here that you can change, and that's you. It's God's job to reach Gabe's heart and change him, not yours."

"You make it sound so easy."

"It's never easy." *It's not, Lord. You and I both know it's the hardest thing anyone can ever do.* "But it's right. Let God be God, and Renee be Renee." She lifted her teacup for another sip. "It works much better that way."

Renee sat in her car, hands on the steering wheel, staring at nothing.

"Let God be God, and Renee be Renee."

The truth in those simple words resonated through her. *I want to. Lord…I want to.*

She knew so much of what Grace had said to her today was right. Especially what she'd said about Renee's childhood, about her parents' marriage—and about her expectations. Renee *had* been holding up her parents and their relationship as a picture of what she and Gabe should be.

But that wasn't fair. She and Gabe weren't her mother and father. They were very different people. Their relationship couldn't possibly be the same. Shouldn't be.

She forced herself to release the stranglehold her fingers had on the steering wheel, then stared at her fingers. *If only I could do that with Gabe, with my marriage—release the stranglehold I've had on all of it. But how?*

"Give up." Grace's words had plowed into her, shaking her more than she cared to admit. When Grace had explained what she meant, it had only made it worse. *Give up my hopes. My dreams. I thought I had. Long ago.*

Apparently not.

"Show me what I'm holding back, Lord. And show me how to let go. I can't do it without Your help." Her voice was soft and pleading in the stillness of the car. "But if I do that, Gabe had better make some changes, too—"

"Let God be God, and Renee be Renee."

She bit off the argument rising within her. Let God be God. In other words, get out of His way. With a slow nod, she pulled the keys from the ignition.

"Okay." She glanced out the side window, only vaguely aware of the flowering bush beside the car, of the bright blossoms dancing in the breeze. "I'll try to do my part, and trust that You'll do yours."

All she had to do was figure out exactly what her part was.

Let me out, God!

I don't want to be here, don't want to deal with this...with him...one more time. I don't think I can handle this. Not any of it. I'm trying so hard to keep trusting, to hold on to the peace and love that was there once. Long ago.

But it's getting harder and harder.

Can't you at least get Satan off our backs? We have the power through YOU to defeat him. So why do we go through so much struggle, so much desperation? Why can't we get past ourselves? What's it going to take, God?

And will I survive it, whatever it is?

28

God wins his greatest victories through apparent defeats.

ANONYMOUS

"Sin is waiting to attack and destroy you."

GENESIS 4:7

JUNE 24, 1992

GABE HAD NEVER FELT SO LOST IN HIS LIFE.

He knew right from wrong. He knew what he should and shouldn't do. He'd never had trouble following that line.

Until Jennifer Jeremiah.

She was young and beautiful and more open than anyone Gabe had ever met.

He remembered the first time he saw her. He'd been called into her department to fix a faulty lamp. She talked with him as he worked, leaning her elbows on her desk, smiling with open ease.

Women had flirted with Gabe before. He was well acquainted with their subtle signals of interest, the unspoken invitation to forbidden territory. He'd never had any trouble turning away from them. Sure, he and Renee had problems, but he still knew what he had with her was something special. Something he never wanted to betray.

But what he felt from Jennifer wasn't flirtation. Instead, it had been like finding an old friend he hadn't even known he had. They seemed to speak the same language. She not only heard him, but understood him. And respected what he had to say.

They'd talked that first day until a call came in on her phone, and Gabe was startled when he realized how long he'd been there. He made a hasty retreat, returning her easy wave, slightly embarrassed by how time seemed to stall while they were together.

He had run into her several times since then. Her smile was always welcoming, and before long their conversations shifted from weather and "how ya doin'?" to issues as broad as politics, religion—and finally relationships.

Gabe shared things with Jennifer that he'd never shared with anyone before. Things about Renee and their struggles. About the guilt that ate away at him, the regret that he was so far away from the man Renee needed and wanted.

He told her how he'd become whatever he needed to in order to win Renee. How he'd played the role to perfection...until after the wedding. Then he let his real self come out. The self that still couldn't seem to get past the anger, the sense that he just wasn't good enough for Renee. For anyone.

Jennifer listened without condemning him or Renee. That was amazing, to find someone who accepted the bad with the good, never passing judgment. She had an uncanny ability to see to the heart of an issue and ask seemingly innocent questions that stopped Gabe cold, turning on the sudden light of realization.

As crazy as it seemed, without ever meeting Renee, Jennifer became a friend to them both. She helped Gabe understand Renee's side, gave him insights on the way his wife's mind and heart worked. She didn't offer advice unless he specifically asked for it. Even then, she was careful with her words, her counsel.

Gabe had made a point a long time ago of not touching women at work, not even as friends. He didn't hug, didn't put a hand on their arms, didn't do anything that could be misconstrued. Thankfully, Jennifer had been as circumspect as he.

Gabe looked forward to their times together. More than that, he found himself protecting those times with a fierce determination.

He had considered telling Renee about Jennifer—several times, in fact. But something always held him back. Which wasn't a problem. There was nothing between him and Jennifer that could or should bother Renee. Besides, she'd probably just misunderstand and they'd end up in just one more pointless argument.

If she knew about her, she'd probably ask you to stop spending time with Jennifer.

Gabe shoved the thought back into the recesses from which it had sprung. All the more reason not to tell Renee. No point in putting her through that kind of emotional turmoil when there really was nothing to worry about.

Or so Gabe told himself—and kept telling himself. So he'd been telling himself all the way in to work that morning. For some reason, he'd been feeling...strange. Apprehensive.

Like he used to feel each night just before his dad came home.

Snap out of it, Roman. He tossed his lunch box on his worktable. *You're not doing anything wrong. She's a friend. That's it. Period. No reason for guilt here.*

Too bad his inner assertions lacked any real conviction. He knew why, too. Lately, things had changed.

It's no big deal. He shoved his way through the doors of the building. So Jennifer had let her hand rest on his arm once a few days ago. So what?

It happened more than once, and you know it.

Okay, twice maybe. Three or four times, tops. And so what that he'd let himself take her hand to help her out of her chair.

She didn't exactly need any help. And you didn't exactly let go right away.

Big deal! Gabe smacked the door to his office and stalked in. *If that's all the evidence you have—*

He halted. A white envelope sat on top of his worktable. He picked it up. The writing was feminine, but it wasn't Renee's.

His pulse pounded an erratic beat in his veins as he opened the envelope and pulled out one white piece of paper.

The first thing he saw was Jennifer's signature at the bottom, and a wave of pleasure washed over him. He hadn't received a card or note from anyone in a long time. Renee used to send him cards when they were dating, and in the first few years of their marriage she often slipped little love notes into his lunch, his coat pockets. But that had stopped long ago.

Which probably explained why he was suddenly feeling really, really good. After all these years of seeing nothing but disappointment on Renee's face, after all the years of battles and being pushed aside…ignored…

He thought he'd grown invisible. Just like when he was a kid. Not worth seeing or noticing.

Now, here was this note, saying he wasn't invisible at all. He mattered to someone. Someone really nice.

He eased into his chair and started to read. The pounding in his veins quickened, grew louder, until he felt as if he had a sledgehammer inside his chest, his head. He looked away, trying to swallow with a throat suddenly gone dry. Then he read the words again. But he didn't think they made any more sense the second time around.

Gabe,

I wanted to talk to you in person, but I couldn't. I knew if I looked at you, saw the hurt in your eyes, I'd never be able to do what I need to do. Your friendship has meant so much to me.

Too much. That's the problem.

Gabe, I believe God brought us together to help each other. But I always knew there was an element of danger in our friendship, because I like you so much. Lately I've found myself thinking of you a lot more than I should. And I've found myself wishing…well, that things were different.

I think you knew something was changing in me, in the way I was treating you. I could see it in your eyes when I touched you. I saw something else, too. I saw the same longing I felt. That's when I knew I had to step away.

Please know this is the hardest thing I've ever had to do. I care about you, a great deal. But I know God isn't pleased with the way I've let that care grow, the direction it's taken. So I need to ask your forgiveness. And I need to tell you I can't see you anymore. I won't become a barrier to you and your wife. That isn't fair to any of us. And it isn't right.

I know this probably won't help much, but I will be praying for you. And for Renee. I hope you guys can work things out. God may have made you and me friends for a time—and I'll always cherish the time we shared—but He's made you and Renee husband and wife forever.

I love you.

Jennifer

His fingers closed around the paper, as though protecting it from the thoughts coursing through him. God had made him and Renee husband and wife? Technically, it was true. But was he really married? Did he *have* a wife?

Bitterness stole the breath from his lungs, squeezing his chest until he almost cried out. A wife? Renee hadn't been a wife to him for years. When was the last time she'd looked at him with even an ounce of the affection and respect he saw every day in Jennifer? And when was the last time Renee had let him touch her, let him show her any physical affection without either grimacing or flinching?

Oh, sure, there was a short time a few months ago when things were better. Renee had actually opened up to him again. He'd been so sure things would be better. But it hadn't taken long for them to end up in the same old place again.

Angry. Cold. Distant.

Gabe crushed the note in his fist. Jennifer cared about him. And she'd wanted to care more. That knowledge ate away at his gut, feeding the anger raging inside. Because he *wanted* her to care. He wanted to feel special, respected...the center of someone's world. Wanted to be what he used to be to Renee.

You mean what you told her you didn't want to be any longer, what you couldn't stand?

Gabe shoved the note into his pants pocket then pushed out of his chair. He grabbed his work belt and a handful of work orders and left the room before he threw something. Didn't he have the right to be happy, too? To be himself with someone? Renee wasn't interested in being that someone. She'd made that abundantly clear for a lot of years. She didn't need him. Didn't even seem to like him.

All good things came from the hand of God, right? Surely God knew how empty Gabe's life had become...how far Renee was from what a real wife should be...how far their relationship was from what a real marriage should be. And God was merciful and loving, right? So who was to say He hadn't brought Jennifer into Gabe's life at just the right moment, just when he was finally ready to open the flood-gates he'd kept closed for far too long?

He should just march up to Jennifer's office, pull her out of her chair, and tell her it was over with Renee. He was ready to start again, with someone who really saw him and cared about him!

Gabe caught his reflection in an office window as he passed, and what he saw in his own gaze startled him. Anger. Resolution. Abandon...

It was the reflection of a man about to go over the edge.

His stride broke and he put a hand on the wall, steadying himself. *God, please...*

The angry thoughts that had been coursing through him had faded to a faint echo, and he tried to close his mind against them entirely. Had he gone completely nuts? What was he *thinking?* Leave Renee?

He might as well rip his heart out and leave it lying on the floor.

Jennifer had been right to walk away from him. Right to remind him that he was a married man. *Happily* notwithstanding, he was married.

And faithful notwithstanding, he still loved his wife.

Lord, I came so close...

More shaken than he could ever remember being, he turned and made his way back to the boiler room. He wrote his boss a quick note, saying he was going home, he was sick.

And so he was, he thought as he left the building and walked to his car. Sick to the core of his faithless, foolish soul.

It's over.

I could have taken anything, God...anything but this.

29

When one has smashed everything around oneself,
one has also smashed oneself.

MARIE D'AGOULT

Let there be tears for the wrong things you have done.
Let there be sorrow and deep grief.

JAMES 4:9

JUNE 26, 1992

THERE WAS SOMETHING SOOTHING ABOUT THE DARKNESS.

A stillness, an enveloping silence that formed a protective barrier between Renee and the world. It was as if everything and everyone else were gone, and all that existed was this room, the slowly dying fire, the dancing light of the flames on the walls, the ceiling.

If only she could stay here, cocooned in the night, protected, sheltered.

She pulled the blanket tighter about herself, rubbing her cheek against its softness, drawing in the fragrance of wood smoke and the out-of-doors. The fragrance of childhood.

I want to be a child again...

Tears, quick and hot, pricked at her eyes, and she closed her lids against them. She didn't want to cry. She was tired of crying. Her eyes were so swollen now that they ached until she wanted to scream against the pain. Ached with such intensity that she was sure it would never stop. The pain would never stop. It would just keep growing until it owned her, until it invaded every bone in her body.

Just as it had invaded her heart.

One fisted hand rose to rub at Renee's throbbing eyes, and she pressed her knuckles hard, as though she could erase the gritty discomfort, the sensation of a handful of sand behind her lids. But she couldn't. It was still there, mocking her, choking her, reminding her over and over that she'd failed—

I've failed?

The rise of anger within her was a tide of heat and anguish; a swirling tempest that took hold of her and shook her. With a surge of sudden energy she launched herself from the chair, casting off the blanket that had mere moments ago offered such solace. Now it was a chain holding her down.

I've failed? She paced, hands clenching and releasing at her sides, as the words screamed in her mind. *I haven't failed! Gabe broke his vows, not me! He's the one who let someone else in.*

Like a dying moth drawn to the flame that was its downfall, she walked back to the table, back to the crumpled note lying there.

The note she'd found in Gabe's pocket when she was doing the laundry.

My life is such a cliché.

Usually Gabe did his own laundry, but Renee had wanted to do something nice for him, something to let him know she was thinking of him. A surprise.

She gave a broken laugh. Looked like the real surprise was hers. She smoothed the wrinkles from the white page and read those words again.

"Your friendship has meant so much… I've found myself wishing…things were different… When I touched you…I saw the same longing I felt… I care about you…"

And then the worst of all: *"I love you."* She closed her eyes, but they stayed there, dancing on the backs of her eyelids, taunting her.

I love you…I love you…I love you…

Bile rose in her throat, and she choked back the acrid taste.

He let another woman into his heart.

Wasn't it bad enough that he'd cheated her out of children? How could he have done this to her? How far had it gone? Had he slept with this woman? Had he given her *everything?* Everything he'd been holding back from Renee?

Images flooded her mind, and though she had no idea what this woman looked like, her imagination had little trouble filling in the blanks, crafting a graphic portrayal of her husband surrendering his heart, his dreams, his love to another—

"God!"

The cry for help echoed around her. She barely made it to the kitchen sink before her stomach surged. Violent spasms racked her body until she was spent. Empty. Void of anything. Any feeling. Any dreams.

Hope was a thing of the past, a fragile creature hunted down to extinction by willfulness and pride.

Renee turned on the faucet and rinsed her mouth, gulping down the cold, clear water. Then, as though she could no longer bear the weight of her anguish, she sank to the floor.

She pulled her knees up and pressed her face into them. If only she could curl up into a tiny ball, curl up nice and tight so that she never had to open up again.

But she couldn't get away that easily. There was no easy escape from the ugly reality that was her marriage. Her life. She'd have to deal with it. Soon.

But not now. For now, she was just going to sit here, not thinking, not feeling. *I just need to rest…*

She let her eyes flutter shut and, with a shuddering sigh, surrendered to the comforting shroud of numbness settling over her.

When Renee opened her eyes, she neither knew nor cared how much time had passed. She turned her head, her cheek resting on her knees, and let her gaze roam the darkened room, almost without interest, until it collided with a shadowed form in the doorway.

Shock jolted through her even as Gabe's low voice broke the stillness.

"It's okay, Rennie. It's me."

Relief washed over her, relaxing her fear-tightened muscles—but only for a heartbeat, only for the time it took for her eyes to adjust to the darkness. That was when she saw he was holding the note. And in one scalding moment Renee knew she wasn't empty after all. Yes, hope was gone. But something had come to replace it. Something wild and surging and heady. Something so potent it left her light-headed.

Hatred.

She realized, in the back of her awareness, that it had flickered to life when she read the words that woman had written. But now—looking at the man she'd trusted, the man she'd loved, the man who had thrown her and his vows aside—it blazed into pure, consuming energy.

She rose with forced control, then reached out to flick on the lights. Gabe stood there, the white sheet of paper clutched in his hand. She allowed herself one look into his eyes—and what she saw there told her more clearly than any words just how far things had gone.

"Rennie, I—"

She raised her hand, cutting him off. "Don't." Her voice came out low, raw.

"But—"

She gave one shake of her head—an abrupt, barely controlled motion—but apparently it was enough. Gabe fell silent.

It took all her focus, all her effort, to keep her breathing even, to keep some vestige of rein on the violence that raged through her, begging to be vented.

She wanted to kill him.

The thought should have at least troubled her, but it didn't. Instead, it left her feeling energized, empowered, almost intoxicated. She should be standing here broken and desperate, weeping for all she'd lost, all he'd given away. But she didn't feel like crying.

"Get out."

"Renee…"

She heard the raw entreaty, the depth of emotion in the one word, and steeled herself against it. She looked him right in the eye, let her contempt show in all its fullness.

"Get…out."

Something flickered in his eyes, and Renee felt a jolt of awareness. Right there in front of her, in those blue depths that she used to love to study, she was seeing the death of hope.

Gabe turned and left the kitchen. She listened to his footsteps as words clambered through her. *Stop! Wait! I didn't mean it! We need to talk this out!*

But her voice wouldn't cooperate. It stayed stuck in her throat, so that the only sound in the dark apartment was the quiet click as Gabe walked out the door.

30

The experience of guilt has always been one of the
most excruciating problems in the history of mankind.
PETER G. VAN BREEMEN

Above all else, guard your heart, for it affects everything you do.
PROVERBS 4:23

JUNE 26, 1992

GRACE INHALED THE FRAGRANCE OF FRESHLY BREWED
coffee and sighed.

Was anything more wonderful in the morning than sitting on
the porch, watching the day emerge while you sipped coffee from
your favorite mug?

She leaned back in her chair and propped her feet up on the
porch railing, not even caring that she sounded like some kind of
sappy coffee commercial. This was living, and she planned to
enjoy it to—how did that go? Ah, yes—to the last drop.

Her satisfaction ebbed a bit when the phone jangled to life,
and she seriously considered just letting it ring. After all, this was
her time. Her quiet time. Why surrender that simply because the
phone rang?

She shifted in her chair when the second ring came, frowning at the odd sense of urgency stirring inside her. "Go...away," she muttered, though she couldn't say if she was talking to the phone or to the feeling.

At the third ring, she clamped her jaw. Why should she answer? It was probably just some salesman bent on convincing her she couldn't live without whatever doodad he was hawking.

So why did she feel as though she'd explode if she didn't get up this instant and answer the darned thing?

On the fourth ring, she couldn't take it any longer. Shoving her chair back, she dashed into the kitchen and grabbed the receiver. "Hello?"

Heart pounding, she listened to the ensuing silence. Had the caller hung up? Was she too late for...for...

She frowned. For *what?* What could be so important about answering this—

"Grace?"

Though the voice was ragged and rough, though it didn't bear any resemblance to any voices Grace knew, instant awareness flooded her. "Renee?"

"Grace, I...I...it's over."

Deep concern hit Grace at the anguish flowing through the phone lines. She drew in a slow, steadying breath as her mind skipped past wondering what on earth could have happened to realizing it didn't matter. Whatever it was, her friend was in trouble.

"Renee, where are you?"

Silence, as though she wasn't sure. "Home," she said at last. "I'm at home."

The words were empty, bleak, and a spark of panic shot through Grace. "Listen, don't move. Don't do anything." *Please, God, don't let her do anything.* "I'm leaving right now. I'll be there in twenty minutes."

This time the silence stretched on for what seemed an eternity. It took all of Grace's control to keep her voice soft and soothing, to hold back the rising alarm and keep it from escaping into her words. "Renee, did you hear me?"

"Yes." One word, so empty and emotionless it sent a chill racing through Grace.

"You'll wait for me?" Grace couldn't explain why, but she was sure Renee understood the question within the question. *Don't go anywhere, Renee. And don't do anything.*

"Yes." One word again, as though that was all Renee could manage. But that was enough.

"I'll be right there."

As she hung up and grabbed her keys, Grace prayed for green lights all the way. Either that, or an absence of police…because not even red lights would keep her from getting to Renee as fast as humanly possible.

It was dark. Black. The color of death.

Perfect. The perfect color for him. For his heart and spirit. Wasn't that what he was? Death. Death to any good he'd known in life. Any hope. Any joy. Any love.

Death to the one thing that mattered most in his world. The one thing he'd thrown away, and for what?

For nothing.

Gabe knew that now. Sitting here in his car with no place to go, he knew that what he'd told himself he might find with Jennifer was nothing. Less than nothing. A lie. His lie. Because Jennifer had seen him for what he was and walked away. She was clean.

It was Gabe who had wallowed in filth. He'd convinced himself that his friendship with Jennifer was more—even that it could be everything. But now, here in the darkness, he knew the truth.

He'd had everything. Everything he ever wanted. In Renee. In their life together. And he'd given it away.

You didn't do anything!

The defense rang hollow. No, he hadn't done anything. But he'd thought about it. He wanted it. Would have acted on it if God hadn't pulled him up short.

Gabe gripped the steering wheel and leaned his forehead on his hands. What a fool he had been. He'd been so proud of himself for walking the straight and narrow with Jennifer, but all the while his heart was digging around in the murky depths of his soul, dredging up one perfectly formed excuse after another to justify doing what he wanted.

God, why didn't You just strike me dead? Why didn't You stop me?

He knew the answer. It screamed at him in the heavy silence: God had tried. Gabe knew those quiet inner warnings were the still, small voice of a mighty God seeking to keep him from destroying himself.

Pity Gabe didn't listen.

"Jesus…"

The ragged word hung in the silence, a desperate plea for mercy in the face of devastating truth. Regret moved through Gabe, taking up residence deep within him, an uninvited guest settling in for the long haul.

Jesus, that's all it was, wasn't it? The way I felt about Jennifer. It wasn't about being cared for or respected; it wasn't about being visible or invisible. It wasn't any of the things he'd told himself.

It was just about doing what he wanted. Like some kind of two-year-old pitching a fit against the rules that kept him safe.

Well, he'd done it. Done exactly what he wanted. And look what it got him.

I'm in a wilderness, a desert of scorching, punishing heat and towering dunes of conflict. Mountains of shifting, burning sand tower over me, proving that I'm defeated before I even begin. I know there was a time before this, a time when I knew joy, but that's long gone.

I used to find rest, small oases here and there of comfort with friends and family. But they are as rare as they are refreshing, and they never last. I always end up back out in the heat and the wind and the sand, fighting my way through the assault, not even sure where I'm going. Or why.

But today, the solution came to me. Why didn't I see it before? I won't hurt if I don't feel. Let the calluses form, cover the tender places, and I won't feel anymore.

31

Afflictions are but the shadow of God's wings.

GEORGE MACDONALD

Open my eyes to see.

PSALM 119:18

DECEMBER 20, 2003
9 A.M.

GABE FLEXED HIS FINGERS, GRIMACING AS PAIN SHOT
through them.

Had he ever been this cold before? If so, he sure didn't
remember it. Though there was blessed little snow this morning, a
biting wind had kicked up and seemed bent on blowing right in
their faces. After just a couple of hours of walking, cold had
seeped through his entire body and come to rest in his hands and
fingers, making them ache all the way to his elbows.

"Oh, no."

Gabe looked up. Renee was leading, Bo at her side. The ter-
rain, though covered in dense woods, had been level, making the
going fairly easy, despite the deep snow. Even so, they'd been trad-
ing the lead position so neither of them had to endure the wind
up front for too long. "What?"

He saw the droop of her shoulders and came to stand beside her and the dog, and felt his own shoulders droop in response.

So much for easy going.

As though it had decided they'd had it too easy, their nice, level ground dropped off into a steep grade. Even on a nice day it would be a treacherous descent. But now, as cold and tired as they were, with the snow to hinder them…

"Great." Gabe looked left, then right, but it was clear there was no way around it. They would have to make their way to the bottom to stay on course for the river.

Renee leaned against his arm. "This should be interesting."

At the apprehension in her voice, Gabe drew in a deep breath and slipped his arm around her shoulders, giving her a squeeze. "We'll be fine."

Her worried eyes scanned his face. "Are you just saying that?"

He forced as much confidence into his words as he could, considering the way his knees wanted to give way from fatigue and pain. "We'll be fine, hon. So long as we take our time and are careful, we shouldn't have any trouble." He reached down to scratch Bo behind the ears. "Let me take Bo, and we'll lead the way. You just step where I do, and take it nice and slow. If you start to slip, let me know and I'll do what I can to catch you."

Renee chewed her lip, then nodded and held out Bo's lead. The dog hopped up and peered over the edge, then looked back at Gabe with what he swore was an "Are you *nuts?*" expression in those husky eyes.

Without a doubt, he thought as he took a step over the edge and planted his foot in the knee-deep snow. When he was sure he wouldn't slip, he grabbed a nearby branch and took another step. And another.

Man, this grade was steep! And the way his feet kept sliding with each new step, it felt as if there was ice under the snow.

Gabe grabbed another branch, forcing his numb fingers to grip and hold, and glanced back at Renee. "Be careful, Ren, it's really slick he—"

His words ended on a yelp as the branch he was holding suddenly snapped. Arms windmilling, Gabe threw Bo's rope toward Renee to avoid getting tangled in it and scrambled to catch his balance. But it was too late. His feet shot out from under him, and the next thing he knew he was tumbling down the hill. He did his best to tuck, but his aching, cold body just didn't want to respond.

He hit bottom with a thud, and his mind filled with bright light—and then went dark.

"Gabe!"

Renee clutched at Bo's lead, holding on to the branch she'd grabbed for dear life as the dog pranced and yelped, clearly anxious to get to Gabe. She gave one quick tug on the leash. "Bo, sit!"

The agitated husky plopped his backside into the snow but never took his gaze from Gabe's still form sprawled at the bottom of the grade. Sending up a quick prayer for protection, Renee made her way down as quickly as she could.

Don't let him be hurt. Oh, please, don't let him be hurt…

When she reached the bottom, she scrambled to her husband's side. Bo beat her there, hunkering down to give Gabe's pale face frantic swipes with his tongue.

He lay on his back, eyes closed, but a low groan slipped from his lips.

"Gabe? Hon?" She knelt beside him, leaning close to hear what he was trying to say. "What? What did you say?"

He pried one eye open and peered up at her. "I said, 'Yuck…dog breath.'"

Semihysterical laughter tickled the back of her throat, and Renee took hold of Bo's collar, pulling him away as she wiped at the dampness on her chilled cheeks. "Sorry about that. He got to you faster than I did." She eased her pack from her back and secured Bo to the straps so her hands were free.

Normally just the pack wouldn't even have slowed the husky down if he decided to run. But Renee knew Bo wouldn't be leaving Gabe's side anytime soon.

"Yeah, well—" Gabe groaned again as he eased into a sitting position—"he's got four legs; you've only got two." He rubbed his hand over his face and grimaced. "Man...that hurt."

Renee figured that was an understatement. She took hold of his arm. "Let me help you stand."

He leaned on her as he pushed himself up—then gave another yelp and fell back onto the snow, his features tense and pale. "Great, just great!" The words came out on a moan.

Renee leaned over him. "What is it? Are you hurt?"

His reply came through gritted teeth, but she couldn't tell if that was because of the pain or his frustration. "I think I sprained my ankle. Perfect. Just perfect."

A sprained ankle. That was all? That was a miracle!

Renee put a hand on his arm, and his gaze came to meet hers. "Gabe, it could have been a lot worse than that." She knew her voice was trembling, but she couldn't help it. Her heart had almost stopped when she saw him somersaulting down the hill. "If you ask me, God took pretty good care of you just now."

His frustration melted away and he nodded. "You're right." With a sigh, he stared down at his ankle. "You'd better help me wrap this ankle with something—"

"First, let's pack it with some ice for a little while."

He started to protest, but Renee stopped him. "We need to keep it from swelling. Besides—" she managed a smile, though she knew it was feeble—"I could use the rest."

An answering smile tugged at his lips. "Okay. You win."

He had to be hurting pretty bad to give in so quickly. As gently as she could, she piled scoops of snow around his already swelling ankle. Sitting back on her heels, she looked around. "I'm going to see if I can find you a walking stick of some sort."

"Good idea." Gabe's voice was strained, but he still smiled at her. "I think I'll wait here."

She smiled back. "Good idea."

1 P.M.

Was the whole world against them?

Gabe leaned on his walking stick, keeping his weight on his good ankle, and stared at the creek in front of them. Not the river, mind you, which would have been an answer to prayer. But a creek. A knee-deep, four-and-a-half-foot-wide creek.

Right in the middle of their path. And if they were going to hold to their bearing west, they'd have to cross it.

"Well—" Gabe could tell Renee was trying to sound hopeful as they stood there staring at the tumbling water— "maybe we can just follow it to the river."

He considered it. Odds were good that it would feed into the river at some point, but exactly *what* point?

Therein, as Shakespeare once said, lies the rub.

"Hon, this thing could meander on for miles. We've had a stretch of good weather since the storm died down, but I'm not counting on it to stay that way. So the faster we get to the river, the better."

Renee looked from him back to the creek. "Which means we cross it."

"Which means we cross it."

She nodded again, then concern touched her features. "What about Bo?"

Gabe started to remove his pack. "Of the three of us, I figure he'll have the least trouble with this thing. All we have to do is give him the proper motivation." He slid a baggie with dog treats from his pack. "I'll toss our stuff across, jump over, then coax him with a cookie."

At the word cookie, Bo's ears perked up and he fixed his two-colored gaze on Gabe.

Renee chuckled and scratched the husky behind his ears. "Can't we just keep our packs on? I don't want stuff to fall out into the snow."

"I'd be more concerned about it getting wet if you don't make the jump."

She looked from him to the creek, then pulled her pack off and brought it to him.

He gave her a smile as she handed it over. "Besides, if for some reason you don't clear the water, last thing you want is stuff on your back, weighing you down."

Gabe lifted the two packs and carried them to the edge of the water. He drew back and gave his pack a heave, watching it arc into the air, then land with a thud on the other side.

"Nice throw."

He tossed a grin at Renee, who'd come to stand beside him, then flung her pack over as well. It landed right next to his. He turned to her, throwing his arms out like a circus performer who'd just done some wonderful trick. "How's *that* for placement?"

Renee applauded, and he took an exaggerated bow. Giggling, she plopped down in the snow and angled a look up at him. "Think maybe we're just a bit tired and punchy?"

Gabe reached down to ruffle her hair. "Yeah, but it's good to be that way once in a while." He held his hand out to her. "Now come on over here and let me show you what we need to do."

She rose and followed him to the water's edge. "Let me guess...jump?"

He poked her with his elbow. "That, Einstein, and fall forward."

Her nose crinkled. "Fall forward? What do you mean?"

"If you feel yourself slipping after you land, try to fall toward me, not backward into the water. I'd really rather not have to deal with hypothermia on top of everything else."

"Speaking of which—" she crouched to probe his ankle, her touch light and gentle—"how are you going to jump with this?"

Gabe let a crooked smile show. "It's not hurting near as much as it was. I think your snowpacks helped. Besides, it's not the jumping that's the problem. It's the landing."

"Ain't it the truth," she muttered as she rose and got out of his way. "Ain't it the truth."

He knew what she was thinking. Jumping into their relationship, into marriage, into trouble—all that had been easy. But landing on solid ground…that was downright tricky.

Gabe put the majority of his weight on his uninjured foot, sucked in a fortifying breath, and jumped. He cleared the creek with no trouble. Then his foot hit the ground, and pain shot up his leg. He staggered, then went down on one knee.

"Are you okay?"

He couldn't answer her. He just held up a hand, begging for time to breathe again. When the pain finally eased, he pushed himself up, careful not to put too much pressure on his throbbing ankle.

Hobbling to his pack, he pulled out a doggie treat.

"Are you okay?"

He looked at Renee as he tucked the dog biscuit into his shirt pocket. "Fine. It wasn't fun, but I made it. Now toss me Bo's rope, then you come on over. I think he'll be less inclined to balk if we're both on this side."

Renee tossed the rope, and Gabe caught it, then tied it off on a nearby tree. Bo danced back and forth in the snow, and

Renee told him to sit and stay. She had to repeat the command, but Bo finally complied—after casting a pleading look in Gabe's direction.

"Okay, hon. Just grab my hand. I'll help you come across." He planted himself at the edge of the water, his injured foot at the back, and held out his hand. She grasped it, keeping her eyes on his face. "Remember, if you feel yourself slipping, fall toward me. Fall forward."

"Okay. You count. We'll go on three."

They both stopped, and Gabe knew from Renee's expression that she was thinking the same thing as he. He beat her to the punch. "Do we go on three, or count one, two, three, *then* go?" It was one of their favorite lines from *Lethal Weapon*.

Renee's laughter wrapped around him like a down comforter on a winter night. She leaned back, dropping his hand in mock defeat. "Sure thing. Make me laugh when I'm about to go over water in freezing weather. Just keep in mind, if I get hypothermia, you have to carry me."

"Sorry." He waggled his brows, then stretched his hand out again. "Okay, go on three. Ready?"

Her quick nod told him she was. "One, two, *three!*"

Between his tug on her hand and her jump, Renee fairly sailed over the creek, landing in Gabe's arms, sending them both sprawling. He grunted on impact with the ground, holding her tightly in his arms. He lay there, catching his breath, fighting the new pain in his ankle, and she rolled to the side, then patted his arm.

"Thanks for the help, Gabe."

"It was nuthin'." It would have sounded far more convincing if the words hadn't come out on a groan.

A soulful yodel brought them both to their feet. Bo was circling and prancing, looking like a kid whose Mom was about to leave him at preschool.

"Bo, hold it!"

"Wait!"

The husky did neither. He coiled and vaulted the river, clearing it, as Gabe had predicted, with far greater ease than either of them. The dog bounded over to them, then wriggled his delight at being reunited. Gabe's laughter only deepened when Bo's nose suddenly fastened to his shirt pocket.

Pushing the dog aside, he fished out the treat and handed it over. "You deserve it, buddy. That was a great jump."

Renee stood, brushing snow from her clothes, and picked up her pack. "So...onward and upward?"

Gabe rose as well, lifting his pack back onto his shoulders. "Forward, into the fray."

Renee fell into step beside him, her chuckle deep and warm. "I bet you say that to all the girls."

Renee walked beside Gabe, unable to keep the smile from her features.

No one could make her laugh like he did. No one could make her feel more secure and protected.

And no one could hurt her more or drive her crazy faster.

If only they spent more time enjoying each other, like they'd done at the creek. Moments like that both gave her hope and filled her with despair. She knew they loved each other, knew they even liked each other most of the time.

If only she could figure out what it was that kept them from resting in that love, in being at peace with one another. *"There's only one person you can change, Renee..."*

Grace's words echoed through her as they'd done many times over the last few years. *Okay, Lord. Okay.*

Renee gripped the straps of her pack and shifted it into a more comfortable position. She'd tried packing and repacking it over the years in an effort to make it lighter, easier to carry, but it never worked. No matter what she did, the pack always ended up being too heavy.

Sometimes she thought the only way she would ever be

able to walk without being weighed down was if she didn't carry a pack at all. She lifted her foot to step over a fallen branch, then paused.

No pack at all...

She lowered her foot to the snow, her hands tightening on the straps of her pack. Then she looked at the ground.

A sudden memory of Gabe's words at the creek flowed into her mind. *Stuff on your back, weighing you down...fall forward...toward me...*

Then her own thoughts echoed again: *The only way to walk without being weighed down is if I don't carry a pack at all—*

"You okay, Ren?"

She looked up. Gabe was standing just ahead of her, waiting for her. "You want me to carry your pack for a while?"

Renee's mouth fell open. *Okay, God, okay. I get it.* "Um, no. I'm okay." She hiked the pack up on her shoulders. "I just needed to make some adjustments."

His quizzical stare followed her as she joined him, but she didn't explain. She just fell into step beside him.

*So show me what I'm holding on to, Lord. What's weighing me down? Because I'll tell You what—*she matched her steps to Gabe's, focused on the sound of the snow scrunching beneath their feet—*I'm tired of hauling it around.*

"Bo, will you knock it *off?*"

Gabe gave a hard yank on the rope, but it didn't help. Bo continued his side-stepping dance, weaving around his feet and whining like a two-year-old at Toys "R" Us.

"What on earth is wrong with him?"

Gabe looked at Renee and saw the frustration he was feeling reflected in her features. The dog had started acting weird about twenty minutes ago, and he was still at it. "Beats me. But if he wraps that rope around me and I fall—"

Renee didn't wait for him to finish his gritted comment.

She came to take hold of the dog's collar, disentangling him from Gabe's legs. "What's up, boy? You still worried about Gabe falling?" She scratched his ears and neck, which usually soothed him, but Bo wasn't having any of it. He whined again and backed away from her, eyes wide.

Even as Renee cast him a worried glance, Gabe's own frustration shifted to concern.

"Gabe—" Renee's voice trembled—"maybe he was hurt in the crash. Internally. And it's just now showing up?"

He studied the husky, taking in the ears flattened to his head, the pacing, the quick glances around them.

No, Bo wasn't hurt.

He was scared.

Gabe followed the dog's darting gaze. What was that in the snow? Sudden understanding dawned, and the hair at the back of his neck rose as he went to study the indentations in the snow in front of them—indentations that went exactly where he and Renee and Bo were heading.

Tracks. Cougar tracks, from the look of them. And Gabe was willing to bet they were fresh.

"Are those what I think they are?"

He looked to find Renee peering over his shoulder. He stood, nodding.

"Cougar?"

He nodded again. "No wonder Bo's been so antsy. He probably caught the cat's scent, and there's nothing like a whiff of a cougar to make other animals go nuts."

Renee was staring at the tracks as they disappeared into the woods in front of them. "He's going our way, isn't he?"

Gabe sighed. "Looks like it."

Renee pursed her lips. "Do we have to go that way?"

He shook his head. "I can't say for sure, but I think it's the most direct route. And if the weather's any indication, tonight will be even colder than last night."

"So we need the most direct route possible."

He looked up at the sky. "At least we're upwind of him. But if the wind shifts..."

Renee didn't hesitate. "We'll just have to pray it doesn't."

Gabe glanced down at Bo, trembling at his side. "Do me a favor and request a supernatural doggie downer while you're at it."

A smile eased the tension from Renee's eyes. "You got it." She took his hands, and they bowed their heads, but Gabe kept his eyes open, fixed on the tracks and the woods.

Just in case.

Because if there was more waiting for them than the river, he wanted to know as soon as possible.

Go ahead, use me.

What difference does it make whether I'm hurt or not?

Angry? Me?

...Could be.

Go ahead, fulfill your needs at my expense. What does it matter if I'm tired and lost and have needs too?

Angry? Me?

...Possibly.

Or maybe not.

Maybe just tired. Tired of dealing and coping and being strong. Of smiling and trying and going along with the laughter when it just isn't real. Yes, tired. So what I need now is to trust, to find rest in a God who knows how I feel.

A God who never gets tired.

32

It is so hard to believe because it is so hard to obey.

SØREN KIERKEGAARD

"If you love me, obey my commandments."

JOHN 14:15

JUNE 30, 1992

GRACE CAME INTO THE BEDROOM AND FOUND OREN still awake, waiting for her.

"Is Renee settled in her room?"

"Yes." She sat on the edge of their bed, then took her Bible from the bedside table and let it fall open. She read the words from 1 Corinthians, words she knew so well: "When you put a seed into the ground, it doesn't grow...unless it dies first."

Oren watched her in silence, waiting. How she loved that about him. That he didn't feel the need to push. Oh, how far they'd come.

She looked up from her Bible. She knew what she needed to do. "I want to tell her about us, Oren."

He nodded without hesitation. "I think we should. But I also think we need to pray about it. To ask God how we should do that. And when." He slipped from beneath the covers and sat beside her. "Gracie, Renee and Gabe are at a crossroads, and not just in their marriage."

She knew he was right—because he spoke from experience. Their experience. She spread her fingers over the open pages of her Bible.

Unless a seed dies...

She knew this death. Knew it well. Knew the pain and fear, knew the cost of surrendering self and rights and taking on Christ instead. "It's not going to be easy. For either of them."

"No." There was a sweetness, an encouragement in Oren's expression that never failed to move her. "But it will be worth it." He squeezed her hand. "And we'll help them, as much as God lets us."

Grace hugged him. "I love you, Oren."

"I love you, Gracie. Always and forever."

Amen. She followed his lead and bowed her head. *Amen and amen.*

Renee couldn't believe she'd been at Oren and Grace's for so long. At first all she could do was weep, and they let her. Sat with her. Prayed with her. Finally, as the three of them sat together in the living room, she started talking, and her struggles with Gabe came pouring out. The distrust, the anger. Finally, "We can't even talk for more than two minutes without ending up in a fight. It's like we hate each other."

Oren and Grace exchanged a look. "Or like you hate yourselves. And who you've become together."

Renee considered Grace's comment. "Yes, that's it. I can't stand who I am with him. But—" she choked on the truth she was about to share—"I don't know who I am without him. I've changed. Everything I think and do is centered on him, but not in a good way. It's as though I'm living my whole life with the sole purpose of not needing him, not trusting him." Shame warmed her cheeks even as it chilled her spirit. "I've closed him out of my heart, but I've welcomed in hatred. For him. For myself."

"For God?"

The quiet words struck home, and she lowered her head. "Sometimes." She held her hands out. "But He could *change* all this if He wanted to!"

Tears silenced her for a moment and she looked away. "You know, when I was a little girl, I didn't care about a career, about having lots of friends. All I ever wanted was a marriage like my parents had. A marriage full of love and laughter." She turned back to study the two who sat there, listening with such acceptance. "And now...now I have this great career, and wonderful friends—better friends than I deserve. And a marriage that's a nightmare."

She tugged the afghan over her lap, wrapping herself in its softness, its warmth...wishing it could somehow remove the chill that seemed to dwell deep in her bones.

Would she ever feel warm again?

Oren watched her for a moment, then patted Grace's hand. "I think I'm going to leave you two women to talk."

Renee started to shake her head. "You don't have to leave, Oren."

He came to sit on the couch with her. "It's okay, Renee. I have some things I need to do. But first I have something for you."

She took the wrapped package he handed her. "What...?"

"Actually, it's from both Gracie and me." He smiled at his wife.

"You said you longed for a relationship like ours?" The older woman nodded toward the package in Renee's hands. "Then you'll want to read that—but not until you're ready."

Renee must have shown her confusion, because Grace smiled. A tender, understanding smile. "It's just a book, and it's not so very long. But when the time is right, I think it will help you."

Grace and Oren shared a smile, and then Grace turned back to Renee. "It will help you understand what having a relationship like ours really means."

Renee looked down at the package. "But how will I know when I'm ready?"

Grace's reply was simple. "Trust God to show you when the time is right."

Oren halted whatever other questions Renee was about to ask when he patted her hand. Then he rose. "Okay, then, I'm off."

Renee watched him leave the room, the gift pressed against her chest, and swallowed the tears that threatened to overtake her. She was so tired of crying. You'd think that with all the crying she'd done, she'd be bone-dry. But no, there always seemed to be more tears.

She focused on the dancing flames in the stone fireplace. How she loved watching the shadows those flames threw on the rich wooden walls. How she loved everything about this room. It smelled of cedar and wood smoke and pine…

It reminded her of her childhood. Of the Oregon woods and camping and nights full of sweet laughter.

"Can't get the thoughts to stop?"

Renee angled a smile at Grace. Leave it to her to understand. "No."

Grace leaned back in her chair, resting her head against the cushion, closing her eyes. "Maybe that's the problem."

Renee frowned. "What is?"

"Maybe you're trying too hard. Sometimes it's better to just…rest. To not try anything, but to just be."

"Be." Renee pushed at the bottom of the afghan with her foot, pressing the covering between the plush couch cushions. *Just be?* What on earth did *that* mean?

Grace's deep chuckle told Renee her confusion was showing. She gave her a smile that she knew was decidedly sheep-ish. "Okay, Miss Know-Everything, how exactly am I supposed to do that?"

Grace wagged a finger at her. "Ah, ah. No *doing* allowed. Just *being.*"

Renee couldn't sit still for that. She straightened, letting the afghan fall away and immediately regretted it when the cool air hit her.

"It's easier than you think." Grace's compassionate tone took the edge off Renee's sudden frustration. "Just settle back on the couch, like you were."

When she didn't move, Grace tapped one slightly bent finger on her armchair. Though Grace's wrinkled hands showed her age, her face was smooth and wrinkle free. Grace said that was because of her weight.

"There's no room for wrinkles when you're fat."

Restraining a smile at her friend's comment, Renee did as she was bid. She settled back into the cushions, pulling the afghan up to her chin.

"Good, now close your eyes."

Renee obeyed. She lay there, eyes pressed shut, waiting for the next step. But only silence followed. She stood it as long as she could, then opened her eyes—and found herself face-to-face with Grace's amusement.

"I didn't think you'd last too long."

Heat surged into Renee's cheeks, and she laughed, too. How well Grace knew her.

When the older woman moved to sit on the edge of the couch, Renee reached for her hand. "I'm sorry."

Grace squeezed her hand. "No, dear, I understand. Women—especially women who grow up in the church—are taught that we're supposed to *do*. Stay busy, take on tasks, find a need and fill it." She shook her head, the reddish high-lights in her hair reflecting the warmth of the fire. "But what we need to pay attention to is what God calls us to."

Renee studied Grace's face, the easy way she smiled, the kindness in her green eyes, the way the firelight seemed to create a kind of corona behind her. *She looks like an angel.*

Well, why shouldn't she? Hadn't she been an angel to Renee, a messenger who brought God's truth and helped Renee see herself and God more clearly? God had known exactly the kind of friend she needed.

"Renee, when was the last time you were silent—really silent—before God?"

The gentle question caught her by surprise. When was the last time?

For that matter, when was the *first* time?

She couldn't remember ever just sitting in silence with God. Praying, yes…sending word after word scurrying to the heavens in appeal or supplication. Singing, too. She'd sung to the Father plenty of times, letting her joy or sorrow fly on the wings of the music that so often brought peace to her soul.

But silence? She shook her head.

"I didn't think so." Grace's comment held no condemnation, only acknowledgment. "Give God your silence, Renee. Remember what He said in Psalms?"

Renee remembered. "Be still."

Grace nodded. "Why do you think He called us to stillness?"

Emotion welled as Renee realized the answer. For a moment she couldn't speak around the lump in her throat. "To…to know He is God. 'Be still and know that I am God.'"

The smile that lit Grace's face filled Renee with envy. Was such radiance, such simple beauty ever reflected in her face? She doubted it. How she longed to know the peace that permeated this woman!

What will it take, God? What will it take for me to know You so well?

"Be still…and *know*. Know that *I* am God."

Grace's whispered words seemed to fill the room, and

Renee closed her eyes as goose bumps skittered across her arms and shivers scurried up her back. Grace spoke with such reverence, and Renee knew she spoke to the One who listened with His whole heart.

The One who'd been waiting for Renee to listen as well.

She let her lids drift shut...and waited. For what, she wasn't sure. But she knew for whom, and that was enough.

At first there was only silence, and then she became aware of small, gentle sounds. The faint crackle of the flames. The slight creak of the couch as she or Grace shifted. The ticking of the clock on the wall. The whisper of the wind as it caressed the windowpanes...

And something more.

It was barely discernible at first, but then it seemed to grow. It was a kind of sweet, trilling musical note—like the singing of a lark or a robin. But...Renee frowned. It was night-time. There weren't any birds singing at night, especially not in the winter. She tilted her head, honing in on the sound, filled with wonder at the haunting beauty of it. It was melodious, and yet so strange. She'd never heard anything like it.

Lord?

All those times she'd sung to Him, and now—

She caught her breath as the truth rocked her very soul: *He* was singing to her.

Renee soaked in every trill, every nuance, every bit of melodious beauty that seemed to come from nowhere and everywhere. She held on to Grace, overwhelmed by the awareness of a holy presence. "Oh, Grace..."

Her broken whisper hid nothing, not the wonder, the honor she felt, nor the fear. How could a holy God come to *her?* How could He speak anything to her but condemnation? She was so weak...so terribly weak...

"Renee."

Grace's gentle voice pulled her from the barrage of questions, and she opened her eyes with a sob. Grace gripped her hands, then nodded to the fireplace. "Renee, look."

She did as Grace bid and her eyes widened. There, in the depths of the fire, in the center of the most intense heat, was a ' log with pitch bubbling forth. A log that sang.

The music was coming from the log.

For a moment, sharp disappointment pierced Renee, but it was almost immediately replaced by an understanding that she knew came from One far beyond herself. God was bringing her a message, and it wasn't one of condemnation, but of hope.

Look, daughter, and see. Only in the most intense crucible can the log finally let loose the song that has been trapped deep within. It gave itself to the flame, sacrificing all, and in so doing, what was held captive is set free.

This was the song God sang to her soul. This was what He'd been trying to tell her all along. No, she wasn't worthy. No one was but Christ. And yet, God loved her—and He'd shown her the way to find the peace, and the love, she longed for.

She'd told herself she could run away. Gabe broke her trust, so she was free. But that wasn't true. She wasn't free until God released her from the vows she'd taken. She had entered into a covenant, and not just with Gabe. She had made promises to both Gabe and God that would stand until death parted them. For better, for worse.

Well, they'd clearly hit worse. But wasn't that exactly what those vows were for? They were a promise for the struggle, a promise to hold to her vows—to the covenant—when the feeling wasn't there.

Fall into the ground and die, My daughter.

Renee lifted her face to heaven.

Die to self, that I may live in you.

She wanted to, but how? She didn't really know. Show me...

Give up your life for Me, and you will find true life.

Give up. Grace had told her that so many times, and Renee had said she would. But she hadn't. She hadn't surrendered anything—not her rights, not her dreams, not her stubborn determination to always be right.

Take it, Father. Take everything, and don't let me hold back this time. Break me, if that's what it takes to make me Yours.

A whisper of joy passed through her, growing until it was more powerful, more intense than anything she'd ever experienced. Renee felt as though she were lifted from where she sat, carried on a wave of holy pleasure, and then held—cradled in omnipotent arms—as a host of heavenly voices rang out.

A touch on her shoulder brought Renee's eyes open. "Are you okay, Renee?"

"Yes." She confirmed the word with a smile. "I'm great." She glanced around the room. She knew what she had to do. "I need to make a phone call."

The light of hope shone in Grace's eyes. "To your husband?"

"To my husband."

Gabe answered the phone on the first ring.

"Hi, Gabe."

Relief at hearing Renee's voice made him weak. "Are you okay?"

He knew she'd been at the Frazier's home. Oren had called and talked with him the night Renee disappeared, saying Gabe needed to give her a few days to think. To pray.

They'd been the hardest days of his life.

"I'm fine." She really sounded as though she was, and terror gnawed at him. *Is this it, Lord? Is she leaving me?*

"Gabe, I'm sorry. I'm sorry I walked out like that."

He shook his head, then realized she couldn't see him. "No, it's my fault…"

"It's both our faults, Gabe. It has been for a long time."
She hesitated. *Here it comes. I knew this would happen one day.*

"Gabe, I want us to work this out."

His mouth dropped open, and he gripped the phone so hard he wouldn't have been surprised to hear it snap. "You do?"

"Yes. But we can't do it the way we've been doing it."

He knew that. He'd known that when he opened his eyes after praying and found her gone. "Tell me what you want, Renee."

"We have to see a counselor. And we can't be together. Not for a while."

Not together? He tried to keep the fear, the anger from his voice. He didn't succeed. "What exactly does that mean?"

"It means we need to live apart, but Gabe, I want you to hear me. It's just for a while. Just until we start to get ourselves straight. That's what we have to do before we can get us straight."

He fell silent, struggling to find words. He expected her to jump in, to make her case, but she didn't. She just waited. Finally he found his voice again. "I'll do whatever you need me to do, Renee." He knew she could hear the emptiness in his voice, but he couldn't prevent that. Couldn't prevent the feeling that they were just delaying the inevitable.

Her response was gentle, patient. "It's what we both need, Gabe. If it's okay with you, Grace and Oren and I will come by tomorrow morning, and we can talk through our options."

He agreed, and they hung up. He sat there, his hand on the phone, and let the sorrow come. *We're not going to make it, are we, Lord?*

Not by might, nor by strength, but by My power.

Gabe heard the words, longed to believe them…but couldn't help wondering if even God had enough strength for what was ahead.

Father, I'm not sure we can overcome all we have to fight to survive. Most of all, I'm not sure I can overcome myself. My weaknesses. My impatience. My uncertainties.

Father, we won't make it without You. Be with us. Take us over. Make us new. I know that's a lot to ask, but You are the God of the impossible, aren't You? I hope so...otherwise, we're lost.

33

How desperately difficult it is to be honest with oneself.

EDWARD WHITE BENSON

You are… [God's] very own possession.
This is so you can show others the goodness of God,
for he called you out of the darkness into his wonderful light.

1 PETER 2:9

DECEMBER 20, 2003
3 P.M.

IT WAS THERE, JUST AHEAD.

"Gabe, look!"

Bo jumped at the excitement in Renee's voice, and Gabe limped to join her. No one had been more surprised than he when the pain in his ankle lessened enough that he could walk unaided. He was far slower than he liked, but at least he wasn't weighing Renee down.

He followed her pointing finger and felt like bouncing right along with Bo.

The river. They'd found the river.

Relief made him almost light-headed. They weren't out of the woods—figuratively or literally—but it was a step in the right direction. "Is that a beautiful sight or what?"

Her eyes shone. "Gorgeous. Just gorgeous."

"Well, what are we waiting for?"

They were next to the rushing water in minutes. Gabe looked from one direction to the other. *Now what, Lord? Which way do we go?*

South.

He wasn't sure if the direction came from God or from logic, but either way it made sense. The closest thing to civilization was Union Creek, and it was south. There were cabins between where they'd gone off the road and Union Creek, so south it was.

"I think we should head north."

Gabe looked at Renee. "What?"

Her nod was decisive. "I'm sure there are some cabins just north of where we went off the road."

"No. Renee, we need to go south."

"Why?"

He knew all he had to do was say he'd prayed about it and felt God had told him to go south. But he was so tired. He just didn't have the energy to explain himself. "Look, hon, I'm more qualified to figure this out than you are."

"What's that supposed to mean?" Her narrowed eyes warned him he was in dangerous territory, but dang it! He was sore and cold and as weary as he ever remembered being. Why couldn't she just accept he was right without challenging him?

"You have to admit, I'm a little more sensible about these things than you are."

"Sensible? I'm sensible."

He pinned her with a glare. "You never should have left the truck, Renee. You should have waited—"

"For what? For us to freeze to death?" She shook her head. "Make sense, Gabe. I couldn't wait."

He sighed, fatigue seeping into his soul as well as his body. "Couldn't, or wouldn't?" Her arms crossed, and he cut her off before she could vent the irritation he saw brewing behind those eyes. "Look, can't you just trust me on this?"

Her silence and her clenched jaw were just too much. "No, you can't, can you? You don't trust me. You don't trust anyone."

"That's not true—"

"Yes, it is." He rubbed a weary hand over his face. "I've worked hard to show you that you can trust me, but that doesn't matter, does it? It never has. What you want I can't give you."

"And what is that?"

"Perfection." He let the word sink in. "You want perfection, Renee. Nothing else will do. You won't be happy until I'm God."

Her eyes glistened with angry tears. "That's not true. I just want you to be you! But you never are, are you? You're always so busy being who you think everyone wants you to be. At work, at church, in the Bible study. Everywhere but at home, with me."

"I've done everything you asked. Given you everything I can. *You're* the one who withholds yourself, who flinches every time I come near you. God forbid I should try to touch you."

The tears overflowed. He expected her to blow up, to rail at him some more, but when she spoke, her voice was hushed, sorrowful. "Yes, Gabe, you have. You've given me everything...everything but what matters most."

She wasn't making sense! "What are you talking about?"

"You." The green in her eyes had deepened, as though to emphasize the depth of her emotions. "The real you, beneath all the barriers and armor. You've never given me yourself. Don't you think I can tell?" She held a hand out to him, and the entreaty pierced his heart. "Don't you think I know you still hold a part of yourself back, just in case? That you don't trust me?"

He wanted to reach out, to take her hand in his. But he couldn't. He turned away from her, trapped in confusion and silence.

∾

Renee stood staring at Gabe's back. A powerful urge swept her to go to him, to touch him, to form some kind of bridge in the one way she knew he would be able to accept.

Physical contact had always been the most effective way to reach Gabe. He craved being touched, needed it to feel grounded, to feel a part of her, of them. She'd learned that long ago.

And you've always resisted it.

Anger flared to life. *Why shouldn't I, when he won't give me what I need? Emotional connections are more important than the physical could ever be. Everyone knows that!*

More important for you, perhaps. But not for Gabe. Never for Gabe.

It's not fair!

I haven't called you to fairness, child, but to obedience. You know what you need to do. Will you do it?

Renee let her surrender ease out on a deep sigh. Yes. She would do it. But just as she started to step forward, he spun to face her.

She backpedaled at the cold hopelessness in his eyes.

"You want it all, don't you, Renee? You actually think you deserve it. Well, guess what? You don't."

She hugged herself, but her arms were little protection from the words pelting her.

"You're so quick to withhold trust, but what have you done to show me *you* can be trusted? All you do is criticize, harp that I'm not doing or being what you want and need. But no one could! Not even *God* could live up to your expectations."

She closed her eyes against the fury on his face, in his voice. "Stop it."

"Oh, you talk a good game. You say all the right things and you look so righteous on the surface, but I've seen it over and over. You talk about trust, but you don't live it. You never have. You don't trust anyone, Renee. Not even God."

His haunted gaze was fixed on her, the pain so clear in his pinched features that a part of her longed to walk to him, to smooth his brow with her fingers and restore the smile he'd worn before she let her mouth get out of control.

But he wouldn't be open to her now. Why should he be? She'd chosen her attack carefully, known just what to say to cut and wound. Well, she'd done a bang-up job.

Lord God, will I ever learn? What is it going to take—

Die.

This time, the word struck home. She'd asked God to speak to her, to show her what she was withholding from Gabe, from Him. And He was telling her.

She held a hand out to Gabe, then let it fall. "I...I'm sorry. I need some time." She turned and walked away.

Bo's leash was still in her hand, so the husky had no choice but to follow her as she walked. But he kept looking back over his shoulder, as though to ask where Gabe was.

Renee just kept walking until she was alone, isolated. She came to a large, snow-dusted rock and sat, tugging Bo forward until he came to rest his head on her knee. She pulled off her mittens and buried her fingers in his luxurious fur, seeking comfort from his warmth.

But there was precious little comfort with Gabe's words pounding at her.

It's never enough...you don't trust anyone...not even God.

She lowered her head to press her face against Bo's back as the voice of conviction struck its mark, slicing through until she bowed her head in surrender and let memory after memory sweep over her.

And as they did so, she could no longer hide from the painful truth: Gabe was right. And she was wrong. Terribly, terribly wrong.

This hurts.

I know I agreed to this, to the counseling and the talking and moving toward healing, but it hurts! It's like that awful, wretched pinpricking you get when you move a foot that's gone numb and the blood begins to pump back in. You know it's best, that it means you'll have feeling again, but you wonder in the midst of the pain if being numb is so bad after all?

So what if I'm coming alive again? So what if this is a step to becoming healthy? Why does it have to hurt so much? And what grates the most is that I'm doing this for him! It's his fault I closed off to begin with, and now I'm doing what I swore I wouldn't do anymore.

I'm hurting because of him.

34

Love must be learned, and learned again and again;
there is no end to it. Hate needs no instruction,
but waits only to be provoked.

Fire tests the purity of silver and gold,
but the LORD tests the heart.

PROVERBS 17:3

JULY 1993

FIREWORKS EXPLODED IN THE SKY, BRILLIANT COLORS splashing across the canvas of darkness, but Renee couldn't enjoy the show.

She was too focused on Gabe. On waiting for the fireworks to really explode. His fireworks.

They'd been getting together like this for a couple of months now. *Trust building,* Steve called it.

She thought it was like dating.

Gabe thought it was ridiculous.

At least, he'd thought so at first. He made no secret of the fact that the rules their counselor had set up chafed at Gabe like prickly heat. Picking Renee up at the front door of the apartment or meeting her at some emotionally neutral spot, not being alone together in an intimate setting, not being allowed to go into his own home...

He hated it. Told her once it was about as weird as it got.

But he agreed to it. And that surprised her. Almost as much as the fact that he seemed to grow more at peace with the situation as time went on. And each time they were together, it was less tense. Less stressful. Maybe Gabe finally understood all this was necessary, that they had to start over, build trust and respect.

That he was willing to do so meant a great deal to her. Usually. But right now…

Well, right now all she wanted to do was get up from the blanket they were sitting on, find her car, and flat get outta Dodge.

When Gabe suggested last week that they celebrate the Fourth of July together, she'd thought it was a great idea. And the day had gone well. They met early to watch the parade, then went to the big carnival the city held every year in the park. Renee felt young and carefree, and when Gabe took her hand as they walked from booth to booth, their troubles seemed miles away.

But they weren't. They'd been hiding there all along, just under the surface, waiting to jump out and nail her. Which they'd done a few minutes ago when Gabe turned to put his arm around her as they watched the fireworks display. She hadn't meant to stiffen, to pull away. Maybe it was just that she was tired. Or that the falling darkness had created a feeling of intimacy, of closeness that she wasn't prepared for.

Whatever the reason, the minute his arm circled her, she recoiled.

And the minute she did that, Gabe exploded.

Exploded? her conscience nudged at her.

Okay, so maybe not. But he'd still gotten angry—

Angry?

Okay, frustrated. Like there was any difference.

There is. A big difference. And you know it.

Fine, but I'm not the one sitting here, staring down at the blanket, my face all tense. I'm not the one about to start yelling...ranting...

Gabe finally looked up from the ground and at her. She tensed. *Here it comes.*

"I'm sorry."

Renee blinked. That was it? No blowup? She looked into his eyes and saw hurt there, some frustration. But no rage. No anger.

"It seemed like we were getting along so well..." He looked away. "I just wanted to be close to you."

"We are close. We're sitting together on a blanket."

His steady gaze only confirmed what her conscience was telling her: The sarcastic comment was careless. Uncalled-for.

Gabe considered her for a moment, as though trying to understand what was going on in her head. Once he figured it out, she hoped he'd let her know, too.

His sigh was quiet, but heavy. "Maybe we'd better go. Or at least I'd better go." He started to stand.

Irritation put her mouth in motion. "Oh, fine. One little disagreement and you want to bail?"

Gabe sat down again and leaned toward her, his jaw tight. He drew in a deep breath. But when he spoke, the words were soft, almost gentle. "What do you want from me, Renee?"

A multitude of answers flooded her mind: *Love me. Forgive me. Be patient with me. Help me understand myself.* But she couldn't get any of that out. She was so tangled up inside, all she could do was wrap her arms around herself.

He watched her in silence, then reached out to touch her arm. This time she didn't pull away. She just sat there, blinking fast.

"Look, I'm not angry. But I think it would be best for both of us if I head home."

She looked up, begged him with her eyes to stay. He shook his head. "I think you need some time...to yourself. Okay?"

Renee swallowed hard, then nodded. He squeezed her arm, then stood and walked away.

She covered her face with her hands. What was wrong with her? They'd been doing so well. Why couldn't she just relax and enjoy it? Why did she have to sit here, like a hawk hanging on a wire, watching Gabe for some sign of anger, some hint that things were going to turn unpleasant?

Renee stood, snatched up her blanket, and strode through the crowd to her car. She threw the blanket in the trunk, slamming the lid. But the action didn't make her feel any better.

No matter how good things went between the two of them, she always seemed on edge. Always prepared, at the first sign of trouble, to bail. To throw her hands in the air and say, "See? See how impossible this is? We'll never change."

Trouble was, she thought as she unlocked the car door and slid onto the seat, Gabe was changing. This wasn't the first time she'd seen him react without anger. Wasn't the first time he'd dealt with an obstacle between them with an attitude of kindness and understanding rather than irritation.

Her hand paused halfway to putting the key in the ignition. She glanced up, caught her reflection in the rearview mirror. "And it wasn't the first time you goaded him into the very behaviors you keep telling Steve you hate."

She let out a sigh and slid the key into the ignition.

Gabe was learning to control his anger. She should be thrilled. Instead, she realized, she was angry.

Angry that while he'd found a way to get beyond the struggles—or at least start to do so—she seemed mired in the past, unable or unwilling to let go of how things used to be.

And she was terrified that would never change.

Lord, following You seems almost impossible. I think I'm doing what You want, that I'm following Your lead—then something happens and I can only question, can only fight the sense that the rug's been pulled out from beneath my stumbling feet yet again.

You'd think I'd be used to being off balance by now. But I'm not. I hate it.

What do You want from me, God? Teach me Your ways. Show me Your paths. Lead me in the way of Your righteousness, because I have none of my own, that's for sure.

Help me, Lord, to understand.

35

Did Sorrow lay his hand upon your shoulder,
And walk with you in silence on life's way?...
He is God's angel, clothed in veils of night,
With whom "we walk by faith" and "not by sight."

STREAMS IN THE DESERT

In every battle you will need faith as your
shield to stop the fiery arrows aimed at you by Satan.

EPHESIANS 6:16

JULY 1993

IT'S HOPELESS. WE'LL NEVER CHANGE.

Gabe stood in the drizzling summer rain and knew the chill
wasn't coming from the warm drops falling from the sky. He'd
been cold long before the rain started. Cold to the bone.

For years.

But these last seven months...

Gabe jammed his hands into his coat pockets. Seven months.
Seven months since he'd packed up his life and moved out of the
apartment he and Renee had shared.

Seven months, three days, fifteen hours, and twelve minutes
to be exact. He didn't know how many seconds. And he counted
that a victory. A small one, but a victory nonetheless.

Within a few days of agreeing to separate, Gabe had moved
out of their apartment and into a spare room at Oren and Grace's

house. Gabe still couldn't believe they'd just opened their home to him, welcomed him like their son rather than some pathetic loser.

The thought had barely formed when Gabe heard Steve's voice admonishing him: *"You have to watch that self-talk, Gabe. Don't give in to the tapes that play inside your head."*

He had to admit, Steve was just what the doctor ordered. When Gabe first met the man who'd agreed to be his and Renee's counselor, he hadn't been sure he could help. Hadn't been sure anyone could help. And he'd been angry that not only did he have to go to two sessions a week, but there wouldn't be any sessions with both him and Renee for the first few months. He'd tried arguing about that. How were they going to work things out if they never saw each other? But Steve had been firm.

"Being together isn't what matters now, Gabe. What matters is the work you and Renee have to do on yourselves."

In the end, Gabe had been glad it was just Steve and him. Steve seemed to understand what Gabe was feeling, to know what he was thinking, sometimes even before Gabe did. He saw past all Gabe's defenses, all the things Gabe did without even realizing to keep his real feelings, his real self hidden. Acting, playing a role...none of it worked with Steve. But what surprised Gabe even more than Steve's ability to see through him was the fact that Gabe was relieved. Relieved he could be himself.

Steve had helped him sort through a lot of garbage deeply ingrained in his head, his heart—stuff that Gabe now knew had convinced him that no one could love him, that had kept him feeling like a failure no matter what he did or how hard he tried.

Some habits died especially hard.

A shiver crab-walked through him, and Gabe looked down. He was soaked. Gee, maybe he'd get lucky and catch pneumonia.

Self-talk, Gabe.

Some habits didn't want to die at all.

He turned and walked to a bench Oren had built at the back of the yard. Several Adirondack chairs were next to it. Renee would have chosen one of those. She loved those chairs, but he preferred the bench.

Opposites at every turn, that was them.

He forced himself to focus on the yard rather than his frustration. It was a big yard, and Gabe liked coming out here, just to have time to himself. Something Steve had helped him realize he needed. Decompression time. Time to get his heart and mind straight before he tried to deal with anyone.

He leaned back against the seat. Yeah, regardless of what happened between Renee and him, he was grateful for the time with Steve.

It had been difficult—

Gabe's laugh was rough. Difficult, nothing. It had been torture. Gabe still recalled his reaction when Steve told him point-blank that he had to let go of the barriers, the defenses that he had built inside himself.

He'd almost walked out then and there. The mere thought of letting the barriers down made his palms sweat, his stomach cramp. If he hadn't had them as a kid, as a young man, he wouldn't have survived. He'd be locked up in a loony bin someplace.

That or dead.

And now, here was this guy he'd just met, sitting there and telling him he was supposed to just let go? Just *"be yourself"*?

No way.

Yet again, Steve seemed to read the direction of his frantic thoughts. "Gabe, holding your emotions in check, not letting anyone inside, not letting yourself trust—even your anger, your rages—those were important safeguards when you were a kid. At the very least, they kept you sane. At the most, they kept you alive."

Finally somebody understood! "Darn straight they did!"

Too bad his victory didn't last long. Steve fixed him with that look, the one that said, *Get ready, 'cuz you're not going to like this,* and fired the shot that almost did Gabe in.

"They protected you when you were a kid, but they're killing you now. And they're killing your marriage. Especially your anger. It's no longer a shield, but a weapon. And you've got to lay it down."

Oh yeah, the last few months had been tough. But Steve hung in there, even when Gabe lost it and let his rage roar. And slowly but surely, Gabe made changes. Little ones at first, like agreeing to make himself take a time-out when he felt his anger build, then bigger things, like letting a few trusted friends—Grace and Oren, mostly—see him as he really was. Not as he thought they wanted him to be, but just as him. Gabe. In all his glorious brokenness.

Funny thing, no one had run screaming from the room. In fact, they'd seemed to like him better when he was just being himself. And Gabe found himself relaxing, even having fun.

More than that, he found himself starting to trust. And, as incredible as it seemed, he was more at peace now. With himself. With Renee.

With God.

If only Renee could see that. But no matter how he tried, all she saw was who he used to be. The woman watched for even the slightest slip on his part, the smallest indication that the man she'd walked out on was still there, alive and well and in control.

She's looking for perfection, God, and You and I both know I haven't got it. If he was never allowed to make a mistake, to even *start* to fall back into old patterns, then he didn't have a chance. He was never going to be what she neede—

He stopped himself. He didn't even need Steve's reminder

this time. The tapes were turned to full volume, and for once he replaced the lie with truth. Satan's lies couldn't stand against God's truth—or so Steve said.

Gabe closed his eyes. Might as well test Steve's theory.

"Don't get tired of doing what is good. Don't get discouraged and give up, for we will reap a harvest of blessing at the appropriate time."

Gabe let the words run through his mind, over and over, relieved when he realized it was all he heard. The tapes had grown quiet. They weren't shut off; he knew better than that. But at least they weren't drowning out everything else in his mind.

"Cool..." He turned his eyes to the sky.

"I suppose it's cooler than it was this afternoon, thank goodness."

Gabe looked to find Oren walking across the grass, coming to join him. As always, Oren was the epitome of unruffled calm. Gabe didn't think he'd ever seen that steady, ever-present tranquility leave his eyes, his features.

Peace.

Everything about the man spoke peace.

Pierced by a sudden, sharp envy, Gabe straightened. "You forgot your umbrella, Oren," he said by way of distracting himself from all this man was—and he wasn't.

"Umbrellas are for sissies." Oren's grin was infectious. "Besides, I like these nice, warm rains." He walked to a pile of wood and pulled out a thick stick about the size of his palm, then came to ease himself down into a chair with a small grunt. He gave Gabe a small smile. "Don't remember these things being so far down when we first got them."

He lifted the piece of wood, brushing at it, studying it. "So," he said, his eyes still on the wood, "I take it you didn't have a good time with Renee?"

The snort escaped Gabe before he even knew it was coming. "Renee wouldn't know a good time if it came up to bite her on the—" he pulled himself up short, then opted for a less offensive word than he'd been planning to use—"nose."

Gabe fell silent. He waited for Oren to tell him what a jerk he was being, but the older man just pulled a pocketknife from his jacket and started stripping the bark from the branch.

Gabe clamped his jaw, trapping the words that wanted to come tumbling out. Frustration and desperation, apology and appeal. It was all there. He wanted to rant and rave and have the man tell him he was right, that Renee was an unreasonable witch. And yet, despite himself, right on the heels of that desire was the urge to ask Oren what he should do. To beg the older man to tell him how to make things right when they'd gone so terribly wrong.

But he didn't say a word. This was his problem. He'd spent years creating it, building layer after layer of miscommunication and misunderstanding. Didn't matter that he'd usually done so without even realizing it. Didn't matter that he'd thought he was doing the right thing.

All that mattered was he'd messed everything up. So what made him think Oren would want to hear it, let alone try to fix it for him?

No. Gabe was on his own.

As the silence between them lengthened, Gabe looked away. Shifted position on the wooden bench. Plunged his hands deep into his pockets. He kept sneaking glances at Oren, but the man just sat there, hands moving with steady precision as he worked on the wood.

Suddenly Gabe was six again, staring at his silent, brooding father, studying body language, stance, features...anything for a clue to what was going on in the other man's thoughts. Was Oren mad at him? That last crack about Renee had been a cheap shot, and Gabe knew it. He opened his mouth to say something, maybe even to apologize, but Oren—who had finished stripping the bark away and now started working on the wood with slow, steady strokes of the knife—spoke first.

"You remember the story of Elijah, son?"

Son.

Lord. O Lord...

Gabe's throat constricted as he leaned back. Son. Oren said it so easily, so naturally...as if he really meant it. Really thought of Gabe that way.

Right. Why should Oren think of you as his son when your own father couldn't stand the sight of you?

The muscles in Gabe's chest tightened into a fierce, aching knot.

"Yes, sir." Oren went on as though Gabe had replied rather than just sat there, staring at nothing, chewing his anger like a pup with a ratty old sock. "That Elijah was something else. Did you know he took his world, and the king—Ahab, I think it was—by storm?"

Gabe folded his arms and angled a look at Oren. Again with the Bible stories. They spilled out of Oren like grain from a silo. What Gabe wanted to know was why this man was even out here talking to him. Didn't he know Gabe was a lost cause?

Apparently not. He just gave a small shake of his head, as though amused by something, and went on. Gabe forced himself to focus on what Oren was saying.

"Of course, it was God's storm, not Elijah's."

"Oh?" Gabe tried to sound interested. It was the least he could do. "How so?"

"Well, Elijah just did one miracle after another. First he greets a new king by telling him there won't be any rain in the land until Elijah says so. Then he gives a widow woman bottomless containers of oil and flour. And when her son dies, Elijah brings the boy back to life."

A frown drew his brow tight. Fine. If Oren wanted to talk Bible, he'd play along. Gabe wasn't exactly uninformed when it came to God's Word. He'd been in seminary, after all. He even remembered Elijah. One of the few gutsy guys in the Bible. "He made a bunch of self-righteous priests look like fools."

Oren's smile broadened. "That he did. Always liked that about Elijah. Challenged Baal's priests to a little contest. Said they should build an altar to *their* gods, and he'd build one to *his*. They'd prepare an offering and pray for the altars to be set on fire. The god who answered first would be declared the true God. Baal's priests figured it was a done deal. So they got everything ready and prayed. For days. But nothing happened."

Oh yeah, Gabe remembered this part of the story. "Elijah said their gods must not hear them because he was off...uh—" he waggled his eyebrows—"*relieving* himself."

Oren's deep chuckle filled the night. "Leave it to you to remember that."

"Hey, at least it proves I *do* read the Bible." The comment was only half joking. Gabe knew Renee thought he never cracked the cover of his Bible anymore. He'd be amazed if she kept that opinion to herself.

Oren stopped his whittling and met Gabe's challenge straight on. "I knew that, Gabe. Never doubted it, no matter what anyone said. Just like I've always known you want to be God's man."

Gabe scrambled for a flippant response but couldn't find one. The emotions rocking made it too hard to think. How could this man say such things? How could he speak with such confidence in Gabe? Especially when those who knew him best—his father...his *wife*—had no confidence in him at all?

He waved the questions away. Things were getting entirely too serious—and entirely too focused on him. "So anyway, what were you saying about Elijah?"

Gabe figured Oren recognized the question for what it was: a ploy to get the conversation off of the one topic he was heartily sick of—himself. So he was grateful when Oren let the moment go.

"Well, you know the priests of Baal gave up, so Elijah doused his altar with water. Even dug a trench around it and filled that with water. Then he prayed to God."

"Once. He prayed one time." That was all it took. One prayer from the prophet, and God answered. In spades.

So why hasn't He answered you? You're not a prophet, but you believe. So what's the deal? Doesn't God care enough about you to answer your prayers? Gabe stiffened against the rush of anger the question brought to life.

"Right. Elijah prayed, and God sent a fire from heaven that consumed the offering, the altar, even the water in the trench."

Gabe felt Oren's steady focus on him. He had the distinct sense that nothing escaped this man's notice. He wasn't sure if that was a comfort or a confirmation that Gabe should stay as far away from him as possible.

Oren tapped the branch he was working into his palm, and Gabe was relieved when Oren lowered his eyes to study the branch instead of him. He watched as the older man smoothed the wood with his fingers.

What was it Oren had told him once about whittling? That he liked seeing the secrets in the wood, discovering what lay deep inside just waiting to come out…

His words came back to Gabe like a whisper on the wind: *"All it takes is patience and a skilled blade."*

"Must have been pretty impressive—" Oren's gaze didn't leave his work—"since Ahab and the people followed Elijah's orders to slaughter the priests of Baal. But Elijah wasn't done, even after that."

"Seems like plenty to do in a day."

Oren's mouth tipped at Gabe's muttered comment. "You'd think so, but he had more in mind. He prayed for rain. And like the fire, it came, ending the drought he'd predicted some three years earlier."

It was fascinating to watch Oren work his small knife.

Gabe could see something taking shape beneath his hands, but couldn't tell what it was. He considered leaning closer, getting a better look, but something held him back.

"Just like that, this one man, a prophet no less, brought King Ahab to his knees."

Gabe looked at the sky. What would that be like? How would it feel to have that much impact on someone of such importance? On someone, period. What would it be like to have people actually listen to what you had to say? "Must be nice."

Oren cupped the piece of wood in one palm, then held his knife like a pencil in the other hand, working the tip into the wood. "For a while, I expect it was."

"A while?"

Oren met Gabe's question with a nod. "Less than a day, in fact. Ahab went home and told his wife, Jezebel, all about it. She was a bit upset that her priests had been killed and sent Elijah a message that she was going to do the same to him." He blew on the wood, and tiny shavings floated to the ground. "Remember what he did?"

Gabe thought about it. "No, but he must have let her have it, too. After all, he'd just seen God use him to do some amazing things. Why would he be afraid of one woman?"

Oren's expression was unreadable. "Why, indeed? It's a good question, and not just for Elijah. Why are any of us afraid of the women in our lives?"

Gabe's spine stiffened at that. "I'm not afraid of Renee."

"No?"

"No."

Oren looked beyond Gabe to the small creek behind them, to the budding branches of the trees around them. "So you're out here because...?"

Gabe opened his mouth, but words didn't come. They couldn't, because he suddenly knew anything he had to say was a lie.

He *was* afraid. Of Renee, of the ways she could cut and wound him, of seeing that weary disappointment on her face, of watching the spark in her eyes sputter and die, leaving a dullness there that cut him more deeply than any blade ever could.

Afraid? You'd better believe it. And he hated himself for it.

"It's okay, Gabe. We all face the same feelings."

He shook his head, trying to dislodge the words from his tight, aching throat. "No...not like this."

Oren slid the wood and his knife into his pocket and stood. He came to lay a hand on his shoulder. "Yes, Gabe. Just like this."

He looked into the older man's face, saw the compassion, the understanding. If only he could believe what Oren was saying.

"It's just like Elijah. Here he'd done all these amazing, impossible things, and then one threat from Jezebel, and what does he do? Pray? Ask God for help? No way. He heads for the hills."

Gabe had forgotten that. "He ran."

Oren's nod was firm. "He ran. Just like so many of us when we're worn out by life, by dealing with the world day in and day out. We go through each day doing the seemingly impossible, even seeing the amazing ways God works in our lives and our work, and then we come home, wanting nothing more than to be loved and appreciated."

Gabe couldn't restrain the nod, the groan of agreement. "That's all I ever wanted. Just to know she appreciated all that I was doing."

"I hear you, son. But you know what? Not many of us get that—any more often than we give it."

Anger escaped Gabe in a snort and he pushed himself up from the bench. The emotions churning within him begged for some kind of release, and since there wasn't anything out here to throw, he settled for pacing. He stuffed his hands deep into his pockets. Kept him from hitting something.

Oren moved back to his chair. "Tell you what I think, Gabe." He pulled the twig and the knife from his pocket and went back to work. "I think Elijah folded out of pure exhaustion. He was worn out, physically and spiritually. What he probably needed was rest. To step away from the intensity of the battle and let God refresh him. Instead, he tried to do it all himself. To take the hits, to handle it. He forgot who was the Shepherd and who was the sheep. Forgot his life wasn't in his hands, but in those of the Master. He ended up letting his emotions take over his thinking, and that led to some mighty bad choices. And like any sheep in a panic, he ran straight for the cliff. It was only God's grace that kept him from going over the edge."

Gabe slowed, then came to a halt. He turned to study the man sitting there. "What are you saying, Oren?" He narrowed his eyes, looking around them at the rain-laden landscape. "I don't think you came out here to teach me a Bible lesson. So just say it, okay?"

A smile peeked out from Oren's face. "No, I'm clearly no Bible teacher. So you want it straight?"

Gabe braced himself. Now it would come, Oren telling him what he'd done wrong, how worthless he was for treating Renee the way he had. Well, he'd asked for it, so he better just take it. "Please."

"Okay, straight out, I think you're like Elijah, son."

Gabe frowned. What was that supposed to mean?

"I think you've forgotten you're just one of the sheep, that it's not your job to make everything work out right. To take care of everything and everyone."

Oren leaned back in his chair, tilting his head as he studied Gabe. "You had a bad start, son. Worse than most. And you've had some mighty hard hits since then. But despite all that, you're doing what you know to do. God is doing some amazing things in your life. He's called you to obedience even in the face of all the doubts, and in many ways, you've done well." There was no denying the sincerity in either his tone or his eyes. "I've seen the changes in you, Gabe. And I know they weren't easy. But there's this thing inside of you that won't let you open yourself up. Won't let you lean on anyone, not your friends or your family. Not even the Shepherd."

Oren stood and came to stand in front of Gabe. He reached into his coat pocket and pulled out his whittling project, then pressed it into Gabe's hand. "I know you're used to standing on your own. I know you've felt like the one who had to protect everyone else for a long time. But that time is past. I'm here. Gracie is here. Your counselor, your friends in the Bible study—" his gaze softened—"even Renee. We're all here for you, just waiting for you to realize it. And God, Gabe. God's here, too. It's time to let yourself join the flock, to be one of the sheep, and rest in the Shepherd's care."

He patted Gabe's arm. "All you have to do is let us in, son. And we'll get through this thing. Together. I know it won't be easy, but I'm here to tell you the best thing you can do is ignore that voice that tells you it isn't safe, that you have to do this on your own. That's a lie, Gabe. And you know where it's gotten you so far." He lifted one shoulder in a slight shrug. "Why not take a risk and give the truth a chance?" He looked to the house, then waved. "Looks like Gracie wants to talk to me, so I'm going to head in." His gaze caught Gabe's and held it. "You okay?"

Gabe nodded, and Oren started back toward the house. Gabe did move. He stood, looking into the sky.

"We're all here for you, just waiting for you to realize it… All you have to do is let us in… Why not take a risk and give the truth a chance?"

Gabe felt his hands clench, then flinched. He looked down at the small piece of wood in his palm, and in the moonlight pouring over the yard, he saw a small, intricately carved lamb curled in his hand. Its head rested on its stretched-out front legs, its eyes were closed, and a look of pure, trusting contentment was on its tiny face.

He tipped it to the light and saw that what the lamb rested on was two simple words: *Trust Me.*

Gabe's hand closed over the lamb as he lifted his face to the stars. "I'll try, God. I can't make any promises beyond that...I will try."

He only hoped Oren was right, that he wouldn't have to do it alone. He was going to need all the help he could get.

I'm sorry, God. I'm so sorry...and I'm not even sure for what.

36

I would not consider any spirituality worthwhile that wants to walk in
sweetness and ease and run from all the imitation of Christ.

JOHN CLIMACUS

If you claim to be religious but don't control your tongue,
you are just fooling yourself, and your religion is worthless.

JAMES 1:26

AUGUST 1993

RENEE LOVED THE QUIET.

So much of her life with Gabe had been filled with yelling
and emotional violence that she'd forgotten the beauty of silence.
But since their separation, she found herself spending night after
night at home, the TV and radio off, just sitting there.

Soaking in the peace.

Tonight, though, peace seemed far away. Ever since she'd
been with Gabe on the Fourth, troubling thoughts had been
plaguing Renee. Why couldn't she just relax? Just trust what her
own eyes and heart were telling her: that Gabe was changing. For
the better.

The answer had come, but she hadn't liked it. Not one bit.

Because I'm afraid. I can't trust because I'm afraid.

And who could blame her? Gabe was a master at playing a
role. What if that was all this was? Just another role until he got

what he wanted? Was she supposed to forget all those years of conflict after a few months of improvement? What if she started to believe in him and it blew up? What if—

What right do you have to judge?

That drew her up short. "Who better than I? I *lived* with him."

You are not a judge who can decide what is right or wrong. God alone can rightly judge among us.

Renee jumped up from the couch, not wanting to hear, to think, anymore. She went to fix herself a cup of hot tea, then put on some of her favorite CDs...any distraction she could think of. As she returned to the living room, the shelf of photo albums caught her eye.

She loved looking through photo albums. Almost every time she went to her parents' house to visit, she'd end up pulling out the albums and paging through her past. It was so much fun to see them all as they'd been back then.

Good. She'd wanted a distraction and now she had one. If she started at the beginning of the albums and worked her way to the end, she'd keep herself busy most of the night.

She pulled out the very first album she and Gabe had started together and padded back to the couch.

Before the night was over, she'd gone through all the years she and Gabe had been married. But the photos hadn't distracted her at all. In fact, they'd done just the opposite.

As she turned each page, studied each face frozen in time, she'd been struck first by the changes in Gabe. In the early photos, though he wasn't exactly carefree, he'd been smiling, hopeful, clearly looking forward to what was coming. In the most recent photos...

Gone was the relaxed, smiling Gabe. In his place stood a man whose features, whose posture, whose haunted eyes screamed pain. This was a man whose spirit was weighed down almost to the breaking point.

Then Renee realized something else. Her own face smiled out at her from the pictures, laughing, clearly happy—but only when she was with her friends and family. When it came to pictures of her with Gabe, it was a completely different story.

Or rather, she was a completely different person.

She stood there, sometimes beside him but usually in the background, looking like one of the most belligerent women she'd ever seen. Disdain, contempt, anger, resentment—it glowered in her eyes, pulled at her features. In almost every shot she had her arms crossed or was leaning away from Gabe, barely tolerating his arm around her.

It was not a pretty picture.

Renee stared, hardly able to believe that the pinched-faced woman was her. But it was. And as she looked into those resentful eyes, all she could think of was how miserable it must have been to live, day in and day out, with a woman like that.

What was it Proverbs said? A contentious woman was as annoying as a constant dripping on a rainy day?

Renee's eyes went back to the photos and she felt her mouth droop. She'd been dripping, all right. And then some.

Gabe had suffered that woman for years. No wonder he'd fallen back into acting a part, keeping his real needs and his real heart hidden. He'd had to protect himself. And now...he was doing everything he could to be real, to be who he was deep inside. To win her back, to earn her trust.

Why? She covered the picture with her hand. Why would he want to be around her ever again?

Because he loves you.

"I know that!" She hissed the words into the stillness around her. "He's always loved me. Or said he has. But that didn't change his behavior, didn't stop the rages—"

He's changing now.

"It's too late. How can I let it all go, just forget about what he's done, what he's taken from me?"

You have nothing but what I have given you. All you have has come from My hand, child.

She closed her eyes, but the hard words weren't finished.

Humble yourself before God. Wash your hands; purify your heart. Let there be tears for the wrong you have done. When you bow down before the Lord and admit your dependence on Him, He will lift you up and give you honor.

Heart breaking, Renee closed the album, letting it slide from her lap to the floor. She followed it, falling to her knees.

All these years she'd told herself the problems in her marriage lay at Gabe's door. They were *his* fault, *his* mess to clean up, because of his childhood, his issues, his anger. Once he got his act together, things would fall into place, life would be good.

Well, he'd been doing exactly that—getting his act together. And she had only grown more demanding, more critical.

More like the woman in the pictures.

Life with that woman would never be good. No matter how much Gabe changed. That woman wanted what she wanted, when she wanted it, and resented anyone who kept her from getting it.

How had Gabe endured her for so long?

Because he felt it was all he deserved.

Why didn't I see it? Why didn't I see what I was doing?

Because you thought you deserved more.

The realization was as swift as it was terrible, and as Renee knelt there, head bowed, the veil that had been over her eyes, over her understanding, finally tore and fell away.

She'd always believed she knew God so intimately that when she finally met him face-to-face in eternity, she would run and leap into his lap with the abandon of an adoring daughter. But now, finally faced with herself, she understood she hardly knew God at all. She had turned Him, in her mind, into some kind of celestial daddy, a tolerant and patient paternal figure who loved and adored her, tolerating her willful heart as just another likable quirk.

Now the truth washed over her. Yes, He loved her. Yes, He accepted her as she was because of Christ. But no, He did not see her willfulness as a quirk. He saw it for what it was.

Sin.

And as such, it had kept her from Him. Even as it had kept her from Gabe.

I'm sorry...I'm so sorry...

Renee wept her repentance late into the night, and when she finally rose from her knees she knew it wasn't enough to ask forgiveness.

She had to extend it as well.

Hope is a delicate thing.

It takes so little to crush it, to grind it into the dirt of disappointment and anger. And yet...

Hope is indestructible.

No matter how we stomp it down; no matter what we pile on top of it, smothering it, blocking the light so it can't grow, be nurtured...

No matter what we do, it's still there. Waiting. And all it takes is the smallest ray of light, the merest drop of water, and it uncoils, reaches, stretches, and suddenly explodes from ground that looked dead and useless.

You amaze me, God. With hope.

37

Marriage is both a gift and a task to be accomplished.

OTTO PIPER

*It is all so wonderful that even the angels are
eagerly watching these things happen.*

1 PETER 1:12

OCTOBER 1993, SATURDAY MORNING

GABE PUSHED THE CAR DOOR OPEN AND SLID OUT.
He hunched his shoulders, trying to ease some of the tension
before he went inside.

There was far too much potential for tension waiting inside.

But not as much as there used to be.

It was true, and that fact helped his shoulders relax. He tossed
the apartment key into the air and caught it, enjoying the feel of it
in his hand. The day Renee returned his apartment key to him
was one of the best days he'd had in a long time. Partly because
he finally had access again to his home, but mostly because of the
gladness he'd seen in Renee's eyes. And the trust.

Gabe had wondered if he'd ever see that look in her eyes
again.

He made his way up the walkway, then slid his key into the
lock and opened the door, making sure his tread on the steps was

loud enough for Renee to know he was coming.

"Gabe!"

The alarm in Renee's voice sent him bounding up the last few stairs. She only sounded like that when something serious was happening, some kind of emergency.

He shoved open the door at the top and bolted into the apartment. "Renee?"

"In here!"

He rushed into the sunroom, then halted. She was standing at the south window, hands pressed against the glass. The early morning sun glinted on her hair, setting the red highlights on fire. Warmth filled him as he studied her, remembering how she felt when she melted against him—

"Oh, Gabe…"

Her broken whisper snapped him out of his thoughts, and he went to her side, reaching out to touch her shoulder, grateful she no longer jerked away from him. Not as often, anyway. She turned wide eyes to him, and the dismay in her features brought a quick frown to his face.

"Sweetheart, what's—"

"Look." She pointed out the window, where, on the phone wires extending from the house, dangled a gray squirrel. It was a tiny thing—obviously just a baby. Where on earth was the critter's mother? A quick scan of the trees brought him an answer. A larger version of the baby was perched on a branch just above the wire, tail puffed out like a bottle brush. Gabe scanned the tree and spotted a nest. The little squirrel must have fallen out and landed on the wire.

From the looks of things, it wouldn't be long until the animal plunged the fifteen feet or so to the concrete driveway below. Gabe shook his head. Nature could be tough…

"A fall like that will kill him, won't it?"

At the tears in her voice, Gabe sighed. *This* was the emergency? A squirrel? "Renee, honey…"

"Can't you do something?"

Her green eyes were fixed on him, and he knew there was no way he was going to turn away from the pleading he saw in them. He studied the situation again. "I don't—"

"Maybe we could catch him or something."

Gabe shook his head again. "No…"

"We can't just watch him die."

He turned to her, about to tell her it was pretty hopeless, but he stopped. If there was one thing he knew about his wife, it was that she loved animals and children and couldn't stand to see either in peril. With animals, especially, she seemed to have some kind of special bond. He'd taken Renee to plenty of action movies, and used to worry that seeing dozens of people shot or blown up would bother her. Not a problem. She wasn't even fazed.

But let a dog or a horse or any critter get injured or threatened, and she lost it. Her tender heart just couldn't take it.

He reached out to pull her close, and as she pressed her face into his chest, he rested his chin on top of her head, breathing in the faint fragrance of vanilla. She always smelled like just-baked cookies. He closed his eyes, letting her warmth seep into him. *Lord, this feels good. I've missed her so much…*

Emotion welled up in his throat, and he swallowed hard against it. To distract himself, he glanced back out the window at the still-struggling squirrel…and sighed.

He didn't know if he could help, but he at least owed the little critter the effort to try. After all, that little ball of fur had gotten Renee back into his arms, even if only for a little while. He gave her a squeeze, then stepped back. The hope on her face as she looked up at him made him feel great. Invincible, even.

"I'm not promising anything, hon, but I'll tr—"

Renee launched herself at him, wrapping her arms around his neck and squeezing until he could hardly breathe.

Laughing, he returned squeeze for squeeze and dropped a quick kiss on her now smiling lips.

"I knew you'd think of something."

An odd pain struck him at her words. If only she held such confidence in him when it mattered...really mattered.

Forcing a smile back to his lips, he pulled away and headed down the back stairs, to the basement. There he gathered a ladder, a broom, a discarded broom handle, and his roll of duct tape. *Gray tape,* his mind corrected him.

He grinned. "Whatever it is, don't leave home without it."

Outside, he could hear the squirrel's squeaky screams as it struggled to hold on to the wire. Gabe scanned the nearby trees again. Last thing he needed was to have the little guy's mom come down on his head while he was trying to play the rescuing hero. She was still on her perch, but she'd spotted him and was directing her angry chatter his way.

"Relax, Mama, I'm the hero."

Clearly unconvinced, the squirrel's tail twitched and she upped the volume a notch. He knelt and taped the broom handles together, then situated the ladder just below the squirrel and made his way up. He perched on the rung just below the top of the ladder and extended his makeshift rescue rod.

It was too short. He grimaced as he realized he would have to balance on the top of the ladder.

"No way."

How often had he made fun of guys who did that, who put themselves at ridiculous risk, no matter how good the reason? No way was he going to do exactly what he'd been telling people for years *not* to do—

"Be careful, Gabe."

He started and had to wave his arms wildly to keep from toppling off the ladder. The broom clattered to the ground as he caught his balance and shot a glare to the windows above. Renee had opened one of the windows and was leaning out, peering down at him, her eyes wide. Even from this distance he could see the red creeping up her cheeks as she realized what she'd just done.

"I'm sor—"

He held up a hand, halting her, and made his way down to retrieve the broom. Drawing a deep breath, he climbed the ladder again, then glanced up at Renee. She was looking from him to the squirrel, and the trust on her face told the whole story. He had no choice.

Shaking his head, he stepped onto the top of the ladder. "I must be crazy…"

"Gabe—"

He tried to keep his words from sounding tense. "I need to concentrate here, Renee."

She clamped her mouth shut and nodded, but worry showed in her creased brow. Well, why shouldn't she be worried? He sure was. Only an idiot stood on the top of a ladder.

Don't think about it. Just focus on the task at hand.

With slow, careful movements, he extended the broom so that the head was just below the little squirrel's scrambling legs. Gabe held his breath as the little guy tried to get away from the broom, then, as though suddenly realizing this was solid ground, let go of the wire and clamped onto the broom head.

As quickly as he dared, Gabe swiveled, extending the broom to the tree, where the mother squirrel kept up her constant, frantic scolding. He nudged the little squirrel against a branch, and as though understanding perfectly, the little furball jumped off the broom and onto the branch. In a heartbeat the mother was beside her baby, snatching him up and scampering back to the next branch, tail twitching like a conductor's baton.

Gabe glanced up to share the victory with Renee, but she was gone. His euphoria vanished in an instant, replaced by a disappointment so sharp and keen that it made it hard to breathe. She hadn't stayed to see the rescue? He clenched his teeth. She'd probably decided he would fail. That he'd end up knocking the squirrel to the ground. He caught an oath deep in his throat, not willing to give voice to his frustration. He threw the broom to the ground, then made his way down the ladder, calling himself every kind of fool for thinking she believed in him.

He had barely reached the ground when the back door burst open and Renee was there, running to him. Before he could take it in, she was in his arms, her face pressed against him, her hands warm and firm at his back.

"Thank you."

Her smile glowed up at him, and instead of the disdain he so often saw in her expression, there was only gratitude. He didn't question or try to analyze what was happening. There wasn't really time. He just took the moment for what it was: a gift.

He gathered her close, savoring the feel of her, and lowered his head, half holding his breath in case she stiffened and backed away. But she didn't. She met his kiss without hesitation, and for a moment they were a part of each other again, connected, sharing the very essence of who they were. Like they'd been at the beginning. Like he thought they'd always be.

When their lips parted, he rested his forehead against hers, breathing in the fragrance that was so uniquely Renee. "I've missed you."

She leaned back, then lifted a hand to cup his face, her touch feather-soft. "I've missed you, too."

They stood there, neither one wanting to break the moment. Renee moved first, stepping back, out of his arms, but she slid a hand down his arm as she moved until their fingers entwined.

"Gabe, I have something I want to ask you."

He held his silence. Whatever it was, he wasn't afraid. And that in itself was a miracle.

"Will you come home?"

Come home? Did she mean…? Well, Steve had been telling him to ask for clarification when he wasn't clear. "I'm not sure I understand, Renee. What do you mean, come home?"

She looked down at their joined hands, then back up at him. "I mean move back home, into our apartment. I miss you, Gabe, and I want you home. With me." She bit her lip. "If…you're ready. If not, I understand. I really do. But I wanted you to know that I'd like you to come home."

Gabe stood there, looking down at her, stunned to find himself at a total loss for words.

Renee stood, waiting. It was one of the hardest things she'd had to do in a long time.

She wanted an answer, and she wanted it now. And she wanted it to be yes. She'd hoped Gabe would react with excitement, enthusiasm, and if she was honest she had to admit it hurt a bit that he didn't.

But she understood his hesitation. They'd made a lot of progress, but things were far from smooth. They still had conflicts, still drove each other nuts at times, still fell into old patterns far too often.

And yet, Renee knew she was ready for him to come home. She'd seen such amazing changes in him over the past year, and she'd worked hard to make changes as well.

Of course, that came a good deal more slowly…

She didn't bother to deny it, was just grateful it had finally come. Of course, changing the way she looked at Gabe was far from easy, and she'd failed more than she'd succeeded, but she was trying. Which was why she didn't try to rush Gabe, to pull the answer she wanted from him. She just waited.

"Renee, I need to think about this. Pray about it."

She let the disappointment come and go. She'd made her request. Gabe had every right to respond to it in his own way, his own timing. And how could she possibly object to his wanting to pray about it?

Renee linked her arm with his. "I think that's a good idea. Now, didn't I hear you say something about ordering pizza and renting a video tonight?"

Surprise lit his features at her acceptance, and then relief. But her best reward came when he smiled—because what lifted his lips was the relaxed, almost happy smile she'd seen in those earlier pictures.

They weren't out of the woods, not by a long shot. But for this moment, at least, they'd reached a clearing.

38

If you wish me conventional happiness,
I will never forgive you. Don't wish me happiness...
Wish me courage and strength and a
sense of humor—I will need them all.

ANNE LINDBERGH

As for me, I am poor and needy, but the Lord
is thinking about me right now.
You are my helper and my savior. Do not delay, O my God.

PSALM 40:17

OCTOBER 1993, SATURDAY EVENING

"GRACE, OREN, CAN I TALK WITH YOU?"

Grace looked up from the book she was reading and found Gabe standing in the doorway of the family room.

Oren laid down his own book and slid his bifocals from his face. "Sure, come on in."

Grace nodded her agreement to Oren's invitation, but Gabe leaned in the doorway. "I just wanted to ask you guys to be praying for me. I...have a decision to make." When they didn't say anything, he went on. "Renee has asked me to move back in with her."

How Grace kept herself from jumping up and bouncing on the couch, she didn't know. If only she could be as reserved and calm as Oren. He just gave Gabe a warm smile.

"We'll be praying for you, son. I know you'll make the right decision."

That brought Gabe into the room, and he fell to pacing on Grace's favorite hand-thrown rug.

"Gabe—" she smiled and patted the couch—"why don't you sit down, dear?"

"I'm not sure I'm ready."

Grace frowned. "To sit down?"

Oren shot her a look, and she bit her lip. "Oh. Sorry."

He turned back to Gabe. "You may never feel ready. Not really."

"But what if…"

"What?"

He turned away. "What if this whole thing is a mistake? What if Renee and I were never meant to be married? What if we're just not right for each other?"

If the pain in his voice was any indication of the ache in his heart, Gabe was really hurting. And really afraid. Grace went to join him, sliding her arm around his waist. She could always buy another rug.

He leaned into her. "If I move back in, it will just be that much harder to walk away when…if it doesn't work out."

Oren leaned back in his chair. "I don't think the question is whether or not you're right for each other. There *is* no right person out there. We're all human and broken. I think you know the key to marriage isn't finding the right person—it's becoming the right person. It's working and struggling and giving up your selfishness; it's being willing to confront at times and confess at others."

Gabe gave Grace a hug and moved to sit on the couch. She followed him with a smile. "Renee and I are doing pretty well right now. I'm just worried that when we're together, day in and day out, well…we'll blow it. *I'll* blow it."

"Of course you will." Oren's smile lit his face. "That's where forgiveness comes in, and mercy. And keeping in mind that your behavior doesn't depend on Renee or what she says and does. It depends on you. You determine your actions, not Renee. You're the one who has to resolve to pursue Renee, to love her, even in the midst of anger, frustration, disappointment, whatever. You made the choice to marry her, and that means you have made a commitment to embrace her, to open yourself to her, and to let God redefine your fears, your resistance, even the hate you sometimes feel, into His love."

Gabe rubbed the back of his neck. "That's a tall order."

"But it's God's order. And that means He'll give you the wisdom and strength to carry it out."

Grace laid a hand on Gabe's arm. "My mother told me a long time ago that when you marry someone, you give him or her the gift of yourself. I think you need to ask yourself if you're ready to do that. Are you ready to give yourself to Renee?"

He fell silent, and after a few moments, Grace and Oren went back to their books. But Grace couldn't hold back a smile when Gabe rose from the couch, determination on his features.

"I'm going to make a phone call."

Grace reached for Oren's hand. "To your wife?"

"To my wife."

Renee pounced on the phone at the first ring.

"Renee?"

Oh, she'd hoped it was Gabe! She held the receiver with both hands, her heart pounding. "Hi, Gabe."

"Can I come back over and talk, just for a few minutes?"

You can come for as long as you want. "Sure, come on over."

"I'll be there in twenty minutes."

Renee set the phone back in the cradle, and her hand rested on top of the receiver for a few seconds. *You know what I want, Lord, and so does Gabe. But even more than Gabe coming home, I want us to do this Your way. So help me be patient and understanding, whatever he's coming to say.*

She made her way down to the porch steps, and true to his word, twenty minutes later Gabe's car pulled into the drive. He walked from the car, and she thought there was purpose to his steps.

"You want to sit out here? It's a nice night."

He nodded and came to perch on the top step beside her. He rested his elbows on his knees and angled a look at her. "Rennie, I don't know what the future holds, but I know this: I want to make us work. And I think you're right. We can't really do that until we're together. Really together again."

Her pulse pounding in her ears, she made certain she was hearing what she thought she was. "Are you saying...?"

His gaze was as steady as his words. "I want to come home."

She took his hand in hers and nodded. A new start. Again. They seemed to end up here so often...

This time, though, it was different. It might not be the last time they needed to start over—she knew herself, and their relationship, too well to believe that—but she prayed they'd never again let things go so very wrong.

Please, Father, don't ever let us pull so far apart again.

She leaned against Gabe's arm, grateful just to be together, sitting under the stars, surrounded by a silence that spoke volumes.

Lord, how you afflict your lovers!
But everything is small in comparison to what you give them afterward.
TERESA OF AVILA

Trust yourself to the God who made you, for he will never fail you.
1 PETER 4:19

DECEMBER 20, 2003
3:30 P.M.

GABE SAT ON A FALLEN LOG, MAKING CIRCLES IN THE snow with the toe of his boot.

Renee had been gone only a half hour or so, but out here—in this white, muted world—it felt like hours.

A half hour. Just long enough for him to get worried…but he wasn't. And he wasn't quite sure why. He'd considered going after her, but something stopped him. It was as though some invisible hand came to rest on his shoulder, holding him there, keeping him silent and still as a parade of thoughts marched through his mind.

What he'd said to Renee was true, but if he was going to be honest, he had to admit there was truth to what she said, too. He definitely had built barriers between them. It's only common sense. *She walked out, remember? Why do I have to open myself, be vulnerable? Where will that leave me when she walks out again?*

When?

He dragged his foot through the snow, erasing all his nice round circles. Why should he think any different?

Because she's still here. After all the pain, all the struggles, she's still here.

As was the anger. Always the anger.

Because you hold on to it. Think you need it. But what you really need is to let it go. Release it...release yourself.

I can't. He tossed a stick onto the fire. *I can't just drop my defenses, just like that.*

You won't.

What if she leaves me again? I'll be alone.

The thought pulled a harsh laugh from him. Who was he kidding? He was *already* alone. He always had been.

Not always. I am with you.

Gabe recognized the whisper of truth and hung his head. God...God...

I am with you. Even to the ends of the earth.

He rubbed a trembling hand over his eyes. *It's not the ends of the earth I'm worried about. It's the end of myself.*

If you try to keep your life for yourself, you will lose it.

The words shuddered through him, raising the hair on his arms, his neck. He thought he knew what was coming next. He was right.

But if you give up your life for Me, you will find true life.

True life. He let this echo through him. True life. Life without pretense, without playing a part...without the barrier of anger...without doing and saying things he regretted the minute they were done or said...

Was it possible? Could he really give up the defenses he'd held on to for so long? For his whole life?

Jesus, I'm afraid.

And suddenly, Gabe knew. This was the core of his struggle. Not anger. Anger was the response, the defense. The real problem was far deeper. Far more powerful.

Fear. Fear of never being good enough. Fear of having everything and everyone walk away from him. Fear of being rejected, abandoned...

Utterly, completely alone.

Come unto Me, all ye who labor and are heavy laden, and I will give you rest.

Rest. How long since he last rested in anyone or anything? He wanted to rest. Oh, how he wanted it.

I don't know how...

The answer rang out with such force that he couldn't tell if it was inside him or all around him, in the snow, on the wind: *Come...and I will give you rest.*

Gabe lowered his head to his hands. Could it really be that simple? A fierce longing stirred within him, a longing to be free of facade. Of pretense. Of images. But most of all, to be free of the anger.

Free? Without anger, you're nothing! Weak. Defenseless. That's not freedom, that's insanity.

The response was so familiar, so predictable, Gabe almost laughed. This he knew well—this voice that crawled through him like some dark stain seeping through the fabric of his soul, turning light to dark, friend to foe, help to threat. But this time he recognized it for what it was.

Fear. The voice of fear.

And he recognized something else.

Fear wasn't truth.

Thoughts tumbled over each other, flowing through Gabe with the force of a rain-swollen river finally breaching its banks.

Fear might reflect his feelings, his deepest emotional struggles. It might even understand and give voice to his deepest longings and needs. But it wasn't truth. It wasn't what defined him. It didn't make him who he was.

Then what does?

His mind stumbled.

Without fear, without anger, who are you? Nothing. No one…

Covering his face with his hands, Gabe fought the familiar pull of despair. *Jesus…I don't know.*

I have called you to be My very own.

Every sound stilled; every thought slowed. The jumble of emotions within him coalesced and became wonder. Astonishment.

Peace.

Gabe's hands lowered as it came again: *I have called you to be My very own. I have brought you here, to this place, to see Me.*

To see God.

It hadn't been an accident. God had *brought* them here…taken them over the edge, literally, to a stark, cold place where they had no one but each other.

And God. Always God.

The truth surged over Gabe like a tidal wave, drowning out the last echoes of his fear, washing them away, cleansing him. Gabe had no words, no way to respond. All he could do was sit here and let a soul-deep quiet settle over him.

It was as though his eyes had been clamped shut, as though he'd been looking at Renee, at himself—at *life*—through a dark and heavy veil. But now his vision had cleared. His eyes were well and truly open. His heart, his mind, all of him was open, and he knew. Really knew it was true.

God was with him.

God was more powerful than the anger. More true than the fear. More effective than any of the masks Gabe had hidden behind. Masks Gabe thought were protecting him, but that he now understood had been holding him back. Keeping him bound.

Well, no longer. Gabe's heart swelled with new determination. The time had come. To open his hands and let go. He could walk forward unencumbered, because God was with him.

He always had been.

I don't get it.

I did my part. I followed You, God, read Your book, did what I'm supposed to. I've gone to church, prayed, sought Your will.

So how come my life is still so far from what it should be? Why am I so far from what I should be? Why can't I stop hurting over something that I should have been over long ago?

You've said You'll give me Your strength when I'm weak. Well, I could use some of that strength now, Father. Please. Before this weakness breaks me.

40

There is never a majestic mountain without
a deep valley, and there is no birth without pain.

DANIEL CRAWFORD

Each heart knows its own bitterness.

PROVERBS 14:10

APRIL 1995, SUNDAY MORNING

SHE WAS IN HELL.

How ironic. The last place Renee had expected to find hell was in church. And yet, there it was. Oh, sure, the church liked to call it Meet and Greet time, those fifteen or so minutes after the service, but Renee knew the truth.

It was hell. Purgatory, at the very least.

She stood at the back of the narthex, watching people sip coffee, laugh, and discuss what seemed to be on everyone's minds: babies.

Renee pressed her eyes shut. How could practically every woman in the congregation be pregnant, trying to get pregnant, or in the process of adopting a child? All at the same time?

Every woman, of course, except for those past the childbearing years.

Oh, yes…and Renee.

Had there been some kind of notice in the bulletin? "Would all the ladies of the church interested in having children kindly procreate—or begin adoption proceedings—within the same two-month period"?

Admittedly, the women of their church were particularly responsive whenever called to meet a need within the church body—but this was ridiculous!

Renee would have laughed if her throat hadn't been clogged with emotion. She looked around for a clear exit, then stopped. Affection warred with agony at the sight that met her eyes: Gabe congratulating one beaming, burgeoning couple after another.

"Oh, Renee. I'm glad I found you."

She turned, relieved for a distraction. "Hi, Wanda."

"As you know, I'm the nursery coordinator this year—"

A stone seemed to lodge in Renee's gut.

"And since you're one of the few of our women who doesn't have children of her own…"

Renee felt her smile turn plastic. *Lord, once…just once, couldn't You make these people realize what they're saying?* What would Wanda say if she chirped back, "Why, Wanda, what a sweet thing to say. I think I'll just cross-stitch that into a sampler and hang it on my wall: 'No Children of My Own.' Why, just the thought of it makes me tingly all over."

The woman would choke on her tongue.

Renee arched a brow. *Hmm, just might be worth it.*

"…I figured you could take a couple of shifts in the nursery this month. You know, to give the moms a break. I mean, they have to be with their kids every day."

Have to? *Have* to be with their children?

"So what do you say?"

"Go away."

At least, that's what Renee *wanted* to say. *Go find someone else to take care of other people's children. To sit downstairs and hold someone else's baby...feel someone else's tiny, perfectly formed son or daughter in my arms, knowing I'll never look into a face that is a mirror of my own...or Gabe's. Find someone else to give them a break from the one thing I'll never have the joy of knowing.*

"Renee?"

She started and focused on the woman before her. Wanda was watching her, a small furrow forming between her pale eyes. "Are you okay?"

Renee realized Wanda's hand was on her arm, and that she'd guided the two of them to a quiet corner in the nearly deserted sanctuary. Wanda's eyes glowed with kind concern. "Renee, would you like to talk?"

She held off the woman's compassion with a firm shake of her head. "No." *Don't be nice to me. I'm barely holding it together as it is...* She forced a smile but knew it was feeble at best, tremulous at worst. "I..."

Tell her the truth.

"I'm fine, Wanda. Really."

Renee wished she could be honest. Maybe help Wanda understand. Of course, that would be a lot easier if Renee understood it all herself. If she understood why this still hurt so much after all these years.

Try.

Renee drew a deep breath. "Do you realize six women from the church have gotten pregnant in just the past few months?"

Wanda tilted her head at the quiet question. "That many? Are you sure?"

She cleared her throat past the pain. "I'm sure. And I went to every shower, listened to all the stories about pregnancy and childbirth and the wonders of parenting..."

Renee had to look away, out the window at the front of the sanctuary to focus on the trees in the distance, the clouds floating by with slow contentment—anything but the ache in her heart and the emptiness of her womb.

God, why can't I get past this? Why, after all these years, is this pain so strong, so constant?

She turned to face her friend again. "Then, with each new shower, there was the added blessing of baby pictures." Which had been nothing compared to the parade of new mothers bringing their little ones to church for everyone to coo at and hold. Every time, no matter how often Renee told herself she would keep her arms at her sides or sit in her pew, she couldn't resist.

Like a mouse drawn to the waiting trap, she'd joined the women gathered around the tiny bundles, opened her arms when the babies were passed to her.

Every time, she'd cradled those tiny forms against her, pressed her cheek to their downy-soft heads, breathed in the fragrance that was so distinctive, so clearly the scent of baby and newness and life.

Every time, she'd handed the baby back, then made her way to her pew as she fought the sinking nausea of despair.

"I can't do it anymore, Wanda." Renee leaned against the wall, wishing she could be as strong, as impenetrable. "Not the showers, not the nursery, not any of it. I can't smile and pretend it's okay, that I don't mind how every woman around me seems to be having a baby when I'm...I'm..." Defeat was an ache in her throat. "I'm not. And never will be."

"Oh, Renee, you don't know that."

She could tell Wanda wanted to say more, was just drawing breath to do so, but she fell silent when she looked into Renee's eyes. Because for once she didn't hide the numbing grief that ravaged her heart, her hope.

"I do know, Wanda." The words were flat, hollow. "I know, and now you know."

"Renee...oh, Renee. I'm sorry."

A mantle of pitying shock fell over Wanda's features, and Renee knew she had misunderstood. She thought Renee was saying she *couldn't* have children. Sometimes she wished that were the case. That might be easier to bear than the truth.

Her first and only pregnancy had ended in disaster. There was no way of knowing if she could have another child. She'd never been given the chance.

Wanda's awkward pat on her shoulder pulled Renee's attention back to the woman at her side.

"I'll make a note for the nursery coordinators to know that they shouldn't...that you... I'll just tell them not to bother you."

Renee managed a nod around the lump lodged at the back of her throat. Relief came in the wake of Wanda's departure, and Renee stood for a moment, soaking in the solitude. Then women's voices and laughter drifted to her from the entryway. Almost against her will, she glanced out and saw, at the end of the chattering crowd, several older women talking to a young mother-to-be. The poor woman looked ready to burst, and one of the other women laughed and patted her swollen belly, a gesture of comfort known well in that particular sisterhood of mothers and mothers-to-be.

A sisterhood forever closed to Renee.

She grappled for some inner comfort but found only the silence she faced lately when she prayed. The barrenness she felt when she stared at herself in the mirror.

Barren. A barren woman.

She'd made the mistake once of looking up *barren* in the Bible. She'd been hoping for some comfort. What she found was verse after verse saying how pitiable, how miserable, it was for a woman to be barren.

Long ago they branded adulterous women with a large *A* on their foreheads. But was Renee's brand any less painful? No scarred *A* glared out to meet those who looked at her, but she was branded just the same by empty arms...a vacant womb...a God-breathed purpose unfulfilled.

She had come so close...

Renee closed her eyes, remembering the joy of a life filling her womb, the wonder as the child within her moved and made its presence known. Her throat caught. What would he have looked like, their little one, if he'd lived? Would he have Gabe's blue eyes or her green ones? Gabe's blond hair or her copper tones?

Would his laugh have been an echo of theirs, his smile a sweet combination of Gabe's dimples and her unrestrained grin?

She'd never know. Not about that little one—or about any other.

She was a female. What she would never really be was fully woman—and the thought turned her bitterness to bile.

Just get out of here. Fast. Before you do anything to humiliate yourself.

Thank heaven she and Gabe had come to church in separate cars so he could attend a meeting after church. She took a deep breath, then walked toward the crowded narthex—and the group of women standing in front of the outside doors.

She felt like a Christian in the arena going to shake paws with the lions.

Dodging smiling attempts to draw her into half a dozen conversations, Renee made her way to freedom, sidestepping the pregnant woman and her court, then letting out her pent-up relief when she finally pushed through the doors—and promptly barreled into someone heading in.

"Whoa, there! Where's the fire, girl?"

Renee took a step back from the petite woman, whose pixie face was framed in a halo of golden curls. "Are you leaving already, Renee?"

Would this morning never end? She did her best to hide the grimace that was perched on the edge of her features. "Yes, I'm not fee—"

But Andrea's attention was elsewhere. She was staring

over Renee's shoulder, through the glass double doors, at the women gathered there.

"Isn't it exciting?"

Oh please…get me out of here… Renee gave a faint smile. "Hmm?"

Andrea inclined her head to the crowd of couples. "All these women pregnant at the same time! So many sweet little babies. If that isn't a blessing straight from God, I don't know what is."

Weary beyond imagining, Renee simply nodded, making what she hoped sounded more like an affirmation than a sob.

Andrea turned to study her. A flash of what looked suspiciously like pity touched the woman's features, but vanished as quickly as it had come. Her slim hand patted Renee's arm. "You know, Renee, natural childbirth isn't the only way to go."

Renee blinked. "I…excuse me?" Andrea slid an arm around her shoulders and gave her what was probably supposed to be a reassuring squeeze, but Renee didn't feel comforted. In fact, she felt far more like she did when she walked on the nature path and felt one of those invisible, sticky strands of spiderweb hit her face.

A shiver rippled up Renee's spine. *Please, just let me go home—*

"Honey, it's no shame that you can't get pregnant."

Astonishment sputtered in Renee's voice. "Can't…who said we—?"

"Believe me, I know what it's like to want a child and not be able to have one."

Renee didn't bother to reply, but she couldn't hold back the bland, pointed stare at Andrea's three beautiful children, who stood just behind their mother.

A pointed stare that Andrea completely missed. "You know, Alan and I are so glad we gave adoption a chance. Our baby boy is just as much a part of us as the children I bore."

Renee knew Andrea meant well, knew that she had a

heart as big as the Sears Tower, but right now the last thing she wanted to hear about was the joy of adoption.

She tried to sidle away from Andrea's arm. "So good to see you, Andrea." She pointed toward her car. "I have to—"

The woman let her arm fall away—then fell into step beside Renee as she walked toward the parking lot. "There are so many children out there who need a good, solid family. A family like you and Gabe could give them."

Renee wasn't sure if she was going to burst into tears or hysterical laughter.

"If you'd like some information, I'd be happy to share it with you. I've even talked with Gabe about it and he seemed interested—"

"Stop."

Andrea didn't even break stride. Maybe she thought Renee hiccupped rather than spoke.

"Adoption is *such* a worthy cause, Renee. Maybe God is calling you two to serve a child in this way."

"Andrea…"

"I mean, look at Gabe. Children absolutely adore him."

Renee looked to the entryway. Sure enough, as on nearly every Sunday, Gabe was surrounded by children chattering away, those cherubic lips smiling up at him, chubby arms held out, begging to be picked up and held close in those strong arms. Gabe was smiling, laughing, and Renee felt her heart choke as he leaned down to gather a little boy up and lift him into a hug. She watched the child's baby hands pat at Gabe's beard.

He caught one of the boy's tiny hands, engulfing it in his huge paw, and nibbled at the wriggling fingers. The boy threw his head back and chortled, then offered his other hand for equal treatment. Gabe's roar of laughter drifted to her through the glass doors. The sound was a balm to Renee's senses, and she drew it in.

"He's so good with children."

So much for the balm. "Andrea—"

"Really, he should be given the chance to be a father. He has so much to give…"

It was true. They both did. But they'd never even tried…never given themselves the chance…

Shouldn't I have had the chance to be a mother, to feel our child growing within me? To hold in my arms the most precious gift God can give a man and woman?

Renee reined in the tormented questions that stampeded her heart, tumbling over each other with such speed that it made her dizzy. *Stop it. Just stop it.* She'd gone down this path so many times. Too many times. And it always ended in the same place. Desperation. Sorrow. Hopelessness.

She was so tired of it all. So tired she could hardly bear it.

Renee didn't waste another minute. She stepped around Andrea, not even caring that the woman was still talking, and went to pull her car door open. She slid in, turned the ignition, and finally, blessedly, she was free.

As she pulled onto the street, she took one look back in the rearview mirror…and wished she hadn't.

Andrea was talking to Gabe, pointing after Renee's car. From what Renee could see of her husband's expression, she knew she hadn't escaped at all. Gained time, maybe. Time to think, to try and understand what seemed crazy, even to herself.

But escape? Not even close.

I feel so inadequate! Sometimes I hate myself. Maybe I need to just let the feelings come, then face them...deal with them. They'll never go away if I don't.

41

Once God has deepened us,
He can give us His deepest truths.

A. B. SIMPSON

Once you were wandering like lost sheep.
But now you have turned to your Shepherd,
the Guardian of your souls.

1 PETER 2:25

APRIL 1995, SUNDAY AFTERNOON

RENEE LOVED THE BASEMENT OF THEIR HOUSE.

They'd bought the house almost six months ago, moving from the apartment they'd lived in since they were married. Renee discovered she had a flair for decorating the rooms, and she delighted in changing the house into their home. Gabe loved working in their large backyard.

In many ways, their house had become a haven for each of them. And that's what she'd needed today: a haven.

She had been sitting on the couch in the basement for hours. Just sitting. Not thinking. Not praying. Just sitting. And waiting. For the sound of Gabe's car pulling into the driveway.

When it finally came, she listened as his car door closed...his steps sounded on the walkway, the stairs...then his key scraped in the door. She drew a deep breath as he came inside and tossed his things onto the counter.

351

"Renee?"

"Down here."

He paused on the stairs to the basement when he saw her curled up on the couch, a comforter pulled over her. The cushion sagged as he sat beside her, and she turned to meet his gaze. His smile was hesitant as he studied her.

Renee laid her hand over his where it rested on the cushion. He turned his palm to hers, surrounding her hand with those broad, powerful fingers.

"You okay?"

She appreciated the way he asked it. Not as if he thought she was going nuts, but more as though he was offering to listen if she wanted. And she did.

"I couldn't take it, Gabe."

He understood immediately. "The babies."

She nodded, looking down at their joined hands. "I know it was the right decision, not having children. I know it would have been a nightmare for us...for them...with what we had to work through. But Gabe..."

Regret crowded into her throat, choking off her words. She'd sworn she wasn't going to cry. Promised herself she wouldn't do that to him. But that was a promise she couldn't keep. So she sat there, helpless with silent sorrow, tears dropping onto their joined hands.

"I'm sorry, Renee."

She squeezed his hand. It was clear in the fathomless blue of his eyes how deep his regret was, how it tore at his heart, his peace.

"I know." She brushed at her damp cheeks. "And that's why it's so hard for me to tell you about all of this, about how much I still struggle. But Gabe, I want you to understand; I'm not blaming you. I just can't seem to get past it."

"How can I help?"

Her heart twisted and the laugh that slipped from her was gruff, ragged as a gasp. "I don't know. I don't think you can. I don't think anyone can but God. I mean, He's the one who created me with this longing. And it hurts so much—" she pressed a hand to her breastbone—"in here. Deep inside."

She floundered at the glimmer of regret in his eyes. Words were so inadequate! How could mere words explain, how could they help him understand without heaping guilt on himself?

Be with us, Father…

"It's a constant ache, a nagging feeling, like a hunger that's tearing at me, that threatens to consume me if I don't satisfy it. Everything inside of me screams to have a child, to share that experience with you, to look down into a tiny face and know that we—you and I—are responsible for that. That we've invested a part of our bodies, a part of our souls, into this little creation who will one day grow up and do amazing, wonderful things."

His grip on her hand was so tight that it hurt, and she looked into his face, startled at the tears making a slow journey down his face. She couldn't help but draw him close and hold him.

His arms encircled her, and they sat there, mute in the face of shared grief. There was really nothing either of them could say to make the hurting go away. They both knew it was their decisions, their choices through a lot of years—a lot of mistakes—that had brought them to this place.

Renee wasn't sure how long they wept together. She only knew that, however long it was, something happened inside of her. The broken place deep within her, the gaping despair and desperation that had snatched and consumed any measure of hope she'd tried to find, began to ease. In sharing her grief with Gabe—*really* sharing it, without flinging accusations or letting anger mask her grief—she could almost dare to believe that maybe, just maybe, something was being born within her after all. Something she'd begun to believe would never be hers.

Healing. Like a tiny seed planted within her, it had found
a spot to implant and take root, ready at last to draw nourish-
ment and grow. No, God hadn't given her a child, but He was
giving her something she needed even more.

Hope.

Gabe straightened, then slowly leaned back against the
couch arm, drawing her with him until she was nestled in the
circle of his strong, sheltering embrace.

"Go on."

In that moment, emotions flooded her heart—affection,
appreciation, gratitude—warming places that had been cold
for far too long. They swept into the chilled chambers and
she could feel the ice pack of resentment beginning to thaw,
break apart.

She did as Gabe requested. She shared more—everything
swirling around inside of her. She told him about her
struggle, her feelings of failure as a woman, how she felt she'd
let God down by not being what He created her to be.

And Gabe talked with her, speaking words of compassion, words that brought her a new understanding, a new
peace. He told her how God had used her to birth life and
hope in him; how He'd used her wonder, her joy and child-
likeness, to open his heart and show him what life could be
like; how she'd taught him about playing, about enjoying the
moment.

Renee not only heard what he was saying, she believed it.
She took it all in, letting the truth of God's hand and work
flow through her, fill her, replace the emptiness that had held
her for so long.

She spread her fingers out across his chest, loving the
solid feel of him, the steady beat of his heart.

It was such a good heart. Despite all the garbage, all the
pain, it was a heart determined to care. To love.

"I just wish…"

Gabe looked down at her. "You just wish?"

"That you'd had the chance to be a dad. To be for your son the kind of dad you always wanted."

His mouth softened, and the warmth of his gaze washed over her, telling her more powerfully than words ever could how she'd touched him, moved him. He pulled the comforter over her, tucking it around her with a touch that was pure tenderness.

His fingers caressed her hair. "I wish things were different, hon." She started to protest, but his hand at her back stilled her. "But I wouldn't give up even a day of our time together. Not even the hard ones. God has used it all to make us stronger, better, individually and together. And I like who we're becoming."

She did, too.

He stroked her cheek. "For now, I guess we'll just have to nurture and care for each other…and leave the rest to God. We can't worry about the future. We just need to be where we are, the way we are, and let God keep working in us." He smiled. "Who knows what He has in store for us?"

Renee nodded. *Who knows, indeed?* The thought held a surprising measure of hope.

The next morning dawned fresh and new. Renee stretched her body to wakefulness, feeling lighter than she'd felt in a very long time.

God was at work. She was as sure of that as she was of the coming sunset. She found herself humming throughout the day, and on her way home from work that evening she made a stop at the grocery store. Steak. Potatoes. Corn. She smiled as she envisioned Gabe's face when he got home and found his favorite meal waiting.

She had just finished setting the table when she heard his truck pull into the driveway. She lit the tall candles she'd set in place and went to check the steaks on the grill.

"Renee, I'm home."

She turned to greet him and stopped when she found him peeking at her from behind the front door.

"Close your eyes."

What on earth? "Why?"

He looked like a little kid bursting to tell a secret. "Just close your eyes."

With a laugh, she did as he commanded.

"Now, hold out your hands."

"Gabe…"

He nudged her at the playful warning in her tone. "Come on, trust me. You're gonna love this."

She lifted her hands and held them out. Something small and soft was set in them…something that wriggled and licked at her hands—

Renee's eyes snapped open, and she stared in stunned delight. "A puppy!"

Gabe was grinning like a Chihuahua with a Great Dane–sized bone. "A Siberian husky puppy, to be exact."

Renee cradled the wriggling body close, burying her fingers in the silky, cinnamon-colored coat. The puppy grinned up at her, tongue lolling, and she saw he had one brown eye, one blue.

A Siberian. She'd always wanted a Siberian.

Gabe came to put his arms around both of them. "I know a puppy is no substitute for a baby." He scratched the little guy behind one velvety ear. "But he's someone we can care for—" his gaze caught Renee's—"and fall in love with together."

Renee hugged him, and the puppy, trapped between them as it was, gave a shrill yip of protest. She and Gabe laughed, and as he went to get the supplies he'd bought out of his truck, Renee sat on the carpeted floor, playing with the puppy, laughing at his unsteady gait and unbridled excitement.

A Siberian husky. She'd already researched names for such a dog. She looked at the little guy and knew the perfect one. Bohdan. A solid Russian name for a Russian breed. And a name with the perfect meaning: *God's gift.*

She tried it out. "What do you think, Bohdan? Does that work for you?"

The puppy tripped over himself trying to lick her face, and she laughed, gathering him close.

"Bohdan it is, then. Our own personal gift from God."

Like renewed hope, Renee thought, watching Gabe as he came through the door, arms laden with doggie supplies. They weren't through the storm...not entirely. But at least she knew they were in the same boat, working together to endure, to survive.

And that was a good start.

I long for peace, for rest. I ache to lean on You—but all I feel is unrest.

I seek peace in Your Word. Solace. Wisdom. I read and absorb, wanting the words to go beyond mere comprehension and become truth. I want to KNOW. To know what it is to rest in You, to know Your promised peace. To know my times are in Your hands and one day, somehow, all will be well.

And yet, my weaknesses, my failures, my lack—they all scream at me, drowning out the still, small voice that calls me to stillness. Battles I thought won long ago spark to life again, and I am defeated. Heartsick.

Help me, Lord. I am weak and wandering. Forgive my fainting heart and teach me.

42

Christ says, "Give me All...I want You.
I have not come to torment your natural self, but to kill it...
I will give you a new self instead. In fact, I will give you Myself."

C. S. LEWIS

My heart has heard you say, "Come and talk with me."
And my heart responds, "LORD, I am coming."

PSALM 27:8

DECEMBER 20, 2003
3:50 P.M.

GABE HADN'T COME AFTER HER.

When she'd walked away from him, Renee thought for sure he would come after her. And when he didn't, she realized how much she wanted him to.

She *wanted* Gabe. Here. With her.

She longed to feel his hands on hers, to hear his deep voice as he talked with her, helped her sort through the jumble of emotions. To lean into him, trade her weariness for his solid strength.

She wanted Gabe.

Renee let the realization roll around in her head, her heart. She clasped her hands together and stared at them, wondering as the truth dawned...grew.

She'd fallen in love with her husband.

Not the little-girl dream of falling in love, where he was perfect and they were always happy. But a deep, abiding yearning that made her ache when they weren't together.

It was a realization that left her reeling.

Gabe was a part of her. Now and forever. She could walk away from him, divorce him, try to pretend he'd never existed, even move into another relationship—but nothing would change the fact that he owned a part of her heart. He was there, a constant thread in the fabric of who she was. And he always would be.

She gave a small laugh. *What ever made me think I could walk away from that?* She wanted to know what held her back, and it couldn't have been clearer: pride. That and fear. And a lack of trust in the One she was so quick to say she followed.

Shame came then, quick and heated, and Renee bowed her head beneath the onslaught.

She'd made herself Gabe's jury, judge, and executioner. She closed her mind and heart to truth and turned instead to embrace bitterness. She'd taken destruction to her breast and nurtured it, fed it, tended it like the babe she'd never been allowed to bear.

And in doing that, she birthed her own ruin.

She had. Not Gabe. Not God. Not even Gabe's father or the liquor that had enslaved him. Only one person was responsible for where she'd ended up, who she'd become—Renee herself.

She'd thrown wide the door of her heart to self-pity and welcomed in the enemy of her soul. Now, looking back with eyes wide open, Renee saw the truth…and trembled. She saw how she'd let pride usurp faith; how she'd taken on self-righteousness in place of kindness; how she'd clutched her rights and placed them not on the altar of surrender, but squarely on the throne of her heart.

Scene after scene from her life with Gabe played through her mind, and she covered her eyes. But that didn't stop the terrible replay of events. She watched as her young self made Gabe, not God, the center of her life. Saw how that burden finally wore him down, until he struck out, leaving her heart shredded, torn…saw how she turned her back on healing and reconciliation, choosing instead to turn cold, to continue in the marriage on the surface even as she shut Gabe out of her heart.

O Lord…

She understood now. Walking away would have been a mercy compared to her emotional abandonment of her husband. She had taken what she knew of Gabe's fondest dreams and deepest fears and used them to beat him down.

No wonder he'd grown angry. No wonder he'd turned away from her. No wonder he'd sought understanding and acceptance from another.

A wretchedness of mind such as she'd never known before settled over her, its weight pressing on her until she thought she would die from the burden. But she wasn't so lucky. Death would not come to release her from the consequences of her foolish choices.

Forgive me… Forgive me…

How often had she complained to God that her life wasn't what it was supposed to be? And why hadn't she seen before now that such a question was the height of arrogance?

Her life was far beyond anything she'd hoped for. Certainly beyond anything she deserved. Gabe loved her. He sacrificed for her. He gave up his own will and way to meet her needs. He sheltered her, protected her. He showed her every day that he cherished her. She had just been too fixated on herself and what she wanted to see it.

Forgive me…

Be still.

Lord, I'm sorry.

Be still. Be still and know. I am God. Trust in me, for I will make all things new.

Renee lifted her face to the sky. It was true. God was here. With her. With Gabe. He'd always been there, and He had made them new. Over and over, one small step at a time. He'd changed them.

And He'd changed her. In spite of herself. Through all she'd had to face—about Gabe, about herself, about life. Despite all her kicking and screaming, her complaints and struggles, despite the fact that she got herself into the trouble she experienced, God had used it all.

To refine her.

And to give her exactly what she'd always wanted—and exactly who she'd always needed.

Father, I saw You today.

And the real miracle is that I saw You in him. In the man I've known all these years, but never really seen before. Oh, I looked at him, saw his features, saw the emotions that filled his face, that drove him so...but until today, I never really looked to see You in him.

Imagine my surprise when I did so, and You were there. I was so sure I knew him...so sure he was closed off to You, that there was no room for You in his heart. But You kept telling me I wasn't seeing truth, and so I finally looked.

And there You were. Right there. Looking back at me.

I'm sorry, Lord. I thought I knew the truth, and now I see it was just my truth. Not Yours.

43

The state of marriage is one that requires more virtue and constancy
than any other. It is a perpetual exercise of mortification....
From this thyme plant, in spite of the bitter nature of its juice,
you may be able to draw and make the honey of a holy life.

FRANCES DE SALES

"Slowly, steadily, surely, the time approaches when the
vision will be fulfilled. If it seems slow, wait patiently,
for it will surely take place. It will not be delayed."

HABAKKUK 2:3

DECEMBER 20, 2003
4:15 P.M.

GABE FELT A HAND ON HIS SHOULDER. EVEN IF THEY'D
been in a press of people rather than alone in the wilderness, he'd
have known it was Renee. He knew the touch of her, the feel of her.

He moved his hand to cover hers.

"I'm sorry."

Gabe couldn't accept her soft words. "No, I—"

She knelt in front of him then. He looked into those green
eyes. Something flickered deep within her that he'd never seen
before. A kind of...brokenness. That was the only word that fit.

Renee reached for his hand, and the simple action warmed
his chilled soul. She lifted his hand, pressed it to her lips, and
looked up at him. "I'm sorry."

He knew she was talking about more than just their argument. Just as he knew she meant it. Something had happened, he

could see it in her face, feel it in her touch.

She was different. Vulnerable.

Gabe knew he had to take the next step. She'd opened a door, and he had to go through.

He laid her hand over his heart. The words he wanted to speak were there, perched on his lips. Easy words, words he'd said over and over through the years. *"I'm sorry, too."* But so many times before when he offered her those words, she turned from him, not accepting, not believing. How often had she told him the words didn't matter if his actions didn't prove them?

Too often.

He didn't want to do that now. To give her words that he knew she wouldn't fully believe, no matter how much she wanted to. He'd used those words too often before without any real change. He wouldn't do that again.

He wanted her to know this was different. He was different. Words wouldn't do that.

If you give up your life for me, you will find true life.

He understood. All or nothing. He'd had his fill of nothing. It was time to try all. *It's in Your hands, Lord.*

Gabe slid his fingers along her face, cupping her cheek in his palm. She turned to press a kiss there. It was a pledge. An offering. Leaning down, he pressed his lips to hers, asking nothing, giving everything.

Another beginning. Another new start. *Please, God, let this be the last. I don't want to end up here ever again.*

Give up your life...

I will. I do.

A high whine broke them apart, and they both turned to look at Bo, who lay in the snow, head on his paws, watching them with thinly veiled impatience.

"I think somebody's hungry." Gabe directed Renee's attention to their pathetic pet.

Her laughter filled the empty places inside him. "I think somebody's internal clock is messed up. It's not even five yet."

Gabe tugged at her sleeve. "Come on, Mom, how can you resist a face like that?"

She looked from him to Bo—whose tail thump-thumped his hopefulness in the snow—then back to Gabe again. She pulled a tissue from her pocket and began to wave it.

Gabe quirked a brow. "Let me guess…a white flag."

She tossed it at him with a flick of her wrist. "You always were a good guesser, Roman." With a dramatic sigh, she stood. "Guess I'll go scrounge up some dinner."

He caught her hand before she walked away, and she hesitated, her eyes resting on his face. "We're going to be okay." He believed it. Really believed it.

The radiance that touched her features, bringing her a new beauty, told him she did, too. "Better than okay."

As she walked to her pack and began pulling out the protein bars, Gabe tried to decipher the feelings surging through him. His eyes widened when it finally clicked.

Freedom. He felt like a man set free. It was as though he suddenly realized a band had been fastened around his heart, restricting it; and now that it had finally been cut, his heart beat solid and true for the first time in a very long time.

He smiled. Welcome to true life. It was even better than he'd hoped.

11:45 P.M.

Gabe fed another stick into the fire, then leaned back to slide his arm around Renee's shoulders. She smiled up at him and nestled close.

Their second night in the woods. He wasn't the least bit disappointed. In fact, he was having a great time.

He and Renee had walked for a little over an hour after they ate, but he could tell each step made her bruised ribs hurt. She didn't complain. She would have kept on going if he hadn't touched her arm.

"Better find a place to set up camp, hon."

She nodded. No argument, no alternate plans. Just acceptance.

They laid out the space blanket, got a fire going, and settled in. They had been sitting here, looking at the stars and talking, for hours. He rested his cheek on the top of her head, tightening his arm around her.

"Hey!"

He looked down at her laughing protest and saw the same peace he was feeling reflected in her eyes.

"Hugs are great, but not so tight. I mean, have mercy on my poor aching ribs."

Gabe knew he looked decidedly sheepish. "Well, they say to bind bruised ribs, don't they?"

"Uh-huh, so it was for my own good?"

"Okay."

Her bubbling laughter was a soothing balm on his healing spirit. He pulled her close again, and they sat in comfortable silence, Bo curled beside them. Gabe leaned his head back to watch the stars twinkling in the sky, then let his gaze fall to the woods.

What the...?

"Renee. Hold Bo. And keep him as still as you can."

She did as he directed, which told him the alarm he felt had come through clearly in his words. He eased away from her, ready to jump in front of her and Bo if he needed to, and nodded toward the woods. She followed the action, and her eyes widened.

There, in the darkness just beyond the light of the fire, were two glowing eyes. Feline eyes. Wild eyes. Watching them.

"The cougar."

At Renee's strangled whisper, he put a hand on her arm,

doing his best to comfort her with his touch. "We'll be okay."

She nodded at his quiet words, though her tension was evident in the rigid muscles beneath his hand. Gabe looked back at the cat and tensed. It had stepped out of the woods and was now standing there, studying them. It was so close he could see the dancing flames of the fire reflected in its large, golden eyes. Flickering light from the fire highlighted its tawny coat, muscular body, and huge paws.

Paws, he knew, that could deliver a deathblow with far too little effort.

And yet...

Gabe wasn't afraid. For no reason he could explain, his alarm simply melted away. He glanced at Renee and saw his own surprise reflected in her features. But the greatest wonder of all came when he looked at Bo. Earlier, the mere scent of the cougar had almost sent the dog bolting into the woods. Now the husky lay there, beneath Renee's arm, watching the cougar watch them, looking completely at ease.

Father, what are You up to?

Gabe looked back at the cougar just in time to see it turn and pad back into the woods. Within seconds, it was swallowed in the darkness.

Gone.

Just like that.

He leaned forward, blinking.

Beside him, Renee squinted into the night-shrouded woods. "Did I see what I think I just saw?"

Gabe's wonder slipped out on a breath, and he shook his head. "If what you thought you just saw was a cougar, then yes. Because I saw it, too."

"But—"

He turned to her and couldn't help but smile at the confusion on her face. He felt the same way.

"Why didn't Bo react? You saw him earlier—"

"I know." Gabe reached for his flashlight and a large stick, then stood. "It makes no sense whatsoever, and yet—"

"It makes perfect sense."

He met Renee's wide-eyed stare and grinned. "Yeah. Exactly."

She shook her head, then pointed at the stick in his hand. "What's that for?"

Gabe looked toward the woods. "I figured I'd just make sure he was gone."

"He is."

He nodded at the confidence in her tone. "Yeah, I know. But I wanted to check anyway."

"We'll wait here."

At the somewhat dazed humor in her tone, he leaned down and kissed her on top of her head. Then he reached out to give Bo a scratch behind the ears. "Curiouser and curiouser…"

Renee laughed. "So now you're Alice in Wonderland?"

Gabe grinned and started toward the woods. "Yeah, but if I see a white rabbit with a pocket watch, I'm sending him your way."

Renee's chuckle followed him into the woods. He turned on the flashlight, shining the beam on the ground in front of him. Large paw prints in the snow bore mute testimony to the fact that they hadn't been hallucinating.

A cougar really had come calling.

He directed the light along the path of the prints, peering into the woods ahead. No sign of the animal. It was as if it had vanished into the surrounding trees.

No wonder they called cougars "ghost cats."

Gabe cast one last look at the woods ahead—and froze. He frowned. Was that…?

He squinted, then flicked off his flashlight, letting the darkness bring it into better focus.

It was. There was a light just ahead. He was sure of it!

Thank You, God! Thank You!

He turned the flashlight on again and hurried back to Renee. "I saw a light out there!"

She jumped up and came to stand beside him. He took her hand and led her to the spot where he'd seen the light. "There—a dim yellow glimmer, beyond those trees. It has to be a cabin."

"Oh my…" Her eyes glowed with wonder. "We never would have seen it if you hadn't made sure that cougar was gone."

He nodded. "And if it hadn't been dark. If we hadn't stopped."

Gratitude, joy, exultation—they exploded through him, carried on the sure awareness of God's provision. Gabe turned to Renee, opening his arms. She moved into them without hesitation.

Renee's heart was full as Gabe's arms closed around her, sheltering her, covering her.

Thank You, Father…

"Thank You, God."

She smiled at his echo of her heart's prayer. And as she listened to him pray, she found herself smiling, loving the sound of his voice as he spoke to the Creator. *God, You really have made all things new…*

"Thanks for Your timing, God. We were lost, not just in the woods, in the storm, and you knew that. Knew we had to come here, had to find ourselves with nothing but each other. And You. You brought us here to show us that we can't live without You. Or without each other. You showed us Your love, and the love we have for each other. You came and walked beside us, letting us know we weren't alone, and You saved us. From the storm. From the wilderness. From ourselves."

Renee felt his lips press against her hair.

"Thank You for the gift of my wife. For the gift of Your Son. And for the gift of renewal. Amen."

"Amen," she echoed and stepped back. She looked down to find Bo lying there, watching them, that husky grin on his face. He looked as happy as she felt.

They returned to the fire and Gabe dumped snow on it. She touched his shoulder, and he glanced at her. "You don't want to check it out first, be sure it's really a cabin, before we put out the fire?"

Confidence glowed in his blue eyes. "It's a cabin. Trust me, Renee." He stopped. "No, strike that, trust *Him.*"

She glanced at the yellow glow beyond the trees, then back at Gabe. "How about if I trust both."

His slow grin was warm and delicious. "Even better."

They were ready to go in minutes, and Gabe laced his fingers through hers as they followed the beam of his flashlight. Renee was amazed to realize she wasn't tired or sore.

Just excited.

Finally they reached the source of the light they'd seen. Gabe had been right. It was a small cabin, nestled in the trees. Renee could just see wisps of smoke rising from the chimney. She started to move forward, but Gabe stopped her.

"Hey, guess what?"

"What?"

He held up his watch for her to see, pressing the button to light it. *12:01 a.m., December 21.*

His arms slid around her. "Happy anniversary, hon."

She went up on her toes to kiss him. "The happiest."

44

What I like about experience is that it is such an honest thing.

C. S. LEWIS

"These are the ones coming out of the great tribulation…
He who sits on the throne will live among them and shelter them.…
For the Lamb who stands in front of the throne will be their Shepherd.
He will lead them to the springs of life-giving waters.
And God will wipe away all their tears."

REVELATION 7:14–15, 17

DECEMBER 21, 2003

4 P.M.

THEY WERE HOME. RENEE HAD NEVER BEEN SO GLAD TO be home in her life.

The couple who owned the cabin, Dave and Laura Burk, had been a kindly retired couple. Though Gabe's insistent knocks had awakened them, they didn't seem to mind in the least. When they realized what had happened, they bustled Renee and Gabe into their home, bundled them with blankets in front of the fire, and plied them with hot soup and coffee. Bo was given a place of honor right in front of the crackling fire, a big bone and a bowl of water at his side.

He'd been in heaven.

After a good night's sleep in a soft down bed, Gabe and Renee had contacted everyone to let them know they were okay. Before the day was over, their truck had been recovered and towed, and the Burks had taken them home. Gabe had resisted at first, saying they'd done enough, but Dave Burk, who was a huge teddy bear of a man, had brushed aside his objections.

"The drive to your home will give you plenty of time to tell us all about your adventure."

They'd been home for about two hours. Gabe was on the phone with his mother again. She had asked him to call once they got home, and Renee told Gabe to take his time. He needed to reassure her they really were okay.

And Renee needed to finish what she'd started on the drive up to the resort.

She had discovered the book while packing for their trip. She'd needed another suitcase, a small one, for incidentals. She knew she had one that would be the perfect size...somewhere. She found the small suitcase in the garage, where she must have stuck it long ago. It was still in good condition—she'd only used it once. Years ago. The night she threw things into it and ran to Grace and Oren's.

The night she found that woman's letter to Gabe.

She'd carried the case into the house, wondering why she never put the thing in a garage sale. It was a reminder of so much pain. And yet every time she considered getting rid of it, something stopped her. Well, at least she could put it to use now.

When she opened the suitcase, she saw it. A gift-wrapped package. For a moment, she couldn't imagine what it was. But as she lifted it, held in her hands what was obviously a book, the memory flooded back—Oren handing it to her, telling her it was a gift from him and Grace.

Shivers had whispered along her spine as Grace's words drifted back to her: *Read that, but not until you're ready... Trust God to show you when the time is right.*

Clarity beyond anything Renee had ever known settled over her as she stood there, the book in her hands. She knew without a trace of doubt that God was indeed showing her. It was time to read what He had for her in the pages of this book.

And oh! What wonders You had for me, Father.

Renee smiled now as she got a fire going in the fireplace. It was amazing how words written so long ago could still resonate with such truth, could speak to her heart and change it.

But then, the one who wrote them understood Renee, understood what she was going through.

She carried a steaming mug of cocoa to her favorite over-stuffed chair and settled in. She pulled the journal from the coffee table, where she'd set it, and opened the cover to the last entry.

Easter Sunday

I never would have imagined it. Never dreamed it was possible. But You've done it.

You've done it.

New life. You've brought it to us for eternity, but in Your mercy I see now that You've given it to us in the here and now. We've found the kind of love I thought we'd never find. Because we stopped looking for it in each other—and looked instead to You.

Why did it take us so long, Lord? Why did we waste so much time, cause each other and ourselves so much pain, when the truth was right there in front of us all the time?

"If you try to keep your life for yourself, you will lose it. But if you give up your life for Me, you will find true life."

True life. True joy. True love as never before. We've found it all. In You first. And then, finally, miraculously, in each other. So many times I thought I'd lost him, that I'd lost myself. But You held us safe all along, even when we couldn't see You.

I know we're not done. I know there's more to learn, more to become, more refinement in store. I'm too stubborn, Lord, for the crucible to be over. But here's the amazing thing: You're more stubborn than I! And more patient. And You will never give up on me. Or on us.

Today is Easter, Lord, and I can hardly wait to go to church. To lift my voice with Oren's and sing those glorious words: Christ the Lord, is risen today, Alleluia!

You are risen. You are alive. And You have brought us from death to life. Praise You, Father God.

Alleluia!
With all my love,
Grace

Renee closed Grace's journal, resting her hand on the cover. No wonder the older woman had seemed to understand her struggles so well. She'd known them more intimately than Renee could have imagined. Not the same details, probably not the same issues, but the same struggles nonetheless.

Fear. Pride. Wanting what she wanted, when she wanted it.

Renee reached up to brush away a tear. She'd never imagined, all those times she watched Grace and Oren together, all those times she'd been steeped in envy, that their communion of heart and spirit had been born from such pain, anger, and hopelessness. If God could take Grace and Oren beyond all of that and make them the way they were now...

"You okay, hon?"

Renee looked up and nodded at Gabe as he came into the room. She watched as he settled into the chair beside her. She understood his silence. If he talked with his mom, he'd also talked with his dad. Gabe always made a point of talking with his dad, of doing all he could to build a relationship with him. It was further evidence to Renee of her husband's capacity for forgiveness and love.

"How's your dad?"

He stared into the fire, and she watched the light play on his features, saw him purposing to relax. "The same. Always the same." There was sadness in his tone, but something else. Acceptance.

She looked down at her mug of cocoa, watching the tiny marshmallows float on the top. "I'm sorry it's hard."

The sigh that eased from him was heavy. "I just have to remind myself that he does the best he can with what he knows." Gabe's eyes settled on her, and his fingers touched her arm in a light caress. "I'm pretty lucky, Renee. I've had a lot of support, good friends, a wife who loves me, and a God who never gives up on me. My dad—" he looked back into the fire—"well, he's never been able to see that he has any of that."

"You're kind of amazing, you know?"

Gabe's smile was rueful as he leaned back in his chair. "I don't know about that. But he's my dad. The only one I'll ever have. And I won't give up on him." His gaze rested on her, and the warmth in those blue depths made her smile. "How could I, when you never gave up on me?"

The silence that fell over them then was easy, comfortable. Renee looked at Gabe.

"Thank you."

He tipped his head. "For what?"

She reached out to take his hand. "For being patient. For sticking it out." She glanced down at their joined hands. "You didn't have to, you know?"

Gabe squeezed her hand and gave her a lopsided grin. "Yeah, I did. I mean, what else could I do?"

"Lots of guys would have walked away. Gotten a divorce." She traced the line of his fingers curled around her hand. "It's kind of funny, you know? I mean, we never really considered that, did we?"

His smile broadened. "Divorce? No…"

Laughter bubbled up within her. She knew where he was going. "I know, I know, we never considered divorce…"

They finished it together: "Murder, on the other hand…"

His chuckle was deep and warm. She tugged on his hand. "Really, though. You ever wonder why we didn't just give in? Why we kept working and fighting when it was so hard?"

Gabe leaned back in his chair, peering at her over the rim of his mug as he took a sip. "Because it's not the legacy I want to leave."

Renee considered that. "What do you mean?"

"We put a lot into this relationship, Rennie. I know it's been hard, sometimes almost too hard, but it's always been worth it. To me."

Her nod was immediate. "To me, too."

"I love you, and I don't ever want to lose that. Or you. Besides, God never saw fit to release either one of us from this relationship." A small smile tugged at his lips. "No matter how much we begged Him at times."

She chuckled. It felt so good to laugh.

Gabe let go of her hand and leaned forward, resting his elbows on his knees. "But beyond all of that, I never wanted the epitaph on our marriage to read, 'It got too hard, so I got out.'" He shrugged. "That's not the legacy I wanted to leave for our family and friends." He held his hand out and she placed hers in it again. "I believe with all my heart that our struggles happened because you and I walked into this relationship without seeking God's heart, His wisdom and guidance."

She couldn't argue with that.

"So how could it *not* be hard? I had a lot of garbage to overcome."

Renee squeezed his hand. "We both did. We still do."

"Even so, God's been faithful. He stood with us—or against us when He needed to—and kept us on the road to healing. And now—"

Her smile came from the depths of her heart. "Now, we're better than ever before."

"Exactly." He slanted a grin at her. "Besides, I'm just getting you trained right. Think how long it would take me to break in a new wife."

She gave his leg a playful kick. "Like any other woman would put up with you."

"Like I'd want any other woman but you."

She sipped her chocolate through a smile.

"You know something?"

She glanced at him. "What?"

"I know our marriage isn't exactly a romantic dream, and I regret that. But I think it's a kind of a shrine."

Renee took this in, pondered it. "How so?"

"To endurance. God's and ours. People who know us know what we've been through, how close we came to walking away. It would have been easy to be yet another example of giving up. But by God's grace, and only by God's grace, we didn't. God's powerful enough to overcome our biggest problems. Our fiercest struggles."

"He's the only One who can."

"Right. I want people to know that. That He's sufficient. That He can bring healing, no matter how broken you are."

Renee fell silent, staring into the fire, content just to be near Gabe.

"So whatcha been readin'?"

She glanced down at the journal in her lap. Grace had told her for years that it would be worth it to endure. She was right. So right. "Something wonderful."

"Hmmm." Gabe stood and pulled Renee up and into his arms, Grace's journal trapped between them. "Wanna tell me about it?"

She shook her head. "Not yet. I will soon, but not yet."

The slow curve of his lips was pure devilment. "Good." He plucked the journal from between them.

Renee pulled back slightly, letting her lip stick out. "Good? You don't want me to talk with you?"

"Nu-uh." He gave the book a gentle toss so that it landed in her chair, then his arms tightened around her. "Matter of fact, I don't think I want to talk at all."

Understanding brought warmth flooding to her cheeks—and her heart. New life. New love. God had given all that to her and more in this man.

Alleluia! she thought as she lifted her face for his kiss. *Alleluia, amen!*

～

6:30 P.M.

Grace almost flew to the door when the bell rang.

She pulled it open. Renee and Gabe stood there on the doorstep, faces wreathed in smiles. Hands joined.

"Thank God!" Grace threw her arms around them, giving them each a sound hug, then bustling them inside. Oren had come into the room and stood watching them.

"So, the adventurers have returned, eh?"

Gabe went to shake his hand, then laughed when Oren swatted it away and hugged first him, then Renee.

"All right, you two. Into the living room with you. I want to hear everything."

Grace perched on the arm of Oren's chair, listening as the younger couple told them all that God had done in those few days in the woods. When Grace glanced up at the clock, she was stunned to see that two and a half hours had passed.

"Oh, my heavens!" She hopped up. "I've got brownies and coffee in the kitchen."

Renee rose from her seat next to Gabe on the couch. "I'll help you." She linked one arm with Grace's as they walked, and when they reached the kitchen, she brought something out from behind her back and held it out to Grace.

Grace blinked. Though she hadn't seen it in years, she recognized it right away.

Her journal.

So many years had passed since she and Oren gave it to Renee. Grace had wondered about it over the years, but she never felt free to ask Renee about it. And now, here it was—and from the look in Renee's shining eyes, Grace knew she'd read every word. And understood.

Ah, Lord God, Your timing truly is perfect. Forgive me for not always trusting that.

"I had no idea, Grace."

Grace took the journal and set it on the counter. "Not many people do. They see us now and think it's always been like this between us." She let a finger trail across the cover of the journal. How many nights had she poured her heart out, weeping, praying, begging for things to change? And so they had. Just not in her timing.

"Gabe and I would like to talk with you more about what you and Oren went through."

Pleasure filled Grace. "We were hoping you would want that. We have so much in common. God brought us through a great deal, Renee." She smiled at the younger woman. "Just as He's doing for you now."

She turned to the coffeemaker and eyed the dark liquid in it. "Hmm, this has been sitting here for two and a half hours. Suppose it's drinkable?"

Renee grinned, and they reached the same conclusion: "Give it to the men."

Grace laughed and put the teakettle on. "Oren and I had a lot of learning to do. A lot of growing up." She turned the burner to the right setting. "A lot of dying."

"Dying to self." Renee leaned on the kitchen counter. "It was the hardest thing I've ever had to do. But when I did, I finally came to life. True life. The kind you get when you give everything up to God and let Him have His way."

"Exactly." Grace straightened and put her hand over Renee's, where it rested on the counter. "I'm so glad you understand."

"And I'm glad you had patience with me." Renee's warm smile was shadowed with regret. She sandwiched Grace's hand between hers. "Grace, you are the truest of friends. God is using you both to help us come to a place of peace."

The teakettle's merry whistle split the air, and Grace turned to shut off the burner and pour the water, then set the cups and a small plate of brownies on a tray. "I knew something was different when I saw you two."

Renee leaned on the counter. "Not something—some*one*. Gabe and I are both different. We've started over so many times, and we know we still have a long way to go. But this time…" She shrugged. "It's different. It's as though we've finally let go of that last little something that we were holding on to, that kept us from putting our whole hearts into each other."

"And now?"

Renee's smile was beautiful, glorious. Free. "Now, for the first time, I think, we're in this all the way. I'm trying to see Gabe for Gabe, not in comparison to anyone or anything else. And I can tell he's more open, more honest than he's ever been before." She rested her chin in her hands, her eyes dreamy. "It's like I'm seeing Gabe for the very first time." A slow smile curved her lips. "And I like what I'm seeing. A lot."

"It makes me so happy to hear you say that."

Renee came to hug Grace. "And it makes me happy that we're not in this alone. You're with us. God is with us." She stepped back, and Grace's heart swelled at the joy she saw shining in Renee's eyes. "And we're going to make it."

Grace sniffled and brushed away the dampness tickling the corners of her eyes. "Well, of *course* you are! I never doubted it for a second." She picked up the tray. "Now, how about we go join those two handsome men of ours?"

Renee's face glowed as she fell into step beside Grace. "I can't think of anything I'd rather do."

The Beginning…

Dear Readers,

No doubt about it, marriage is hard. It's one of the hardest things we humans can do. And when marriages hit rocky times—as most marriages do—it's easy to feel that things will never get better, that we've "fallen" out of love, and that the only recourse is to walk away and start over with someone new. I considered it, believe me. But I found the bad times, like the good, go in cycles. If we can hold on to God and His truths, His commandments, during the bad, the good *will* come. Because He wills it. Because He honors obedience.

Never forget that God has called us to holy living. While He promises us joy, He also calls us to show His servant-love to those around us; to place our rights on the altar; to take up our crosses and follow Him into the light. It doesn't sound like fun—obedience often isn't—but oh, it is worth it.

I know some marriages can't be salvaged; both spouses must be willing to work, to submit themselves to God's refinement, for healing to come. I was fortunate in that Don was even more determined, more willing than I to seek God's will and be obedient. I never want to speak condemnation to those who've already suffered so much through divorce. But I do want to testify to those who are still in troubled marriages: God *is* sufficient. *Nothing* is too hard for Him. He can restore you and your marriage—and He will do so if you surrender to Him.

Grace joked with Renee that many women long for a man who is a combination of Solomon, John Wayne, and Cary Grant. Well, I've got him. And I'm glad God didn't let me walk away from Don before I realized just how blessed— and grateful—I am to be his wife.

In 1998, nineteen years after we were married, ten years after a year-long separation and years of counseling, Don and I reaffirmed our wedding vows. I want to leave you with what we shared with our family and friends back then. I hope it helps you see that it's worth it to rest in God, to lean on Him, and to endure.

May God bless you and grant you His peace.

Karen M. Ball

As always, feel free to drop me a note through Multnomah at:

Karen Ball
c/o Multnomah Fiction
12265 Oracle Boulevard, Suite 200
Colorado Springs, CO 80921

WEDDING AFFIRMATION CEREMONY
OF
DON AND KAREN BALL

DON:

When I met Karen in the fall of 1978, I had no idea how unprepared I was for a healthy relationship. My definition of love was nowhere near what it is today. I struggled for a long time with feelings of inferiority, hopelessness, and rage. But nothing was ever *my* fault, always somebody else's.

As a new Christian in October of '78, I figured all that was behind me. Wrong! Karen and I started dating in the spring of '79, were engaged in November of '79, and married in December of '79. After nine months, the honeymoon was over.

I was a hypocrite, going to church and then going out of control at home. The problems only grew until, in 1992, we separated. That's when I started counseling. We got back together after a year of being apart and started over, trying to rebuild trust. But the rage in me continued. There have been many times over our nearly twenty years of being together that I was sure our marriage was over. Somehow I clung to the promises I made to Karen and God and vowed not to give up.

With God's grace, hard work, and lots of friends who also wouldn't give up, I stand before you now, made new in Christ. I love my wife, my partner, with all my heart. For me, marriage is a commitment made for life—and because of it, I truly have life.

KAREN:

Over the years of our marriage, I've adopted certain credos:

- Divorce isn't in my vocabulary. *Murder,* on the other hand...
- Forget time. *Chocolate* heals all wounds.
- We've been happily married for ten years, and that's not bad out of nineteen.

But the most important credo I've learned is this: God is in control.

Life may be going crazy, feelings of love may be nonexistent, every day may be a struggle, but none of that changes this fact:

God is in control.

Let circumstances, chaos, and conflicts do their worst—and believe me, they will. Let all our dreams seem to disappear, let sorrow walk beside me every step of the rocky way...it still doesn't change: God is in control.

Growing up, I watched my parents laugh and love and be each other's best friend. I knew what marriage was. I had it figured out. Then I got married and discovered I didn't have *anything* figured out. It took a lot of years and a lot of pain, but God finally showed me that my dream of marriage had become an idol. My focus was on it, not on God or on Don. All I saw was what we weren't, not what we were. It wasn't until I could release the stranglehold I had on that dream that I could start being a wife, serving my husband as God's representative in our house, acting out of obedience to Christ and the vows I'd made, not out of warm fuzzy feelings.

And that's when it happened. Without the illusion clouding my vision, I saw the truth. Not only was God in control, but He was at work refining both Don and me, making us exactly who we need to be. For Him. And for each other.

Today, through God's grace, and thanks to faithful friends, hard work, and learning when to keep silent, I can tell you my dream is here and now. I have the husband—and the marriage—I've always wanted. We live in love and laughter and the sure awareness of God's presence, grace, and provision. And when things get rough again, as they're bound to because we're human, I know God will be sufficient.

He always has been. He always will be.

Recommended Reading

The books listed below are those that Don and I have found to be especially helpful, truthful, and effective both as we dealt with the challenges we faced and for strengthening our bond. Of course, the most vital resource you have is God's Word: the Bible. If you could read only one book, that is the one we both suggest. These books are offered as a supplement.

Sacred Marriage by Gary Thomas (Zondervan Publishing). This is the best book either of us has read concerning a godly marriage. When I saw the subtitle—*What If God Designed Marriage to Make Us Holy More than to Make Us Happy?*—I knew I had to buy it. Thomas has a wonderful way of sharing truth to encourage, challenge, convict, and refine you. We strongly recommend this book.

The Five Love Languages by Gary Chapman (Northfield Press) A powerful tool for helping couples understand effective communication. We worked on these kinds of things in counseling, but reading this book helped me understand why it's so important to learn your spouse's "love language." Especially if you're in a relationship, as Don and I are, with someone who is your polar opposite.

The Joy of Listening to God and *Marriage on the Mend*, both by Joyce Huggett (InterVarsity Press). I'd recommend that anyone, married or single, read the first book. But married people especially need to be reminded of the importance of being silent before God, listening to Him, and building a strong relationship with Him. The second book is a wonderful testimony to God's restorative power in broken relationships.

Streams in the Desert, by L. B. Cowman (updated edition, edited by James Reimann; Zondervan Publishing). Powerful truths from those who have traveled the path before us. This was an anchor for me during terrible times and a reminder during good times. It points your attention directly where it should be: to the only One who can help and heal—God Almighty.

DISCUSSION QUESTIONS

1. Scripture speaks often of the dangers of idols and idolatry. Consider 1 Samuel 15:22–23; Psalm 78:56–59; Isaiah 44:9–11; Habakkuk 2:18–20. But idolatry is more than just worshiping a false image of God. Read Colossians 3:5 and Ephesians 5:5. For Renee, having a marriage similar to her parents' was so important it became an idol, something she focused on rather than looking to God. Is there anything in your life that could become an idol, a barrier between you and God? What can you do about it? When is it time to let go of a dream?

2. Renee struggled with unanswered prayer, both in relationship to her marriage and to having a baby. These things were not selfish or wrong desires. Why would God keep such blessings from a child of His?

3. How do you reconcile such Scriptures as Matthew 11:7, Luke 11:9, and John 14:13 with what seems in your own life to be unanswered prayers?

4. What gives you a sense of fulfillment in your life? Where should you look to have your needs met? Why can't other people fully meet your needs? How can you rely on God rather than other people to meet your needs and give you a sense of being complete? What does it mean to really believe that God is sufficient?

5. What is the worst part about making a poor or careless decision? Have you ever made a decision without seeking God's counsel? What were the consequences? Has God used that situation to teach or refine you or your faith? How?

6. How can you be sure you're making decisions that are wise and godly? Consider 1 Kings 22:5; Psalm 16:7; Proverbs 3:5–26, 13:20, 15:22; John 14:16; Titus 2:4–8. To whom do you go for counsel when you need to make a wise decision? How do you keep yourself accountable for the decisions you make?

6. What do you believe is God's purpose in marriage? What are we, as believers, to learn from marriage? What is your individual call as a wife or husband?

7. Read 2 Corinthians 1:3–11; Romans 5:3–5; Romans 8:17–32. What is the "fellowship of suffering," and what does it mean to you? How does going through your own suffering enable you to minister to others who suffer?

8. Renee and Gabe's struggle lasted for years. Many people would have given up on such a relationship, looking instead for happiness elsewhere. What kept Renee and Gabe from walking away? Have you ever faced a long-term struggle in your own life or marriage? How can you stay faithful to God's call when it seems as though a struggle lasts for a long time, when you're in what feels like an emotional wasteland?

9. So many people today talk about their "rights," about what they "deserve." What does Scripture have to say about that? (Consider Galatians 5:13–15; Philippians 2:3–11.) What does it mean to be a servant in your relationships and, specifically, in your marriage?

10. In light of Romans 12:1–3, 9–10, and 16–21, what sacrifices is God calling each of us to make, and why?

11. Many of us wrestle with the reality that life often doesn't turn out like we thought it would. Our dreams and plans too often go awry. Why is life so full of struggles and conflicts? Doesn't God want us to be happy? Hasn't He promised us a life that is peaceful and joyful? How do our struggles fit in with that promise?

12. Though they faced many painful moments, Renee and Gabe did have times of joy and laughter. Read Romans 5:1–5, 12:12; James 1:2–4, 19–27. How can you find joy in the face of trials?

13. Gabe's greatest challenge was letting go of the lies planted deep in his heart during his childhood and embracing God's love and truth. How can you overcome a difficult past, turn your hurts over to God, and open yourself to His love and plans for you?

Three Novella-Sized Escapades in One Hilarious Anthology!

Warning: Laughter ahead! Liz Curtis Higgs delivers again with "Fine Print," where a businessman and the speech coach he's hired have no idea there are matchmakers at work on their behalf! Her novella is part of a delightful triple-header in *Three Weddings and a Giggle*. The "giggle" comes from Carolyn Zane, whose "Sweet Chariot" drops readers in on two little old ladies who purchase a motor home sight unseen, then drag their adult grandchildren along for cross-country antics. In Karen Ball's "Bride on the Run," an heiress defies her father's demand that she marry a man she doesn't love. If only she hadn't waited until her wedding day to do so! So it's out the window, down the rose trellis…and headlong into one escapade after another. Thoroughly fun!

ISBN 1-57673-656-3

Love and Faith—Pushed to the Limits

This rerelease of Karen Ball's first romance novel tells the story of a young widow who learns to love again. Taylor Sorensen has a secret: There are wolves on her ranch. Taylor's new ranch hand, Connor Alexander, has a secret, too: He's a wildlife biologist who's been sent to find out if, after sixty years, wolves have returned to Wyoming. Caught in a fierce battle against angry ranchers and centuries of superstition, Taylor and Connor are drawn together by their desire to protect these wild, majestic animals. What they don't know is that there's someone else out there who hates the wolves—someone who's as determined to get rid of them as Taylor and Connor are to protect them.

ISBN 1-57673-597-4

Taylor couldn't remember a spring this hot in years.

She shifted in the saddle, pulled her hat off, and fanned herself. What a rotten day.

You'd better appreciate this, Josh. She urged Topaz forward. If any horse could make it to Reunion in this blistering heat, it was her buckskin.

Taylor breathed a small sigh when they reached the top. Now there was only the descent left. Tricky, but nothing they hadn't done hundreds of times.

Never for this reason. The thought came unbidden, unwelcome...and images flooded her mind. She saw her husband standing at the bottom of the steep path, the picture of rugged masculinity. His electric blue eyes laughed up at her; his gaze was warm and aware as he reached up. She slid from the saddle into his embrace...

A sudden jerk startled her. Topaz whinnied once, and then Taylor was airborne. She landed with a thud on the rocky ground, then lay still. Was anything broken? With slow care, she pushed herself into a sitting position, then eased to her feet, feeling the anger rising again. "If you weren't already dead, Josh..."

She bit off the rest of the words, then straightened her shoulders and looked around. The beauty of the valley never failed to stir her. No one would ever imagine it was here, nestled as it was in a rocky outcropping. She'd found it when she was a teen, exploring her parents' Wyoming ranch. She hadn't told anyone about it.

Until Josh.

They had met in college and married six months later. Josh brought her love and laughter and the certainty that life was good.

Or at least, it used to be.

All that changed on the youth group trip.

Josh loved those trips. He loved the kids, the adventure, sharing his faith. He took every experience by the horns and rode it into the ground. It was what made him a favorite with the kids.

It was what got him killed.

Pushing her thoughts away, Taylor went to reach into her saddlebag. Her hand closed around the cool ceramic container.

Josh's ashes.

"If anything happens to me, will you bring my ashes here?" he'd asked her on one of their last visits to the valley. *"I like the idea of being a part of this place, this beauty. Besides, that way we'll always be together, Taylor."*

At the time it had been a nice sentiment. Now it was reality. Undeniable, dreadful reality.

Summoning every ounce of determination, she moved to the small lake at the center of the valley.

What good does it do to let someone in, Lord? I trusted Josh, and he risked it all... She hugged the ceramic container. *How do I live without him?*

Silence answered her, bringing a wretchedness of mind and spirit she'd never known. Icy fingers seeped into every pore, leaving something deep within her—some part that had been vital and living—brittle, ready to shatter.

Taylor turned the container upside down. The ashes spilled out with a slight *whoosh,* and she smiled through her tears. Even in death Josh was in a hurry.

Then she sank to the ground and surrendered to the grief she'd been wrestling for the last six months.

It was dusk when Taylor lifted her head. Wasn't crying healthy, cathartic, the beginning of healing? So why didn't she feel better? Maybe some pain went so deep that even tears couldn't touch it.

She stared across the pool…and froze. She was being watched.

There, at the edge of the rock face, sat a wolf.

There weren't any wolves in Wyoming! Hadn't been for sixty years. *So this is what it's like to go crazy.* She squeezed her eyes shut, then opened them.

The wolf sat there, head held high, ears perked, amber gaze fixed on her—clearly unaware his presence was an impossibility.

Taylor shifted, and the wolf crouched, ready to flee. She froze, and after a moment he seemed to relax. His haunting, penetrating eyes glittered with intelligence.

His demeanor was positively aristocratic; he gave the impression of a sovereign surveying his domain—and one of his subjects. His coat—a study of light grays, browns, and flecks of black—was so thick and luxurious that Taylor's fingers itched to touch him, to bury themselves in what promised to be remarkable softness. For all that it was watchful, the look on his gray face was disarmingly sweet. She had the distinct impression that he found her fascinating.

A quick and disturbing thought coursed though her. Was this majestic beast looking at her with such interest not out of curiosity, but because she was a threat? Or an enemy?

Or, worse yet, an item on the dinner menu?

Loath to move and precipitate any response, she could only continue the hypnotic exchange of glances. Then, for one incredible moment, her eyes met the wolf's golden gaze. The contact lasted a heartbeat, but before his eyes flicked away something clicked in her mind.

She was in no danger.

Her apprehension melted as the assurance resonated within her, filling her with a strange peace. It was as though the wolf were watching her out of concern. And a kind of protectiveness.

Taylor stared. The wolf was barely-controlled power coiled in a slender frame; he was everything that was wild and graceful and beautiful.

And then, as suddenly as a wink, he was gone. It was as though he'd simply melted into thin air.

Taylor blinked twice, then frowned. *Okay, God...what are You doing now?*

KAREN BALL

A Test of Faith

Her daughter Faith is the answer to Ann's lifelong prayer to be a mother. But her dream is shattered when the teenager rejects Ann's love and the love of God. After years pass, and God heals their relationship, Ann falls seriously ill. Faith watches her mother weaken, struggling with role reversals and leaning on God as never before. Through all the intricacies of their relationship, all the joys and trials, they are reminded that God is with them. He brings them peace in the darkness, joy in the midst of sorrow, and hope in the face of death.

ISBN 1-59052-265-6

Favorite Novelists Tell
Tales About Home

Combined in one volume, Christian readers' favorite fiction authors—including Randy Alcorn, Terri Blackstock, Angela Elwell Hunt, Melody Carlson, Nancy Moser, and Karen Kingsbury—offer delightful new short stories about hometown faith and foibles. This hard-to-put-down book, which features story settings all around North America in a variety of time periods, reminds readers what values really spell 'home.' And the contributors celebrate a home-based ministry by donating their royalties to Prison Fellowship!

ISBN 1-57673-820-5

Printed in the United States
by Baker & Taylor Publisher Services